T0265718

BEST BE PREPARED

BEST BE PREPARED

Gwen Florio

**SEVERN
HOUSE**

First world edition published in Great Britain and the USA in 2023
by Severn House, an imprint of Canongate Books Ltd,
14 High Street, Edinburgh EH1 1TE.

severnhouse.com

British Library Cataloguing-in-Publication Data
A CIP catalogue record for this title is available from the British Library.

ISBN-13: 978-0-7278-5078-2 (cased)
ISBN-13: 978-1-4483-0688-6 (e-book)

All Severn House titles are printed on acid-free paper.

Typeset by Palimpsest Book Production Ltd.,
Falkirk, Stirlingshire, Scotland.
Printed and bound in Great Britain by
TJ Books, Padstow, Cornwall.

Praise for Gwen Florio

About the author

Gwen Florio grew up in a farmhouse filled with books and a ban on television. After studying English at the University of Delaware, she began a decades-long career in journalism that has taken her around the country and to more than a dozen countries, including several conflict zones.

Her first novel in the Lola Wicks mystery series, *Montana*, won the Pinckley Prize for Crime Fiction and the High Plains Book Award, and was a finalist for the Shamus Award, an International Thriller Award and a Silver Falchion Award. Four more books followed in the Lola Wicks series, as well as two Julia Geary legal thrillers and a stand-alone novel, *Silent Hearts*. *Best Laid Plans* was the first book in the Nora Best series and her first with Severn House.

www.gwenflorio.net

ONE

The sirens went off on a day of record-breaking September heat, the air thick and syrupy, the kids sluggish, whiney, rolling their eyes and dragging their feet.

Nora Best caught her breath. She looked at her watch, fixing the time in her mind: 1:20 PM. They had fifteen minutes. 'Emergency backpacks, *now*. Go, go, go!'

'I hate these drills.' Damien Austin, reliably zigging when she needed him to zag, stood still as a boulder in midstream, forcing the rushing current of seventh-graders to flow around him.

Nora took his upper arm and spun him toward the cloakroom where the packs, full of water bottles and power bars, wet wipes and space blankets, waited. She pinched the soft skin just above the inside of his elbow and twisted, impermissible for a teacher, excusable – or so she told herself – under the circumstances.

'Owww. You're not allowed to touch me! I'm gonna tell my mom and she's gonna tell Principal Everhart and then you're . . .'

Nora dropped his arm. 'Not a drill,' she hissed. 'Look at the sky.' She willed him to see a yellowish tinge to the clouds, hanging so low their watery tendrils reached toward the black-green Sitka spruce just beyond the dunes. A few raindrops left inkblot splatters on the just-poured concrete footings for the new tsunami evacuation tower beside the school, mockingly highlighting the tower's lack.

Nora looked at her watch again then raised her voice. 'We've got thirteen minutes to get to the top of Highview Hill. *Go*.'

The grimace slid from Damien's face. His eyes widened and he lowered his voice to match hers. 'For real?'

She looked at her watch again. 'Twelve minutes.'

It worked. Damien shoved his way past the uneven line of Nora's twenty social-studies students and assumed command, albeit with a crack in his voice. 'Hey, everybody! Let's race. Let's our class beat all the others.'

As they joined the mob streaming from the doors of Peninsula

Middle School, Nora mentally took back everything she'd thought about Damien, her reliable tormenter since her first day in the classroom, when he'd taken one look at the nameplate on her desk and dubbed her Ms Worst.

He was largely responsible for her last-period class being the day's most challenging, telling his fellow students she wasn't a real teacher, even though her on-the-job certification program qualified her as such. That her dog, the elderly and amiable Murph, a pure-bred Chesapeake Bay retriever, was part pit bull and had fleas, too. That she was trailer trash because she lived in her Airstream.

On her best days, she'd have cheerfully killed him. On her worst, she fantasized about precisely how.

Now the boy whose sole mission appeared to be making her life a living hell might be responsible for saving it.

Seventh-graders are a weird bunch.

They teeter on the knife-edge between child and teenager, some still soft of face and body, eyes trusting, easily enchanted. Others slouch into the classroom, shoulders bent against unaccustomed height, their only defense against their bodies' sudden betrayal – the boys with their low, raspy voices, the girls unsure whether to hide or flaunt their new breasts – a sullen, sarcastic attitude toward everything and everyone. Including Nora.

Her previous job involved working with teenage girls or, as she thought of them, Creatures from Hell, never mind that she herself had qualified for archfiend status during her own high-school years. She'd jumped at the chance to work with younger children. Surely they'd be more malleable, easier to win over.

They weren't.

She tried to slough off the disdain of the bigger ones, hoarding the regard of the smaller the way a perennial dieter stashes pieces of chocolate to offset the pangs of hunger and yearning. Now those same little ones, their short legs achingly slow, could get her killed.

Hours earlier and nearly five thousand miles away, the Earth's floor groaned and heaved beneath the Pacific's churning expanse, its plates shuddering like boxers locked in a thrusting embrace until one finally prevailed, the other sinking beneath it in defeat.

Needles quivered and leapt on monitors and apps flashed alerts, the numbers initially reassuring to the blissfully inexpert, who shrugged at the quake's distance from anything other than a few uninhabited atolls in the Pacific.

Except.

The Earth's jolt traveled up and up, through churning miles of water, mounding six feet high in a wave that rolled inexorably eastward toward the peninsula where Nora now lived and worked, a peninsula so synonymous with sea level that brackish water sometimes bubbled up from the ground around the wheels of her Airstream.

A mere mile across at its base, the peninsula ran north for ten miles, gradually narrowing to just a few yards wide. To its west, the Pacific lunged and retreated in accordance with the pull of the Moon, constantly rearranging the configuration of its sandy beaches. Along its eastern flank, oyster flats – the remnants of an industry that once supported the entire peninsula – gridded a shallow bay.

Near the tapered tip, a hill stood like a callus on a finger, a mere bump, only sixty feet high. That sandy, rounded blip on the horizon became the difference between life and death for the peninsula's northern residents, the pupils of Peninsula Middle School among them. Those at the southern end, blessed with wide, soaring bluffs, would give thanks to a multitude of deities for the dumb luck of geography.

But the hill was a quarter-mile from the school and already the smaller kids were faltering, unable to keep up with Damien and his scampering minions.

As their teacher, Nora was bound to stay with the slowest, urging them on, her feet pounding a hopeless rhythm, her gaze dragged toward her watch as though by magnetic force.

Six minutes. Five minutes.

Four.

Three.

Two.

That's how long they had to get to the top of the hill before the water hit, chewing across the yards of beach, hopping the dunes, scooping up shops and houses and cars, and bounding merrily up the sides of the hill and the little ones, oh, the little ones.

She hefted poor Abby James, chubby and nearsighted and slow, exhorting the others on, panting now, no way to keep the panic from her voice. Her class was the last, the bigger kids far ahead, the eighth-graders already standing like sentries at the top. They shouted and waved, but the only sound that registered was the beeping of her watch, the alarm she'd set as soon as the sirens sounded, the one that meant they were too late.

They weren't going to make it.

TWO

Principal Louann Everhart brandished a stopwatch and spoke through lips thinned with rage.

'Congratulations, Miss Best. Almost half your class made it. But a dozen children died on your watch. I want you to take a moment and think exactly how you're going to tell their parents. We have a template for such notifications in our tsunami information packet. I hope you've memorized it.'

The principal's tongue-lashing was nothing compared to what she faced from Damien, who hadn't bothered to contain his own distress.

'You said it wasn't a drill. You let me think it was real.' Tears stood in his eyes. His voice shook.

Nora had thought things were as bad as they could get. But Everhart overheard him, meaning they were about to get worse.

'Is this true, Damien? Is it, Miss Best?'

Nora clung to the hope that Everhart's question indicated a justifiable lack of trust in Damien's account.

Everhart didn't even wait for an answer. The principal took that hope and stomped the bejesus out of it.

'You traumatized a student. You realize we have to send him to counseling.' The manual about tsunami drills emphasized the importance of balancing the need for speed with not unduly frightening students. When it came to Damien, Nora had failed. Badly.

'And because your . . . your . . . *partner*' – Everhart spat the word – 'is our new school counselor, we'll have to contract with someone outside the district to avoid the appearance of a conflict of interest. I only wish we could take the cost out of your salary.'

Nora and Luke, their relationship still young, were nowhere near ready to commit to marriage. They didn't even live together, Nora's Airstream being far too small to accommodate two people for more than a few days. Luke rented a place nearby in Lane's End, the northern peninsula hamlet so small it was impossible not to notice how often Nora's truck sat overnight beside Luke's house, or his Subaru snugged next to her trailer at its beachfront campsite. Most people seemed not to mind – or at least, were too polite to say so if they did – but Everhart had pointedly and blatantly illegally asked during their job interviews whether they intended to marry and had sniffed at their stammering responses.

Now, Everhart delivered her remarks just loud enough to be heard by some of the other teachers lounging nearby, keeping a desultory eye on their pupils. They'd deliberately turned the rest of the final period into school-wide free time, knowing from previous experience the necessity of giving the kids time to settle down before they went home after the excitement of a drill.

But first, they'd had to chase away a man who sprawled either asleep or drunk or maybe both in the clearing atop the hill. In her short time in Lane's End, Nora had already come to know Harold Wallace. He limped up and down the hamlet's few streets, leaning heavily on his stick and muttering just loud enough to be overheard about the perceived injustice of a years-ago ruinous injury on an oyster boat. He'd sued the company for negligence, only to see himself countersued for showing up to work drunk. There'd been a settlement, a small one, quickly exhausted. Disability payments. The occasional handout. None of it enough.

Stories about Harold usually ended with, 'but he's harmless.'

Nora, whenever she encountered him – peering wild-eyed beneath the shade of his ball cap, hair hanging nearly to his shoulders in greasy strings, his stick waving and spittle flying as he ranted against the perceived injustice done him – remained unconvinced.

On this day, though, perhaps because of a gentle shake and soft admonition from one of the teachers, he roused himself and limped off without complaint. The bigger kids promptly took over the space he'd just vacated, digging through their emergency packs and swapping power bars and juice boxes. They were supposed to save the supplies for a real emergency. Everhart had probably already taken note. Nora would have to fund replacements out of her salary.

A glowering Damien sat in the middle of their circle as befitted his alpha-male status, which Nora attributed to a combination of swagger and looks. He'd probably always been a beautiful boy, all golden ringlets and big brown eyes and ready smile. Only twelve, but already the babyish prettiness was transforming into full-on handsome, his shoulders widening, the smile turned sardonic, his dark eyes even more striking in contrast to the blond curls that nearly obscured them.

He and the other seventh-graders crouched in wary groups, as though rehearsing for the savage judgment of high school, while sixth-graders –still too young to be alert to the hovering threat of their teen years – ran back and forth atop Highview Hill.

Eventually they'd all move on to the high school at the south end of the peninsula, where the craggy two-hundred-foot bluff offered reasonable protection should a tsunami ever hit. But the middle school was miles to the north, so silly little Highview Hill was their only hope, as long as an earthquake wasn't too strong, the waves weren't too high.

It was all theoretical anyway, as Nora had periodically reminded herself, ever since arriving on the peninsula and noting the loudspeaker-topped tsunami-warning towers. She hadn't lived there two weeks before she heard about the 1700 tsunami known in the local tribes' oral traditions as the Great Drowning, its devastation – a wave that might have reached thirty feet high, racing nearly three miles inland along the Pacific Northwest – only belatedly recognized by science.

But once she saw it termed a five-hundred-year event, she comforted herself with the thought that she was probably safe for another two centuries. At which, point, she had ceased to worry about tsunamis. At least, until her disastrous performance in the drill.

She forced herself to meet Everhart's gaze. The principal was at least ten years her senior, nearing – Nora hoped – retirement age; wiry and tough as one of the peninsula's knobbed shore pines. She'd reminded Nora repeatedly that she'd grown up on the peninsula. Her vocal disdain for the newcomers flooding the area was frequent and unfiltered.

Sweat from her sprint up the hill bathed Nora's forehead and stung her eyes. She blinked it away. The sun, a rare visitor to this part of the world, muscled the clouds aside, sending them back out over the ocean, flat and pewter-hued in the distance. The sunshine, while welcome, combined with Everhart's glare to make Nora feel as though she was under a spotlight.

The sound of her own name in Abby James' high, piping voice was all the excuse she needed to flee.

'Ms Best! Ms Best!'

The girl ran toward them, face pale, eyes wide, mouth open and closing soundlessly after the effort of calling Nora's name.

Nora dropped to one knee and held her arms open to the girl, ignoring Everhart's quick head-shake. Physical contact with kids was discouraged, but clearly something had upset Abby and she needed comforting. She trembled within Nora's embrace.

'There's a . . . there's a . . . Ms Best, you have to come and see.'

She grabbed Nora's hand in her chubby damp one and pulled her toward a brushy spot on the hill. Hardhack grew close there, nearly impenetrable. Nora had discovered as much in her early days on the island. She'd gone in search of a view of the waves she could hear pounding the sand somewhere close by and attempted to push her way through the woody thickets with their deceptively delicate fuzzy pink flowers. She'd finally given up and had driven her truck to a spot a quarter-mile away where someone had cut a rough track to the beach.

Abby pointed to a shrub a few feet in and buried her face against Nora's thigh. 'Hardly any flowers are left. I wanted to pick some. But then I saw that.'

A man lay prone, his dark hair spread across his face.

'Oh, for heaven's sake.' Harold Wallace hadn't gone far. He'd just crawled into the hardhack to finish sleeping off whatever he'd downed the night before. Nora looked around for Sheila Connor, who'd earlier roused him. The math teacher, whose brisk, no-nonsense manner reflected the certainties involved in her subject, seemed to have a way with Harold.

But Sheila was organizing a group at the far end of the clearing into a cleanup crew, handing out garbage bags and assigning some of the kids to collect and sort recycling, while others picked up trash.

Nora stooped beside Harold and tried to emulate Sheila's manner. Her timid shake elicited no response, and she tried again, jostling him so hard the hair shook away from his face, dark with dried blood.

She stuffed her first in her mouth and fell back.

The person before her wasn't Harold.

He was, however, dead.

Nora, already in hot water for having traumatized one student, managed to choke back the scream that might have terrified another.

She hustled Abby over to Sheila. 'Can you and the others please round up the kids and get them back to the school?' She leaned close and whispered the reason, adding, 'I thought it was Harold.'

'Holy hell,' Sheila breathed. 'He must have had a heart attack.'

'He didn't have a heart attack and it's not Harold. It's—' But she'd only met the man once. 'I'm not sure who he is.'

Sheila bent and took Abby's face between her hands. 'You're safe. You were smart to get an adult right away.' She straightened and held out a hand. Abby took it. 'All of us are going to go back down to the school now. Don't you even think about letting go of my hand.'

She looked at Nora and mouthed, 'You're going to have to tell EverJerk.'

Nora indulged a momentary twinge of gratification. At least she wasn't alone in her opinion of the principal.

She waited until Sheila and the other teachers had corralled the kids and started shepherding them down the hill, then approached Everhart, who waited with arms crossed.

'What's this about?'

Nora could have told her. Should have told her. But the sight of Everhart's pursed lips and narrowed gaze, the one that routinely judged her and found her wanting, quashed any impulse toward charity.

'You'd better come see. I'm afraid this is well above my pay grade.'

Everhart muttered something that Nora didn't quite catch, though she imagined Everhart thought every single job at Peninsula Middle School, including the custodian's, was above Nora's pay grade.

She led Everhart toward the clump of shrubbery.

'Oh-oh.' Damien's voice sounded behind them. 'Taking a walk with the principal, huh? Looks like you're in trouble, Ms Best.'

'Miss Best,' Everhart snapped. The principal did not, she'd informed Nora upon her arrival at the school, believe in the use of 'fake honorifics'. Nora hadn't dared ask Everhart about her policy on the use of the students' preferred pronouns, figuring she was better off claiming plausible deniability.

'What's going on, Miss Best?' Damien turned a routine question into a singsong taunt.

Nora turned. 'Damien, please go with the others.' But the boy sauntered toward them, his smile holding both eagerness and contempt. If Nora was in for a shellacking, he wanted to see it – and, of course, tell the whole class about it and further undermine what little authority she had.

'Damien, no.' She tried to wave him back, but Everhart pushed past her into the hardhack.

'If we need to pick up trash, you're certainly capable of doing that yourself,' the principal huffed. Then, 'Dear Lord. Oh, dear Lord in heaven.' She fell to her knees in an intercession to a deity who deigned not to intercede.

Because nothing stopped Damien's headlong rush toward this scene of unanticipated drama.

'Wait!' Nora caught at him just as he reached the shrubs.

All traces of the cocky, taunting child of seconds before drained from his face, confirming Nora's guess as to the identity of the unfortunate before them.

He twisted in her grip, his intermittently deep voice cracking on a single word.

'Dad?'

THREE

'Oh, Luke. You should have seen it. That boy's face.' Nora covered her own face, trying and failing to blot out the memory.

They sat in Luke's apartment on the second floor of an aging cottage whose cedar shakes, warped and silvery and furred with moss, attested to decades of the peninsula's battering winds and lashing rain.

Murph lay at their feet, waiting for Luke to 'accidentally' drop a chunk of barbacoa. Mooch, her orange cat, lay across the back of the sofa, too dignified to fight with the dog over scraps and secure in the knowledge that a dish would be prepared for him later.

Luke held out a basket of just-warmed tortillas wrapped in a towel. Nora took two and forked barbacoa onto them, drizzled the meat with salsa verde and sprinkled diced onions and cilantro atop it, finishing with a squeeze of lime.

'Isn't Damien the one who's always needling you?'

'The same.'

Luke waited as she chewed. He'd been at the high school at the southern end of the peninsula all day, in his role as a rotating guidance counselor, and hadn't heard about the grim discovery until he'd arrived home and found Nora curled in a fetal position on the sofa, shivering beneath a quilt she'd pulled from the bed.

Upon hearing the barest details, he'd poured her a shot of tequila, then dished up the shredded beef from the crock pot, commanding, 'Eat first. Then talk.'

'I thought it was a homeless person at first. Harold Wallace, or maybe someone else.' Despite the seemingly unending rain, the Pacific Northwest's relatively mild temperatures rarely dipped below freezing. That fact drew legions of transients, although they tended to congregate in cities like Portland and Seattle, with their robust social services.

Still, in her few months on the peninsula, Nora had glimpsed the occasional flash of dirt-streaked neon-bright nylon tents tucked deep beneath the pines, far from any official campground. Men with heavy backpacks tramped its parallel main roads – one along the ocean, the other bayside – and occasionally pestered her for change outside the lone supermarket.

'Harold was up on the hill when we got there. One of the teachers asked him to leave. I thought it was him. In retrospect, the boots should have been a giveaway.'

After that first ghastly glimpse of the man's face, she'd focused on his footgear to steady herself. Not the cheap, cracked variety, soles worn nearly through, of the constantly on-the-move road and sidewalk denizen, but the sturdy, engineered sort featured in REI catalogues with a price tag worthy of the glossy come-on, their Vibram lugs meant to withstand scrambles over boulder and scree, during days or even weeks on a wilderness trail. The kind of boots likely worn – she hadn't noticed at the time – by the bearded fellow who'd shyly slipped into her classroom a few weeks earlier as back-to-school night was winding up, introducing himself as Damien's father.

She'd shaken her head at him in confusion. 'But I thought . . .'

She'd jotted surreptitious notes during each meeting with her students' parents, and clearly remembered the couple who'd introduced themselves as Damien's parents. Even without the signifiers – the rock the size of Gibraltar weighing down Delilah's left hand; Spencer's loafers so buttery soft that Nora guessed Italian – they had the burnished, well-tended look conferred by money.

'You met his mother and stepfather,' Ward Austin said. He tugged at the leather lace dangling over one shoulder, shook free his hair, and bound it back into its short greying ponytail, shrugging away her stammered apology as he pulled the lace tight.

'No worries. For future reference, their last name is Templeton.'

Nora apologized again. She hadn't written down Spencer's and Delilah's last name, assuming it was the same as Damien's.

'Really, it's fine. Whenever I can, though, I try to avoid crossing paths. Tough divorce. My wife accused me of being more invested in my cause – I run a nonprofit dedicated to preserving the peninsula's environment – than our relationship. "Your mistress", she called it. To say she grew bitter is an understatement.'

Nora, who'd found out too late about her husband's serial infidelity, thought she could teach Delilah a thing or two about true bitterness.

Ward must have mistaken her wordless nod for some sort of encouragement.

'She said she just wanted a normal life. Honestly, I can't hold that against her. I'm surprised she put up with me for as long as she did.'

Sympathy swelled for the absent Delilah. How often had Nora's single friends complained about newly divorced men, their nonstop carping about their exes? If her ex had lived, would he too have blabbed about her to whoever would listen?

But then Ward leaned in, voice quivering with intensity, his eyes fixed on hers in a gaze so resolute and sad that an electric finger ran up her spine.

'To me, normal means passive and that sort of life is not worth living. Do you know what I mean?'

She did not. She'd ended up on this spit of land on the western edge of the continent because she was in search of the very normalcy he eschewed. Her recent life had been marked by the sort of emotional temblors that in geologic form would have sent a tsunami sloshing across half the continent. Passivity was, for her, a life-saving strategy.

Yet she suppressed an urge to lay a hand atop his arm, to assure him that she too aspired to a life of purpose rather than one of simple, trouble-free existence.

'Sorry. Sometimes I get carried away.' He leaned back.

Nora hoped her weak smile masked the foolishness she felt. She cut her eyes toward the clock. She shouldn't even be having this conversation. Back-to-school night was supposed to have ended ten minutes earlier. Ward Austin and his son shared one trait in common – the ability to screw up her day.

He took the hint. 'All that was by way of explanation. There've been . . . confrontations. I don't want to drag you into our business, but please understand that when you come to a Little League game and see me sitting in the opposing team's stands, it's because I don't want to make things any tougher on Damien. They've been known to get up and leave if I dare sit on the same side of the field as them. Speaking of Damien.'

She failed to suppress an audible sigh. Finally, a segue into the reason for the meeting; her chance to lay out her plans for the school year, the achievements expected of her pupils and – the thing all parents most wanted to hear – a glowing evaluation of their children.

Sheila, the math teacher, had prepped her with useful phrases for such meetings and Nora trotted them out now.

'Damien is one of our most promising students.' *In terms of ending up in some sort of juvie facility, that is.*

'He has a lively imagination.' *Always thinking up new ways to get under her skin.*

'A natural-born leader.' *See: instigator, agitator, rabble-rouser.*

Ward threw back his head, setting his ponytail swinging. He had a surprisingly loud laugh for such a soft-spoken man.

'You mean he's a pain in the ass.' His face grew serious. 'I know Damien's a handful. He's still trying to adjust to the schizophrenia of a two-household life. His mother's new existence, and hence his, is quite a bit different than mine. Shinier, let's say.'

He shook his head and stood. 'I've taken up enough of your time. All I ask is your patience with my son. And if he truly gets out of line, please don't hesitate to call.'

Nora gave Luke an edited version of the conversation, leaving out the part about the marital woes that led to Ward's divorce. Luke, too, was a divorced father, something they rarely discussed. This didn't seem the time to start.

'Until today, that was the only time I'd seen him. I feel guilty even saying this, but at least it got Everhart off my back about the drill. You know what? I looked it up later. The model they used – it was based on one of the world's biggest tsunamis. That wave would've gone halfway up the hill. A bunch of kids – teachers, too – would have drowned no matter what. That woman hates me.'

'From what I hear, she's pretty tough on everybody.'

Nora thought of Everhart on her knees, stoicism shattered at the sight of Ward's body. 'She wasn't tough today, that's for sure.'

Luke's phone dinged an alert.

He picked it up and tapped the screen, studying it a moment before handing it to Nora.

A single story – 'Prominent local activist found dead' – filled the homepage for the *Peninsula Press*, the local newspaper. It quoted the county sheriff.

'Mr Austin had a severe injury, possibly after stumbling and striking his head on a rocky outcropping. But that's preliminary. We're ruling nothing out.'

FOUR

'Prominent' turned out to be an understatement.

The *Peninsula Press* followed up the next day with a far longer story. Luke held his phone close to his face and read aloud the lengthy recitation of Ward Austin's work on behalf of his beloved region. Ward was that increasingly rare creature, a peninsula native, and often cited his childhood exploring its spruce groves and tide pools as his reason for obtaining degrees in marine biology and ecology.

His nonprofit, Preserve the Peninsula, raised money to buy private property whenever it came on the market, with the aim of linking parcels to the wildlife refuge at the peninsula's northern tip, a lonely wind- and water-swept expanse of dunes and salt grass, the province of seals and otters and swooping seabirds.

Preserve the Peninsula filed suit after suit aimed at stopping the burgeoning development on the peninsula's southern end and steadily creeping northward – the ostentatious shoreline-hogging second homes that blocked the sea breezes from the cottages that had housed the summer people of Ward Austin's youth, the new motels with their unnecessary swimming pools surrounded by swaths of thirsty green lawn; an outlet mall beloved by day-trippers. His acolytes called themselves Ward's Warriors.

It didn't take much to suss out the unwritten story between the lines of the just-the-facts account: Ward's persistence earned him the enmity of the peninsula's so-called champions of progress, the business owners, real-estate agents and contractors, and especially of one Spencer Templeton, the peninsula's largest contractor and head of the Chamber of Commerce – aka, husband of Ward Austin's former wife Delilah and stepfather to Damien.

Luke laid his phone aside.

'Looks like we've settled into a regular little Peyton Place here.'

Nora, dozing with her head on his chest, murmured agreement.

It was Saturday, their day for a lazy morning of lovemaking, followed up with multiple mugs of coffee, after which they turned their attention to doughnuts from a bakery and restaurant that was one of the few businesses on the peninsula's still relatively lightly inhabited north end. Nora had never considered herself a doughnut aficionada until she'd tasted the offerings from Betty's, at which point she understood how the bakery thrived so far from the main traffic flow.

Nora reached an arm from beneath the quilt and sat up just enough to take another sip of coffee. Luke made it the way she liked it, with a hint of cinnamon.

This, she thought as she sipped. This man, this place, this life. This is enough. More than. Ward Austin had touted a life of passionate purpose, and where had it gotten him? Dead.

'When's the memorial?'

Luke picked up the phone again and scrolled down. 'Eleven Friday morning.'

'Damn. I'll have to ask Everhart for permission to take the morning off. As Damien's teacher, I should be there. But she'll hold the request against me.'

Luke took the mug from her and drained it of its contents, then filled it again from the Thermos on the bedside table.

'No, she won't,' he said over the gurgle of coffee into the mug. Mooch, curled beside Nora, yawned and stretched and flexed his forepaws, the quilt's thickness shielding her from his claws. Murph lay heavily across both their feet.

'How do you know?'

'Because I called her last night to suggest that whenever they scheduled a service, she close the school for the day to allow both faculty and families to attend. And of course I'll be available for counseling all week for anyone who feels the need. Best practices.'

She winced at his use of a phrase that had governed their former jobs at a private program for troubled girls, where they'd met and where the practices had been anything but.

'Sorry,' he added. 'But in this case, it really is.'

Nora snuggled down beneath the quilt. Luke's bedroom was cozy by default, tucked as it was under the cottage's eaves, but the peninsula's persistent damp chill somehow seeped through. 'Ward said something about confrontations between him and Damien's mom and stepdad.'

Luke grimaced. 'Happens. It's a shame. Wish people would think about their kids and keep their differences to themselves. Although, kids usually figure it out anyway. Observant little buggers. Like spies in a way.'

Nora thought of her class, their eyes following her every move, assessing, probing for weakness – the catch of her breath, the break in her voice, the jump of muscle in her jaw – that meant they'd gotten to her. Filing it away to be analyzed, their technique honed for greater effect the next time and the time after that.

She had to stop herself from searching out the friendly faces – Abby, Zeke Miles, Jeannie Graves – and calling on them over and over again, knowing that to single them out would only get them slotted into an enemy camp. Sometimes she feared she even went harder on them because of that.

But she, too, was honing her own tradecraft, gleaning bits of useful information from overheard playground chatter, the expression on one student's face as another spoke, even from things parents let drop. She sat up abruptly, jostling both cat and dog.

'His dad said something on parent–teacher night – *ow*.' This time, Mooch's claws dug deep. She shoved the cat away and he sprang to the floor, back arched, hissing dissatisfaction. 'He called Damien's life with his dad and stepmom "shiny". It's a strange term, don't you think?'

Luke chuckled. 'It's the right word. I didn't make the connection between Damien and Spencer Templeton until I read this story. Have you seen their house?'

'No. At least, I don't think so.'

'Yes, you have. Think shiny.'

Nora thought. 'Wait. You mean the spaceship?'

It was their name for a house that commandeered prime oceanfront real estate, a modern curvilinear monstrosity whose steel and concrete construction was at odds with all the other sprawling new homes. Those, despite their size, at least gave a nod to the area's aesthetic with their dark shakes that appeared to be weathered cedar but upon inspection proved to be a compressed-plastic composite, rubbery and weird.

The rounded contours and oval windows of the steel-clad house, along with the fact that it floated atop high concrete pillars, lent the unoriginal nickname.

'The one and the same.'

She'd thought it a vacation home, one rented for vast sums by moneyed outsiders hosting family reunions or wedding parties or just weeklong getaways with twenty of their closest friends in the perfect Instagrammable location. She glanced around Luke's two-room apartment and tried to imagine three people rattling around in a space six times that size.

Especially if one of them was a kid.

Maybe Damien liked it. Maybe life in the spaceship was like those old-time movies that showed poor little rich kids frolicking in mansions, sliding down banisters, begging treats from a rosy-cheeked cook, palling around with an avuncular butler.

Her other students expressed open envy over Damon's marshmallow-y sneakers, apparently some trendy, hard-to-procure variety. His iPhone and MacBook were newer than hers, and she guessed he'd be presented with a car – new, not used – when he turned sixteen.

As with nearby Portland and Seattle, the peninsula paid lip service to a green ethos, one to which the middle school dutifully subscribed, what with its recycling bins and compost container and student-tilled garden that yielded a few stunted vegetables ostensibly for use by the cafeteria. But its students were as avariciously materialistic as any bombarded by a stream of online ads, and Damien's ostentatious stuff went a long way toward conferring top-dog status.

Like Nora, he was an only child. But her parents had always been close at hand, instantaneously summoned by a mere shout through a closed bedroom door. Maybe the spaceship had some sort of speaker system, or a button you could press, the way people used to summon servants in days of old. A house that size might even have servants; at the very least, a regular cleaning person.

She imagined an interior full of vast echoing spaces, interrupted only by strategically placed furniture so stylish as to negate comfort. How long would it take to go through it, buffing each surface to gleaming perfection? To wipe away the grubby fingerprints of a child just returned from playing outdoors with his friends, to pick up the jackets and toys and electronic gadgets he'd probably left strewn about? To scrub away all traces of him?

Did Damien really like all that shiny newness? Or did its glare hurt his eyes, leaving him irritable and casting about for an acceptable target upon which to vent his bile?

Nora threw off the covers, stood and stretched, trying to shake off an overactive imagination.

'Let's go for a walk. It's supposed to rain later.' It was always supposed to rain later, if it wasn't raining already. Nora found the fat drops comforting as they drummed against her Airstream's aluminum roof, but less enjoyable if she happened to be caught outdoors, which she invariably was.

Then: 'Where does Damien's dad live?' She caught herself and amended it. 'Where did he live?'

Luke rose and stepped into the jeans he'd left on the floor the night before. It was the weekend, after all.

'Damned if I know. But you can be sure it's nothing like the spaceship.'

FIVE

Nora was glad she'd included a suit in her bare-bones wardrobe when she'd stocked the Airstream for its long-ago maiden voyage.

The trailer had been procured with a book in mind, one that would follow the adventures of a middle-aged couple stepping off the career treadmill and roaming the country. This was before the #vanlife craze had swept social media, and the book aimed to break new ground, with Nora paving its way with posts on their travels. She'd envisioned the occasional local television station interview; hence, the suit.

But the book deal fell through when Nora left her husband and took off alone in the Airstream, and the suit had lived crammed into the far end of the postage-stamp closet, wrinkled and forlorn.

The night before Ward Austin's memorial, she hung it in her sardine-tin bathroom, turned on the shower hot and full-force, and closed the door, hoping to steam it back to freshness. When she retrieved it, it was passable – just – if a little damp. Under the circumstances, she wished she'd chosen something more sober than its dusty rose hue, but she paired it with a gray shell, forced her feet into black pumps – oh, ouch – and accepted the slow, appreciative sweep of Luke's gaze when she opened to the door.

'I'm just glad it still fits,' she told him as they walked to his car. Luke had turned out to be an excellent cook, presenting her with full protein–vegetable–starch dinners and a variety of fresh breads, and one teasing reason she gave for refusing to move in with him was she feared the weight gain that would come with eating his meals every night.

He'd donned a blazer – as neglected as her suit, she guessed – and a pair of dress pants, and had buffed cowboy boots to a high gloss, 'a holdover talent from the Marines,' he said.

But after taking so much care with her appearance, Nora got a shock when entering the community center at the island's south end for Ward Austin's memorial.

Other than the close family members seated in the front rows, people dressed mostly as they did every day. Jeans abounded, although the men had switched out T-shirts for collared button-downs and a few women wore skirts.

She turned to Luke, eyebrows raised. 'It's not the city,' he shrugged as they squeezed into a row near the back of the packed space.

Nora took stock. Most of the middle-school teachers were there and more of the students than she would have expected. She didn't remember going to any funerals as a child; even her grandparents had lived until she was in her twenties. But then, none of her friends' parents had died when she was a youngster.

Everhart sat near the front – of course she would have arrived
early – and she twisted around, surveying the crowd, as though
taking attendance. Nora shifted in her seat. Too late. The principal
grimaced, no doubt mentally marking Nora as a latecomer.

Nora's vantage point gave her a slanting view across the room
to the front row where Damien sat next to his mother, his stepfather conspicuous by his absence. Someone had inflicted a bow
tie upon poor Damien and he slid a finger inside his shirt collar
as though trying to loosen a noose. He jerked – Nora suspected
a quick elbow to the ribs – shot his mother a dark look and
dropped his hand.

Delilah Austin sat straight-backed and dry-eyed as Ward's,
friends and relatives, and even some of Damien's teachers, rose
to eulogize the man she'd left for the peninsula's most prominent
citizen, not even flinching when one speaker pointedly stared at
her while praising Ward Austin's 'unwavering fight against those
who would sell our beloved island's beautiful natural resources
to the highest bidder.'

She wore her pale blond hair in a shoulder-grazing bob, swept
back from a high forehead so smooth that – along with the
absence of crow's feet – made Nora suspect Botox. Delilah gazed
at some point past the lectern, her gaze never once straying to
the photo of her former husband on a table beside it. It showed
Ward Austin in profile, silhouetted against the endless expanse
of the Pacific, his pants rolled to his knees, his bare feet planted
firmly in the sands of his beloved peninsula.

Another speaker rose and walked to the podium. Nora didn't
recognize Sheila Connor, the math teacher, until she turned
around, probably because Sheila had straightened her unruly curls
for the occasion, and had donned a dress, rather than her practical
workaday outfits of slim slacks and overblouses.

She looked first to Ward Austin's parents and siblings, folding
chairs pulled close, their clasped hands forming a chain along
the row.

'I've never met many of you before today, and I'm so sorry
to get to know you under these circumstances. I hope the words
you've heard here bring some comfort to your family. Ward
was so very loved in this community, and even those few who
disagreed with him admired his passion.'

Nora could only catch glimpses of the family's faces, but thought she saw a wan smile flit across his mother's.

'Ward loved this peninsula and opted to stay, even as so many others moved away into the wider world. The only thing he loved more was his son, Damien.'

She turned slightly to face Damien and spoke to him directly.

'His life's work was to preserve the fragile beauty of this region so you could have the same sort of childhood all of us who grew up here did, exploring its wild places and drawing strength from them. Every time we spoke, he mentioned how proud he was of you, how—'

Damien leapt to his feet.

'Bullshit! Whatever he told you, it was just to get you in the sack. And it worked, didn't it?'

He wrested free of his mother's grasp and spun to face a room comprising a collective held breath. 'All of you, you're all full of shit. A bunch of losers. Just like my dad and his stupid nonprofit.'

Sheila stepped from behind the lectern, reaching for him. 'Oh, Damien.' He ducked away. His mother made another grab, wobbling off balance on skinny high heels. Everhart rose and shoved past the others in her row to stand in the aisle and block a possible escape.

The funeral director who'd led the service rushed to the lectern to announce a brief, hasty closing song, performed by a trio of Ward's friends, as Everhart helped Delilah wrestle Damien into submission, and the service ended with an unsteady tune as murmurs of polite horror rippled through Ward's mourners.

SIX

Nora and Luke shared a booth that night with Sheila Connor in Betty's Bakery Café.

Betty's was a BYOB joint. Nora and Luke had arrived with a six-pack of a local IPA, but set it aside when Sheila pulled a bottle of Scotch from her tote. 'After that funeral, something stronger seemed in order. Ice?'

'God, no.'

Sheila waited as they drained their water glasses. Nora held up two fingers; Luke, three.

'Luke, I think you've got the right idea.' Sheila poured generously for everyone.

Nora had invited Sheila to join her and Luke in the trailer, thinking Sheila might need privacy, but Sheila had waved away her offer. 'It's no secret that Ward and I were seeing each other for a while. It was all above-board – each of us was divorced by then, but not for long. Classic rebound on both our parts. It was fun for a while, and then we both came to our senses. No regrets. Besides, no way do I want any of these people to think a twelve-year-old has shamed me into hiding.'

Around them, the café hummed with an energy seemingly strong enough to lift it from its foundation, every booth and table full. People clustered outside, waiting for a table or, reluctantly, for takeout. Janie, the lone server, hot-footed among the tables, pad and pen in hand.

Betty's, catercorner across the street from the school, was a Friday-night hangout, host to a communal kicking-back at the end of the work week – especially a week that had ended like this one.

At every table, every eulogy would be parsed, every gesture and facial expression analyzed, every possible meaning squeezed from them and reinterpreted, with Damien's outburst Topics A, B and C, and Sheila attracting more than her share of furtive glances.

'I feel terrible,' Sheila said for the dozenth time. 'If I had any idea, I'd never have said anything. I knew he'd taken his mom's side in the divorce, but I never expected anything like that. I'm just glad he's not in any of my classes.' Whatever discipline she'd applied to her hair had long been vanquished as she ran her hands through it again and again, tugging at it in agitation until the curls reasserted themselves and formed their customary unman-ageable corona.

Like everything else about Sheila, they were lush, abundant, and whenever they were together Nora felt keenly her body's angularity, and her lank straight hair that hadn't looked good since she'd abandoned the ministrations of her top-dollar stylist in Denver.

'Damien might not be in your class but he is in mine.' Nora turned to Luke. 'You're the counselor. And a divorced parent, too. That makes you a double expert. He'll be back in class in a few days. Maybe sooner. How do I handle this?'

Sheila, who'd been studying the amber liquid in her glass as though it held the answer to one of the equations she posed daily, looked at Luke with renewed interest. 'You, too?'

'Me, too, what?'

'Divorced. Do you do the kid handoff routine? How does yours work? Every other week? Weekends? Three days on, four off, and then switch?'

'I'd take any of those. My son's in New Mexico with his mom. I only see him four times a year. Phone calls once a week.'

Nora winced, thinking of the hushed, too-brief conversations that left Luke tense and uncommunicative for hours afterward.

'That's rough.' Sheila held out her glass for more. 'Boy? Girl? How old?'

'Son. Thirteen.'

'What's his name?'

'Gabriel.'

Information that comprised nearly the sum total of everything Nora knew about Luke's son. How had she never learned more? Because she'd never asked. Luke returned from his New Mexico visits so despondent that she usually made herself scarce until he emerged from his funk.

Luke sat up straighter. 'What about you?'

'Two boys, eight and eleven. Bill and Lannie. Troublemakers, both of them.' Her fond tone implied anything but.

'How do you handle it?'

'You mean the custody schedule, or the whole divorce thing in general? For custody, every other week and alternate weekends. We tried trading off midweek but it was too hard. As to the divorce, what can I say? Better for me but sucks for the kids.'

'Ain't that the truth.' Luke raised his glass and they clinked, faces mirroring rueful understanding.

Nora tried to wrest the conversation back to the matter at hand. 'At least it sounds as though neither of you has the kind of situation Damien is dealing with.'

'I'll say.' Sheila twisted a hand in her curls again, as Nora breathed relief. The danger of being exposed as knowing next to nothing about Luke's son appeared to have passed for the moment. She resolved to find out more, lots more. What kind of woman never asked about her partner's child?

'I'd never have pictured Delilah throwing Ward over for someone like Spencer. She and Spencer actually dated in high school – we all went to school together – but once she took up with Ward, that was it. Kindred spirits, they were, at least back then. She was your basic peninsula hippie chick, granola out the wazoo. If anything, she was even more of an activist than Ward.'

Nora recalled the formidably put-together woman she'd seen earlier in the day. She mentally lengthened and darkened Delilah's hair to a sandy, waist-length braid, swapped out her tailored dress for a loose Indian-print smock and harem pants, her tennis bracelet for jangling bangles, and her vertiginous pumps for shuffling huaraches. She could see it, just.

For sure, Delilah's former life must have been a lot more comfortable than the regimen of weekly hair blowouts and monthly stylings, the chemical peels and serums and mani-pedis, the gym membership and personal trainer, all necessary to maintain the sleek appearance demanded of her present life – the sort of routine that had once been Nora's own. She didn't miss it.

Janie arrived with three orders of fish and chips. Much as with the doughnuts, Nora had thought she didn't love fish and chips before she'd had Betty's light and perfectly crisped variety. More to the point, the substantial portions would help soak up the whisky they'd already consumed, and the beer they were about to, cans hissing as Luke popped their tops. At least they were all walking home.

Luke doused his chips with malt vinegar. 'What happened with Ward and Delilah?'

Sheila shrugged. 'Maybe she just got tired of being poor. A lot of the people working for the nonprofits around here are trustafarians, or tech refugees from Seattle, living off their earnings and fending off the guilt that comes with all that privilege. But Ward and Delilah paid themselves peanuts for salaries at Preserve the Peninsula. They didn't have any fallback funds. And you can only go to so many marches for so many years, and file so many lawsuits that go to one appeal after another, before you realize nothing is ever going to change, or at least nothing of substance.'

'But for Damien to choose one parent over another,' Nora broke in.

Luke and Sheila exchanged glances and broke into laughs wholly free of mirth.

Luke patted her shoulder. 'Oh, the joys of ignorance. Savor them.'

She knew he meant well. But she couldn't shake the feeling of being on the outside, looking in at a club nobody wanted to join.

A crash saved her from the need to respond.

Conversation stopped. Necks craned. A mechanical yellow beast dropped a load of steel girders beside the foundation for the tsunami platform.

'Ward Austin must be rolling in his grave,' said a man at a table just beyond their booth.

'Why?' Nora couldn't help herself. She quickly introduced herself and Luke. 'Mr Austin's son is in my class.'

'Gerry Fields,' he said. 'Ward's a friend. Was a friend.'

'Still a friend,' said his companion, introducing himself as Clark Stevens. 'He's with us every step of the way. He lost that fight.' He nodded to the construction across the street. 'But there'll be more.'

He and Gerry had the same weathered look as Ward Austin, men whose out-of-doors time went beyond weekend warrior excursions and leaned more toward days bent beneath heavy packs, one foot placed deliberately before the other, with exquisite attention to the smallest wildflower as well as the sweeping views on all sides.

Nora watched with them as the machine reversed, leaving deep tracks in the damp, sandy soil. She was hesitant to contradict two people she'd just met but couldn't help but ask. 'What's wrong with the tsunami tower? Seems like a good idea.'

Gerry shrugged. 'Never did find out. Ward dropped his objection but didn't have anything to back it up. It's Spencer Templeton's other project that really set Ward's hair on fire. But if Ward was against it, that's good enough for us.'

They'd assumed identical postures, arms folded across chests, jaws set. Ward's Warriors indeed. They didn't need a reason, just Ward Austin's word.

She wanted to ask about the other project, but feared a holier-than-thou lecture, something she'd gotten her fill of back when she'd held a university public relations job. All those student groups, so inspiring and infuriating at once, pursuing their various causes with single-minded energy, and quick to label a sellout anyone who mentioned the dirty word *compromise*.

'Nice talking to you,' she said. Her none-too-subtle exit strategy didn't work.

'Not that Templeton cares what we think. He wouldn't be caught dead eating in a place like this.' Clark hoisted his beer with pinky aloft and mimed a prissy sip.

Janie swept up to the table and slammed a check between them.

'You two pissing and moaning again?'

She put her hands on her hips and played to her audience of Nora and Luke and Sheila. 'Some people want to keep this place in the Dark Ages, everybody scratching and scraping with two or three part-time jobs just to get by. Just look at that!'

She swept a hand toward the window. 'My Ron's over there right now, getting extra hours working weekends and evenings until it's dark. That's real money, money Ward would have kept from going into Ron's pockets, and it's just for this piddly-ass tower. I can't wait for Templeton's next project. Maybe then I can quit this job and not have to listen to the likes of you anymore.'

She stomped away, leaving the men shaking their heads.

'She's hardly alone,' Clark said. 'All that lovey-dovey stuff you heard this morning? That's just because it was a memorial service.' Clark looked around and lowered his voice. 'For all the people who loved him, Ward had enemies, real enemies in this town. People who said right to his face they were fed up with him.'

'You two are more full of crap than my grandson's diapers.' Janie was back. 'You and everybody else in this room and their little conspiracy theories. I happen to know exactly what happened to Ward, and it had nothing to do with Spencer's project.'

Gerry half-rose from his chair. 'You know? What was it?'

Betty stuck her head out of the kitchen. 'Janie! Order up!'

Janie pinched thumb and forefinger together and zipped them across her closed lips. She pointedly eyeballed the bills they'd placed atop on the check.

The two men dug in their pockets for a few more singles, added them, and left.

SEVEN

'**K**eep them busy' was Luke's advice on how to handle her students when everyone returned to class the Monday after the memorial.

'Load them up with so much work they don't have time to think about what happened at the memorial. They will, of course, but guiding them through it is my job. Yours is getting them back to normal. Kids thrive on routine.'

Nora wasn't so sure. Her students, at least some of them, seemed determined to disrupt routine at every opportunity. Further complication came in the form of an all-school notice from Everhart that plans for the first semester class project were due by the end of the week.

'What's the deal with this project?'

Nora and Sheila were in the teachers' lounge during their half-hour lunch break. Nora snapped the plastic lid off the container Luke had prepared, revealing a salad of arugula, avocado and baked sweet potatoes with a miso dressing, and a thick slice of focaccia.

Sheila, already halfway through a peanut butter-and-jelly sandwich, looked on in undisguised envy. 'Must be great to have time to make your own lunch. I just throw together whatever I've made for the kids. They'd never eat anything like that, anyway.'

'Oh, I don't make my lunches. If I did, I'd be eating PB&J, too. Luke makes them all. It's his mission to keep me healthy.'

To keep me alive, she almost added. Because if it hadn't been for Luke, her former job literally could have killed her.

Sheila nearly choked on her last bite of sandwich. 'You

shouldn't tell other women something like that. Be glad I'm a friend. Otherwise, I might try to steal him out from under you. Haven't you ever heard that Bonnie Raitt song "Women, be wise"?'

Nora shook her head. 'I don't know it.'

Sheila hummed a few bluesy bars. 'Something like that. Basically, if you've got it that good, keep it to yourself.'

'He's a good one,' Nora agreed. But hadn't she thought her husband a good man, too, long past the point when she shouldn't have?

She bit into the focaccia and tried not to close her eyes in bliss. 'A little stale,' she lied. She knew it had come out of the oven that morning because she'd awoken to its scent and had successfully begged a piece for breakfast. 'What about these projects? I have no idea what to suggest, or even what kids this age are capable of.'

'More than you'd think.' Sheila gave the focaccia a look worthy of the most winsome puppy.

Nora tore the piece in half and handed it to her.

'Forget woman be wise,' Sheila said after wolfing it down. 'Turn your back for a New York second, and I'm going after him. Just joking. Really.'

Really?

'But, as to the project.' Sheila outlined a plan so generous that Nora forgave her awkward maybe-joke on the spot.

'Let's double up. I was thinking of having my class build a model of the tsunami evacuation tower.'

Nora had been wondering about the planned platform ever since she'd seen the foundation beside the school and said as much.

'It's exactly what it sounds like. When it's done, it won't be quite as high as that ridiculous excuse for a hill, but a lot closer to the school and easier to get to for the people on this end of the peninsula. And it's still higher than any tsunami this place has seen in—'

'Oh, I know,' Nora interrupted. 'Three hundred years. You'd think it's something to brag about, the way people here talk about it.'

'Exactly. These towers are in Japan, and in coastal towns north and south of here – and those places aren't nearly as vulnerable as this peninsula. You might have seen one if you've spent any time in this part of the world. Couple of platforms, with sides open to let the water flow through if it ever gets that high, even though the chances of that ever happening are about a jillion to one. Anyway, it's a perfect project for my class, because building the model will involve lots of math.'

That made sense to Nora. 'But I teach social studies. With seventh-graders. How would that fit in with your project?'

Sheila flung her arms wide, indicating endless possibilities. 'They can study the community impact. There are always people who will object because of the aesthetics. Who wants a big ugly tower obscuring their pristine beachfront? Never mind all the big ugly houses that are going up.' She gave an exaggerated cough, speaking through it: 'Spaceship.'

'Exhibit A,' said Nora. For all its *Architectural Digest* styling, she found the spaceship grotesque.

'Your class could do a survey of local attitudes. My kids could tabulate the results – more math. Your kids could write the narrative.' Sheila grew more and more animated as she spoke and Nora nodded along, catching her enthusiasm. Not just for the project itself, but because of the fact she wouldn't have to come up with an idea on her own.

'Will Everhart approve a joint project?'

'Please.' Sheila wadded up her paper napkin and tossed it toward the recycling container. It fell far short. She looked at it and shrugged. 'There's a reason I don't teach gym. Don't worry about Everhart. The semester-end projects check some sort of box required by the state. As long as we complete them remotely competently, she'll be thrilled.'

Nora retrieved the napkin and deposited it, then put her own containers – reusable – in her insulated lunch bag.

'Speaking of Everhart, we'd better get back. I swear she stands outside my classroom door with that stopwatch of hers. As for the project, count me in.'

Nora's relief over the solution to the class project buoyed her through the rest of the day and for once she left school without the stone-in-her-stomach realization of all the ways in which she'd fallen short.

The school was barely a mile from her campsite, both of them bordering the beach, making for the most pleasant commute of her life.

Low tide left a wide stretch of yielding sand, and she stumbled across it before reaching the darkened area pounded to a hard surface by the retreating surf. She kicked off her shoes and socks and carried them, having learned from earlier experience about the occasional wave that outran the rest, sweeping in high and fast and soaking an unwary beachcomber to the knees.

A few cars and pickups sat parked facing the waves, their owners relaxing within, watching the waves while protected from the fog that clung to surfaces like a chilly, wet sheet.

The sight of the vehicles startled her at first until she'd learned it was legal to drive on the beach. The trick was to stick to the few entry points that offered a hard-packed surface all the way to the shoreline, and to let a little air out of the tires for traction beforehand, just in case.

'You can always tell the tourists,' Sheila had pointed out. 'They're the ones who get stuck.'

As warm and dry as it must have been inside the cars, Nora couldn't abide the notion of viewing the waves through a windshield. The peninsula's cool, misty weather discouraged cheek-by-jowl crowds deploying beach towels and umbrellas. It made for solitary walks, perfect for shedding the stress of a day spent with a bunch of preteens, their hormones simmering toward a full boil.

She nudged the edge of a whitened sand dollar with her bare toe and found its fragile surface remarkably unbroken. She carefully blew away as much sand as she could and tucked it into her jacket's breast pocket, where she was unlikely to bump into something and shatter it. She passed block after block of the showy new houses fast replacing the traditional cottages a fraction of their size. Most sat shuttered and still, used only for those few weeks of high summer when visitors could reasonably hope for sun.

The spaceship was the last in line, unusual not only for its bizarre shape but in the obvious signs of habitation. A pair of Mercedes, one black, one cream – his and hers? – sat beneath its concrete pilings, along with an array of mountain bikes that must have been for use on vacations in places far from the strap-flat peninsula.

Ovoid windows, in keeping with the home's overall shape, stared blankly out at the sea. She stood on tiptoe, peering upward, hoping to detect a hint of life within.

'I'm out here.'

Nora spun around so quickly she nearly fell.

The man who'd walked up silently behind her caught her arm and steadied her.

'Careful. The last thing I need is a slip-and-fall suit.' He smiled to underscore the joke, teeth flashing white in a face so tanned she suspected either bronzer or regular visits to a booth. For sure, he didn't acquire it on the peninsula.

He dropped her arm and held out his hand. 'Spencer Templeton. We met at back-to-school night. Damien's stepdad.'

'Yes, of course. I'm so sorry.' The rote phrase rose to her lips. But sorry for what? For a loss that wasn't his? 'This must be a difficult time for your family.' It was the best she could manage.

'I'm the one who should be apologizing to you.'

'Whatever for?' She was the one who'd been caught snooping.

'For Damien's behavior at the service. Care to come inside? I'll make you a cup of coffee and explain.'

No explanation needed. That's what she should have said. Plus, coffee this late in the day would leave her bug-eyed and twitchy at three in the morning. But the opportunity to gain insight into her most problematic student, not to mention the chance of seeing the interior of the spaceship, overcame knee-jerk courtesy.

'That's very generous of you. Lead the way.'

She followed him to a narrow metal staircase that spiraled up and up. 'It goes all the way to the roof. We have a deck there. But perhaps you'd rather take the elevator? This is so open it makes some people nervous, Delilah among them, I'm afraid.'

An elevator! Nora was tempted by the sheer novelty of it. But she didn't want to be seen as obviously gawking. 'I'm fine.'

He started up the stairwell. 'I hope you like espresso,' he called over his shoulder.

An elevator and an espresso machine, too? Wait until Luke heard about this.

'I love it.'

EIGHT

Her first reaction to the spaceship was disappointment. Then, a smug satisfaction.

It was so *ordinary*. She'd expected more than the same sort of granite-countertop, stainless-appliance kitchen she'd had in the Denver home she'd shared with her husband, back in marital prehistory. Beyond the kitchen island she glimpsed curved white leather sofas (surely leather was impractical in this region of damp and sand?) and glass accent tables, all seemingly designed for effect rather than comfort or utility. Large paintings filled the wall space; tasteful, skilled versions of the same sorts of insipid beach scenes sold in the schlock shops in Seacrest, the peninsula's main town.

Behind her, a machine gurgled. Spencer handed her a tiny cup filled just shy of the brim with liquid the shade of the darkest chocolate and smelling as nearly delectable. So what if she'd be up half the night? The brew, unlike the decor, *was* superior.

As was the view, which she belatedly noticed. The home's height lofted its occupants above the sight of the street and beach below, framing nothing but sky and rolling waves cut by the occasional glistening flash of dolphins or, farther out, the barnacled bulk of a gray whale.

'It's as though you're in a ship,' she breathed. All this time, she'd thought of it as a spacecraft, soaring through the inky heavens, swerving among the glassy shards of stars. But it was so like a seagoing vessel that she planted her feet a little farther apart as though to counter the undulation of the waves.

'That's the idea. Join me.' He indicated one of the colossal sofas.

She perched on the edge, clutching her coffee cup, afraid of splashing as much as drop on that pale, glove-soft surface. She was afraid he'd sit beside her, but he took an armchair, though not before producing a whisky decanter. He raised a questioning eyebrow. 'We've all had a rough week.'

She nodded and he splashed a few drops into her coffee.

He leaned back in his chair and crossed an ankle atop a knee. 'About Damien.'

'Yes. I so enjoy having him in my class.' Which is what she was supposed to say. Except even Damien's stepdad didn't buy it.

'You so enjoy being called Miss Worst?'

Checkmate, right out of the gate.

'As nicknames go, it's a natural. I once had a music teacher named Mrs Horney. You can just imagine.'

The smile turned genuine. 'You're right. That makes Worst look mild by comparison. But what can I tell you about Damien? That's what you want to know, isn't it?'

Nora put her cup down very carefully on the glass end table, fearful she might choke if she took another sip, and took still more care when she spoke.

'Obviously, he's very traumatized by his father's death.'

'You mean the man he called a loser? Who he found so intolerable he couldn't even sit quietly through his funeral?' Spencer fiddled with the tassel on his loafer. 'I agree Damien is a troubled youngster. But he seems quite certain about his feelings for his father.'

'I mean,' Nora floundered. She half-wished he'd dosed her coffee more strongly but was also glad he hadn't. She was already way too off balance. 'Divorce has to be really confusing for kids, without the added complication of his father's death.'

'Not necessarily. I assume you'd met Ward Austin? I seem to remember him slinking into the school as we were leaving on back-to-school night.'

Nora offered up another platitude. 'He seemed nice.'

'Nice, sure. If you're a tree, or some obscure endangered mollusk. But I shouldn't complain. If he hadn't been so wrapped up in trying to sequester every last grain of sand on this peninsula for anything other than humans, I wouldn't be with Delilah. The way he neglected his wife and son – it was criminal. Before this happened, Delilah and I were working with a therapist to build Damien's confidence back up.'

Nora wondered if that involved buying him every trendy new thing on the market. Anyway, as far as she could tell, Damien had confidence to spare.

Spencer let go of the tassel and leaned forward, hands clasped, just shy of being folded in prayer. 'We hope you'll prove an ally in that effort.'

Why did she feel as though she were being courted? And, considering the goal, did it matter? Given the stories she'd heard from other teachers about indifferent parents, she knew she should be glad when one sought her help. Meet him halfway, she lectured herself.

'Of course, I'll be alert to any concerning signs. But I've seen nothing in the classroom that exceeds his behavior at the funeral.'

'Inexcusable,' he agreed. 'I can't imagine what that must have been like for Delilah. I wish I'd been there. We felt it would be better if I stayed away. Ward had legions of supporters. I'm sure you saw that. Ward's Warriors – more like Ward's Worriers, wringing their hands over the least change. They even tried to stop the tsunami platform I'm building next to the school. Can you imagine? Something that could save hundreds of lives! But Ward was more concerned about one of those microscopic sea creatures than the lives of children, including his own son.'

He caught his breath and raised his hand, as though to stop himself. But he wasn't done.

'The way those people treated Delilah after the divorce – scandalous. You'd think she was the Whore of Babylon for finally opting for some happiness for herself and her son.'

Anger blazed in his eyes, so hot and raw that Nora suppressed a flinch.

'I finally had to tell him to get them to back off. It was unpleasant. But necessary. Anyway, I'm hardly the only person Ward picked a public fight with.'

Ward Austin had mentioned confrontations with Spencer and Delilah. Nora considered her initial impression of the man. Made some readjustments. Once again, she thought of her years in academia, which attracted crusaders of all stripes, along with their fanatically devoted acolytes, some of them inevitably star-struck young women. These men – they were almost always men – threw all their energy into their causes. Spencer had termed Ward's treatment of his wife and son 'neglect'. Nora thought it probably wasn't too strong a word.

'Were there a lot of public fights?'

He nodded. 'Some. You're not from here, so you don't know how quickly things are changing. People relied on fishing and oystering for years, but those jobs are fast disappearing. The peninsula's whole economy is changing. Now it's all about development – construction, hospitality, eco-tourism, everything opposed by Ward's Warriors. But every one of their wins means that many fewer jobs. You can just imagine how people feel about that. You should hear the talk among my construction crews.'

'I don't have to imagine. I saw it in action.' She described the dressing-down Janie dealt Ward's friends.

He gave a grim nod. 'Add a lot of testosterone to that equation and you can just imagine. Ward got into it a couple of times with my foreman, Ron Stevenson.'

'That name sounds familiar. Janie's his wife, right? If he hates Ward's Warriors half as much as she does, those must have been some showdowns.'

'Oh, they were. At least they never came to blows. Unless . . .'

He stopped. Their eyes met. What was it one of the men in Betty's had said? *Ward had real enemies in this town.*

A door banged open. Quick, light footsteps sounded.

'Oh, hello! What a surprise.' Delilah rearranged her features into a smile so quickly Nora was nearly persuaded of her delight in finding her son's teacher in her living room. She wore a hot-pink windbreaker over a matching polo shirt and pink-and-green plaid slacks, colors so aggressively feminine that Nora wondered if she were overcompensating for her boyish build. She swept a neon-green cap from her head and shook out her hair.

Spencer rose and went to her, brushing her cheek with a kiss. She was nearly as tall as he. 'Espresso for you, too?'

'Heavens, no. I'm impressed, Ms Best. If I had espresso at this hour, I'd be up all night and thoroughly incapable of teaching tomorrow morning.'

Nora squirmed. She had the same concern, compounded by the knowledge that Damien would gleefully report the least slip-up.

Delilah pointed to the bottle on the coffee table. 'But I'll take a little of that, please. I need it after today's session.'

She took the other end of the sofa, angling her body to face

Nora. 'I've been working on my putting with the pro. Not that it's helped.'

Spencer retrieved a glass from a cupboard and held it under the dispenser in the refrigerator door. 'The new putter didn't do the trick?' he called over the rattle of ice. 'I thought the pro said it would make all the difference.'

Delilah rolled her eyes. 'Oh, the new putter is great. The problem is that I'm the same old golfer.'

She blotted her forehead with the back of her hand.

Spencer handed her the glass. 'You're flushed. Are you all right?'

She smiled up at him. 'I jogged over and back. Helps me warm up beforehand and work off tension afterward.'

'What about the Maxwells' dog?' Spencer turned to Nora. 'The Maxwells are the nicest people on the whole peninsula. Unfortunately, they have the meanest dog. We've all complained about him, but Animal Control says as long as he hasn't hurt anyone, they can't do anything. The Maxwells keep him on a lead in the yard, but we're all terrified that he'll get loose someday. He loses his mind whenever anybody passes the house on foot.'

'Or on a bike. I pedaled past there once.' Nora folded her arms around her torso as if protecting herself against the slavering beast who'd charged her bike, only to be yanked up short by a line that looked far too insubstantial. 'Never again.'

Delilah nodded sympathy. 'I always carry my putter if I'm going that way. I might not be able to hit a golf ball worth a darn, but I figure it gives me a fighting chance against Booyah.'

She poured and lifted her glass toward Nora. 'Cheers. Maybe I should drink this before practice rather than afterward. It couldn't hurt. What brings you here, Ms Best? Is there a problem with Damien? I assume you already know we've lined him up with a child psychiatrist. We have to drive to Portland, but we wanted the best. We're fortunate he would accommodate a weekend schedule so Damien doesn't have to miss school.'

Spencer spoke over Nora's demurral. 'Ms Best was passing by and I invited her in. She assured me that Damien is doing remarkably well, given everything he's dealing with.'

She had?

'That's right.' Nora's fake smile was nowhere near as practiced as Delilah's. Time to extract herself before Delilah could quiz her more closely about Damien. 'Thanks so much for your hospitality. Good luck with your golf game.'

Delilah rolled her eyes and gave a little wave. 'I need all the luck I can get. Nice to see you, Ms Best.'

Spencer collected their espresso cups. 'I'll see you out.'

He walked Nora to the door that opened on to the stairwell and raised his voice so his wife could hear. 'Please stop by anytime, Ms Best. Take care on the stairs. Damien runs up and down them all day, but it takes a while to get the hang of them.'

He stepped close to Nora and pitched his voice low. 'What you said about Janie. And what I saw with her husband and Ward – you're wondering the same thing I am, aren't you?'

Probably. She pushed the thought away. Ridiculous.

'Thanks again for the coffee.' She started down the stairs, moving cautiously. The stairway, for all its visual appeal, was wildly impractical. She couldn't imagine climbing it with supermarket bags slung over her arm. But of course, she reminded herself, there was the elevator.

His voice followed her.

'You're thinking maybe Ward pissed somebody off enough to get himself killed.'

She hadn't been. But she was now.

NINE

As promised, Nora watched Damien closely for signs of distress. But he seemed his usual irritating self, always the last to comply with any request, opening his book only after someone else had already started reading aloud, letting his hands drop just to his knees during hourly stretching and toe-touching breaks, and groaning louder than anyone else when Nora announced the end-of-year project.

They quieted when she added they'd share responsibility for the project with Sheila Connor's math class.

'Her students will design the model of the tsunami evacuation

tower.' She flicked the switch that lowered the screen in front of
the whiteboard, then tapped a key on her computer to display an
image of a soaring steel platform, fifty feet high with another
platform ten feet below the top, both surrounded by sturdy safety
fences to which people could cling in the face of lashing winds
or pummeling waves.

'We'll ask people in town how they feel about it. Let's list
some questions.'

She'd prepared her own, just in case, but to her surprise, they
chimed in, with suddenly-not-shy Abby James leading the charge.

'People will worry about the' – she lost the struggle with
'aesthetics', finally resorting to, 'They'll say it'll scare the tourists
away.'

Nora raised an eyebrow and made a mental reminder to check
her notes from back-to-school night. She had a vague memory
that Abby's mom was on the County Commission. Clearly, Abby
wasn't one of those kids who zoned out over her phone when
her parents were talking.

'How much will it cost?' This from Zeke Miles, which figured.
The freckled budding entrepreneur turned a healthy profit each week
by deputizing his mom to buy oversize bags of candy and chips at
big box stores on the mainland, then repacking small amounts in
paper lunch sacks – better for the environment than baggies – and
selling them at recess. Those who wrote their name on the sacks
and re-used them got a nickel discount on each purchase.

Nora had wanted to discourage him, but Sheila told her he
wasn't breaking any rules. 'Anyway, you should see his spreadsheets. Every month, he puts his profits into the stock market.
He picks the stocks and his mom invests the money for
him. He's saving up to buy a car when he's sixteen. The way
he's going, he'll have enough for a down-payment on a house
by the time he hits college.'

Nora raised the screen so she could jot Abby's and Zeke's
questions on the whiteboard. 'Anyone else?'

'How many people should it hold? Just us kids? Our families?
Everyone on this end of the peninsula?'

'Won't there be traffic jams if there's a tsunami warning? Should
they build a bigger road so everybody can get to it in time?'

'It's all metal. Won't it attract lightning? Is that a problem?'

'What's it going to do to the environment? Will any endangered species be affected?' If Nora had to guess, Maryann McGinnis' parents were among Ward's Warriors. What had Spencer Templeton said? Something about a tiny sea creature. It must not have been too terribly endangered, given that the tower rose higher by the day.

She soon filled all the space on the whiteboard, beaming as they vied with one another to ask the next question and the one after that. Maybe, just maybe, she was getting the hang of this teaching business.

'That's enough for now. Let's break into small groups and decide how best to survey people. Do we interview them in person? Send out emails?'

They winced. 'Oh, I forgot. Email is too old-school for all of you. What about social media? And if so, which sites? Think about those things and come up with a plan.'

She counted them off in groups of five and told them to arrange their desks in circles. 'Each of you appoint a group leader. Work on this for the rest of the period. Tomorrow, your leaders will present your plans and we'll decide as a class how to proceed.'

A knock interrupted them. Everhart entered before Nora could answer. Now what? Was the principal going to scuttle her Hail Mary plan for a joint project with Sheila's class?

'I'm here for Damien Austin.'

Had Everhart been listening outside her door and mistaken the kids' enthusiasm for misbehavior? On this, the one day that things were going well, was Nora about to face some sort of lecture later about an inability to control her class?

But Everhart ignored her. 'Damien, please come with me.'

He left to a mocking chorus of 'uh-ohs' from his classmates. Nora got them quieted down just as the electronic chime that had replaced school bells of old sounded. She followed her pupils into the hallway and headed for the principal's office, hoping for enlightenment on Damien's latest misdemeanor.

But she stopped at the sight visible through the glass panels of the school's main entrance: Spencer Templeton, holding open the door of his black Mercedes and ushering Damien inside.

'I suppose you want to know what that's about.'

Nora jumped, inadvertently glancing at Everhart's feet, half-expecting to see slippers, so quietly had the woman appeared beside her.

'I was just getting ready to call a meeting to tell the teachers. I might as well start with you. Harold Wallace has been arrested in connection with Damien's father's death.'

TEN

Nora and Luke sat at opposite ends of the plaid sofa in his apartment, bare feet entwined, hunched over their phones. Murph lay on the floor beside them, luxuriating in having them all to himself. Mooch was back in the trailer, probably wreaking the sneaky sort of havoc that Nora would discover upon opening the bathroom door – had she really left it ajar? – and finding the entire roll of toilet paper in festive coils across the floor.

'Got it!' Luke held up his phone. Murph raised his head and thumped his tail against the floor, hopeful the outburst presaged a walk.

The *Peninsula Press* story about Harold's arrest was finally online.

Nora thumbed her phone to bring up the story, reading bits aloud. 'Local vagrant taken into custody last night,' she mumbled. 'Arrested without incident . . . held on a potential homicide charge . . .'

Luke, scrolling faster, summarized for her. 'That original theory that maybe Ward stumbled and hit his head on the rocks up there? That's not what happened. There was blood on the rocks, sure, but it says they also found droplets of blood – Ward's blood – all the way up the hill to where Abby found his body. Listen to what the sheriff says: "It appears as though he was assaulted at the bottom of the hill and then fled on foot to the summit, where he collapsed and died several hours before his body was found."'

'Summit makes it sound like a mountain,' Nora groused. 'And "fled on foot". Why can't he just say "ran away" like a normal person?'

'Because maybe he didn't run. Maybe he staggered. Or stumbled.'

Nora kicked at his feet. 'Maybe you should be an English teacher instead of a counselor. However he got up there, that's a pretty gruesome scenario.'

'Poor guy. I wonder if he went into the bushes to hide from whoever attacked him. But it kept him from being seen by anyone who might have helped him.'

Nora thought about the early-morning runners using the hill for a cardio boost. They'd doubtless passed within feet of him without noticing, focused as they were on the judgmental numbers displayed on their various fitness devices. Not to mention the schoolkids frolicking in the clearing – although, by then it had been far too late to save Ward Austin.

She went back to her phone, leapfrogging ahead of him to the end of the story. 'Listen to this.'

It seemed someone – unnamed – had witnessed a stormy encounter between Ward and a person presumed to be Harold the night before Ward's body was found. The person had brandished a long stick. The witness couldn't hear what the other person said, but Ward shouted his response:

'I'm sick of your threats! Just back the fuck off!'

The witness said Wallace then shoved Austin so forcefully that Austin threw up his hands to defend himself. 'At that point, the witness feared being seen, so she left.'

Nora's breath caught. Luke's head snapped up.

'*She*,' said Nora.

Luke said it even as Nora mimed a zipper across her lips. 'Janie.'

They were both too wired to sleep and it was too early, anyway. Luke proposed a walk on the beach.

Their steps crunched across the driveway of crushed oyster shells. Nora cast a worried eye toward the first floor, relieved to see the flickering light of a television through his landlady's window. Mrs Robbins was an early-to-bed, early-to-rise sort, and while the latter part jibed with Luke's school schedule, the former made for a lot of tiptoeing and hushed lovemaking in the apartment above.

The sun had slipped below the cloud cover and hovered just above the sea as they walked onto the beach. Murph bounded ahead of them, plunging into the gentle waves with a thunderous splash.

Gulls lofted from the surface, screaming imprecations. Murph paddled back and forth, tail feathering the water in bliss. Chesapeakes had been bred to withstand hours in the frigid waters of the bay for which they were named, snatching ducks and geese by hundreds for bounty hunters, and Murph always made a beeline for even the smallest puddle. Nora wondered if swimming were even more enjoyable in his dotage, providing a soothing respite for his aching joints.

They walked toward town, with its lengthening stretch of what Luke called 'statement houses', the spaceship making the most emphatic statement of all.

'Don't even think about it,' Nora warned him when his steps slowed as they passed it. 'In fact, don't look at it. Bad enough he already caught me standing outside gawking. Twice would feel like stalking.'

'I'll bet everybody gawks when they first see that thing. And maybe the second and third time, too.'

A Frisbee soared past Nora's head and landed at Luke's feet. 'Sorry!'

Sheila trotted up, trailed by two boys. 'Bill. And his little brother, Lannie. My rotten kids are good at throwing, but the art of catching eludes them.' She proved her point by winging the Frisbee back toward Lannie who watched it sail past him and fall just short of the waves. Both boys raced for it, each trying to shove the other out of the way. Murph's head swung toward them. He liked retrieving almost as much as he liked swimming.

Sheila fell into step beside them. 'I'm trying to tire them out before bedtime. At least, that's my excuse. I love walking this beach. No matter how bad a day I've had, it all falls away the minute my feet hit the sand.'

'Same,' said Nora. 'I worried that I'd hate the fog and rain, but this makes up for it.'

Sheila gave them a sidelong glance. 'I guess you saw the story.'

The Frisbee floated toward them. Luke snatched it from the

air and sent it soaring with a backhanded flick of the wrist. 'Yeah. Are we right in thinking Janie was probably the witness?'

'For people who haven't been here that long, you two sure catch on quick. Who knows if you're right but based on the texts blowing up my phone, pretty much everyone else in town has come to the same conclusion.'

Nora had found the story frustrating in its lack of detail and said as much. 'There was nothing about where she saw this argument, or when. And how come nobody else saw it? And, based on my own limited experience, Harold yelled at everybody about everything.' Sheila gave a quick nod of confirmation. 'Has he ever hurt anybody before?'

The kids detected Murph's interest and skimmed the Frisbee along the waterline, tantalizingly close to the sand. He leapt after it, snatching it away just as Bill's hand touched it, and rewarded Bill with a mighty shake that left him soaked and squealing.

'Serves you right,' Sheila admonished him.

Nora called to Murph, but he ignored her and plunged back into the water.

'As to your question,' Sheila said, 'for all his yelling and stomping around, I don't think Harold's ever even gotten into a physical fight, let alone killed anyone.'

'That's probably the case with a lot of murders,' Luke pointed out.

'Yeah, but there are people in town who were way more upset with Ward than Harold ever was.'

'Those guys at Betty's the other night said Ward took a lot of crap for protesting the tsunami tower and some other project that Spencer Templeton is working on.'

Sheila scuffed her toes through the sand, kicking up gritty rooster tails with each step. 'That's a tough one. You've already been through the tsunami drill so you know how vulnerable this place is. And Templeton's donating the tower. It's hard to turn down an offer like that. You want to see some real excitement? Come to the County Commission meeting Tuesday night on the new hotel.'

'What new hotel?'

Sheila danced away from an incoming wave. It curled and hissed just inches from her feet, leaving a frothy line of yellowish spume as it receded.

'It's Spencer's other project. He wants to put up a big luxury hotel on the last empty block of beachfront in Lane's End. We call it Templeton's Wet Dream. Half the town can't wait to see it built and the other half says it's the beginning of the end of our little peninsula. Check out the meeting. Normally those meetings are a reliable cure for insomnia, but people have gotten so hot and bothered over the hotel project that the commission brings in cops to keep order. Ward led the charge against the hotel, as you might imagine.'

The Frisbee flew straight at Nora. She threw up her hands and it bounced off, rolling across the sand. She chased it down and lobbed it back. It traced a wobbling trajectory, falling well short of the kids.

She was pretty sure she heard a 'you suck' from the direction of Bill and Lannie, but Murph, miraculously rejuvenated by the combination of water to swim in and kids to play with, charged out of the waves and grabbed it between his teeth, setting off a chase. Luke stared so wistfully after them that Nora's heart knotted.

'Those three are made for each other,' Sheila said. 'Where was I? Right. The hotel. Ward had filed suit to stop the construction. But now that he's gone, Spencer will go full steam ahead.'

'How can he? Won't the nonprofit – Preserve the Peninsula, right? – carry on without him?'

'Kids! Come back!'

They were too far away for Nora to see their expressions, but she caught the slump of shoulder, the exaggerated drag of each step that signaled full-on sulking.

Sheila shook her head at them. 'I suppose I should be grateful that this is as bad as it gets, at least for now. Can't wait until they're teenagers.'

'Speaking from experience, you should enjoy every minute of the wait.' Luke's words reminded Nora afresh that she knew so little about Gabriel. Was he indeed a recalcitrant teen? If so, what form did his rebellion take? And how did Luke deal with it from so very far away? She was grateful when Sheila returned to the matter of Ward's death.

'Ward *was* the nonprofit. Well, along with Delilah, until she threw him over for Spencer. Preserve the Peninsula limped along for years, always on the verge of bankruptcy. Ward wore himself out, pestering lawyers all over the state to donate their time. He had a real fight persuading the board to go along with the lawsuit against the hotel project. I figure it'll just die a natural death now, along with Preserve the Peninsula. It's a shame. Ward got a lot of good things done over the years. But the hotel suit was a long shot and he knew it.'

Nora longed to ask Sheila about her relationship with Ward. She seemed largely unperturbed by his death. Had there really been nothing more than rebound sex between them? Or had she smothered her wails with a pillow upon finding of his death, and arisen dry-eyed in the morning, braced for a community's judgment? But she figured such questions were best posed, if at all, over coffee or better yet, a few glasses of wine and definitely when it was just the two of them.

'Why was it a long shot?'

'You've seen Spencer Templeton's house, right? Anyone who can build something that grotesque can throw lawyers at a suit from now until the end of the world. Besides, a lot of people in town want the hotel.'

Nora thought of Janie, exulting over the pay her husband was earning on a small-potatoes project like the tower. Spencer, talking about the grousing among his crews about Ward's opposition. A hotel would take dozens, maybe even hundreds, of workers months to build, and afterward would need front desk staff, housecleaners, bellhops, chefs and kitchen crew, servers and bartenders.

She knew that ever since settlement by Europeans, peninsula residents had looked to the sea and the bay for jobs, spending weeks at a time on trawlers where the pay was good but the work backbreaking – sometimes literally so. More recently, white-collar workers commuted for hours, balancing the lure of city wages and prestige against the pull of a home they loved.

'Still, Ward must have been a major pain in his ass,' Luke suggested. 'You think the police questioned Templeton?'

Sheila laughed so hard she bent double. 'That's a good one. Spencer Templeton bought the department two new cruisers last year.'

She straightened, sobering at their expressions. 'Seriously,

Spencer fights with lawyers, not with whatever it was that killed Ward. I get why you think it's not Harold – I'm right there with you on that one – but Spencer Templeton is the last person anyone should suspect.'

She collected her kids and the Frisbee and waved goodbye.

Nora watched the trio as they passed the spaceship. The only time she'd met Ward, he'd mentioned bad blood between him and Spencer Templeton, but only in the context of post-divorce rancor, the sort of pettiness that sent him to the opponent's bleachers at Little League games.

But Spencer had sketched a longer-term conflict, one that included people harassing his new wife, calling her a whore – the sort of thing that might spur a more personal response than that crafted by lawyers. Could it push a man from the ledge of respectability?

Luke likewise watched them go, but his thoughts were elsewhere.

'Bill's just a little younger than my son. Can't help but wonder what it would be like to see him every other week, maybe even more often if we lived in the same town.'

'You never wanted to move back to New Mexico?'

Nora held her breath, waiting for the answer. What if he said yes? What if he wanted her to come with him? What if he didn't?

He almost never talked about Gabriel. On the other hand, Nora never asked. A school photo on Luke's refrigerator door showed a slim-faced boy with a shock of dark hair that gave her an idea of what Luke's would look like if he ever grew out the buzz cut he'd kept, even after leaving the military.

In a second photo, a framed candid shot beside the bed, Gabriel hugged a black-and-white dog of indeterminate parentage. The same picture served as the wallpaper on Luke's phone.

Luke's sigh verged on a groan. 'Sure. But it's better this way, or at least that's what I keep telling myself. His mom was pregnant when I went to Iraq and we split not long after I got back. She married his stepdad about a minute later.'

An old story. Nora already knew the bare-bones outline and had never really wanted to hear the story fleshed out. Who liked talking about being cuckolded?

'He's a nice enough guy, and his mom's a good woman. Not

her fault I came back messed up. Anyhow, Gabriel has a stable life with them, and he tolerates my visits reasonably well. Why push for more? It might only upset him.'

Or, thought Nora, you could enjoy something as simple as a Frisbee toss without having to make every single second count. She wondered how often that very thought occurred to him.

'You cold? You're shivering.' He put an arm around her.

She shook her head and offered what she hoped was a plausible explanation. 'Just thinking about Ward Austin. It's so sad.'

They'd reached his street. He glanced inland. 'Your place or mine?'

She hesitated. Somehow, she'd never thought twice about the bedside photo of Gabriel, other than the initial cliched boy-and-his-dog comment. Now she imagined the child's reproachful eyes staring at the woman in his father's bed.

Or would it be the other way around? Did Luke, as she lay sleeping beside him, ever look at the photo in the moonlight and wish the gentle snores from the next room were coming from his son and not Nora's aging dog?

'Murph's soaking wet. I don't think your landlady would appreciate him dripping all over the carpet. And I still have papers to grade. Rain check?'

As if she had to ask. She told herself it was her imagination that he'd agreed a little too readily.

ELEVEN

Harold Wallace's initial court appearance was set for 4 PM Thursday and if Nora hadn't known better, she would have sworn the day was a holiday.

As soon as school let out, she jumped in her truck and headed for the county courthouse on the mainland, rolling past one business after another with a 'Closed' sign on its door. Her truck joined the traffic streaming toward the county seat, not quite stop-and-go, but moving well below the speed limit.

If this was what it was like for a mere court hearing, Nora

wondered what would happen during a tsunami alert. How could everyone possibly get to high ground or off the peninsula in time? She didn't know what Ward's objection to the evacuation tower had been, but to her the tower seemed like a good idea, providing it would stand for another two hundred years, or whenever the next earthquake was supposed to trigger a peninsula-swallowing wall of water.

She'd texted Luke to ask if he wanted to go with her, only to receive a frowning emoji and a one-word accusation: 'Ghoul.'

Easy for you to say, she thought. *You didn't find the body.*

She drove instead with Sheila, who was Luke's polar opposite in terms of her attitude toward the biggest thing to happen on the peninsula in recent memory.

'Just think – when it goes to trial, we'll probably be called as witnesses. Won't that be exciting?'

Nora's stomach performed energetic calisthenics. It was one thing to watch the proceedings. But to be part of them? She'd had enough experience with police and courts to last a lifetime. 'No,' she managed.

Sheila chattered on, heedless. 'Not just us, but Everhart, too. Hah. That's something I'd like to see. I pity the lawyer who goes up against her. You think they'll call Abby and Damien, too? I mean, they'd have to testify – Abby's the one who found him, and Damien saw him, too. But it seems so traumatizing. Don't they usually let kids testify by video? And Janie – do you think we'll find out any more today about what she said?'

It turned out not to matter.

They arrived at the courthouse only to find a restive crowd outside, surrounding Harold Wallace and a woman in a suit.

Nora parked and she and Sheila pushed their way through.

'What's going on?' Nora whispered to Janie.

'They're letting him go. Lack of evidence or some such bullshit.' Janie didn't bother lowering her own voice, and the woman in the suit – 'Harold's lawyer,' Janie sneered – turned toward them.

'The witness' – she stared hard at Janie – 'acknowledged she was too far away to identify with any certainty the person arguing with Mr Austin as my client. In fact, she said it was so dark at that hour she only saw the two people as silhouettes. She made her assumption based on generalities. "A tall person, maybe about five-ten, five-eleven" – that estimate based on a comparison to Mr Austin, who the witness has known for much of her lifetime, as she has the victim – "in a ball cap and swinging a stick."'

Arden Talbott, the newspaper editor, stood nearby, recording the exchange on her phone. She lifted it high and snapped a couple of photos as the lawyer continued: 'Honestly, if anyone else had brought forth such slender so-called evidence, charges never would have been filed. With all due respect to our law enforcement and prosecutor, they may have relied a little too heavily on our witness's familiarity with the area and the people allegedly involved.'

The public defender turned and swept the crowd with her gaze. 'Consider this: put a stick in the hand of any of our solid citizens and that could apply to a fair number of people here. Yes, my client was a longstanding, and quite vocal, foe of Mr Austin's work. Nor can he offer proof to back up his claim that he was at home that night. But no proof – other than this very vague assumption – has surfaced to indicate otherwise. I hope some emerges quickly, to erase any remaining taint from my client's name.'

Harold looked even worse for wear than usual due to the time he'd spent in the county lockup. 'I told you so,' he said to no one in particular. 'I told you I didn't do it.'

'I know what I saw,' Janie muttered.

The lawyer's expression softened. 'And I don't doubt that a bit. But are you certain of *who* you saw?'

She took Harold's arm. 'Come on. I'll drive you home.'

People turned their attention to Arden Talbott, jostling to supply her with outraged quotes. For once, Ward's Warriors appeared to be united with their opponents. Gerry and Clark stood just behind Janie, arms folded tight across their chests, nodding as Janie sputtered indignance.

'They shouldn't be so upset,' Nora whispered to Sheila. 'If he was never formally charged and more evidence comes forward, they can charge him.' She'd learned that last through personal experience, grateful that there'd been no additional evidence in her own case.

She'd spoken too loudly. Janie overheard her.

'You hear that?' Janie demanded. 'They just need more
evidence. This isn't over yet.'

Harold's release might have proven a disappointment, but the
next County Commission meeting loomed large in Nora's expectations. After all, Sheila had termed the meetings entertaining
and despite Nora's appreciation for the quiet life the peninsula
offered, sometimes it was a little too quiet.

She was ready for entertainment. Luke, not so much.

'I was just going to hit the couch with the remote and that
new IPA from the Store of Everything.' He'd adopted Nora's
mocking nickname for the peninsula's main supermarket/hard-
ware store but was serious about sampling the selection of beers
that comprised the store's entire rear wall.

'Save the beer for later. There's nothing on TV. Even I know
there's no such thing as Tuesday night football. Come on. If it's
as crazy as Sheila says, it'll be fun. Interesting, anyway.'

'Should I bring popcorn for the theatrics? Or maybe just
earplugs.' In the end he acquiesced, even putting on a fresh shirt
and running a wet comb through his bristly hair.

Nora had suspected Sheila of exaggerating when she mentioned
a police presence, but two uniformed cops flanked the door to
the county building on the mainland, across the street from the
courthouse that had seen Harold's brief hearing. A metal detector
stood in the open doorway. Luke unbuckled his belt, slid it from
the loops of his jeans, handed it to the officer and passed without
a beep.

Nora was glad they'd arrived early. Half the seats were already
occupied and the room filled fast. She recognized several parents
from back-to-school night. She studied the crowd, guessing who
might be for the hotel and who against. She saw Gerry and Clark,
two of Ward's Warriors, across the aisle and belatedly picked up
on the vibe from their side of the room.

People folded arms across chests and glowered at the three
commissioners seated behind a long table. Nora recognized one
of them, a woman with strawberry blond hair beside the chairman.
She propped an iPad before her and sat straight-backed and alert
as the other two fiddled with pen and paper and whispered among
themselves. Nora finally placed her as the mother of Abby James,

the student she'd have called her favorite if she'd admitted to having one.

On her own side of the aisle people chatted easily among themselves, expressions bright with anticipation. Nora saw Janie from the bakery café, holding hands with a man whose corded arms were a thicker version of the veins in his neck. Sheila waved to her from the back of the room. She'd come in late and joined people standing against the wall.

Spencer Templeton had positioned himself in the front row. He'd donned a navy blazer for the occasion, making him the second-best-dressed person in the room. He was accompanied by a man in a full suit, with a laptop on the seat beside him. Something about him – maybe the smudged glasses, the goofy cartoon tie – belied the suit, as though it might hide a pocket protector on the shirt beneath the jacket.

The secretary called the meeting to order. Chairs creaked as people fell back into their seats after an uninspired Pledge of Allegiance. People on Nora's side of the aisle fiddled with their phones during the minutes and old business. Across the way, Ward's Warriors held their stoic stare. Impressive, Nora thought, who'd long been accustomed to the sight of people scanning their phones while waiting for everything from a red light to their espresso drink. Or, maybe Ward's Warriors disdained the accepted necessity of smartphones as just one more thing hastening the end of the planet.

The secretary read a jumbled combination of numbers and letters, and the room snapped to attention. 'The proposed Mare Vista hotel,' she added unnecessarily.

The chairman – Brock Bailey, his nameplate read – bent the skinny table mic toward his mouth.

'I received notice from the court today that the lawsuit against the project has been dropped.'

A long hiss snaked through the room. Bailey leaned toward his microphone. 'We'll have no more of that.' His glare swept the room until people quieted. 'That leaves us free to vote on the project after tonight's public comment. Each speaker will state his or her name for the record and will have two minutes. Civility and decorum will be maintained. Anyone in violation will be escorted out by one of these officers.'

The patrolmen stared at the wall, faces blank.

Several people rose and started toward the microphone stand facing the commissioners. Spencer, by virtue of being in the front row, reached it first.

'Those who wish to speak please line up behind Mr Templeton at the mic stand. And give him – and one another – plenty of room.'

Nora smiled at hearing him direct toward adults the same sort of instruction she applied to her seventh-graders, so prone to shoving, hair-pulling and whispered insults.

Spencer grasped the microphone, detached it from its stand, and turned to face the room.

'I'm glad the withdrawal of the lawsuit filed by Mr Austin's group gives the commission the legal ability to move forward. The Mare Vista will bring innumerable benefits to our peninsula. Not only will it provide jobs, both during construction and after it opens, but it will bring an entirely new class of visitor, people with very deep pockets indeed. They'll eat in our restaurants, shop in our fine establishments, hire our fishing guides.

'I'm confident that once they see what our peninsula has to offer – and of course, the world-class accommodations at the Mare Vista – they'll return year after year. The Mare Vista will benefit our peninsula for generations to come. I ask that the commission grant final approval tonight.'

Half the room applauded wildly.

A renewed hiss from the other half arose, fading when Bailey tapped his mic. 'Thank you, Mr Templeton. Next, please.'

Templeton replaced the mic in its stand. Gerry Fields' elbow shot out as he moved toward it, barely grazing Templeton's arm as they passed. One of the patrolmen took a step forward. Gerry ran a hand through his thinning hair, as though that had been the gesture he'd intended all along.

The room underwent a reversal, Nora and Luke's neighbors united in shooting visual poison darts at Gerry, while those across the aisle offered encouraging smiles and a few fist-pumps.

Bailey had accorded Templeton a 'mister'. Gerry dispensed with the courtesy.

'Spencer would have you believe the Mare Vista will be the best thing to happen to this peninsula since somebody first cracked open an oyster here. He loves to talk about jobs, but neglects to point out that the best-paid ones –the construction jobs – will vanish the moment the last nail is driven and the paint dries. After that, it's nothing but part-time, minimum-wage, no-benefits work, the same sorts of jobs already making it near-impossible to afford to live here.

'Then he's got the nerve to say the kind of people who'll be staying in his four-hundred-dollar-a-night rooms will throw their money around in our town. You think people like that will want to eat at Betty's?'

His eyes sought out Janie. 'No offense.'

Janie's expression showed offense was very much taken.

'Sorry.' Gerry cleared his throat and continued. 'Think they'll want to pick up a few "Peninsula Proud" T-shirts in our stores? Head out to fish with our local outfitters? What a crock. Mr Templeton neglected to mention that the Mare Vista will have not one but two high-end restaurants, plus a breakfast bistro and a bar. The gift shop will sell clothes from the kinds of designers few of us have heard of, let alone can afford. As to fishing, I guarantee you a number of people will cruise to our shores in their own boats – no doubt including a few yachts – and wouldn't be caught dead in one of our low-rent tubs.'

An ominous muttering arose around Nora.

'Time,' Bailey called.

'The hell it is!' Gerry looked at his watch, but Janie was already out of her seat and pushing to the front of the line. She grabbed the mic from him with an unmistakable don't-fuck-with-me air.

'Pretty words from Gerry Fields, with his cushy job at the research station, nothing to do all day but look at birds and plants and come up with one so-called endangered species after another to get in the way of building so much as another backyard storage shed on the peninsula.'

'Yeah!' A man in Nora's row leapt to his feet.

'Officer?' Bailey said.

The man sat back down. 'Won't happen again.'

'See that it doesn't. Janie, please continue.'

'Gladly. You, Gerry, and all of you who call yourselves Ward's Warriors. Quit your salaried jobs and come live hand-to-mouth like the rest of us, no time for running around yammering about the environment. You wouldn't last two weeks before you'd be begging for the kind of work Spencer's hotel is going to offer.'

Gerry's buddy Clark was next in line but Janie reached around him and handed the mic to her husband, who stood behind him.

'Hey!' Clark said. Abby's mother leaned toward her own mic, but Bailey beat her to it. 'Settle down,' he admonished Clark.

'Ron Stevenson,' Janie's husband introduced himself. 'All of you people talk like Spencer is trying to destroy this peninsula. But he's saving it. Look at the tsunami tower he's building. *We're* building. When the big one hits, if we live through it – if our kids live through it – it'll be because of Spencer. And this is the thanks he gets? What's wrong with you people?'

Across the aisle, a man in a Hawaiian shirt and paint-spattered jeans cried out, 'There's something wrong with the tower! And that means there's something wrong with the hotel, too.'

Spencer Templeton rose. 'Our project engineer can address this last point.'

'Excuse me. I believe I was next.' Clark might as well have been speaking to the wall. Abby's mother said something to the chairman, but he shook his head and recognized the man in the suit sitting next to Spencer. 'But please make it brief.'

The engineer rose, introduced himself as Richard Cox, and reeled off a series of numbers and calculations so mind-numbing as to lower the emotional temperature of the room almost to comfort level.

'Bottom line,' he finished, 'we have complete confidence in its structural integrity. The Mare Vista will be able to withstand the most severe storm.'

Clark Stevens didn't even bother to try for the mic. 'Come on, everybody. Let's not honor this farce with our presence.'

Luke tugged at her arm. 'Come on. Let's go, too. I've seen enough.'

'No. We have to wait a minute.' Nora hoped that by lingering a little after Ward's Warriors had left – but not so long as to be slotted into the pro-hotel camp – she could continue to claim neutrality.

Even so, she insisted to Luke that they wait outside with the tense, silent group for the inevitable moment when the secretary cracked the door to tell them that the commission had just voted to approve Spencer Templeton's grand new hotel.

She looked for the man in the Hawaiian shirt who'd been so vocal. But he was gone.

TWELVE

Luke and Nora and Sheila sat at the dinette in Nora's trailer, taste-testing Luke's latest find from the Store of Everything, a sour cherry gose he'd picked up on their way back from the meeting.

Sour fit Nora's mood. 'It's not right.'

'What's not right?' Luke held his glass to the light, examining the reddish contents. 'The first sip seemed really odd, but this stuff grows on you.'

Nora wasn't so sure about that, but it didn't matter. 'Not the beer, or whatever you call it. The meeting.'

'I'm with Luke on the gose.' Sheila examined the label. 'Never heard of it before. Glad I tried it. As to the meeting, welcome to our world.'

'But is it always like that? I thought it was so one-sided, the way the chairman catered to Spencer and his supporters and shut everybody else down.'

Sheila drained her bottle and reached for another. 'What do you expect? There's a school of thought – justified, I might add – that Spencer Templeton's projects keep this place afloat. I know this hotel thing seems like a big deal, and for the peninsula, it is. But it's just par for the course for Spencer. Most of his work is on the mainland. He's built shopping centers and office complexes all over the Pacific Northwest. The guy's got more money than God. He could live anywhere. But he grew up here and wants to stay. That's why he built that weird spaceship house.'

'Gotta give him credit for that.' Luke, like Sheila, was on his second beer.

Nora leaned from the dinette and pulled open a cupboard. She grabbed a jar of mixed nuts and, from another cupboard, a bowl.

She filled it to the top with nuts and sat it between them. She scooped up a handful and pushed the bowl toward Luke and Sheila, hoping the nuts would help soak up the alcohol. The ABV wasn't particularly high, but microbrews had a way of sneaking up on her.

'It just made me uncomfortable, the way the commission didn't even make a pretense of treating people evenhandedly. Is it that way for everything, Sheila?'

She shrugged. 'Don't know. I don't usually go to the meetings. I've gone to the ones on the hotel for the same reason you did; as much for the entertainment value as anything. For starters, it's a great way to keep up on gossip. Take Janie and Ron Stevenson. I'd heard their marriage was on the rocks, that she was seeing somebody else on the sly. But nobody ever knew who, which made me think it's not true because everybody knows everything about everyone in this place. But she and Ron were there together tonight, practically playing kissy-face.' She caught Nora's look. 'Give me a break. Remember, not much happens around here.'

'Which is why I like it.'

'Give it a while. But I have some sympathy for the commission. Ward's Warriors can wear you down, and I say that as someone who was involved with the man.'

She'd given Nora another opening to ask about her relationship with Ward; alas, once again in Luke's presence. Nora tiptoed into the subject, anyway.

'What do you mean?'

'Gawd.' Sheila blew an exasperated sigh. 'They're all so single-minded. Get Ward going on one of his causes and that would be all he'd talk about morning, noon and night. Well, not *all* night.' She grinned and winked. 'Sometimes that sort of single-minded focus could be a good thing, know what I mean?'

Nora knew and she was pretty sure Luke did, too. He shifted beside her on the seat. 'Excuse me,' he said to Nora.

'What for?'

'For kicking you. I didn't mean to.'

'That was me,' Sheila said. 'Anyway, after dating Ward for even a little while, I could see why Delilah left. She must've been desperate to live like a normal person instead of spending every waking moment on this cause or that. Now Spencer whisks her off to Aspen to ski in the winter and then to Hawaii when it gets too cold and rainy here – you know, for *fun*. Which was a concept Ward never quite grasped. Sometimes when I walk by the spaceship, I see Delilah and Spencer on their rooftop deck, drinking cocktails and watching the sunset, and all I can think is, "Good for you."'

Nora flinched at the raw envy in her voice. Did Sheila wish she'd been the one who'd caught Spencer's eye? Imagine herself breathing the Aspen's crystalline air, or dog-paddling through turquoise waters up to a floating bar in Maui?

Nora got it. She really did. Her recent past had been entirely devoid of fun. She'd left behind house and husband in quick succession, under the worst possible circumstances, and seen her possessions reduced to the animals and the Airstream.

Which Sheila now admired. 'This thing is so cool. You've got everything you need within reach. And you can just pick up and go whenever and wherever you want. What's it like to have that sort of freedom?'

People were always asking her that. Someday, she'd fire off the retort that always came to mind: *What's it like to have stability?*

'Electra's pretty great,' she agreed.

'Electra?'

Luke rolled his eyes. 'She named it for Amelia Earhart's airplane.'

Sheila choked on her gose. 'But didn't she . . .?'

'Yeah.' Nora was used to this one, too. 'She disappeared.' No matter what had happened to her, Earhart would be long dead by now. But Nora liked to think that Earhart, sick of the expectations heaped upon her, had *chosen* to disappear, living out her life in some off-the-map locale, a kind of freedom even greater than that afforded by the vast skies.

She turned the conversation back to the meeting. The chairman's behavior still nagged at her, and she said as much again.

Luke snagged the remaining bottle in the six-pack and offered to split it with Sheila. 'Jesus, Nora, give it a rest. After all, it's not exactly our fight.'

We live here now. So, isn't it?

But she sipped her beer in silence and kept that thought to herself, too.

THIRTEEN

Nora might have indulged in the occasional bout of self-pity about the lack of fun in her recent life, but she was determined to supply some for her students.

For all their digital savvy, they'd elected to do their tsunami tower survey in person, probably because it would afford an escape from the classroom – something she, too, relished, even though it meant the herding-cats responsibility of keeping track of twenty youngsters, not to mention alleviating the principal's concerns.

She dealt with the latter by styling the project as a lesson in journalism, emphasizing details such as accuracy and ethical standards, with an entire unit on the First Amendment. She'd shown her class images of old-style reporters from films like *The Front Page* and *The Philadelphia Story* (though it had taken her far too long to find examples without cigarettes or a glass of whiskey). Then she brought out a giant cardboard box and opened it to reveal stacks of child-size fedoras, with cards stuck in the brim reading *Daily Wave*.

Nora had decreed the name after belatedly nixing Damien's straight-faced suggestion to use the school's initials, which would have dubbed their nascent publication the PMS Press.

A smaller box contained reporters' notebooks. She'd expected some whining – those with phones wanted to use them to record interviews – but not everybody had a phone. Rather than turn the wrath of the privileged on those few students, Nora termed it a matter of professionalism.

'Real reporters know their equipment can always conk out on them, and usually at the worst time.' She'd had more run-ins with reporters than she cared to remember. Unfortunately, all their gear had worked perfectly, capturing front-page photos of Nora and quotes that enlivened their stories.

She quashed the memories, mollifying the kids with phones by appointing a few of them photographers.

'Before we head out, let's go over the rules. Class?'

Abby's hand shot up. 'Always ask permission before inter-viewing someone.'

'Very good. Zeke?'

'Identify ourselves by name and school and say why we're interviewing them.'

'Exactly. Jeannie?'

'Ask them how to spell their names. Or better yet, give them our notebooks and ask them to write their names so we'll be sure to get them right.'

Nora beamed. 'You guys are making me so proud. Yes, Damien?'

'If they say words like shit or' – his lips worked, re-forming the single syllable – 'an F-bomb, tell them we can't print it.'

Nora didn't censure her own internal F-bomb. Luke had promised her a special dinner that evening. She was going to need it.

'Damien's right, even though the way he phrased it just earned him an extra homework assignment. Everybody got their hats? Notebooks and pens? Let's go.'

Nora had delayed their expedition until the forecast guaranteed sunshine.

The kids fanned out in groups across the beach, bearing down on the unsuspecting throngs taking advantage of the weather after calling their workplaces with excuses that fooled no one. Nora moved from group to group, trying to keep a respectful distance while remaining within earshot in case any problems arose.

The junior reporters' minimalist costumes had the exact effect she'd hoped, with people smiling indulgently, turning away from their impromptu late-season picnics.

And how could you resist Abby James, her serious mien as she posed her question: 'Although the tsunami tower is being donated, other costs come with it – things like improving the roads and adding signs. Are those costs worth the expense to taxpayers? Why or why not?' She bent over her notebook, tip of her tongue protruding from one corner of her mouth, as she scrawled the answers.

Nora moved to another group and caught Zeke's eye as he handed his notebook to a young mother helping her twin toddlers scoop sand into a plastic bucket. 'Just my name or my kids', too?'

Nora gave Zeke the slightest nod.

'If you'd like them to be in our story, then their names, too, please.'

'Of course I want their names in the story! Spencer Templeton is building this tower for them.'

Nora flashed Zeke a thumbs-up and moved on, getting to the next group just as Damien approached two young men lounging on the hood of a muscle car. A skunky scent wafted toward her. Damien's grin let her know that was exactly why he'd selected these two. The other kids in his group hung back, noses wrinkling.

Nora moved closer. Weed was legal in their state, but surely this was inappropriate? As inappropriate as the answer Damien likely hoped for. But he posed his question – he, too, had been assigned the one about tax dollars – seriously and got a serious response.

'Heck, yeah. Look at this place.' One of the guys pushed himself up and took an unexpectedly lithe leap onto the car roof. Damon fumbled for his phone and snapped a photo. The guy pointed toward the sea, smoke trailing from his vape pen. 'Look at all that water.' He pivoted and indicated the land behind them. Damien's camera app clicked steadily. 'And look at that land. Flat as a pancake. This place would be underwater in a minute. Far as I'm concerned, we could use two or three more of those things and whatever improvements it takes to help us get to them.'

Damien went off script. 'What if they raised the taxes on your, uh – that' – he pointed to the smoke trailing from the vape pen – 'to pay for it?'

The two guys looked at each other and shrugged. 'Sure. Why not?'

Damien handed up his notebook and asked them to write their names.

Nora had to give him credit. The kids had been told to stick to their questions, but Damien's instincts for the follow-up were spot-on.

She forced herself to mouth a sotto-voce 'good job' in response to the look of triumph he shot her way.

Nora checked her watch. She'd managed to wangle an extra period for her students' interviews, negotiating with teachers in their previous-period classes, who seemed frankly relieved to have a few less students to deal with. But they were nearing the end of the school day.

'Time, everybody!'

They straggled back in animated groups, their fedoras tilted far back on their heads or, in some cases, pulled at a low, daring angle. Nora pulled out her phone and took a photo. Part of their project would be to compile an online newspaper with stories detailing the results of their survey.

She counted heads. Counted again. One was missing, and it wasn't the usual suspect. Damien stood at the center of his group, imitating one of the two stoners he'd interviewed. 'Flat as a pancake!' he announced, then mimicked a long toke on an invisible vape.

Nora twisted, scanning the beach. There. Fifty yards away, Abby stood before a man Nora recognized from the County Commissioners' meeting. As before, he wore a Hawaiian shirt and work pants so splashed with paint their original color was undetectable. Abby scribbled furiously in her notebook as he spoke.

'The rest of you stay here. I'm going to let Abby know we're leaving.'

As Nora jogged toward them, Abby stopped writing. She must have asked him a question because he shook his head so violently his hair whipped his cheeks.

'Please.' Abby's voice reached her now. 'It's just for our class project.'

'Not on your life. Or mine.' He looked up and saw Nora. 'You remember what I told you, though.'

'Hey!' Nora called. He took a few stumbling steps backward, then turned and walked away. 'Abby, are you OK? What did he want?'

Abby bit her lip. 'I'm fine. He just wouldn't give me his name.'

They walked slowly back toward the rest of the class. 'He

seemed . . . intense. Are you sure you're OK? Did he say anything bad to you?'

Nora hated asking but she had to. You couldn't be too careful.

'Oh, no. Nothing like that.' Abby's voice, wobbly a moment earlier, rang with certainty. 'But Ms Best?'

They were almost back to the rest. Nora stopped. She loved Abby, if for no other reason than that the girl called her Ms, rather than the Miss the principal insisted upon.

'What, Abby? You can tell me.'

'I don't know if it means anything.' Her lower lip went between her teeth again.

The others had started to move toward them.

'Ms Best he said we had to find the architect who signed off on the tower. He made it sound really important. "You *have* to talk with him," he said. He just kept insisting. But that's not part of our project, is it?'

'No,' said Nora. 'You don't have to worry about it anymore.'

'Honestly?' Abby offered an uncertain smile.

'Truly. As far as I'm concerned, you can forget it ever happened. Look, here's our group. Let's everybody get back to school before Principal Everhart gives us all detention and gives me two detentions because I'm the one in charge.'

As humor went, it was minimal. But it got a few laughs, and another smile from Abby, which was all Nora really wanted.

She trailed them into the building, nodding to Everhart, who stood in her doorway, looking at the large hallway clock that registered one minute before the end of the school day.

She'd told Abby not to worry about what the man had said. But she couldn't forget what he'd said at the meeting – that there was something wrong with the tower.

What the hell. As soon as the kids went home, she'd call the engineer who spoke at the commission meeting about Spencer's hotel project. He'd probably know about the tsunami tower, too.

FOURTEEN

Nora stared at the phone in her hand, its screen fading to black as the call ended.

'I had nothing to do with that project,' was all Richard Cox said, not even a goodbye as he clicked out of the call.

Nora stood in her empty classroom, watching through the window as the last of the kids climbed into their parents' cars, or walked to homes only a few blocks away. If the engineer hadn't worked on the project, who had?

He'd gone before the County Commission, documents in hand. Surely similar documents existed for the tsunami tower?

She tapped her phone back to life. The commission's website told her its offices closed at four thirty.

She had an hour. Plenty of time, even considering the drive to the county complex on the mainland. She waved goodbye to a few lingering students and headed out.

As it turned out, an hour was just barely enough time.

Governed by a vague impulse to secrecy, prompted by the engineer's abrupt manner, she told one clerk after another only that she sought help navigating the county's online records system so she could find the plans for the new hotel. 'For a class project,' she said. She figured the same online search process would apply to the tsunami tower plans.

She drove home with a list of instructions that filled nearly a page in one of the reporter's notebooks she'd filched from her students' stash. Although the County Commission's records were ostensibly public, it seemed to have done everything possible to foil an ordinary citizen's attempt at accessing them.

Even with the notes in hand, it took her forever to navigate the labyrinthine system, which ticked her off if she hesitated too long in clicking through to the next step, or if her query contained a typo. It didn't help that Mooch stalked back and forth across the dinette table as she worked, occasionally pawing at her keyboard, while Murph lay heavily across her feet, whining softly in hopes of a treat.

There were screens full of information about the tower, various permissions and amendments, approvals from subcommittees and committees. By the time she finally found the actual plans for it, she'd cursed so frequently and with such increasing volume that Mooch and Murph had retreated to the far end of the trailer, huddling together on her bed, seeking rare comfort in one another.

She could hardly believe it when the blueprint for the tower finally appeared on her screen, all right angles and precise printed words, so tiny she could barely make them out. She enlarged the image and moved it around the screen, viewing it piecemeal.

There: In the top right corner, Spencer Templeton Associates. Below it: Nothing.

Nora moved the image around again, searching the margins and each corner. But nowhere on the blueprint, or in the bare-bones document that accompanied it, did she see an engineer's name.

She slumped back against the dinette and started to close her laptop. Then she sat upright.

'Architect!'

She'd called the engineer, remembering how he'd detailed the hotel's specifications at the commission meeting. But the man on the beach had said architect, not engineer.

She smacked her forehead, then clicked double-time through her previous screens, scanning more and more slowly as she verified what she already knew. Each was as devoid of an architect's name as it had been an engineer's.

She glared at Mooch and Murph.

'For all I know, a unicorn designed this damn thing.'

She stood, stretched, her fingertips brushing Electra's ceiling. She arched her back, then bowed low, trying to unkink a spine bent too long over a computer screen.

'And you know what? Engineer, architect, I no longer care. I can't believe I wasted all this time just because of something some nutcase said.'

FIFTEEN

Someone pounded on her door so hard the trailer shook.
'Nora! Are you in there?'
She opened the door to see Luke, face red and fist raised
for another assault on her door.

'Luke! Come on in. What's going on? Is something wrong?'

He lowered his fist and crossed his arms, maintaining a
wide-legged stance on the trailer steps.

'Yeah, you could say something's wrong. I expected you for
dinner an hour ago.'

She closed her laptop and rubbed her eyes. 'What time is it?'

'Seven. Dinner's cold. If you were going to be late, I wish
you'd called. That would have been the courteous thing.'

He was right. It would have. So why did she feel the combination of guilt and resentment particular to a scolded child?

'I tried to call you, but you didn't answer.'

'I'm sorry, I—' She'd silenced her phone while at the county
offices to comply with their rules and had forgotten to turn it
back on. 'Never mind. I'm coming. No, wait. I have to feed these
guys and let Murph out.'

'You forgot about the dog, too?'

She didn't bother to respond as she shoveled kibble into their
respective bowls and gave them fresh water.

'Murph can do his business on the walk over to your place.'

He sat on the step with a theatrical thump. 'Sure. At this point,
what's another fifteen or twenty minutes? I hear there's a whole
cold-food movement these days.'

Murph usually inhaled his food. But on this night, he seemed
to chew with special consideration, lifting his head and gazing
around for long moments between bites. Nora wondered if he
was channeling her own recalcitrant mood in the face of Luke's
pissiness. She slipped an extra treat into his bowl before finally
leading him from the trailer.

On the silent walk to Luke's apartment, she caught the

occasional whiff of cologne. She cut her eyes toward him. He'd changed from his school day attire into similar clothes – khakis and a collared shirt – but the khakis were fresh-pressed and he'd shed a pale-blue shirt for a maroon one starched so stiff it looked uncomfortable. And was that a new haircut? He'd mentioned a special dinner, but this seemed over the top.

She started babbling about her day, anything to break the mood. She told him about the kids, their fedoras and notebooks, the way they took to their job seriously – even Damien, although she wished he'd chosen less problematic interview subjects. She'd hoped for a laugh as she pantomimed the scene, but Luke's features remained stubbornly immobile.

'And then this weird thing happened with Abby . . .' She launched into a recitation of the strange man and his insistent request; her frustrations with the county's computer system.

Yet he didn't speak beyond monosyllables until they'd reached his apartment, and then it was to Murph, who stood eyeing the stairs with weary trepidation. 'Not tonight, old man. You stay down here.'

Luke had laid a folded quilt on the soft grass beneath the spruce tree, along with a water bowl and a bone. Murph flopped down onto the blanket and attacked the bone. Nora looked back at him as she climbed the stairs. She anticipated another lecture and would have liked the comfort of the dog close at hand.

Luke opened the door and moved aside. She stepped through it and beheld the two-top covered with a snowy cloth, the single rose in its wine-bottle vase, the plates holding steaks gone gray and once-melted butter solidified in unsightly blobs atop cold mashed potatoes. Even the salads had wilted.

'Um, what's the occasion?'

He opened the refrigerator door, pulled out a bottle of champagne and yanked at the cork. It flew against the wall with such a loud pop that Nora tensed for a call from the landlady.

He put the bottle to his lips and drank directly from it, heedless of the foam cascading down his chin and over his beautiful clean shirt.

He sat the bottle down without offering it to her and ran his sleeve across his face.

'What *was* the occasion, you mean?' He pointed to a piece of paper on the table between the forlorn plates.

She pinched it between thumb and forefinger and held it away from her as though it might bite. She saw a photo of a bungalow, slate-gray, with a deck on two sides. Smaller photos beneath showed an orderly interior and an expansive back yard,

'It's small. Just two bedrooms and one bath. But it's still bigger than your trailer and my apartment put together. There's a fenced yard where Murph can run around all day instead of being cooped up in your trailer. And did you see the raised beds? We can have a vegetable garden.'

Nora decided it wasn't the time to mention she'd never successfully kept so much as a houseplant alive.

'But what about Electra?'

'We'd use her for travel, just like normal people.' He didn't say it and he didn't have to: the way Nora had intended when she and her ex had first bought it.

She picked up the flier again. She wanted to flinch at the price, but it wasn't . . . awful.

Luke answered her unspoken question. 'We can afford it, just, because of the mortgage help I'll get from the VA. It's not on the water – that's why it's affordable, but it's only a couple blocks back. And it's on the far outskirts of town, which is another reason the price is so reasonable. We couldn't walk to work anymore, but we're still only talking a five-minute drive. It's perfect.'

It was.

And yet.

'I'm just not sure.' She took a breath and forced the rest of the sentence. 'That I'm ready.'

He sat and hacked at the meat on his place with a steak knife, severing a piece and biting down on it as though annihilating an enemy.

'Oh, for heaven's sake.' Nora snatched his plate away and put it in the microwave. She covered it with a paper towel and punched some buttons.

'What aren't you ready for, Nora? The money part? I don't know how much that insurance settlement you finally got for your husband's death was, but surely you can spare part of it toward a down-payment.'

The microwave beeped. She swapped out his plate for her own.

'It's enough.'

'Then what is it? You don't want us to move in together?'

'I'm just not sure that I'm ready.' It was easier to say the second time.

'Because you'd rather spend time messing around on your computer because of something some crazy guy said than have a special meal with me?'

Nora retrieved her plate from the microwave and slammed it so hard onto the table she had to stab the steak with her fork to keep it from flying to the floor. Finally, anger.

'Consider this, Luke Rivera. If – *if* – we move in together, we'll be part of this community. I'm just taking an active interest in something that's happening here. It's what we should do as responsible citizens.'

It wasn't the world's best argument. But that *if* seemed enough to mollify him; that, and what she said next.

She pointed to the photo of the house. 'It's lovely. But I wasn't expecting this. It's a lot to take in. I'd like some time to think about it.'

He'd just taken another bite of the steak. He nodded, chewing and chewing.

'Fair enough,' he said finally. Then: 'This is awful.'

'You know who won't think it's awful? Murph. How about we give him the best night of his life, and you and I go to Betty's?'

A few minutes later, they were heading down the street, Murph crouched over his bowl in ecstasy behind them.

Crisis averted, Nora thought.

But she kept swallowing, trying to rid herself of the bad taste brought on by her knee-jerk attempts to mollify a man for criticism that felt both unfair and disproportionate, and especially for his presumption that she'd jump at his plan to move in together.

SIXTEEN

Nora put her foot down the next night when Luke asked if he could join her and Sheila at Betty's.

She was still unnerved by his sudden swerve toward domesticity even though she had to admit to herself that looked at one way, the house purchase made sense. But she didn't like the way he'd surprised her and couldn't help but wonder what other surprises might be in store as their relationship progressed. What if he was one of those guys who thought a traditional living arrangement meant traditional gender roles, too?

'Girls' night out,' she said, lobbing an uber-traditional phrase just in case he turned out to be Mr Traditional.

She'd offered to bring wine, but Sheila emphatically forbade it. Nora found out why as soon as they sat down.

'Drink your water.' Sheila pointed toward her glass.

'What?'

Sheila lifted her own glass and demonstrated. 'Chug-a-lug. All of it.'

Nora followed suit, glad that at least the glasses were on the small side. 'Why?'

Sheila pulled a Thermos from a tote bag and poured. The faint tang of juniper wafted toward Nora.

'Check it out.' Sheila reached into the tote again, emerging with a jar of Sicilian olives. A final dive into its contents brought up a container of toothpicks. She speared two fat olives on each and dropped them into the glasses. 'Martini time.'

'Oh, lord,' Nora sighed after the first astringent sip. 'This is fine. You have no idea how badly I needed this.'

Despite her intention to quiz Sheila about her brief relationship with Ward Austin, her own dilemma tumbled out, a nascent romance that seemed to be careening into high gear before she even had a chance to fasten her seatbelt.

Sheila fended off Janie – 'We'll each have the special' – and studied Nora over the rim of her glass. 'Tell me again what's so awful about moving into a sweet little house with a guy who worships you. Is there something I'm missing? You don't seem the type to put up with abuse or addiction, so what is it? Does he squeeze the toothpaste tube in the middle? Leave the toilet seat up? Wants blow jobs but won't go down on you?'

'Hush!' Nora looked around, fearing a sea of shocked faces. But Betty's was only half-full and Sheila had kept her voice low.

'None of the above,' she said as a blush crept up her neck and bathed her face in heat.

Sheila's left eyebrow shot toward her hairline. 'Lucky you. Shoot, I'd move in with Harold Wallace if he'd promise those things. So what's the problem?'

'It just feels too soon. We've barely known one another a year. We went through a pretty rough time in our last jobs.' The understatement of the century. She'd nearly been killed, escaping only when Luke – with her help – dispatched her assailants, something of which they'd never spoken since, not even with the counselors they'd seen. Justifiable homicide? In their minds, sure. In the eyes of law enforcement? Maybe not so much.

'Anyway, what if it's just a rebound thing? Like you and Ward.' Nora mentally patted herself on the back for steering the conversation back to what she really wanted to know. She took a sip of her martini and stepped farther out on the limb. They didn't call it liquid courage for nothing.

'Did *he* squeeze the toothpaste tube in the middle? Leave the seat up? And, ah, that other?'

'That other? Look at you, red as a schoolgirl. Let's just say that other was so good I wouldn't have cared about the toothpaste or the toilet seat. No, the main problem with Ward is that any woman in his life would always play second fiddle to the Almighty Cause. Only person he put above it was Damien.'

Nora wondered if the booze had hit her harder and faster than she'd expected. Because what Sheila had just said didn't make sense.

'But Damien hated his dad. That performance at the memorial service – ouch.'

'Damien's a twelve-year-old boy. By definition he's a mess, even without factoring in a divorce. Kids always feel like they have to choose. His mom loves him, too, and you know how boys love their mamas.'

Nora didn't, but she wasn't about to interrupt Sheila.

'He could make either his dad happy or his mom happy, and making Mom happy came with a big new house and every toy and electronic gadget a kid could want. If you'd ever seen Ward's house, you'd understand.'

Their specials – fried oyster sandwiches, with sides of coleslaw and fries – arrived. Nora bit through her baguette into an oyster so plump and juicy that for a second she forgot what they'd been talking about. Right. Ward's house.

'Never seen it,' she mumbled.

'Good, huh?' Sheila paused to attack her own sandwich. 'They probably pulled these oysters out of the bay this morning. And Betty's smart enough not to load them up with breading. Anyhow, Ward's house. You've probably gone by it without ever noticing it. It's easy to do. Blink and you'd miss it. Ward believed in what he called "living lightly". It probably started off as an oysterman's shack and then went on to be somebody's summer cottage, back when people didn't mind rustic. Only one bedroom, and a living room futon for Damien. One bath with a shower that reeked of mildew.'

She shuddered. 'How three people lived in it as long as they did, I don't know. I'd spend weekends there sometimes when my kids were with their dad and Damien was with Delilah, and let me tell you that, by the time Sunday night rolled around, I was glad to go home.'

Nora, who'd lived the last couple of years in a roughly two-hundred-square-foot Airstream, didn't think it sounded so terrible, except for the mildew part. After moving from the cool, dry mountain West onto the rain-drenched peninsula, she'd kept it at bay with every-third-day applications of a vinegar solution and so far, was winning the battle.

Sheila read her silence. 'It wasn't just that it was small. But every surface was covered with Ward's work – legal papers, pamphlets, books for research. You'd barely know anyone else lived there, and for all I know, it wasn't like that when Delilah was still around. You've been in the spaceship. What's it like?'

Nora spread her arms. 'Huge. And not a thing out of place.'

She thought she was starting to understand. Her trailer was small, but it was hers and everything in it was exactly the way she wanted it. The nights Luke stayed caused a disturbance in the field, his clothes on the floor beside the bed, toothbrush and razor and shaving cream taking up space on her tiny bathroom sink, his big shoes kicked off wherever she was most likely to trip over them. She was grateful for his presence in her bed, it's just that his presence was everywhere else, too.

'You put your finger on it. People called Delilah a gold-digger when she left Ward, just as you'd expect. But I don't think she wanted all those nice things as much as she just wanted space to call her own. You know, she and Ward were the only two employees of the nonprofit. That was how they kept costs down. Ward wanted every possible penny to go to the cause.'

'How did she feel about the cause?'

'Oh, she loves this place as much as all of us do. But she's willing to accept the fact that it's changing. Ward, though, he fought every change tooth and nail. Even the good ones, like the tsunami tower.'

Sheila emptied the remaining contents of the Thermos into their glasses. 'Now you've heard my story and theirs, too. Tell me yours. How'd you and lover man meet?'

The martini iced Nora's brain. She and Luke usually had beer or wine with dinner, along with the occasional glass of whiskey, but she'd forgotten the delicious lethality of straight gin kissed by vermouth. She was already glad she'd walked to Betty's instead of driving. If the drink played this much havoc with her thoughts, what might it do with her words?

'We both worked at the same school. Workplace romance. Not terribly original.' She held up the remains of her meal. 'I think this is the best oyster sandwich I've ever eaten.'

Sheila was undeterred.

'You two rescued those girls. Seems pretty original to me.'

If Nora had learned nothing else in the last few months, it was how to fend off the inevitable questions about her recently lurid past. Sometimes she wished she'd opted for life in a city, with its welcome anonymity.

But she and Luke had ended up on the peninsula when they freed two runaway girls from men bent on harm, and the resulting publicity – the term 'hero teachers' instantly appended to their names – had led to their present jobs.

Sooner or later, everyone she met asked about it, not all of them with the same roundabout finesse Sheila had just attempted – in much the same way, she had to admit, she herself had tried to weasel information from Sheila.

She set her glass on the table with a practiced tremor, then ran a hand over her eyes, blinking rapidly behind it to summon moisture. 'It was such a traumatic experience.' She lowered her hand and dabbed at her eyes with her napkin. 'I still have a hard time talking about it. Nightmares, panic attacks, that sort of thing.'

She had to be careful not to overplay her hand. The principal had quizzed her in far blunter terms, and Nora was convinced the woman watched her daily for the signs of crazy. She appeared to have struck just the right note with Sheila, though.

'I'm so sorry. I can just imagine.'

Which was bullshit because she couldn't.

But enough people had said something similar that she'd perfected a response for that, too, a sad smile and a murmured 'thank you' followed by a quick change of subject.

'There's a girl in my class, Abby James. What do you know about her?'

'Noooo.' Sheila held the Thermos over her glass, but only a few sparkling drops slid from it. 'I thought work talk was off limits tonight. If I'd known it was on the agenda, I'd have brought a second Thermos.'

The contents of the first had already rendered Nora's lips numb. 'If you'd brought a second, you'd have to roll me home in a wheelbarrow. Anyhow, this will just take a minute. It's more about something she said.'

Sheila capped the useless Thermos and stowed it in her tote. 'Shoot.'

'Her mom's on the County Commission, right? Abby seems so knowledgeable about things happening on the peninsula. Not typical kid-type stuff, but about tourism and development.'

'Her mom's worked for the county for years, which means she knows more about what goes on in this town than anybody on the commission. She's already announced she's running for chair next year, which must give Brock Bailey fits. He seems to think of himself as chairman for life. Why so curious?'

Nora attempted to project nonchalance. She shrugged and picked at her coleslaw, which unlike far too many versions was light on the mayo and had a fine, peppery bite. 'No reason. She's just one of those kids who stands out, and in a good way.'

'I know what you mean. She's the same way in my pre-algebra class.'

Nora nearly choked on her coleslaw. 'How did I not know that? And how is that possible? She's a seventh-grader. You teach eighth grade.'

'They just moved her in this week. She was finishing all her quizzes in half the time it took the rest of the kids in seventh-grade math and acing them besides.'

'That's exactly how she is in my class. I hope they don't put her in eighth-grade social studies, too. I really like having her in class. She's quiet, but whenever she opens her mouth, it's worth hearing.'

Sheila's eyes narrowed. 'Why ask about her mom?'

The martini didn't seem to have muddled Sheila's thinking at all. 'Just trying to match up kids with all the parents I met at back-to-school night. How long does it take to get everybody straight?'

'Depends how long you stick around.'

They were back on familiar, if uncomfortable, ground. The principal hadn't minced words during Nora's and Luke's job interviews.

'People come here in the summertime, during the three months of the year we actually get sunshine, and fall in love with this place. A lot of the new people work remotely – they're the only ones who can afford houses here anymore. They swan around for the first few months, talking about how charming everything is. Then September comes, the tourists leave and all the cutesy little shops and cafes they love so much shut down, and the rain starts – and it doesn't stop for nine months.

'Next thing you know, our newbies are heading out of here for long weekends in the city. It rains just as much in Seattle as it does here, but at least the lights are bright and there's more to do than stare at the beach all day. Their long weekends turn into a month, two months. We take bets on when the "for sale" signs will go up in front of their houses.'

Sheila fixed Nora with a gimlet eye. 'Just how long do you think it will be before your own sign goes up?'

'The kind of quiet you describe is exactly what I'm looking for. I've lived in a city most of my adult life. I'm more than ready for a change.' No need to mention that her desire for change had nothing to do with her years in Denver, and everything with the chaos of her life since leaving there.

Now she told Sheila the same thing she'd told Everhart. 'I plan to stick around for a long, long time.' She thought a moment and added, 'Whether Luke and I move in together, or not.'

SEVENTEEN

She left Betty's just buzzed enough that she headed for the water, hoping for a sobering shock to her system.

She left her shoes and socks behind and waded in, trying to balance as the waves sucked at the sand beneath her feet.

But she couldn't lose herself as usual in their hiss and crash. A low, grinding sound underlaid the waves' soothing rhythm. She opened her eyes and looked down the beach toward town. The yellow machines at work on the tsunami tower had been joined by their larger, even noisier brethren. Spencer's contractors had lost no time in starting work on his grand hotel.

She splashed back onto the sand and headed to the construction site. A sign hung on the fence with a schematic of the hotel's final appearance.

It paid homage to the peninsula's fishing camps, its bungalows covered with those faux shakes, their verandas draped in nets, and exterior walls hung with clusters of multicolored glass floats. But the bungalows, like the spaceship, would sit atop the pilings that would allow even the highest tides or, God forbid, a tsunami, to flow beneath. Despite their humble appearance, luxury lay within.

Nora was already getting inundated with online ads for the

Mare Vista, even though she couldn't imagine why. She'd never be able to afford its king-size beds mounded with throw pillows, bathrooms with soaking tubs and walk-in showers whose multiple nozzles would aim jets of water at whatever body part most needed caressing. A dining area featured a fridge stocked with champagne and charcuterie, while a butler would roam the premises, ready to fetch anything a guest might desire. Bicycles and sea kayaks would be stocked discreetly beneath the cottages and chartered fishing expeditions were part of the deal, with the added fillip of having one's own catch served up at dinner by a Cordon Bleu-trained chef.

'Pretty great, huh?'

A burly man in hard hat and safety vest advanced upon her. He pushed his hat back and she recognized Janie's husband.

'Ron, right? I'm Nora.'

He took the hand she offered and crunched it into jelly. 'Yeah, I know. One of the hero teachers.'

Nora rescued her hand and rubbed her fingers together, willing feeling to return, and retrieved one of her standard responses. 'The longer I teach, the less I feel like a hero. Seventh-graders, sheesh.'

'Yeah, well.' He took a step toward her, doing that thing that big men do, standing too close, smiling too hard. Nora tried never to cede ground – who the hell did these guys think they were, anyway? – but she was out of practice and Ron was particularly large, both tall and wide, with the beer-barrel gut that balanced out the side-of-beef slab of shoulders.

'You didn't seem like much of a hero at the County Commission meeting the other night, walking out with all the greenies.'

Greenies? Oh, environmentalists.

Nora searched and found her backbone. 'We left later. Anyway, last I checked, it's still a free country for people to leave whenever they want.' A level of rejoinder on par with her students, but at least she'd pushed back.

'You really think the peninsula is part of the rest of the country? We're in our own little world out here. And that's how we like it.'

'And yet.' She couldn't help herself. She pointed to the sign. 'Something like this invites the rest of the world in.'

'Something like this is what lets the rest of us continue to live here.' If he'd taken a single step more, this encounter would turn into a chest bump, but he merely leaned in. *Loomed* was more like it. 'So you might want to think twice about who you associate with. Whose side you take. What kind of questions your baby reporters are asking – oh, yeah, I know all about that. About the trouble they're stirring up. Look what happened to Ward Austin.'

Nora tried to read another meaning into his words. Couldn't.

'Are you honestly threatening my students? Over a silly class project? They're just kids!'

'I know.' He clapped her on the shoulder, suddenly avuncular.

'But you're not. As to threatening anyone, I'd say you have an overactive imagination. I'm just letting you know how things work around here. You know, so you can fit in better. We need all the hero teachers we can get.'

She made a snap decision to take advantage of his change in mood. 'I should have my students talk to you. After all, you're the main expert on the tower, out here every day the way you are.'

He grinned and nodded. 'That I am.'

'And you probably know the architect who designed it, right?'

His giant paw lingered on her shoulder. She flinched, fearing the same sort of damage it had earlier imposed on her hand. But he merely let it sit there, its weight more ominous for the possibility of pain rather than actual injury.

'That's the sort of question that gets people in trouble.'

She jerked away.

Ron sauntered back to the worksite, donning his hard hat and swinging up into one of the yellow machines.

Her knees had gone as rickety as the steps to Luke's apartment.

The tower's struts rose black against the dusk-purple sky. The man who'd pestered her at the commission meeting and Abby on the beach wanted her to find out more about it. Ron had just warned her, in both words and actions, to back off.

She'd abandoned her search for the architect as a waste of time.

It didn't feel like that anymore.

EIGHTEEN

The good thing about being a teacher was a ready excuse to meet with a parent.

Sheila had said Melanie James knew as much about the workings of local government as anyone. Surely she'd be able to clear up the architect/engineer business.

Nora jotted down a script so as not to stumble over her words.

'I'd love for us to get together to discuss Abby's progress. When would be a good time? I'm happy to meet outside school and work hours if that's most convenient.' She was glad she'd gotten Melanie James' voicemail. The lie was easier over the phone.

Melanie called back within minutes. 'Does today work? My lunch break is in half an hour. Are you free then?' Whatever Nora had to say, Melanie wanted to hear it fast.

Nora sighed. Calls from a teacher, no matter how reassuringly she pitched her voice, always seemed to set parents on edge.

'That's fine, but it's nothing bad.' She spoke to a connection gone dark. Melanie must have gone into full parental panic mode, a guess confirmed when Nora found her hovering outside the classroom door when she dismissed her pre-lunch-period class. Melanie had said half an hour. She'd made it in twenty minutes.

Nora dragged a student's chair beside her own and invited Melanie to sit. But she remained standing, knuckles gone white around the straps of her purse.

Nora took her own seat, hoping Melanie would follow suit. 'You didn't give me a chance to say this on the phone, but you should know that Abby is one of the top students in my class, if not *the* top student.'

Melanie sat so suddenly the movement verged on collapse, her palpable foreboding moments earlier at odd with an appearance that – from the subtle highlights in her hair, the clear varnish on her nails, the nipped-waist blazer and knife-creased slacks – bespoke an understated competence.

Indeed, she was already regaining the straight-backed, professionally pleasant bearing that Nora now remembered from back-to-school night and the County Commission meeting.

'If Abby's your best student, what's the problem? And how can I help?'

Nora lifted her hands. 'There's no problem. Or, at least it's a good one. I'm just looking for ways to challenge her. She processes information so quickly and well that I'm afraid she'll be bored. I know she's already been moved up to eighth-grade math. Does she have any particular interest I might incorporate into her curriculum? I don't want to burden her with extra work, but I do want to keep her engaged.'

'Horses. Like every other twelve-year-old girl. And she likes the newspaper project your class is doing. Now she wants to be a reporter. Maybe she'll report on horses.' Melanie's laugh had a giddy edge. 'Forgive me. I was so worried that she'd had some sort of issue relating to her finding Ward Austin's body. She's met with a counselor, of course. And she doesn't seem to be any more upset than you might expect. But I'm a mother. I worry. You know how it is.'

Nora felt as though she were constantly being reminded that she didn't know how it was. She waved away Melanie's apology and tried to recall Sheila's advice on dealing with parents. 'Start by validating their feelings, no matter how unreasonable they seem. It builds trust.'

Melanie had been worried. Nora would give her something innocuous to worry about.

'I do have one concern.'

Panic flared anew in Melanie's eyes.

'It's just a small one. Abby is so smart, but she's also shy. I'd like to bring her out of her shell. Give her some sort of leadership role. After all, she has the perfect role model in you.'

Shameless. But it worked.

Women – far too many, far too often – responded to compliments by brushing them aside, declaring themselves unworthy. Melanie went up several notches in Nora's opinion when she accepted Nora's praise as a simple statement of fact.

'I've worked hard to be where I am, and Abby's seen that. She knows my job demands a lot of extra hours – all those

evening commission meetings – and that I'm never going to be
the mom who can volunteer for playground duty or bring cupcakes
for the whole class. But she also knows I love my job and that
it makes me happy.'

Nora lost herself for a moment in a wistful reverie. What if
her own mother had championed such a stance? Impossible of
course, in that time and place. Until recently, she'd thought her
mother had perfectly fulfilled the only role available – decorative,
gracious and above all, *nice*. Something in Melanie James'
demeanor, now that her concerns for Abby had eased, said that
nice wasn't a high priority.

Anyway, she'd just handed Nora the perfect opening.

'Your being on the commission – that explains Abby.'

'What do you mean?'

'She's so organized. And I imagine a job like yours, having to
keep track of so many things, you need to be also. I can just
imagine her watching you and learning.' Maybe she was laying it
on a little thick. 'How long have you been on the commission?'

'Years. And I was county clerk before that. When you talked
about a leadership role for Abby, what did you have in mind?'

Nora thought back to her days of interminable interdepart-
mental meetings. There'd always been a Melanie, someone who
applied a firm hand when discussions wandered off track. At
least, she'd thought through a plan for Abby.

'This newspaper project that we're doing – the kids really like
it. I'd like to make Abby the editor. It plays to her strengths.
And, frankly, it takes some of the organizational burden off me.'

'Delegating. Always a good strategy.'

'Maybe you can help her prepare for it. Google "what a newspaper editor does". That sort of thing.'

Melanie brightened. 'I can go one better. I'm in touch on a
regular basis with Arden Talbott, the editor of the local paper.
The commission often runs op-eds in the paper. I'll ask if she'd
be willing to let Abby come by the office one day after school
to watch her at work.'

Nora sat back in her chair. 'That's a great idea. In fact, I'd
like to build on it. Do you think we could turn it into a class
visit? I know Abby will benefit from a one-on-one with the editor,
but I'd love to let the whole class see a real newsroom in action.'

'Perfect. I'll make the initial contact with Arden about Abby and let her know you'll be following up concerning a class visit.'

She stood and offered her hand. Her palm was cool and slender, her shake firm. 'I've enjoyed brainstorming with you, Ms Best. I wish our commission sessions were this productive.'

'I've enjoyed it, too.' She hoped Melanie hadn't noticed the wistful tone in her voice. Their brief interaction had carried a whiff of her old life as a public relations specialist, back before the implosion of her marriage, her estranged husband's murder, the terrifying experience at the wilderness program for teenage girls – all the things that made the peninsula's quietude so attractive. Still, as much as she loved the fact that she'd apparently never have to wear heels again, she missed . . . what, exactly? The sense of striving, the barely concealed ambition, so tiresome some of the time but that once lent an undeniable frisson to her days.

Melanie slung her purse over her shoulder.

'Before you go,' Nora said. 'Maybe you can help me with something.'

NINETEEN

Nora had practiced her delivery. Thought she'd perfected it – the careless aside, the casual tone, suggesting her question about the tsunami tower was just idle curiosity.

But Melanie's eyes went wide, then narrowed to slits. 'You looked at the plans?'

'Because of the school project, yes.'

'Because of what that man told my daughter,' Melanie shot back.

Busted. Of course Abby would have told her mother about the man on the beach.

'He was so adamant. That's why I looked at the plans. They didn't list an architectural firm. I even called the engineer who spoke about the hotel at the meeting. I thought he might know something. But he said he didn't have anything to do with it and then he hung up on me.'

Nora watched the gears creak into motion behind Melanie's eyes. She nodded, short and sharp.

'Let me get back to you on that.' She spun on her heel and left, her purposeful bearing at odds with the woman who'd hovered in the classroom doorway only a little while before.

Nora was doubly surprised to get a text from Melanie seconds after the final bell rang. 'Can you meet me at Betty's a little after 5?'

This time, Nora – mindful of Luke's understandable reaction when she showed up late for the special dinner he'd prepared – texted him that she'd be late. 'Meeting with a parent,' she added, tamping down her resentment at the self-imposed need to justify herself.

A platter of a dozen oysters awaited when Nora slid into the booth,

'I took the liberty,' Melanie said. 'I know the old guidelines about never eating oysters in a month without an "r" no longer apply, but I always wait until September before ordering them again. I took a chance that you liked them raw. Believe me, I can eat the entire dozen if you don't.'

'Sorry to disappoint.' Nora squeezed a few drops of lemon juice onto a glistening oyster, lifted the shell to her lips and slurped, holding it in her mouth for a moment, savoring the briny tang. 'Oh, that's good.'

She waited, barely able to contain her curiosity as Melanie followed suit, posing her question as soon as Melanie swallowed. 'Did you have more ideas on how I can best help Abby?'

'That's not why I called.'

Nora endured another oyster-slurp before Melanie deigned to enlighten her.

'I went back over the transcripts of the commission's discussion on the tower. The planning board had already signed off on it, so it was just a matter of us approving it – a rubber-stamp sort of thing, especially since Spencer was donating it. We're talking a three-million-dollar project. But Ward came to the meeting and spoke against it during the public comment period.'

She reached for another oyster, making her way around the tray in double-time.

'What was his objection?'

They were down to the last three oysters. Melanie reached for one, then pulled her hand back in a reluctant concession to good manners.

'Go ahead,' said Nora, her own reluctance equally obvious. 'I'll take the last two.'

'He didn't really have anything specific, which was weird, because usually Ward would show up with a stack of paperwork this high' – she held her palm a foot above the table – 'to bolster his point. But this time he was empty-handed. Just a gut feeling, he called it. Bailey has had his fill of Ward over the years, so he didn't hold back. "We don't make decisions on gut feelings," he said.'

'So you approved it.'

Melanie nodded.

'How'd *you* vote?'

Melanie fiddled with the empty oyster shells, balancing them atop one another. 'I voted for it.'

Nora added her oyster shell to the stack. Melanie had downed eight to her four. Nora wasn't inclined to let her off the hook. 'How do you feel about that now?'

The tower of shells wobbled, hung sideways for a moment, then slid back onto the tray with a clatter. Around the room, heads raised among the early-dinner crowd.

Melanie finally met Nora's gaze. 'Uncomfortable. Even without any supporting evidence, Ward felt so strongly about this that it gave me pause. When I reviewed the records, I saw the same thing you did – no one listed on the plans other than Spencer's firm. So I called Spencer.'

Nora kicked herself under the table. She'd been going at things sideways, not wanting to call attention to herself after Ron's warning.

It didn't matter now. Melanie had done the obvious. She made a mental note for her students' journalism project: just be straightforward.

'He did one of these.' Melanie mimed an exasperated sigh. 'He said, "I suppose this is for your daughter's school project.

Pretty weird project if you ask me, sending kids poking around into something that was settled a long time ago."'

Nora retrieved a shell that had bounced out of the tray onto the table. 'Ron Stevenson said something along the same lines to me. I can't believe people are worked up about a kids' project.'

Melanie gave her a pitying look. 'I could have told you. Development – even something as innocuous as a tsunami tower – is the peninsula's third rail. When Abby came home and told me about it, I was worried about exactly this sort of thing. But I get so tired of having to tiptoe around everything having to do with development. And Abby was so excited about it, so I just kept my mouth shut.'

'I'm so sorry. If I'd known, I'd have gone with another idea.' Except, she hadn't had one.

'Don't apologize. It's good for the kids to dip their toes into something controversial. God knows, living here, they'll get enough of it. They might as well be prepared. Anyhow, Spencer said he'd forgotten the name. "A Portland firm," was all he said. But not before another one of these.' A second heaving sigh. 'He made it pretty clear I was wasting his time.'

'He couldn't remember?'

Melanie raised an eyebrow.

'So he says.'

Nora's own eyebrow twitched in response.

Melanie James waved off Nora's attempts to split the bill. 'Tell you what. I'd feel better if we could talk to that architect.'

Apparently, they'd now become *we*.

'I'll do some computer sleuthing to try and track him down. But if I find him, maybe you can be the one to visit him?'

'Sure,' said Nora. 'I'm curious, too. But why not just call him?'

A voice sounded behind her. Janie sidled into view. 'Hope I'm not interrupting official business.'

'Not at all. Just getting to know Abby's teacher a little better.'

Janie lofted the tray of empty oyster shells. 'I'll get these out of your way.'

Melanie flashed her a smile. 'Put it on my tab, would you please, Janie? And this is for you. Thanks for taking such good care of us.' A bill disappeared into Janie's apron pocket.

'Anytime I have a work meal, I try to do it here. Social occasions, too. Support our local businesses, you know? I settle up at the end of each month.'

Maybe she hadn't heard Nora's question. 'Is it really worth driving all the way to Portland just to talk with someone?'

Melanie glanced over her shoulder at Janie. She took Nora's arm and led her outside. 'Call me a control freak. But it's too easy to just hang up on someone if they call. If I've learned anything in politics, it's that face-to-face interaction is always best. Speaking of politics, that's the other reason: I'm so busy getting my campaign going right now. Surely you can understand. So – deal?'

'Deal.'

TWENTY

Nora hurried from Betty's, stopping only to text Luke that she was on her way.

She'd agreed to go with him to look at the house for sale. Though *house* seemed like too grand a term. Even Naomi Stillwell, the real-estate agent, called it a cottage although she couldn't resist appending *charming* as she threw open the front door and led them inside, scattering still more adjectives in her wake.

'It's just darling. And perfect for two people – a rare find on the peninsula. Most of our homes are designed for families, or more often these days as vacation rentals. An elderly couple spent their whole married life here. They never had children. He's only selling because she died a few months ago. You'll have a difficult time finding anything else that meets your needs within your price range, and certainly not anything so desirable. Just look at the space in this kitchen.'

Nora bit her lips against a smile. If the kitchen was spacious, it was only because the previous owners had knocked out a wall between it and the living room. To be fair, the space accommodated a two-top table in the kitchen area.

A few steps brought Nora into the living room, where she plopped down on the sofa and stretched her legs toward one of the kitchen chairs. Add a coffee table, and one person could take the sofa and prop their feet on it, while the other could do the same from the kitchen chair. 'You're right. Plenty of space!'

She rose, ignoring Naomi's flustered laugh and Luke's glare, and headed for the bedrooms. 'More space!' she crowed. The larger, at least, would accommodate a queen bed and an end table; the smaller, a single bed.

'The office could go in here,' Naomi trilled in recovery mode. 'Or bunk beds. Do you have children? Because this would be perfect . . .'

Their simultaneous response cut her off.

'No,' said Nora.

'Yes,' said Luke.

Naomi looked from one to the other. Her mouth hung open for a long beat. 'Let's look at the backyard,' she suggested, her voice gone flat.

And that's where she got Nora. Thanks to the home's corner lot the yard was spacious beyond her imagining. French doors opened on to a mossy flagstone patio. Beyond, a tall redwood fence enclosed a space shaded on one side by leaning spruce, while the other sat ready to capture the sun whenever it chose to shine.

'You'll have your barbecues here,' Naomi promised, having shrewdly detected some rearrangement in Nora's attitude. 'I understand you have a dog. It would be the matter of a mere hour's time to install a dog door that would let him – him, yes? Murph, I believe – go in and out so that you could sleep through the night.' Oh, she'd done her homework, apparently with plenty of help from Luke.

Murph, like any aging gentleman, awoke often in the middle of the night and Nora, like any woman of a certain age, had trouble getting back to sleep after being roused, resulting in bleary-eyed mornings and days during which her brain lagged a beat behind. The idea that Murph could take care of his own business held an undeniable appeal.

Naomi wisely urged Luke across the yard to examine the raised beds, leaving Nora alone with her thoughts. Their conversation

– something about varieties of tomatoes – floated back toward Nora.

'Hey!' She held up her hand for silence. Listened hard. No. It wasn't there – the undulating whoosh of the waves that soothed her to sleep each night in her beachfront campsite. She'd always known the campsite was only a temporary solution. As it was, she had to switch sites every few weeks to comply with limits on occupation. But always, the sound of the waves followed her, along with the enticing whiff of brine through windows she left cracked open on even the coldest nights.

She knew she couldn't stay there forever. But she wasn't ready to leave.

She wasn't ready.

But.

She left Luke and Naomi in the yard and wandered back through the house. The kitchen appliances were new-ish and, most important, the sneaky crevices between stove and counter were crumb-free, no fingerprints smeared the fridge surface or the brushed-metal cupboard doorknobs. The floor – unlike her own – lacked the faint outline of pawprints. Flowered paper lined the cupboard shelves and even the Tupperware was arranged by size, each piece matched with a lid, something Nora had never managed to achieve. A house-proud cook had occupied this space.

She'd just glanced into the bathroom before. Now she took a longer look at the wide and deep tub. For months she'd limited herself to hasty showers in Electra's cramped bathroom. She leaned against the doorjamb and indulged in a fantasy of stretching out in near-scalding water up to her chin, lingering until the water cooled and stepping out into a space that would allow her to towel herself dry without bruising her elbows against the walls.

A step sounded behind her. 'Well?'

She turned to face Luke. If she wanted this – the yard where Murph could romp free while she lounged on the deck with a book and a glass of wine, the bright kitchen where she might once again cook more than egg scrambles and pasta, and oh, that tub – he'd be part of the deal.

Luke, who'd helped save her and two teenage runaways.

Luke, with whom she shared responsibility for their attackers' deaths – a responsibility that, so far, remained a secret buried so deep it nudged the Earth's molten core. He'd never use that against her. Would he?

But she wasn't ready.

Or was she?

After all, it wasn't like they were getting married.

'Do we have a deal?'

She watched as her hand reached out to be confined within his and, for the second time that day, heard herself say, 'Deal.'

TWENTY-ONE

Nora meant to tell Luke about her conversation with Melanie.

She'd even started to.

They'd gone with Sheila to the Mall, the locals' name for the roofed-over community garage sale/swap shop behind the library in Seacrest, shopping for the house. Nora's furniture amounted to a couple of camp chairs for evenings under Electra's awning, and her kitchen supplies would barely fill a single cupboard. Luke had more pots and pans, but his apartment was furnished and Naomi had informed them the home's owner wasn't interested in including any of his belongings in the house sale.

'Consider the bright side,' Luke said now. 'You won't have to look at that plaid sofa anymore. How about that one?' He pointed out a tufted gold Victorian-style number perched on carved wooden talons hooked around wooden orbs.

'Not on your life.'

Sheila gave a snort of laughter. 'I'd forgotten about the compromises of married – or whatever you two are – life. I'll leave you to it.'

Distraction was in order. 'I had an interesting conversation with Abby James' mom the other day, right before we looked at the house.'

A sofa was a major commitment. Nora had hoped to start with something small, kitchen gadgets maybe, before moving on to something as sizeable and anchoring as a sofa. She moved toward the tables holding dinnerware, willing Luke to follow.

'She's helped me find the name of that architect. The one who signed off on the plans for the tower.'

'Seriously? In just a month, we're going to move into a bunch of bare rooms and that's what you're worried about?'

Nora stopped and opened her arms wide. 'Luke, look at all this. We'll find everything we need and then some within an hour.' The cavernous space was arranged into department-store sections: furniture here (sectioned off into living room, bedroom, office and so on); linens there, kitchen and bath items against the far wall. It hummed with activity, people bringing items no longer needed or wanted, others piling goods into carts or balancing them on hand trucks.

'I'm so glad you showed us this place,' she called to Sheila who, divining that they'd moved out of the danger zone, had returned.

'I can't believe you didn't already know about it. It's one of the peninsula's treasures. I'm here almost every weekend, whether I need anything or not. I don't think I've ever bought a new bike for either of my kids. I just come here. It's a single mom's dream, in terms of making things affordable. Oh, look! Houseplants.'

She was off again, making for a table that resembled a mini-garden center, everything from seedlings to low flowering shrubs in large pots sold by a man in his early forties with a square jaw, an easy grin and – even from a distance, Nora could see – a naked left hand.

She grinned and strolled toward the kitchen goods, stopping at a table displaying stacks of dinnerware. She had four place settings of serviceable Corelle, but surely they'd need more? She'd left her husband more than a year ago and had surprised herself by so quickly adjusting to a solo life. Now she'd have to relearn how to factor another person into nearly every equation.

She picked up a dinner plate, started to put it back, then examined it with more interest. A dun-colored shorebird strode across its surface, its spear of a beak nearly as long and slender as its legs. She turned the plate over. 'Marbled godwit.'

She picked up another, this time recognizing one of the peninsula's ubiquitous gulls. The plate informed her otherwise. The showy silvery bird with the black crown and scarlet beak was a Caspian tern. Nora made a mental note to look up the difference between gulls and terns, and scanned the table. The plates were part of a set – bowls, dessert dishes, cups and saucers.

Behind her, someone muffled a gasp. A hand reached around and caressed one of the dishes.

Nora turned and looked into Sheila's moist blue eyes, peering through the broad leaves of a large aspidistra she cradled in one arm.

'Sorry.' Sheila's voice roughened. 'Those were Ward's,' she said a moment later. 'His things must have gone to second-hand brokers. I ate a lot of yogurt and granola out of those bowls. I always teased him that I was going to sneak in some Frosted Flakes for breakfast.'

'Ward's?' Nora picked up one of the bowls and held it to the light, admiring the near-translucent china. 'From everything I've heard about him, these don't seem like the sort of thing he'd have.' She amended her sentence. 'He and Delilah would have had.'

'Wedding present,' Sheila said. 'If memory serves, it was from Spencer. You could look at it two ways. On the one hand, it was a pretty classy gesture, considering that after going out with him all through high school, she threw him over for Ward when Spencer went East for college. On the other, at every single meal they'd serve as a reminder of what she'd given up – or what she could still have. Say what you want about Spencer Templeton, in the end he always gets what he wants.'

'They're beautiful,' Nora agreed. She made a snap decision. 'And now they're mine.' She tried to divine Sheila's expression behind the wavering leaves. 'Unless, of course, you want them.' She held her breath.

'God, no. I'm so done with these incestuous peninsula relationships. Next person I get involved with cannot have signed my high school yearbook.'

Nora made the easiest of leaps. 'Where's plant guy from?'

'Expedition!' She named the nearest mainland community. 'Does that count?'

Sheila winked. 'Seeing him Friday night.' She held out her free hand for a fist bump.

'What are you two laughing about?'

Luke's face bore the look common to men who come upon women excluding them from a conversation.

'Our new dishes.' Nora held up a plate, then turned to negotiate a price, happy to leave Luke stewing, sure – as men conclude – that he'd been the topic.

Luke wandered off as the person selling the dishes took her sweet time wrapping each in layers of newspaper.

Nora found out where he'd gone when she toted the box full of china outside, only to see Luke tying down the gold sofa in the bed of her pickup. Sheila dropped her plant and grabbed the box of dishes as it slid from Nora's arms.

'You've got to be kidding. That thing is hideous.'

Luke shrugged and grinned. 'Fancy-ass sofa to go with those fancy-ass dishes.'

Nora reached for the box, but Sheila held tight. 'I don't trust these with you right now.' She placed them in the bed of the truck beside the sofa and fondled one of its clawed feet. 'What are these supposed to be, giant chickens? C'mon, Nora, it's fun. For sure, it's the only one like it on the whole peninsula.'

She bent and righted her plant, which had landed on its side with only a minimal loss of dirt. 'This was supposed to be a move-in present for you two, but do you mind if I keep it for a while? I want my new friend to see it when he comes over Friday night.' She put a finger to her cheek and affected a wide-eyed, innocent stare. 'Hmm, where should I put it? I know – the bedroom!'

Nora and Luke laughed together on cue and waved goodbye. 'At least you've got a bed. That's our next stop.' They headed off-peninsula to another mall – a real one, this time featuring new furniture.

'Think we'll ever see that plant again?' Luke teased. 'Maybe we should just buy one of our own.'

Nora mustered a smile but couldn't help sneaking peeks in the rear-view mirror at the gold monstrosity looming behind her. She'd forgotten the constant push-pull of marriage, the way compromise was touted as a saving grace. She was going on her second year without having to compromise. She'd liked it.

But now – she glanced in the mirror again and gritted her teeth – she was going to have to learn to like that goddamned gold sofa.

TWENTY-TWO

Shopping for beds was almost worse. All those mattress choices! Foam, innerspring, or combo? And then there was the matter of a frame, leaving Nora so exhausted that Luke offered to drive home.

At some point in the process, she'd forgotten that she hated compromise. After they'd flopped on to the fifteenth mattress – or was it the fiftieth? – she'd ceased to care about having a say in the matter at all. 'Anything. Just get anything in our price range. As long as it's firm.' The one thing they'd agreed upon.

Luke had walked her out of the furniture store to a coffee kiosk and ordered her a latte with a quad shot. 'Take a breath,' he said.

She took a sip instead, then a larger one. 'Ahhh. That helps. It's just that, living in Electra, I haven't had to make many choices. Hardly any. I don't think I realized until today how much easier that makes my life.'

Luke took her coffee cup, set it aside, and clasped both her hands in his. 'Same. Look at me. I haven't had my own stuff for years now. First the Marines put me up, then after my divorce I had free room and board at Serendipity Ranch' – the program where they'd met – 'and now I'm in a furnished apartment. We've both got a lot to figure out. The good thing is, we get to figure it out together.'

The tension drained from Nora at his words, nearly as quickly as she'd drained her coffee cup. 'Let's go get a bed,' she'd said.

Now, nearly home with a bed scheduled for delivery, she glanced out the truck window and saw – 'Pull over. Quick. Right there.' She pointed.

'Look,' she mouthed as the truck coasted to a halt. She angled the rear-view mirror so he could see.

Spencer Templeton stood on the sidewalk, arguing with a brawny man in overalls and a hard hat. Rather, Templeton stood with arms folded as the very agitated man got in his face.

'Isn't that . . .?' Luke whispered.

Nora nodded. 'Janie's husband. He's working on the tsunami tower. Maybe something went wrong on the site.'

Whatever Ron Stevenson said jolted Spencer from his studied cool. 'Don't forget who gave you this job,' he yelled.

'Don't forget why you gave it to me,' Ron shot back.

Spencer stepped close and lowered his voice. Nora didn't hear the rest of it, but Ron swept his helmet from his head and hurled it at Spencer's feet. Spencer danced backward as Janie's husband stalked away.

Spencer spat a curse and looked their way.

'Shit,' said Luke. 'He sees us.'

'Drive away.'

Luke threw the truck into gear, then eased it back to neutral. 'Too late.'

Spencer's face appeared in the window. 'I'm sorry you saw that. But you're both teachers. You know how it is. Sometimes, managing employees is a lot like managing schoolchildren. Or at least, never having been a schoolteacher, I imagine it is.'

So smooth, thought Nora. His comments could have been taken as condescending until he'd thrown in that last remark.

'Is there a problem with your truck? Do you need some help?'

'Excuse me?' Nora leaned forward.

'You pulled over. Is something wrong?'

The only thing wrong was that they'd been caught spying on a personal confrontation.

Nora hopped out of the truck and tugged at the bindings holding the gold sofa in place. She'd hoped someone might steal it while they were bed shopping, but no such luck.

'I thought one of these had come loose.'

Spencer gazed at the sofa with an expression so blank it spoke louder than any appalled words. He joined Nora in testing the bindings.

'They seem fine. Good thing. You'd hate to lose something as . . . unique . . . as this.'

He lingered by the tailgate.

'Damien's told us about your class project. It puts him in a tough spot, don't you think?'

Nora cocked her head. 'In what way?'

'Forcing him to dig up negative information on his dad's project.'

Stepdad's. But maybe, with Ward gone, he'd been promoted.

'That's hardly what we're doing. It's just a middle-school project. Honestly, there's no hidden agenda here.'

'Isn't there?'

He slapped the side of the truck before she could answer. 'All good,' he called to Luke and made his goodbyes.

Nora climbed back into the passenger seat.

'What was all that about?'

'He let me know he doesn't like my kids' project on the tsunami tower.'

He shrugged, put the truck in gear and eased from the curb. 'People are entitled to their own opinions.'

'What about the fight between them?'

He shot her some side-eye. 'I think we can't know what's going on between two people.'

Standard psychologist advice, something he trotted out whenever she speculated on someone's motives, and that she found profoundly annoying.

'But—'

'And I think we need to unload this stuff in Sheila's garage before it gets dark.' She'd offered them space to store their accumulations until they moved into the house.

Nora wasn't ready to let it go. 'Ron Stevenson got in my face the other day. He could use anger-management classes.'

She finally had his attention.

'What do you mean?' The truck swerved as he twisted to look directly at her. 'Define got in your face. Yelling? Or did he get physical?'

'Eyes on the road. And, neither. He didn't like the class project, either. He told me in no uncertain terms just how important the hotel is to this place and made it clear he didn't take kindly to anyone who objected to it. He thought we did because we left the commission meeting right after all of Ward's supporters did.'

'See? I told you we never should have gone to that thing. But all he did was talk to you?'

'Yes. That's all.' Even though it wasn't. *He stood too close. Leaned over me.* Even as she imagined saying the words aloud, she imagined his puzzled response. *So?*

In a way, she envied the open hostility of Ron's confrontation with Spencer. A raised voice, a thrown hard hat – anybody would understand that for what it was.

'I just think it's weird. Him yelling at me about the project and now yelling at Spencer. And Spencer up in my face about the project, too.'

'You just said Ron didn't yell at you,' he reminded her. 'And you don't know what he was yelling about with Spencer. It might just have been some sort of personal thing. Anyway, it's none of our business.'

'Uh-huh,' Nora offered in the spirit of compromise. Which was bullshit. She very much intended to make it her business.

TWENTY-THREE

She couldn't change course on the class project even if she'd been so inclined – which she was not.

They were already a few weeks into the semester. Anyway, not only had her students embraced the original concept, they wanted to expand it.

The unlikely duo of Abby and Damien confronted her Monday morning in their roles as editor and chief photographer. Damien held up his phone, displaying the *Peninsula Press* webpage.

'There.' He put a finger on a small notice sandwiched between a larger story about the annual oyster festival and another about the high school football team's first victory in two years.

'Groundbreaking scheduled,' read the headline.

'What groundbreaking?' Nora enlarged the page. She'd recently noted an increasing need for cheater glasses and had purchased several pairs that she stashed by her bed, at the dinette, at Luke's and in her purse, which she'd forgotten in her morning scramble. For months she'd brushed aside Luke's suggestion that she see an optometrist, but now thought maybe he was right, a thought she intended to keep to herself.

'For the new hotel. We should do a story about it. Maryann could write it,' Abby said. 'She's our lead reporter.'

Just as both her mother and Nora had hoped, Abby embraced her responsibilities as editor, making sure everyone had a title and duties to go with it. Jeannie Graves was the page designer. Matthew was appointed to solicit ads from local businesses. Everybody else was either a reporter, photographer or copy editor.

'The copy editors write the headlines and captions. But they call captions cutlines,' Abby explained after a day's excused absence to shadow Arden Talbott. 'And they make sure there are no typos or grammatical errors. Copy editors are really important.' Zeke Miles, the budding entrepreneur with acute attention to detail, was put in charge of the copy editors.

Damien took his phone back, waggling it at Nora. 'And I'll choose the photos.'

The rest of the class, confident that Nora was otherwise occupied, deployed their superpower – a lightning descent into anarchy. Matthew opened a baggie of Gummi Bears, probably purchased from Zeke, licked one, and lobbed it across the row into Jeannie's short Afro.

'Let me think about it,' Nora called back to Abby and Damien as she darted from behind her desk, managing to catch Jeannie's arm before she launched a well-deserved beatdown on Matthew.

'Matthew, you'll apologize this minute and stay for detention after school. Jeannie, here's a bathroom pass so you can wash that out of your hair. Oh, and Matthew?' She held out her hand.

He deposited the baggie in her palm and muttered an apology to Jeannie, whose death stare promised off-premises revenge, which was just fine with Nora. Matthew was one of Damien's most devoted minions.

She refocused them with a reminder that the written reports on Asian countries were due, and that they'd be giving their oral presentations in just a few minutes. 'That way, we can all learn from each other.' She'd assigned each child a different country so as not to end up with a dozen papers on China, each illustrated by a snaggle-toothed drawing of the Great Wall.

Handing in their papers gave them time to settle down, and Nora time to come up with a plan.

'Before we start the oral presentations, your news editor and photo editor would like to cover the groundbreaking for the new hotel.'

'Yeah!' An affirmative chorus arose. Nora wasn't an idiot. She knew an excuse to get out of the classroom when she saw one. But the kids weren't the only ones dying for the occasional escape.

'Only one problem. Can anyone tell me what it is?'

She'd just about given up hope of an answer when Jeannie's hand inched up.

'Our project doesn't have anything to do with the hotel.' Jeannie touched a hand to her damp hair and shot a triumphant glance at Matthew, who'd been one of the most vocal respondents to the idea.

'Exactly. At least, not at first glance. But Abby and Damien clearly think it's a good idea. I'm sure they were just about to tell me why but first, I'd like your thoughts.'

'Because Damien's dad is building it? And he's putting up the tower, too?' Zeke's expression was a little *too* blank.

'So what, you little suck-up?' Damien glowered.

Nora shot him The Look. His apology was just shy of inaudible, while Zeke's face did an equally inadequate job of concealing a smirk. Nora wondered if one of his spreadsheets kept track of classroom one-upmanship.

'To Jeannie's point, what if anything does one project have to do with the other?'

'I know! I know!' Madison Everett, dressed as usual in head-to-toe Seattle Seahawks gear, practically jumped out of her chair. Abby had appointed her the sports editor. When Nora asked what could possibly comprise a sports story about the tsunami tower, Madison had a ready answer: the track team could hold regular drills for students, building their endurance for a double-time sprint to the tower. Now, she had the answer for Nora's question, too.

'We watched a program on tsunamis before last year's drill. There was that big one, on some island.'

'Indonesia. That's the country for my report,' Abby interjected.

Madison rushed on, probably afraid Abby would pre-empt her. 'It killed millions of people.'

Abby couldn't contain herself any longer. She stepped forward, in front of Nora. 'Not millions. But more than two hundred thousand. My report talks about it. A lot of them were tourists in hotels. Just like the one that Mr Templeton is building.'

'Not just like that,' Damien asserted himself. 'Those got washed away. My d-dad's will stand.'

Nora noted the slight hesitation and wondered anew whether Ward's death had promoted Spencer from stepdad to dad, or whether Damien was just trying out the notion.

'Anyway,' he said, 'Abby and I think it's all related. That the tsunami tower will make tourists feel safer.'

Nora took a moment to digest the concept of Abby and Damien as allies. 'Fair point. But the hotel's a long way from being built, so you won't have any tourists to interview – beyond the ones you've already talked to, that is.'

'But it could be a practice story for our final report. We could . . .' Nora watched him fish for the words. 'Work out the kinks.'

'He's not wrong, Ms Best.' This from Jeannie, who couldn't help but add, 'For once.'

Nora threw up her hands. If this was what it took to unite the warring factions within her classroom, she was all for it.

'You've convinced me. But, Abby, I want your reporters to talk with every single town official who's at that groundbreaking, along with a good sample of anyone who's come to watch. And of course, nothing's set in stone until we get Principal Everhart's permission. Now, because Madison brought up Indonesia, Abby can start with her oral report on that country. Please show her the same respect you yourself would appreciate when it's your turn.'

She sat back and made the appropriate sounds of approval as Abby reeled off her facts – the world's fourth-largest country! Seventeen thousand islands! But then Abby moved on to the tsunami, and the room fell silent as new figures populated her presentation: Sumatra on the northwestern tip of Indonesia had the misfortune of being just a hundred and fifty miles from the epicenter of the third-strongest earthquake ever recorded, and it took only about twenty minutes for a thirty-foot wave to smash ashore. It surged three miles inland across pitifully flat expanses of sand and palm trees, swallowing buildings whole, turning entire towns into heaps of rubble and killing nearly a quarter-million people.

If Nora turned her head just the slightest bit, not so much that Abby would think she'd stopped paying attention, she could see across the street and the beach to the ocean beyond, so very calm on this day, a tentative sun turning its surface pearlescent.

Beautiful.

Inviting.

Just as those other seas must have looked seconds before the ocean floor heaved beneath them.

She could see the water from where she sat but she couldn't see Highview Hill. It didn't matter. For all its lofty name, she knew it wasn't high enough.

Abby had moved on to Indonesia's economy. Nora pretended interest in palm oil and tourism, even as the watery images she'd painted caused a tectonic shift in Nora's own thinking about the tower. Abby persuaded herself a tsunami wouldn't hit the peninsula for another two centuries. But what if she was wrong?

As far as she was concerned, Spencer Templeton couldn't build that tower fast enough.

TWENTY-FOUR

Everhart granted permission for the outing so quickly that Nora should have been suspicious.

But she lingered in blissful ignorance until the day of the groundbreaking, when the principal fell in step beside Nora and her students as they walked the two blocks to the construction site.

'I've been so curious about this newspaper project of yours. I've certainly heard a lot about it around town. I thought I'd see for myself.'

Nora stiffened. 'Aren't they cute in their little hats and with their little notebooks?'

'Cute isn't the word I'd use. Not everybody likes the press or trusts it. Are you sure this is a safe practice for children?'

Have you read the First Amendment lately?

But Nora kept the retort to herself.

'It's part of our unit on democracy. Not only do they learn that we have a free press, but they learn how a responsible, ethical press works. Plus, it's done wonders for some of the shyest students. It's amazing how much more outgoing they become in search of a story.'

'I see.' Her tone told Nora she didn't, or maybe that she didn't want to. Someone called to her. 'To be continued,' she said, leaving Nora wondering: promise or threat?

The hotel site, at this point only a collection of concrete stilts and yellow machines caged within a fenced-off lot, loomed before them. As Nora understood it, the official groundbreaking had been delayed to accommodate an appearance by a congressman known for his pro-development stance.

A woman holding a reporter's notebook, just like the kids, turned at their approach, a smile spreading across her lightly freckled features. 'Abby! There's my next employee. We're holding a spot for you in – what grade are you in again?'

'Seventh.'

'Let's see – five more years of school and then four of college. But after that, there's a job for you at the *Peninsula Press*.'

'Be careful.' Melanie James left the group of county officials and joined them. 'Abby has a mind like a steel trap. Don't be surprised to find her knocking at your door in nine years, expecting you to have a desk ready for her in the newsroom.'

Nora held out her hand to the woman. 'You're Arden Talbott. I'm Nora Best, Abby's teacher. I was hoping to arrange a class visit to the newspaper, but it seems as though Abby beat us to the punch.'

'Any time,' Talbott said. 'Abby told us about your project. I appreciate anything that helps people better understand the realities of journalism. But speaking of realities, I'm a bit of a one-man band today. Editor and reporter and photographer and videographer. Welcome to the never-ending world of staff cuts. When you visit our newsroom, there won't be many of us to see. Excuse me.'

She hurried to the congressman's side, phone at the ready, her recording app blinking.

Nora stood to one side and watched with pride as Abby shepherded her charges. She assigned a different student to each speaker. Damien did the same with his photo crew – the kids with smartphones.

Nora's eyes glazed over during the speeches, a collection of platitudes that could have been offered by anyone, anywhere at any similar event. 'Jobs blah blah blah economy blah blah blah bright future blah-de-blahbitty-blah.' But the kids scrawled ferociously in their notebooks as though listening to the Gettysburg Address or King's 'I Have a Dream' speech.

'I can't believe the school lets them do that,' someone near Nora muttered. She snapped to attention and looked around. The kids' initial foray had involved quizzing people on the beach, many of them day-trippers who gave every indication of finding them adorable. This day featured a darker vibe.

While some in the small gathering actually appeared to be listening to the dog-and-pony show, others glared at her students, shook their heads, whispered asides to one another.

Someone sidled up to her and said something too low for her to make out. She folded her arms and turned away.

The person raised his voice. 'Have you found him yet?'

Nora yanked away from the gangly man she recognized from the commission meeting and the beach, the one who'd pestered Abby to find the architect. He sported the unruly tangle of graying hair, same paint-crusted pants, the same Hawaiian-style shirt, although this one featured outsize blue flowers and she remembered the other as red.

'Found who?' Just in case her recall was off. It wasn't.

'The architect. You have to talk to him.'

'Who are you?'

He began to edge away. 'A friend of this peninsula. And of the people who live here.'

Someone shushed them. Templeton wielded a shovel painted gold. Damien pushed close for a photo. Everhart twisted to glare at Nora, probably seeing his actions as rude and expecting her to intervene, even though Damien was doing exactly what he was supposed to do. Nora didn't have time to deal with a paranoia-pushing stranger – even though she was starting to share his paranoia.

'You're one of Ward's Warriors, aren't you? Just tell me your name. And how I can be in touch.'

'I'll find you. But you find him first. Before anybody else does.'

TWENTY-FIVE

Nora shook out an old copy of the *Peninsula Press*, freed a page, and wrapped it around one of Luke's cast-iron pans.

She'd had trouble finding enough newspaper to package even their meager goods, now that the *Peninsula Press* only printed on weekends. Luckily, Arden Talbott had come through with some yellowed copies languishing in a storeroom along with all the unused desks and chairs that harkened to the days of a far larger staff.

Nora eyeballed the available boxes and selected one of the smaller ones, in the interest of saving the back of whoever ended up carrying it.

'Honestly, Luke, it was like something out of a B movie.' Nora lowered her voice to a growl and spoke out of the side of her mouth. 'You find him first. Before anybody else does. Dunh, dunh, dunh.' She mimicked crashing piano chords.

'I thought you'd decided all of that was a bunch of hooey,' Luke called from the bedroom. Nora could see him through the open door, folding his shirts beside a plastic storage container waiting on the bed. Cardboard boxes and more storage containers sat in various stages of being filled.

Nora wrapped another piece of cast iron, this time a Dutch oven. 'How much of this stuff do you have?'

'Not enough. And when we move in together, you're not to touch it. Just my luck, you'd scrub the finish right off.'

'Fine by me.' The less dishwashing Nora had to do, the better. 'I'd almost forgotten about the architect,' she said. 'But then that guy reminded me. He seemed obsessed.'

Luke smacked the lid down onto the storage container with perhaps more force than necessary. 'He is obsessed. Which is why you should ignore him. Hey, I have an idea.'

He hefted the storage container, added it to the fast-growing stack in one corner of the living room, and came up behind her and put his arms around her, nuzzling her ear.

'Now?' Nora pretended indignation, even as she relaxed against him. She'd rather do just about anything else than pack boxes, and what he had in mind was a lot better than most things.

'Not that.' Luke's arms tightened around her. 'Although, now that you mention it . . .'

Later, as they lay in a hastily cleared bed, he roused Nora from a happy daze when he murmured, 'Actually, that wasn't my first idea. Helluva substitute, though.'

'What was your first idea?' Nora hoped it was a nap. She was half-asleep anyway, and the idea drifting wholly into sleep appealed.

'Let's take the weekend off from packing. We don't close on the house until the end of next week anyway, and it's not as though either of us has much to pack. Let's hitch up your trailer and head off somewhere fun. I've never been camping in anything but a tent. I'd love to see how the other half lives.'

'Fun? What could possibly be more fun than moving?' Nora congratulated herself for subterfuge masquerading as snark.

'I'm serious.'

She pretended a little more reluctance, hoping it wasn't overkill. 'Oh, all right. But I have an idea, too.'

'Shoot.' Now Luke was the one on the edge of sleep, his voice soft and slurred.

'Let's do the best of both worlds. Let's find a campsite somewhere outside Portland – maybe near whatever that famous waterfall is – but let's spend a day in the city, too. We've been away from civilization so long I've nearly forgotten what it's like to be a culture vulture. We could hit a coffee shop in the morning and a martini bar in the afternoon and maybe wander through the Japanese Garden and the Rose Garden in between.'

'You're on.' A soft snore followed his words.

Nora smiled – if you could call it that; more a baring of teeth – into the lengthening shadows.

*And we could, on our way to one of those places, stroll by the
house of one Kirk Lopez, architect.*

Melanie had whispered the name into the phone as Nora
strained to hear over the din of a seventh-grade classroom
that erupted into chaos upon realizing their teacher's
distraction.

Normally she'd never have answered her phone in class, but
it had vibrated with a call tagged urgent.

'His name is Curt?' she'd said. Then, 'Damien, fold that middle
finger down this instant!'

Melanie's snort came through loud and clear. 'Kirk. You're
right; his name wasn't on the final plans. But I found an earlier
document, deep in some subcommittee stuff. Here's the phone
number and address. At least Spencer told me the right city.'
She named a street in the Portland's southeast district. 'Don't
suppose you're going there anytime soon, but now you know.
Oh, and I'm having a campaign barbecue in the park next week.
I'd love to see you and your guy. Monday, five o'clock. Did
you get that address? Good. Hope to see you at the barbecue.
Gotta go.'

Nora had to go, too. She estimated she'd been on the call for
less than a minute, which was all it took to tilt the class toward
chaos. There was probably a mathematical formula involved,
maybe something Sheila's class could calculate for her.

She corralled their attention with a request. 'I'm designating
all of you my brain trust.'

They cocked their heads, wary of a trick, flattery wrapping
something that would end up being more work.

'What's a brain trust?'

'It's a group of people who are experts about something. In
this case, I'm a dummy and you're the experts.'

'I'll say!'

'Thank you for the, uh, support, Damien. In this case, I'm
serious – although I wish I'd chosen a word other than dummy.
All of you have lived in this area far longer than I. How many
of you have been to Portland?'

Every hand shot up accompanied by a chorus of descriptions
of class trips and family outings.

'Well, I'm going there for the weekend and I'd like some help planning my trip. What should I see?'

Their recommendations skewed to their age – an amusement park. The science museum. The zoo – although that last brought objections from Madison and Jeannie that zoos were cruel.

Somewhat to her surprise, they also mentioned the falls. She reserved a campground near there and, upon arrival, forgot for a moment the trip's clandestine purpose.

She stood at their base, head tilted backward to watch the ribbon of water unspool from high above, rainbows shimmering in the mist.

'Oh,' she breathed.

Luke took her hand. 'I know.'

This, she reminded herself. The fact that he did know and knew that nothing more needed to be said. Her marriage had, in retrospect, been so performative, its surface buffed to an Instagram gloss years before the platform even existed. With Luke, there was no high-wattage facade, just an understated, reassuring warmth. *I know.*

Then he spoke again. 'You know who would love this? Gabriel. There's nothing like this in New Mexico. I can't wait to show it to him. Now that we'll have the house, he could spend summers with us. What do you think?'

Nora dropped his hand and stepped closer to the waterfall, taking a spray of icy water full in the face. She dashed it from her eyes, resisting an urge to plunge into the pool and let the falls beat her into oblivion, eliminating the need to say the only thing she possibly could say in response.

'Sure,' she spluttered. 'That'd be great.'

Now she was glad the trip had an ulterior motive. Focusing on it let her avoid the gut-churning possibility Luke had just mentioned.

Gabriel was thirteen, just a year older than her students. She tried imagining spending days on end – not just school days, but breakfast-to-bedtime – with any of them, even sweet, industrious Abby. The thought made her want to head for the nearest exit, tearing at her hair. Except there wasn't an exit.

She'd already contributed her share of the earnest money and added her signature to appropriate documents. If you loved someone with a child, the kid was part of the deal, right? Until this point, though, Gabriel had only been a shadowy presence, limited to the fridge photos, the tinny voice on the other end of the phone during Luke's weekly calls, the reason for Luke's every-three-months trips to New Mexico.

All of which, she lectured herself as they tiptoed along the mossy paths of the Japanese Gardens and inhaled the fragrance from the Rose Garden's late-blooming varieties, she would think about later. She was on a mission, one demanding the manipulative skills of a Cold War spy.

'Let's take a break this afternoon,' she suggested. 'No sight-seeing, no nothing. Spend an hour or two just hanging around in a coffeeshop like real Portland hipsters. Except we'll have books instead of laptops or phones – although maybe going old-school is a hipster thing? Anyway, I found one that sounds really good. It's in Southeast, just a couple of blocks from Mount Tabor. We can walk up there afterward, check out the reservoirs and get a great view of the city. How does that sound?'

He allowed as to how it sounded good. Better than good when he spied the baked goods on offer at the coffeeshop, which in addition to the usual croissants and scones included an array of savory hand pies. He ordered one with feta and spinach, while Nora opted for the garbanzo and sweet potato version.

Luke coopted a table by the window, opened his book – one of the fat World War II histories he was forever reading – and threw Nora a grateful look. 'This was a terrific idea. If we were at home, I'd be working on reports for school, or heading to the Mall to get more things for the house. I didn't realize how much I needed a break.'

Nora, who'd spent the previous day at the waterfalls, and much of this day wandering gardens, counting the minutes down toward the whole reason for the trip, wanted nothing more than to sprint for the door. Instead, she forced herself to take a bite of her hand pie, a sip of her decadent Mexican mocha, all while making appreciative – authentically so – murmurs. But – 'My book! I left it in the truck. You don't mind if I go back for it, do you?'

Luke waved her away. 'Sure. I'm deep in the Siege of Stalingrad here.'

'I might take a spin around the block, stretch my legs a little.' Which was ridiculous, given how much walking they'd already done. But he merely nodded, already far away on Stalingrad's frozen streets.

The address Melanie had given her was two blocks from the coffeeshop, in a neighborhood of spacious Craftsman bungalows so beautifully maintained that Nora automatically assigned them seven-figure price tags.

They'd only lived on the peninsula for about a year, but she'd already become accustomed to its sandy soil and scrubby pines. Portland was all lush lawns and showy fall flowers, blooming so riotous that Nora felt faintly claustrophobic amid all the vegetation. The architect's house perched on a hillside above the street. Wide steps led from the sidewalk to a deep front porch. Nora paused to let her eyes adjust to the gloom before ringing the bell.

Almost, she hoped no one would answer. Then she could tell Melanie she'd tried and gotten nowhere and that as far as she was concerned, the matter was closed. Which it would be. Wouldn't it?

She never got to resolve her internal debate because a series of thumps sounded and then the front door swung open, revealing a small, bent man with a shock of white hair and faded brown eyes behind wire-frame glasses. He clutched a cane with a three-pronged base.

'Yes?'

'I'm looking for Kirk Lopez.'

'I'm Kirk Lopez. Who's asking? And why?'

Too late, Nora realized she hadn't thought this part through.

'My name is Nora Best. I'm a teacher at Peninsula Middle School in Lane's End.'

He brightened and straightened to the extent that he could. 'Oh, yes. What brings you to Portland, Ms Best? Some sort of class trip? And . . .' His voice trailed off.

He was, Nora thought, of an age where he'd been raised not to ask prying questions. Such as: If this is a class trip, where are the students? And why come here? What in the world are you doing on my doorstep?

'Sort of. My class is doing a project on the tsunami tower.'

Lopez's face went blank. 'Tsunami tower?'

Nora tried a quick visual assessment, one she hoped fell short of a stare. His hand on the cane was steady; his gaze, while watery, was sharp. His clothing – a navy cardigan over a plaid shirt, and khaki pants with a near military crease – free of stains and wrinkles. Despite the physical frailty indicated by the cane, she saw no obvious signs of mental decline.

She started again, not wanting to make it an accusation. 'I was told you were the architect.'

His eyes narrowed. 'Someone told you wrong, young lady. I've never designed such a tower. Nor would I.'

Now she almost wished he'd been the doddering gent she'd first feared. Because there was nothing tentative in the look he gave her, nor in his abrupt dismissal.

'I don't know where you get your information, or why you think it's necessary to travel so far to disrupt my well-earned retirement, but whatever your assumptions, they're mistaken. Good day.'

'Wait.'

But he'd already closed the door.

Nora raised her hand to knock again but let it drop at the audible slide of a deadbolt.

'Mean old man,' she muttered as she trudged down the steps and stalked the block to the coffeeshop, not realizing until she'd slipped into the seat opposite Luke that she'd forgotten to grab her book from the truck.

TWENTY-SIX

Nora swung by Betty's on her way to school the next morning.

She'd been deputized to pick up an obligatory birthday cake for Everhart. There'd be a party in the teachers' lounge at the end of the day, hopeful 'jokes' about Everhart's surely approaching retirement, watery off-brand juice sipped from paper cups, everyone wishing it were something stronger, eyeing the clock and wondering when they could gracefully slip away.

Nora left the house early, trusting a forecast that despite gray skies promised a dry day, which meant she could ride her bike to school. She missed her morning walk along the beach, but biking was the next best thing. At least Betty's was across from the school, so she wouldn't have to try and balance a cake box as she rode.

Janie greeted her with box in hand. 'Saw you through the window. You want a peek before I tie this up?'

'I don't dare. It'll just tempt me. What are you doing working a morning shift? I've only seen you at lunch and dinner. Don't you ever sleep?'

Too late, Nora registered the dark circles under Janie's eyes, the slump in her spine. Nora guessed her to be in her early forties, at the age when working a twelve-hour shift one day and coming in at dawn the next took a progressive toll. But she reminded herself, so did living paycheck to paycheck, which Janie once again made clear was her reality.

'I fill in whenever we're short. You have any idea how well hungover folks tip when you hand them hot coffee and a still-warm pastry? What I made in tips today means I can pay my cell phone bill.'

She threw Nora a wink that belied the weariness in her eyes and the set of her jaw. Was it the hours? Nora wondered. Or the strain of being married to someone with the sort of hair-trigger temper Ron Stevenson seemed to possess?

The door opened. Delilah Templeton breezed in on a cloud of perfume that overrode the lingering scent of fresh-baked bread and pastries. Once again, she was in golf gear – neon-green like her cap this time; her plaid slacks shot through with yellow stripes. Despite the cloud cover, dark sunglasses shaded her face.

'I'll take a baguette,' she said to Janie. And, to Nora, 'How was your weekend in Portland?'

'How did you . . .?' Oh, of course. Damien must have said something at home.

'Shoot,' Janie muttered. 'We're out of bags.' She stooped and Nora heard drawers opening and closing.

'It was great. But we'll have to go back sometime. We barely scratched the surface.'

'Of course you'll go back. It's what people do when they

realize that life on the peninsula is not for them.' Delilah smiled sweetly.

'Same goes for people who grew up here,' Janie said from somewhere behind the counter.

Was it Nora's imagination or had the temperature just dropped a couple of degrees? Janie was taking longer than Nora would have thought possible to locate a long paper bag for Delilah's bread.

'Those things are around here somewhere. What are you up to today, Nora? Still stirring up trouble about the tower?'

Nora blinked. 'Um . . .'

'Ron told me you were asking about the architect, of all things.'

Did he tell you he warned me off? In the creepiest possible way?

Janie stood with a long cardboard box in her hand. She tore it open and extracted a sheaf of bags. 'I don't know why you went to him. Anything to do with the architect would be way beyond Ron's pay grade. That's more Spencer's territory. Delilah, maybe you can help her?'

Delilah ignored her and tapped a lacquered fingernail against the glass over the few remaining baguettes.

'Are these fresh?' She lowered her sunglasses to peer at them.

Nora started at what looked like a bruise high on her cheek, imperfectly disguised by a shading of blush. But Delilah raised the glasses so quickly she couldn't be sure.

'Delilah. When have you ever known this bakery to have enough of anything left over to sell day-olds?'

Said one way, Janie could have been joshing her. But there was no mistaking the disdain in her tone, and Delilah returned it in spades.

'I suppose they'll do.'

'You want any fresher, you'll have to roll out of bed at the ass-crack of dawn like the rest of us.'

Delilah lay a bill on the counter. 'Keep the change,' she said.

This time, Nora knew she wasn't imagining things. Delilah's manicured fingers were bluish and swollen, and her pinky turned inward as though something – or someone – had wrenched it.

She'd seen Spencer Templeton and Ron Stevenson nearly come to blows. At the time she'd thought Ron the aggressor. But what if it were Spencer?

'What happened to your hand?' she blurted.

Delilah's eyebrows climbed above the outsize glasses. 'Car door.'

Janie slid the baguette into its paper sleeve and jabbed it so fiercely toward Delilah that Nora took a step back. But Delilah held her ground, taking the bread and tucking it under her arm in a single smooth motion.

'Always nice to see you, Janie. And you, too, Ms Best.'

Nora stepped aside to let her pass. The cleats on her bike shoes clacked against the tile floor.

Delilah glanced down. 'You look as though you're ready for a leg of the Tour de France.'

'And you look as though you're headed to the Master's.'

It was the only golf tournament whose name she could pull up. It was the wrong one.

'Women don't compete at Augusta.' Having scored her point, Delilah turned sunny. 'But maybe someday Damien will. He's taking lessons now. We were supposed to have one after school today, but I hear it's going to rain. Enjoy your ride home, Ms Best.'

'Bitch,' Janie muttered.

Delilah hadn't said anything inappropriate. But Nora was inclined to agree with her. She also thought that, in Janie, Delilah had probably met her match.

TWENTY-SEVEN

Nora spent much of the day in a protracted struggle to control a class full of pre-teens rested and ready for renewed battle.

Nate Gilmore sassed her when she gave him an F on his nonexistent homework. 'It fell out of my bookbag on the way to school. Are you accusing me of being a liar? Let me go look for it. I'll prove you wrong.'

'You really think you can trick me into letting you out of class for this whole period? Unsupervised? An F it is.'

He sulked his way back to his desk with a threat – 'I'm telling my mom' – she only pretended to shrug off. She hadn't had to deal with helicopter parents, yet, but had heard the horror stories.

The ongoing feud between Jeannie Graves and Matthew Dexter inked a new chapter when Jeannie's foot edged into the aisle as Matthew passed, sending him into a sprawl so spectacular that Nora suspected amateur theatrics, and spurring a round of escalating accusations.

Jeannie: 'I was just bending over to tie my shoe.'

Matthew: 'I think I chipped a tooth.'

'Matthew, open your mouth – your teeth look fine. And do your laces, Jeannie. I've half a mind to assign you two to detention. Together. Don't like that idea? Then let it guide your future behavior.'

Compared with them, Damien seemed almost subdued, contenting himself with making fart noises by running his fist up inside his T-shirt and working it in his armpit, supplementing the effect with a few raspberries, to the point where Abby sank down in her chair, hands over her ears.

'Make him stop, Ms Best. Please.'

'I'm going to make all of you stop. Pop quiz.' She had one ready, having learned early on that they were particularly squirrely on Mondays. 'Hope you all memorized your Asian capitals. Pencil and paper, please.'

Amid the groans, she walked between the rows, holding a basket for their cell phones. She'd have liked to confiscate their phones for the whole period, but the never-ending nationwide threat of school shootings made that inadvisable. Who wanted to be responsible for an inability to call 9-1-1, let alone send a last message to a parent?

'Mini-Snickers to anyone who gets all ten questions right,' she added, to an instantaneous and nearly palpable shift in mood.

'When all else fails, go for bribery,' Sheila had advised her during the first week. Not only did that strategy work, it necessitated keeping a stash of small candy bars (she went with Snickers only after ascertaining no one had a peanut allergy), something she raided nearly as often as she awarded them to the kids. She'd learned to make sure that multiple students got the awards; if she limited it to the highest grade, Abby would be up to her elbows in Snickers.

Nora made it a mix-and-match, listing ten countries, then ten capitals, and asking the students to pair them. 'Extra credit for anyone who can tell me where Naypyidaw is the capital. Double extra credit if you spell Naypyidaw correctly. Triple extra credit if you can tell me something about it,' she coaxed, to more groans. But at least they'd quieted, glaring down at their papers, drawing tentative lines between countries and capitals, then dragging their erasers across them and trying again.

Nora sat down and awarded herself a surreptitious mini-Snicker for having looked up Naypyidaw's pronunciation first. She herself had been surprised, when reviewing the lesson plan for Asia, that the capital of Myanmar – the much contested name of the country also known as Burma; at least, she'd known that much – was no longer Yangon, formerly Rangoon. She'd known that much, too. Some days she felt herself learning alongside her students, sprinting through lesson plans to stay a half-step ahead of them.

Abby, of course, garnered two candy bars, but enough other students netted perfect scores that Nora texted herself a note to replenish her stash. The quiz and subsequent awards took her to the end of the day.

She and Luke had a strict no-public-displays-of-affection around the students, but she let herself lean against him for a second as they stood at the school's main door, waving goodbye to the same students who'd been slumped in boredom only minutes before, now leaping and racing away from the building.

'I'm so glad Melanie's having the barbecue tonight,' she said. 'The last thing I want to think about is preparing dinner.'

'Get real,' Luke reminded her. 'I'm the one who does the preparing. Your version of dinner is takeout.'

'True' she acknowledged. 'But I'm too tired even to think about what to order.'

She edged away, creating the scant inch of space between them necessary for social acceptability. She forced a smile in Damien's direction as he and Matthew slouched past, heads together, no doubt planning the next day's mayhem.

'OK if I pick you up a little before five? I want to run home and get the Wiffle ball stuff first.'

'What Wiffle ball stuff?'

'I've had it ever since Gabriel was a little boy. I figured I could organize a game at the picnic. You know, keep the kids occupied. Sheila said hers liked to play. You up for pitching?'

'Love to.' She hated ballgames of all kinds. But told herself the unease pricking her spine at the mention of Luke's eagerness to please Sheila and her kids had nothing to do with her quick assent.

Nora had hoped to pull Melanie aside for a few moments at the barbecue to recount her odd experience with Kirk Lopez. But she'd forgotten about the campaign part of the barbecue. When they arrived, she saw Melanie across the park, flitting from group to group, shaking hands and chatting. Portable tables and folding chairs dotted the park, and the scent of sizzling meat wafted from a large grill, presided over by a sweating man in an apron whose red and white letters proclaimed Melanie Makes It Happen.

Nora recognized him from back-to-school night as Abby's dad. Beside him, Abby flipped patties on a smaller grill. She wore a matching apron, this one reaching nearly to her ankles.

'Child labor?' Nora teased.

'I'm Chief Campaign Minister of Serendipity.' Abby pronounced it syllable by syllable.

Nora turned away to conceal her wince. Abby had no way of knowing it was the name of the program for troubled girls where she and Luke had met, and where they'd discovered the program itself was infinitely more troubled than its clients.

'What in the world does that entail?'

'It means that vegetarians will feel welcome at Mom's barbecue because we're serving veggie burgers along with hamburgers and hotdogs, on a separate grill so there's no cross-contamination.' Abby's voice took on a singsong, well-rehearsed tone. 'In Melanie James' administration, everyone will be welcome.'

'Good job, Abby. But as much as I'd like one of your veggie burgers, I'd like a hotdog even more.'

'Coming right up, Ms Best.' Abby's dad – 'George,' he reminded her – slotted a dog into a bun and handed it to her. 'All beef,' he said. 'Melanie doesn't cut corners on food and she won't on services, either.'

'Does every meal come with a campaign slogan?'

'Yes. And' – George James deposited a crosshatched burger onto the whole-grain bun on Luke's recyclable paper plate – 'and just as you'll find that burger perfectly cooked, you'll find that Melanie delivers on her promises.' He winked. 'Couldn't help myself. You handed me the straight line on a silver platter. Condiments and napkins are on the table over there, and beers and soft drinks are in the coolers under the trees.' He turned to the next person in line.

Sheila waved to them from one of the tables.

'Oh, good,' she said, when she saw the bag full of gear slung over Luke's shoulder. 'This'll give the kids something to do while Melanie makes her speech.'

Luke took the hint. 'I'll round up some players. I'll send one of them over when we're all set up.'

Nora glanced from him to Sheila but saw nothing untoward in either of their expressions, not even the studied indifference that would have set off the loudest alarm bells. She chided herself for her earlier twinge of suspicion. For heaven's sake, she and Luke were buying a house together.

'There's a speech?' Nora had planned only on grabbing a quick meal and a word with Melanie. Now she'd been roped into a Wiffle ball game and a speech besides.

'It's a campaign barbecue. Of course there's a speech. These, too.' She slid a stack of envelopes toward Nora, pre-addressed to Melanie's campaign office, with suggested donation amounts printed on the back. 'Politics-wise, this race is the hottest thing going on the peninsula. Brock Bailey has been commission chair forever. Most elections, he doesn't even have an opponent. Now here comes Melanie aiming to make a real race of it. Brock must be taking it seriously because' – she glanced around and lowered her voice – 'people are getting mailers. Negative stuff about Melanie.'

Nora took a bite of her hotdog, which she'd garnished with organic ketchup and stone-ground mustard. Melanie had spared no expense on feeding her would-be constituents. 'What sort of negative stuff? The kind they always dredge up – an affair, money issues?'

Sheila threw back her head and laughed. 'An affair? Melanie? Good lord, when would she have time? I swear that woman has every minute of every day mapped out on her calendar.'

Nora managed to laugh in response. She'd thought the same thing about her husband, who turned out to have been the horndog from hell.

'Anyway,' Sheila said, 'it's way worse than either of those, at least as far as the peninsula is concerned. They're painting her as being anti-development.'

'Is that a bad thing? Ward's Warriors seem like a sizable contingent here. For sure she has their vote.'

Sheila lifted a shoulder bare but for an angel-hair wisp of a spaghetti strap. She wore a shimmery tank top and slim cropped jeans and – just to make sure, Nora leaned across the table on the pretext of retrieving a paper napkin, inhaling as she did so – a hint of perfume.

'Got a date with Plant Man tonight?'

'Had one.' Sheila flashed a wicked grin. 'The kids had after-school activities, so he stopped by. Didn't stay long. Just long enough.'

Nora remembered the early days with Luke, when their relationship had tipped over from collegial into something more, with a swiftness and intensity that surprised them both. Once, driving home from a teacher training, he'd pulled off the highway into a secluded cutoff and they'd scrambled into the back seat like a couple of teenagers. She blushed, even as she fought a wave of regret. How had they fallen so quickly into routine?

'Spare me the details. What's that on your neck? A mosquito bite?' Nora teased.

Sheila's hand flew to her neck. 'What?' She held up her phone, flipped the camera view as though for a selfie and peered into it. 'There's nothing there. Shame on you, Nora Best!'

Nora chuckled. 'Gotcha.'

'Anyhow, Ward's Warriors. They're outspoken, sure. But they can afford to be. Trustafarians, a lot of 'em, with the money and time to run around sloganeering and filing lawsuits and going to all those meetings. Most people on the peninsula are too busy just trying to stay financially afloat to have any energy left over for that sort of thing. They don't have it easy the way we do.'

'We've got it easy?' Nora's salary was adequate, but no more. She'd been far better paid at Serendipity Ranch, although that job had taken an emotional toll from which she was still recovering.

'Sure. We might not make much money, but we have regular hours, a guaranteed salary and benefits. Those are like unicorns here. Something like Spencer's hotel comes along, with decent wages for the construction workers and a whole variety of jobs once it opens – well, people start to care a little less about saving some shorebird as opposed to saving their mortgage payments.'

'Now you're starting to sound like Janie.' As far as Nora could tell, the server at Betty's sounded off on the subject every chance she got.

'Face it. Janie has a point. Would you trade jobs with her?'

Now Sheila had a point. She waggled an empty beer bottle at Nora. 'Another?'

Nora spied Melanie near the coolers. 'I'll get them.'

She hurried to Melanie's side, touching her arm as she started to turn from one person to another.

'Melanie! Great barbecue! Can't wait to hear your speech!' She raised her voice and underscored every comment with an exclamation point, just another enthusiastic participant in democracy.

Melanie played her part perfectly, pumping Nora's hand and simultaneously pulling her away from the others, saying, 'I read your email. I really want to hear more about your proposal.'

She bent over the coolers with Nora, selecting bottled water while Nora fished out two beers.

'Well? Did you find him? Was he home?'

'I did and he was. But when I said I'd been told he was the architect on the tower project, he basically slammed the door in my face.'

Melanie straightened abruptly. Droplets flew from her water bottle, patterning her polo shirt and khaki pants. 'Shoot. I'm going to have to wait for this to dry before I give my speech. Otherwise I'll look like a speckled idiot in the photos. Here.'

She handed her water to Nora, who already had a beer in each hand. Nora tucked one of the beers under her arm and took it. Melanie held her shirt away from her body, attempting to catch a drying breeze. 'I don't get it. I saw his name in black and white.'

'He acted as though I was delusional. Honestly, I wondered

if he might have dementia – he's pretty old – but he seemed sharp.'

Melanie sighed. 'Maybe I misunderstood something. But I don't see how I could have.' She glanced down at her shirt, the blotches paler now. 'This is probably as good as it's going to get. You know, I opted for a picnic because I wanted something informal instead of standing up on stage, yakking down at everyone. Now I wish I had a lectern to stand behind.'

Melanie took her water back and headed for the center of the park, where her husband was already motioning people to gather round.

Nora caught Sheila's eye and held up their beers, then inclined her head toward the fast-coalescing group. She called to Luke. 'OK if I listen for a bit?'

He motioned toward the motley assortment of ballplayers, a peanut-size batter waggling his slugger toward a tote bag that marked a spot for a mound. 'Go for it. I'll pitch for now.'

Nora nodded and joined Sheila at the edge of the crowd.

Maybe she'd given up too easily on Kirk Lopez. Melanie had advised an in-person approach, but the man clearly felt his privacy had been invaded. Melanie's discovery of his address had included a phone number. When she got home, she'd call him, point out the discrepancy, and oh-so-meekly seek an explanation.

Thus equipped with a new plan, she raised her beer to her lips and turned her attention to Melanie's stump speech.

Melanie had said she didn't want to talk down to people, but she'd hopped atop a plastic milk crate to give her a slight height advantage.

She spoke without notes, and Nora wondered how much practice it took to seem so relaxed and conversational, managing to score points on her opponent without ever once mentioning him by name.

'We're rightfully proud of our traditions on the peninsula. They've stood us in good stead for decades, and that's what makes this peninsula such a desirable place to live and work. And our traditions are not so hidebound that we haven't managed to adapt to changing times. It's fashionable in some quarters to gripe about over-regulation, but new regulations are what saved our precious oyster paddocks – and protected those who work under sometimes dangerous conditions in our fisheries.' She scanned the crowd and nodded toward Harold Wallace. 'We can only wish they'd been adopted sooner.'

Nora noticed Spencer Templeton in the semicircle that had formed with Melanie at its center point. He crossed his arms at the mention of regulations.

Melanie must have noticed, too, because she turned and spoke directly to him.

'That's why we're so fortunate to have a developer who brings new business to our peninsula while ensuring the strictest compliance with all environmental and safety regulations. It's a source of both pride and comfort that he is local. It means he cares about the peninsula – cares enough to pay a living wage to his workers and provide health care, ensuring a stable, healthy and happy *local* workforce on our peninsula.'

Spencer looked as though he'd bitten into a lemon. He managed to twist his grimace into a smile as the crowd applauded. Nifty bit of work on Melanie's part, Nora thought. She'd heard nothing about employer-provided health care – nonexistent for most of the service-industry jobs that were prevalent on the peninsula – for hotel workers.

Now Spencer would have to supply them or risk looking like a Scrooge. Or – Nora thought of the negative mailers Sheila had mentioned, the sort of surreptitious campaigning designed to undercut one's foe – he'd likely do everything within his well-financed power to make sure Melanie lost the election.

Melanie appeared to be wrapping up her remarks. Nora edged away from the crowd. Maybe she could lure Luke away from the Wiffle ball game and head for home.

'Did you find him? Did you?'

It was the man from the beach, the one who'd been so insistent about the architect.

Nora groaned. 'Not you again. Don't you have anything better to do than follow me and my students around? What's your name?'

'Nunya. Did you find him?'

She stared toward Luke, willing him to look her way and call a greeting that would disrupt this unwelcome conversation.

'Nunya what?'

'Nunya Business.' He shrugged. 'Sorry. Old joke.'

As if she didn't hear enough such nonsense dealing with her seventh-graders.

'Yes.' She picked up the pace. Luke stooped beside a tiny batter, putting his hands over hers and guiding her through a swing. He ran a few paces away and lobbed a ball that took its own sweet time getting to the batter. She swung unaided. A plastic thwack sounded. Luke made a fake grab as it floated lazily past, landing with a bounce and rolling through the spraddled legs of the second baseman.

'Run!' Luke urged his charge, who stood staring in wonder as the ball wobbled to a stop.

'Not only did I find, I met him in person. He said he didn't have anything to do with the tower. So there.'

Nora, too, could stoop to a seventh-grade level. It felt surprisingly good. She barely stopped herself from sticking out her tongue.

'You met him?' Nunya went wide-eyed. 'Did anyone see you?'

'I have no idea. What does it matter?'

He stood staring. 'You don't know what you're dealing with. Of course he said he had nothing to do with it.'

Zealots, Nora thought. They were all alike, even the best-intentioned, seeing conspiracies everywhere.

'He truly seemed to have no idea what I was talking about. I took him at his word. Anything more would have been harassment. Now, if you don't mind, I have a Wiffle ball game to join.'

She stalked off with as much dignity as that last ridiculous sentence would allow.

But she wasn't free yet. Someone fell into step beside her.

'Jesus, give it a rest,' she snapped, only to see Spencer Templeton flashing his professionally whitened smile.

'How's our hero teacher today?'

'I'm sorry. I thought you were someone else. You know, I wouldn't mind just being a regular teacher.'

Every time someone hit her with that damned phrase, things she'd prefer stay buried forever swam to the surface, toothy things with razor-sharp fins, shredding her psyche anew.

'All of that was so long ago,' she said, nearly as much to herself as Spencer.

Not nearly long enough.

Spencer echoed her unspoken response. 'Not that long. At least, not in law-enforcement terms.'

The teeth dug deep. The fins raked. Drew blood.

Nora didn't even try to pretend indifference. 'What are you talking about?'

'There's an investigating officer over on the mainland . . . oh, what was his name? Let me think.' Spencer knit his brow. Tapped a finger against his cheek. Gave every impression of a man trying to dredge up a fact that he already knew cold.

Nora mouthed the name along with him.

'Detective Eberle. I wonder what he'll find?'

Nora should have kept her mouth shut. Too late. 'Nothing. Because there's nothing to find. The investigation is closed.'

'Tell that to our Detective Eberle. He seems a persistent sort. By the way, I recently found out something interesting about the criminal justice system in this state. Would you like to know what it is?'

Oh, hell, no. She would not.

'Accomplices to felonies get treated just like the actual perpetrators. That means they face the same penalties, up to and including for murder.'

Message delivered, Spencer strolled away, hands in pockets, whistling a happy tune as Nora watched the edges of her world – her new, safe world – grow dark and crumble.

TWENTY-EIGHT

Nora dashed onto the ballfield and grabbed Luke's arm. The ball dropped from his hand.

'Nora, what . . .'

'We have to go. Right now. Luke, we have to get out of here.'

Luke picked up the whistle dangling on a lanyard around his neck and blew it hard.

'Hold up, everybody. I've gotta talk with our relief pitcher for a minute.'

'I'm not going to pitch and neither are you. We have to leave.'

He dropped his glove and jammed his hands into his pockets. 'We were supposed to meet up with Sheila and her boys afterward, maybe get a pizza.'

We were? Whatever. It didn't matter.

'What's got you in such a tizzy, anyway? Is it important enough to stop our game? For Chrissakes, Nora, you're causing a scene.'

She took in the circle of gaping children around them. A couple of parents, who'd chosen to watch the game rather than listen to Melanie's speech, headed toward them. 'Is everything all right?' one called.

Nora looked up. Spencer Templeton stood beyond the outfield fence, far enough that she couldn't see his expression, just his face turned toward them. Oh, how he must be enjoying this.

'Everything's fine,' she stammered. 'Just trying to convince Luke that it's in everyone's best interest that he keep pitching.'

She walked on shaking legs to the sidelines and sat cross-legged on the grass, pretending to watch the game but in reality waiting until Spencer Templeton finally wandered away and she could breathe almost normally again.

She managed to stick it out until the game, such as it was, ended. But she nixed the outing with Sheila and her boys.

'What am I supposed to tell her? We were really looking forward to this.'

Nora was sure she would have been, too, if she'd been involved in any way. Now she thought she had about a fifteen-minute window before her frayed nerves snapped and she started screaming,

'Tell her I feel sick. Really sick.' It was as true a statement as she'd ever uttered.

He picked up the ball and tossed it from hand to hand. 'You were fine when we left the house.'

'Maybe it was that organic hotdog. How can you trust a hotdog that's supposed to be good for you?'

Luke threw the ball and bats into their bag and stalked off to find Sheila. Eyes front, Nora told herself, resisting the urge to swivel her head to the right and left, searching out Spencer Templeton. He'd left – or at least, he'd seemed to leave. But what if he were lurking somewhere, waiting to torment her further?

She so feared that possibility that she refused to enlighten Luke until they were safely home. Spencer fights with lawyers, Sheila had said. Apparently he fought with private investigators, too. Unless he'd called Eberle himself – but no. He'd want to keep his hands clean. Wasn't that how these things worked? And what exactly was this, anyway? Blackmail? Over a kids' project?

Nora's thoughts swooped and dived, banging themselves against her skull, so that by the time they got home she'd pressed both hands to her forehead, trying to push back against what felt like the first migraine of her life.

Luke's attitude shifted from annoyance to concern. 'You really do look bad.' He helped her into the house and on to the sofa. 'Can I get you anything? Tea? Ibuprofen? Whiskey?'

'Maybe all of the above. But first, just listen to me.' She pulled him onto the couch and clung to his hands as she repeated Spencer's warning, watching as he just . . . shrugged.

'So?'

'So? You know what happened in that van as well as I!'

Another shrug. 'Do I? Things happened so fast, I can't remember the details. I was acting on instinct. As for you – you'd been knocked around pretty severely. How can you remember anything with any sort of clarity?'

How could she? The better question was, how could she forget? She'd remembered everything every single day since.

She started to say as much but Luke laid a finger across her lips.

'You can't remember anything. And neither can I.'

She tried a last time.

'But those injuries. Identical. At least the fatal ones.'

His finger pressed harder, mashing lips into teeth. She tasted blood and with it, the urgent necessity of his words.

'You can't remember anything. And neither can I.'

TWENTY-NINE

In a nod to Nora's migraine, or whatever it was attacking her skull from the inside with tiny buzzing drills, she and Luke turned in early.

He fell asleep almost immediately, his easy soft snores echoed by the dog on the floor beside them. But the cat picked up on Nora's agitated wakefulness, pacing the bed with measured footfalls, stopping occasionally to arch his back and hiss a warning to the unseen threat.

Nora told herself Luke's unconcern was warranted.

But something about her students' seemingly innocuous project had stirred Templeton's wrath.

Which didn't make sense. As far as she could tell – a sense underscored by her students' reporting – people generally liked the project. None of the objections people lobbed at the hotel – its huge footprint, its thirsty heated swimming pools just yards from the ocean, the shitty service-industry work required to run it – applied to the tower. Their taxes weren't even paying for it.

But Spencer essentially had declared war over it.

Maybe she should drop the project. Invent some stupid excuse for Everhart, and come up with a bullshit, last-minute replacement. She picked up her phone from the nightstand and typed into her search engine: 'easy fast middle school projects social studies' and the Internet predictably spat back dozens of possibilities.

She started scrolling. Quickly at first, then slower and slower still.

Dough maps. Timelines. Flip books.

Baby stuff compared to what her kids had turned their project into.

She thought of Abby James, handing out assignments and directing her reporting staff with such confidence. Damien, who became almost human when aiming his camera phone and, later, swiping through the results, holding up the phone to show Abby different shots for her approval. Zeke, solemnly shaking his head at a classmate's attempt at a headline and advising him to 'kick it up a notch'. Jeannie, moving stories and photos around on her screen to design the perfect page.

Bowing to Spencer's threats would take all that away from them.

She remembered Ron Stevenson, looming over her, underscoring the difference in size and strength. Everhart always picking at her, looking for ways to discredit her. Now here came someone else, trying to push her around.

What if she pushed back?

But Spencer's threat was so much worse than the others. Just hearing Eberle's name brought her back to that night in the van, the full-body terror of it. But there'd been something else. She'd fought back then, too. And she – along with Luke – had won.

For some reason, Spencer wanted her to look away from the tower. What if she probed deeper? Found whatever it was that so provoked him?

Nora sat up in bed.

'Fuck you, Spencer Templeton.'

Mooch leapt to the floor and yowled.

Murph started from his sleep, rose halfway to his feet, and muttered a warning to the invisible foe.

Luke rolled over and snored anew.

Nora smiled into the dark.

First order of business: get back to the architect.

Nora was committed to battle, but that commitment didn't extend to driving all the way to Portland again.

She'd call, and if he hung up on her, she'd call right back again. Throughout the school day, she jotted down questions for Kirk Lopez, starting with the obvious – a follow-up to his cryptic declaration that he'd not designed the tower and 'nor would I.'

He hadn't given her time to ask what he meant by that. But she had other questions, too. Did he know Ward? Had they discussed the tower? What was the problem with it? She assumed it had to do with an endangered species – maybe habitat destruction – but for what? Something cute and cuddly like a seal? Or something harder to build enthusiasm for – a small, obscure, unlovely fish, given the ocean just yards away, brimming with millions of others. Or worse still, a plant or lichen.

People – especially those who didn't live in the affected areas – would make accommodations to save so-called charismatic megafauna like wolves and grizzly bears; not so much snail darters and bog turtles.

She called as soon as she got home from school. But her lightning rejoinder – 'This is Nora Best. Please don't hang up.' – never left her lips. Because a woman answered.

Why had she assumed Lopez lived alone? But the woman's voice, while hoarse, sounded decades younger than anyone who might conceivably have been Lopez's wife.

Nora stumbled through a new introduction. 'My name is Nora Best. I'm a teacher in a town called Lane's End. Mr Lopez and I spoke last week and I'm calling to follow up on our conversation.'

The woman's laugh ended on a sob.

'I'm afraid that's impossible,' she said, her next words barely intelligible as tears won out. 'Daddy's dead.'

Nora didn't dare call back.

She tapped Lopez's name into her browser, along with 'architect' and 'Portland' and 'obituary,' and within seconds Lopez's visage – younger, handsome, smiling – stared out at her.

The accompanying obituary was standard fare – his degree from MIT, various awards, and well-known projects that included an office tower, historic renovations, the luxury homes of tech kazillionaires. Nora scrolled through photos of understated designs lauded for their environmental integrity, even as she wondered: why the heck would someone of Lopez's talent bother with a dinky tsunami tower?

A paragraph low in the obituary told her why: 'Mr Lopez's works were known for their harmony with their settings, something he attributed to his childhood on the peninsula, which instilled in him a deep appreciation for nature.'

So noted. But couldn't he have passed off the tower design to an underling, maybe even an intern? Maybe he had. Maybe his name on whatever document Melanie had seen was some sort of formality. She'd ask Melanie to doublecheck, a final step toward putting Nunya's weirdness behind her – which, of course, still left the problem of Spencer.

She clicked out of the obit and started to put her phone away when the item below it caught her attention.

She'd included 'obituary' in her search terms. The notation below the thumbnail had crossed out 'obituary' but her other search terms led to a trove of news stories with details she found far more interesting than those in the obit.

Several news organizations had run essentially the same story: *Noted Portland Architect Kirk Lopez Found Dead in Home.*

Lopez's daughter, after not having heard from him for a day, stopped by to check and found her father dead at the bottom of the basement stairs. The daughter declined to talk with reporters, but a neighbor had no such reticence.

'He insisted upon living all alone in that big house after his wife died. He was so proud of it. He'd fixed it up himself, of course. Given all the work he put into it, why he didn't move the laundry room to the first floor is beyond me.'

Nora could imagine it: the creaky stairs, the dim light, the washer and dryer at the rear of a dank space. She hoped the fall had killed him instantly. He'd been borderline rude to her, but she flinched at the thought of him lying hurt and terrified in the basement, his cries for help growing steadily weaker, unheard beyond the thick walls of his beautifully restored home.

Police termed it a likely accident, appending the standard 'no sign of forced entry' phrasing. But they added that the home was unlocked and that, as a precaution, they were seeking to talk with anyone seen visiting Lopez's house within twenty-four hours of his being found.

Kirk Lopez had been alive when she'd seen him just two days ago. He'd been found on Monday morning. The stories had all been posted Monday evening, while she and Luke were at the barbecue. She ran the timeline in her head, over and over. Each time, it was the same.

If her timeline was correct, Kirk Lopez took his fatal fall shortly after she had left his house.

She closed her laptop with shaking hands. It didn't mean anything. Accidents happened all the time. Lopez wouldn't be the first elderly person to succumb to a fall.

But Nunya's words clanged in her mind. 'You don't know what you're dealing with.'

She didn't. But she was starting to be afraid that she might.

THIRTY

She couldn't tell Luke.

He didn't know she'd gone to Lopez's house. Anyway, she'd done everything to create the impression that she no longer cared about the tower, beyond the elementary limits of her students' project.

Melanie was an obvious choice of confidante, although the twin demands of her job and the campaign made Nora reluctant to burden her further. She'd at least forward the notices about Lopez's death, along with her question about whether someone else in Lopez's firm could have designed the tower. Then she could try and track down that person – carefully, very carefully this time.

But first, she needed to shake off the initial shock. She shucked out of her work clothes, pulled on her running gear, and whistled to Murph to rouse him from his day-long slumber.

Minutes later she'd set a leisurely pace to accommodate Murph's arthritic legs, loping along the stretch of firm, damp sand on the water's edge, dodging the occasional outsize wave that sought to submerge her to the shins.

The sun sneaked below the cloud cover. The waves turned luminescent. Shorebirds lifted at her approach and wheeled away with high, mocking cries.

With each step, the concern raised by Nunya's enigmatic insistence on finding the architect, heightened by the news of Lopez's death, seemed more and more fantastical.

The traumas of the past two years had crept too deeply into her psyche. She took deep breaths, lengthened her stride, and followed the advice gleaned from the therapy sessions a doctor had advised after her experience in her last job: reciting the myriad upbeat realities of her new life.

She lived in a beautiful place. She had a secure and engaging, if challenging, job. She and Luke were moving into a new phase of their relationship.

Not everything, especially not vague insinuations from sketchy people, meant her life was once again in danger. She was so busy lecturing herself that she didn't see the wave until it crashed against her, flowing up and over her feet, splashing so high and hard that it knocked her off balance. She wavered and then went with it, falling into the water, laughing at herself as it receded with a satisfied slurp.

'You got me,' she called after it, even as Murph cavorted around her, puzzled but delighted by this new game.

She scrambled to her feet, brushing wet sand from her clothes, shaking it from her hair, sending the last of the bad feeling away with it. The beach had worked its reliable magic.

Murph, trotting ahead of her, stopped so suddenly she almost tripped. His head swiveled back toward the beach, ears up, tail rigid.

Nora stepped around him and called back. 'Come on, old man. We're done playing.'

But he didn't move. She turned and saw what had gotten his attention.

A boy, shouting incoherently, retrieving something from the water and throwing it back in again.

Nora squinted. Was that . . .?

She headed back down the beach, Murph now leading the way.

'Damien?'

The boy yelped again, and this time fear eclipsed the rage she'd sensed.

'Miss Best? What are you doing here?' He darted toward the water and retrieved something.

'Walking on the beach, same as you. What's that?'

'What's what?' As if he stood before her empty-handed.

'That golf club. What are you doing with it?'

His face contorted. 'Throwing it away. I hate it! I hate it!'

He darted toward the water and gave a mighty heave. The club soared high and landed with a splash within the curl of an onrushing wave that delivered it within moments to the shallows, where it spun a taunting circle.

Damien leaned and snatched it up. 'Goddammit all to fucking hell.'

'Damien, language. And stop it! Those things are expensive!'

Stupid, she told herself. As if Spencer and Delilah couldn't afford a replacement.

She tried again. 'If you hate it so much, why don't you tell your mom you don't want to play anymore?'

'Because . . . because . . .' He looked on the verge of tears. 'Get out of here, Miss Best. Go do whatever fuck it is you do when you're not pretending you know what you're doing!'

Nora opened her mouth. Closed it. He was right. She was off the clock.

And she had better things to do than deal with an asshole student who was probably going to grow up being just like his asshole stepdad.

She turned away but couldn't resist a last look back.

'Oh, for God's sake.'

Damien had stripped down to his underwear and, as she watched, raced across the sand, club in hand, into the icy gray water, diving as he reached the breaking waves, ducking under wave after wave until he was beyond them. At which point, treading water, he launched the offending club a final time, presumably now beyond the reach of the traitorous waves.

She withdrew her phone, ready to press 9-1-1, and watched until he was safely ashore.

She wondered whether to set up an appointment with Spencer and Delilah. They'd wanted to know if Damien showed any troubling signs and this fit the bill. But it didn't have anything to do with school.

She told herself it was between Damien and his mother, and made her way across the sand, reminding herself she had some phone calls to make.

THIRTY-ONE

S he couldn't call Nunya. She didn't even know his real name. But she had a good idea how to find out.

Gerry Fields and Clark Stevens, the two men she'd initially met at Betty's and who'd been front and center with Ward's Warriors at the County Commission meeting, had to know him. They were easy to find online, listed as members of several environmental groups. Another click took her to Clark's business, a gallery featuring local artists. She smiled. She and Luke would need something to hang on all those blank walls at their new house.

The only thing resembling art in her Airstream was the coffeepot from her mother's silver tea service, one of the very few things she'd saved from her childhood home and the single useless object in a trailer devoted to functionality. It took up too much precious counter space, but she kept a tin of silver polish and a drawer full of soft cloths to maintain its gleaming elegance. She brushed her fingertips across it whenever she entered or left Electra. It was a talisman of sorts, a reminder of her mother's final missive praising Nora's bravery. But that note also carried a warning that Nora's hometown was by no means unique.

'Danger lurks in every town.'

'Stop it right this minute,' she told herself. Something else her mother might have said. Murph thumped his tail in agreement.

She turned back to the gallery's website. It listed extended summer hours until nine PM. It was eight. She had just enough time to shower and change out of her running clothes, still damp and sticky with salt water. She texted Luke – 'Running errands, see you around nine' – and turned her attention to the task of making herself presentable.

The gallery was open, barely.

Empty parking spaces lined the block. Clark sat immobile

at a desk, head drooping toward his chest as though he were asleep, a suspicion confirmed when he jerked upright to the jingle of the tiny copper bells strung on the door as Nora pushed through it.

'May I help you?' he asked automatically through an inadequately stifled yawn. Then, 'Oh, it's you. I didn't recognize you at first. We don't get many people at this hour, especially at the end of the season.'

'No problem. Sorry to disturb you. This is just an impulse visit. Luke and I are buying a house and we'd love to have some local artwork for it. I'm just browsing tonight.'

'Take your time,' he said. 'And don't worry about the closing time. I'm happy to keep it open until you're done.'

Especially if he might make a sale, Nora thought. Business was likely slow to nonexistent this late in the season. It effectively ended on Labor Day, but there were a few hangers-on, older people mostly, who didn't have to worry about kids' school schedules and could take advantage of the shoulder season's lower rates before shops began to close altogether for the winter.

Nora wandered among shelves displaying functional ceramics and trays of handmade silver jewelry. Watercolors of peninsula scenes – ocean sunsets were a particular favorite – dominated the walls. Neatly lettered cards displayed each artist's name and photograph, with an accompanying paragraph about their work.

Nora stopped before a half-dozen works in an out-of-the-way corner. At first glance they appeared to be more beach scenes, albeit darker-hued than the tourist-pleasing pastels in the main part of the gallery. Charcoal-hued waves charged at the sand in a roiling fury. A handful of surfboards, randomly scattered across the sand, provided the only dots of color, their abandonment hinting at a grim fate for their owners.

What appeared to be small, mountainous islands in another turned out to be the peaked roofs of submerged homes. Yet another seemed more peaceful, a nearly abstract rendering of curved, speckled shapes. Closer inspection revealed a pod of beached whales, ravenous seagulls perched atop them, tearing at their rubbery flesh.

A soft football sounded behind her. 'Those are Jeremiah Wendover's climate change series. Hardly among our bestsellers.

Nobody wants to be reminded of what human occupation costs the peninsula.'

'But they're beautiful.' Nora looked again and amended her comment. 'Maybe that's not the right word. But I've always liked the ocean most when it's stormy. These evoke some of the same feelings.'

Clark offered a sad smile. 'I'm grateful to hear it. Most of our buyers want pablum and our artists are no fools. They need to eat and pay rent just like the rest of us, so they paint' – he waved his arm toward the main room – 'those. Can you blame them? But Jeremiah refuses. Of all of us who call ourselves Ward's Warriors, he's the one most like Ward.'

Nora looked again at the first painting and checked the price. She blinked. Then reminded herself of the point Clark had just made. This Jeremiah needed to fund a roof over his head, just as she was about to fork over a considerable portion of her salary toward her new mortgage. But every time she tried to look away, the image of that churning, restless sea drew her gaze back.

'We offer layaway plans,' Clark, a canny salesman, murmured at her side.

'I'll take it,' she heard herself say.

'Just give me a minute to enter it into the computer. And I'm happy to send it home with you early. But if you don't mind, I'd like to leave it up for a few days with a red dot beside it.'

Likely because the visible proof of one sale might encourage others to take a chance on the sort of thing they wouldn't usually buy, Nora thought. But she could hardly begrudge his effort.

She bent to examine the card containing the information about Jeremiah Wendover and straightened with a gasp a second later. She studied the tiny photo again, although the closer inspection was unnecessary.

At least she wouldn't have to come up with a bunch of idiotic questions to get Clark to divulge Nunya's name. She'd instantly recognized his face in the photo on the card.

'I'd love to talk with the artist directly about this painting,' she called across the room. 'I don't suppose you'd share his contact information, would you?'

THIRTY-TWO

He would and he did.

Which meant that five minutes after leaving the gallery, Nora had punched Wendover's name and phone number into a search engine, found an address, pasted it into her map app, and gunned her truck toward it.

Her phone directed her on to a dirt road white with crushed oyster shells. She eased up on the gas. The peninsula was so narrow that nothing was truly isolated – or so she'd thought as she followed the track through a thickening bramble of hardhack. She was close to the ocean – the waves' rhythmic crash sounded through her open window – but all signs of human habitation had vanished.

The track jogged left so abruptly she hit the brakes. She eased up, rounding the corner to see a small wooden house with a beat-up bicycle leaning against it, a south-facing wall of streaked glass overlooking a warped and splintery deck, and Nunya – Jeremiah – standing in the open doorway.

She turned off the engine. The cooling truck ticked a warning into the silence. The sky's characteristic gray was fast shading darker. It occurred to her, even as she opened the door and stepped reluctantly from the safety of the truck, that she hadn't told anyone where she was going.

'I guess you heard me driving up,' she said by way of greeting.

He held up a cell phone. 'Clark called from the gallery.'

So at least one person knew, she thought, pushing away her initial surprise at the sight of the cell phone. Something about him – the raffish appearance, his home's isolation, his apparent lack of a vehicle – made her expect an ascetic sort who would eschew such aggressive modernity.

'Come on in.' He disappeared into the house. 'I'll make tea.'

She hesitated again. He'd pestered her repeatedly to find the architect, and now the architect was dead. Even beyond that, she knew better. Every woman did. How many movies showed the consequences? You walked into a strange man's house and ended up in a makeshift basement dungeon, only to have your dismembered body parts turn up all over town later. But this was the peninsula, where everyone knew everything about everyone else, and surely she would have heard by now . . .

She was still berating herself for her lurid imaginings when he re-emerged from the house, a steaming mug in each hand and a tactful acknowledgment of her reluctance in his words. 'On second thought, let's sit on the deck. It's such a nice evening. Won't be long now before it rains every day. Might as well enjoy this while we can.'

He gestured toward a pair of time-darkened Adirondack chairs, striped green with the moss that furred their grooves. She sat and took the mug he offered, indulging her lingering paranoia with the barest sip. It tasted like . . . tea.

She took a larger sip, wondering why his open gaze didn't spark more discomfort. It was because there was nothing furtive or leering about it, she thought, just one person taking the measure of the other. She returned it in kind, noticing the gray strands in the sandy hair, the sharp cheekbones and beaky nose offset by the full mouth.

'Do I pass muster?' It was the first time she'd seen him smile.

She lifted her mug in acknowledgement. 'You don't look like an ax-murderer. Whatever that means.'

'It was thoughtless of me to invite you in. I don't blame you for being cautious. It's smart, especially after what you've been through.'

Nora groaned and held the mug to her face as though to hide behind it. 'I suppose everyone knows about that.'

'It was the talk of the peninsula. At least' – the smile vanished – 'until Ward was killed.'

'You're one of the Warriors.' How quickly she'd fallen into his direct manner of speaking, no wasting time on small talk, as refreshing as it was unnerving.

His gray eyes met hers again. 'I never liked the name. Too, well, warlike. The only war being waged is by the developers, chewing up this peninsula faster than I'd thought possible. I wish you could have seen it the way it was when Ward and I grew up here.'

'Which was?'

'Wild. Outside of places like Seacrest and Lane's End, most
of it was like this, just a few houses tucked away here and there.
We could run loose all day long, exploring the bogs and the
woods. We'd see eagles, those little Roosevelt elk and even a
black bear once in a while, dig clams and oysters and then build
a bonfire on the beach and roast them.'

Nora could identify. Her own childhood, in a Revolutionary
War-era Maryland farmhouse on a river leading to the Chesapeake
Bay, had been similar. She said as much. 'Only we caught and
steamed blue crabs. Oysters, too, but crabs were the main event.'

'Then you know.'

'Yes.' There was more, much more, and none of it pleasant,
but like him she decided to focus on the good memories.

'Things change,' she added. 'The Eastern Shore has seen its
share of development. Some people there blame the Washington,
D.C., crowd, the same way you look at people from Portland
and Seattle. Of course, plenty of the people I grew up with are
only too eager to cash in. Half of them spent their summers
driving a tractor across corn and soybean fields. It must have felt
great to sell it for some exorbitant price and lounge on the beach
like everyone else.'

He nodded. 'I'd like to be judgmental' – he caught her look
and threw a wry grin back – 'even more than I already am, but
I get that it's almost impossible for people to resist the impulse
to cash in. Or, even just to get a little ahead of where they are
now. Ward was unusual in that regard and it cost him a marriage.'

'What did it cost you?' The conversation was straying far
afield of where she wanted it to go, but she found herself genuinely curious.

'I was smart enough not to get married. At the risk of sounding
like one of those asshole men who run around proclaiming Art
is All, I knew early on that I could either have a wife and kids
or—' He turned in his chair and pointed to the wall of glass
behind him. 'That.'

Nora craned and looked with him, into a room full of canvases
in various states of completion.

'That is exactly what one of those asshole male artists would
say,' she teased.

He offered a smile in return. 'And to think I invited you in and made you tea.'

'But there's nothing assholic – is that a word? – about your work. I love your paintings. I bought one tonight.'

'Clark told me. Thank you. You're the reason I'll be able to pay this month's electric bill.'

Nora sat back. 'You must not use much electricity. I bought it on layaway. Teacher's salary and all that.'

He finished his tea in a long swallow. 'Whenever something sells on layaway, Clark advances me the full price. But I'm guessing, despite what Clark said when he called, that you didn't come here to talk about my work.'

THIRTY-THREE

Now that he'd brought it up, Nora felt almost reluctant. Once they dove into her real reason for being there, the conversation would be over and she'd have to go back to Luke and the myriad small tensions that accompanied even the smallest preparations for their move.

'Why were you so set on me talking to the tower's architect? It's such a small project. What's wrong with it?'

'I don't know. But there must be something.'

Nora set her own mug beside her feet. 'Given the way you've been pestering me and my students, you must know.'

'Look.' He leaned forward and for a moment Nora thought he was about to take her hands. She folded them in her lap against the possibility.

'Ward was adamant that the tower not be built.'

'Why?'

'He wouldn't say. He came by one night – this was after he and Sheila had split – and we had a few beers. You know how it is.'

Nora wished she did. She'd been so mortified by the revelation of her husband's cheating – even though she'd been the one to expose it – that she'd run away from everyone and everything she'd known. There'd been no satisfying gripe-fest over too many glasses of wine, no sad and cynical reassurance that she was hardly alone in her plight. But this had been a different type of commiseration.

Jeremiah must have taken her silence for assent because he continued, 'More than a few beers. He was upset about something. I figured it was the breakup. Which was weird, because everybody, Ward most of all, knew that relationship had a short shelf life. But it turned out he and Sheila were over way before the rest of us had realized it. He'd moved on to someone else. He wouldn't say who, which wasn't like him. Not that Ward was the kiss-and-tell type. Just the opposite. But he was my best friend, and if there was someone new in his life, I'd have expected to hear about it.

'Anyway, that wasn't what was bugging him. He finally owned up it was about the tower. "They can't build it," he kept saying. "We've got to stop them."'

'And he didn't say why?'

'He wouldn't – or couldn't. Neither of us was in any great shape. I made the mistake of trying to keep up with him when he switched from beer to whiskey. When I asked him about it the next morning, he told me to forget he'd said anything. Not in a nice way, either. It almost felt like a threat. And if you'd ever met Ward, you'd know he was a pretty mild-mannered guy.'

She remembered that shy, diffident man, standing in her classroom, apologizing for going on too long about the family issues that might explain Damien's behavior.

'Anyhow, I let it go. Figured I'd ask him about it later. Never got the chance.'

The shadows had deepened so imperceptibly Nora was surprised to find it was too dark to see his expression. 'Any ideas?'

'My best guess is that it has something to do with an endangered species. He'd been looking for something that could halt Spencer's hotel. Maybe he found it near the tower. I'm no biologist, but I've been researching as best I can, and I haven't found anything.'

Nora retrieved her cup and took a surreptitious sniff, wondering if he'd dosed her tea with some of the same whiskey he and Ward had drunk that night. Jeremiah wasn't making sense.

'If you think there's an endangered species involved, then why in the world were you bugging me to talk to the architect?'

Jeremiah's tone reflected her own puzzlement. 'I know it seems far-fetched. Heck, it *is* far-fetched. But Ward said he was going to try and talk with the project's architect. I thought if I could find the architect, he'd tell me. Ward must have gotten his name somehow, but he never told me and I couldn't find it on my own.'

Fair enough. 'Why didn't you sic your crew on it? All of you warriors seem like smart people.'

She couldn't see his face but heard the slide of khaki across the chair as he shifted within it. 'Somebody killed Ward. I figured if one of us came snooping around like Ward had been, maybe the same thing would happen to that person.'

Nora jumped up from her chair. Her hand struck her mug, sending it careening across the deck's warped boards.

'So you sent me?' Her voice climbed an octave. 'Worse yet, you asked one of my students? Just a little kid? To go poking around and maybe get killed? What the hell is wrong with you?'

He rose.

She flinched. She never should have come to this man's house, never should have let herself be taken in by his gentle, retro-hippie shtick. When was she going to learn?

'Hey, hey. Sorry.' He stepped back, so far she feared he'd tumble from the deck. 'Let me stress that I think it's unlikely that Ward was killed because of this. But environmentalism isn't as popular as it once was. The warriors even get the occasional threat. You know what the online world is like these days.

'But you – you've got this cute class project about the tower. As to asking one of the kids, I knew they'd go straight to you. And no one knows you. You're not affiliated with any group. I thought if someone like you asked around, you actually might find out – which you did – and then I could take it from there.'

'Trying to find out has already made me at least one enemy.' She told him about the encounter with Ron Stevenson.

'For what it's worth – and I know this comes too late – I'm sorry. It was stupid of me.'

She felt herself softening. When was the last time a man – any

man, from her ex to Luke and even down to man-boy Damien
– had acknowledged that maybe, just maybe, his actions had
caused her distress? She'd folded her arms tight around her chest.
She let them fall.

'Apology accepted.'

'I'm glad. If you'll just give me his name, I'll take it from here.'

'His name is Kirk Lopez. But that doesn't much matter now.
He's dead.'

'*What?*'

She started to tell him about the newspaper story she'd read,
but he held up a hand. 'I can barely see you. I feel as though
I'm talking to a ghost. Let me fix that.'

He disappeared into the house. She expected the flick of a
switch, a harsh light flooding the deck, throwing everything into
unforgiving relief, but he returned with a fat candle. He put it
on a low table between their chairs in a silent invitation to sit
back down.

Invitation accepted. Candlelight puddled around them, just
enough so they could see one another, but not so much their
conversation felt like an interrogation.

'Better?'

'Much. But maybe it's not as nefarious as it sounds. The police
said it was probably an accident.'

Jeremiah lifted his mug and swung it in a wide arc, sending
a sludge of wet tea leaves over the edge of the deck.

'You said probably.'

She shrugged. 'He was an old man. He fell. It was a bad fall,
down some basement steps.' She shuddered, once again imagining
Lopez's broken body on the basement floor, his unheard cries.

'An accident.' His voice was flat. 'Call me paranoid, but . . .'

'I mean, he used a cane. I saw it.' But she'd also seen his firm
grip, his steely gaze, his steady voice.

'So, you're not sure.'

Their eyes met and she saw her own hesitation reflected in his.

'No. I'm not sure at all.'

They stood simultaneously. It happened so fast that afterward,
she wondered if she'd imagined it. As she stepped close to give
him her empty mug, he moved toward her at the same time. They
stumbled into one another and he reached to keep her from falling

and his arms went around her and . . . that was it. He didn't press close. Plaster his mouth against hers, send his hands wandering.

But, for the briefest second, his hold tightened. 'Be careful,' he whispered, his cheek against hers. 'Please.'

He backed away and cleared his throat. 'I'll look through court records. Maybe this has to do with one of the suits Ward filed. Can you try Janie's husband again?'

She nodded, not trusting herself to speak, remembering Ron's heavy hand on her shoulder. His mirthless grin. *'That's the sort of question that gets people in trouble.'*

'But only if you feel up to it. What you just told me about the way he reacted the first time you stopped at the tower sure sounded like a threat.'

Something Luke hadn't acknowledged.

THIRTY-FOUR

Of course summer decided to ignore the calendar in favor of staging a last hurrah on moving day.

An exuberant sun pumped out heat that in the rest of the country might have ranked as uncomfortable at worst, but when contrasted with the peninsula's usual damp chill ranked as near-suffocating. It kicked the clouds to kingdom come and unleashed wattage of a strength that wouldn't be seen again until the rains had collected their annual toll of suicides, drunkenness, drug overdoses and general despair.

For a few hours, Lane's End came to life with smiles and cheer. But as the temperature crawled higher, people shed outer layers, retreating beneath trees and shaded porches. Business owners grumbled at the cost of cranking air conditioners on again. Pores sprung leaks. Work on the hotel and tsunami tower continued, but in seeming slow motion.

Nora's phone dinged with alerts warning of record-breaking heat predicted to last into the long weekend. The peninsula schools scheduled a three-day fall break in mid-October, which is why she and Luke had scheduled their move then.

She tried to cheer herself up with a reminder that she wouldn't have to teach in such heat. In a bow to the reality of climate change that brought an increasing number of days exactly like this one to the peninsula, the school district was installing air conditioning in its buildings. But the work was being done on a staggered schedule, and the middle school had yet to see its turn.

Nora's T-shirt stuck to her skin. She'd drained and refilled her water bottle three times already. At least they were on their final truckload of household goods and furniture.

They'd saved the worst for last. She and Sheila each grabbed a leg of the awful gold sofa and waited until Luke had hefted the other end. 'Now,' he called and they lifted, wrestling it toward the front steps.

'Think if we drop it, it'll break?' Nora muttered.

'Aw, c'mon. It's not *that* bad. Oof!' Luke had just taken the first step, and much of the sofa's weight fell to Nora and Sheila. 'I'll bet it's a genuine antique,' Sheila gasped. 'The kind of thing you see on one of those shows that turns out to be worth thousands of dollars.'

Luke paused. 'Ready for the next step? On three.'

Nora braced herself. 'I'll sell it to you for a buck. You can take it to one of those shows and say I told you so.' She felt with her feet for the next step.

'Three,' Luke called, and despite herself, Nora lifted. Next, the ordeal of tilting to one side and then another, trying to find the angle that would allow them to maneuver it through the front door and finally into the living room, where it nearly filled one wall.

Luke went into the kitchen and came back with three open bottles of beer, foam bubbling down their sides. 'I think we've earned this.'

Nora turned her back on the sofa and drank deep.

'It doesn't look . . . bad,' Sheila said behind her.

'Wait a minute.' Nora guzzled the rest of her beer, a feat not accomplished since college. 'I've got something that'll make it look better.'

She blotted her chin with the back of the hand and headed back out into the heat, returning with a large flat packet tied in brown paper.

'What's this?' Sheila and Luke crowded close as she laid it on the sofa. She unwrapped it and swept the paper to the floor, revealing a framed, face-down art work. She flipped it over and stood it on the back of the sofa, leaning it against the wall, and stepped back to regard it.

Luke spoke first. 'What the hell is that?'

Sheila bent to peer at the signature in the bottom right corner. 'I thought so. It's one of Jeremiah's.'

'Whoever Jeremiah is, he must have been having a really bad day. I get depressed just looking at this thing.'

Nora smirked. She felt the same way about the sofa. 'That's the whole idea.'

'Jeremiah's one of us. He grew up here,' Sheila chimed in. 'He's all about climate change and how it affects the peninsula. He and Ward were friends.'

'Do you honestly expect me to look at that thing? Can't we put it somewhere else? The bathroom, maybe?'

Nora gave him her sweetest smile. 'If you're sitting on the sofa, you won't have to look at it. Personally, I like it.'

Sheila bit her lip. 'I wouldn't say I like it, exactly, but it does make you think. Sort of like Jeremiah himself. Have you met him? That guy doesn't know the meaning of small talk.'

Sheila said it as though it were a bad thing. Personally, Nora found Jeremiah's directness refreshing.

'We bumped into him on the beach when the kids were doing their interviews.'

'I'm surprised he talked with them. Normally he's one of those quiet, keep-to-himself types.'

Nora thought about her initial wild imaginings of Jeremiah as an ax-murderer. Maybe she should have paid attention. But the way they'd parted that night she'd gone to his house . . . no.

Luke dusted his hands, startling her out of the memory. 'This was the last of it. Sheila, we can't thank you enough. But could you do us one more favor?'

He lifted the painting from the back of the sofa and held it out to her. 'Could you drop this off at the city dump on your way home?'

'Hey!' Nora snatched it from his hands. 'Not cool, Luke. Not cool at all.'

Sheila stepped between them. 'Look at it this way. If the worst disagreement you two ever have is about a sofa and a painting, you're in luck. A piece of advice. Hang the painting over the sofa, just like Nora suggested. Then christen the damn sofa. You'll like both the sofa and the painting a whole lot better afterward, I promise you.'

With a wicked wink and a wave of her hand, she was gone.

'That woman has the dirtiest mind of anyone I know,' Luke said. He looked at the sofa. 'But she might have had the right idea.'

Afterward, Nora once again resorted to subterfuge.

'I left a couple of things in Electra. I'll need to get them.'

He tightened his arms around her. 'Don't go yet. This is so nice.'

They lay twined on the sofa, which proved broad enough to easily accommodate their antics. It was surprisingly comfortable, too, so much that Nora – despite her planned mission – relaxed into Luke's embrace, happy to remain horizontal after a day of hauling furniture and boxes.

'Sheila was right, wasn't she?' Luke murmured.

'About what?'

'The sofa. Do you like it better now?'

She did, but damned if she was going to admit it.

'Look up.' She directed his gaze to the painting. 'Like that better now?'

He was no more willing than she to concede. 'I take your point that the best way to deal with it is to sit on the sofa with my back to it.'

She swatted him and rolled off the sofa onto the floor. He stood and stretched and helped her up. Nora cast a belatedly nervous eye toward the windows. 'Uh, maybe we should get some curtains before we cavort around naked.'

The house wasn't like her campground, where Electra sat on an isolated site, or Luke's apartment, safe on the second floor. Now they had neighbors.

'I suppose. Dibs on the shower.'

She heard water running as she dashed to the bedroom, to which they probably should have retreated in the first place except that it lacked curtains, too.

'Your turn.' Luke came in, wrapped in a towel, and tossed her one, too. 'I hate to be That Guy and dash off afterward, especially with all the unpacking we need to do, but I've got to catch up on some school paperwork. I know classes don't start again until Thursday, but I'd rather get it out of my hair now so we can enjoy the rest of the weekend without it hanging over my head. Do you mind?'

She did not. But he didn't need to know why. 'As long as you don't expect me to do all the unpacking while you're gone.'

'I wouldn't think of it. In fact, don't do any. Let's save it until tomorrow.'

He came in for a hug. She whipped the towel from around his waist and ran laughing to the bathroom, locking the door behind her.

'So help me God, if the neighbors report me for indecent exposure, I'm diming you out,' he called through it.

She was still smiling when she turned off the water. Her phone, sitting on the sink, vibrated. She grabbed it before it could jounce onto the floor. 'EverJerk' flashed on the screen.

She stopped smiling.

Just when she thought the principal couldn't get any more annoying, Everhart was texting her on a weekend.

'My office. First thing Thursday.'

Nora wondered which of her many sins would be the topic of discussion. But she had more important things to deal with than Everhart's relentless nitpicking. Everhart would know she'd seen the message. But she would be damned if she'd reply.

She pulled on her cycling shorts and a T-shirt and headed for the tsunami tower.

THIRTY-FIVE

Sweating workers in safety belts scrambled around on the tower, earning serious overtime given the weekend. A crane swung a semicircle, dropping a pallet of metal fencing at

the base of the tower. Nora had to shout to someone on the
ground to be heard over the din.

Her request triggered a chain reaction of shouts and arm-
waving, which finally made its way to a man on the highest
scaffold. He turned, saw Nora, and made his way monkeylike to
the ground.

'Come on.' He led her a few yards away, where they could
better hear one another. 'What brings you out here at this
hour?'

His query held no hint of the belligerence of their earlier
encounter. He stood at a respectful distance and radiated genuine
curiosity. Maybe Luke had been right – that she'd misread their
previous interaction.

'I'm sorry to bother you so late,' she began.

He waved a hand. 'No sweat. I'm glad for the break. I'm
running ragged, supervising both this and the hotel project. Just
to make life extra-fun, we've got to put up a fence around the
tower. Kids keep climbing on it at night. Last thing we need is
for one to fall and break his neck. Anyway, we're just about
done for the day. So?' He cocked his head.

'This probably comes out of left field,' Nora began again.

'I'll say. Why would a teacher want to talk with me? Especially
now that you've come to your senses and dropped that project.'

'*Excuse me?*'

Nora had heard the phrase 'shit-eating-grin' her whole life
and was never quite sure what it meant. Now, gazing into it, she
understood perfectly,

'Oh, you didn't know?' Ron taunted.

My office. First thing Thursday.

Her fumbling recovery wouldn't have fooled one of her
students, let alone an adult already inclined to disbelief. 'Of
course I knew. I'm just surprised the rest of the world does, also.'

'You know the peninsula. No secrets here.'

Oh, she was getting to know it better every day – and, increasingly, what she knew was that there were secrets everywhere.

'Right. This doesn't have anything to do with the school. I'm
in the midst of a wild-goose chase. I thought maybe you could
help.'

He glanced toward the tower, put two fingers to his lips and emitted a piercing whistle. 'Time!' he shouted, lifting his wrist and pointing to a nonexistent watch. The workers began to descend.

He turned back to Nora. 'Shoot.'

'Remember before I asked you about the architect? I know his name now. Kirk Lopez. Does that ring a bell?'

Just like that, the Ron she remembered was back, moving so close she leaned so far backward that she barely managed to avoid toppling as she tried to hold her ground.

'Listen, lady, I don't know what your game is but you'd better knock it off. How often do I have to tell you?'

He stalked away, muttering. All she heard was 'Ward.'

Nora forced her legs into motion, stumbling back up the beach toward her trailer. She'd locked herself inside before she realized it wasn't her home anymore.

But for the moment it was the right place to be. She'd left it stocked, yes she had, and the supplies included a half-full bottle of whiskey. She poured a generous splash into one of her Lexan wine glasses and sipped until the shaking stopped.

Then she texted Jeremiah.

'Just saw Ron. You weren't paranoid. Not even a little bit.'

THIRTY-SIX

Thursday morning, Everhart had said.

It was Sunday. She had four full days to lose her damn mind.

'What's going on with you?' Luke asked after she'd knocked over her coffee cup, dropped the cereal box on the floor, and stumbled over Murph, who was standing in plain sight.

'I'm just really restless.'

'I can see that. What's up?'

Deflect, she thought. 'How about a bike ride?' Maybe she could pedal her anxiety away.

Luke scraped a palm across his weekend stubble and grimaced. 'I didn't finish everything I needed to do yesterday. I've still got a pile of student evaluations waiting. I could be there most of the day. Do you mind a solo ride?'

Did she mind? It meant she wouldn't have to spend the whole day acting like nothing was wrong. And it meant she wouldn't have to think of an excuse to leave the house on her own so she could drop by Jeremiah's and tell him what Ron had said.

Luke nudged a cardboard box full of pots and pans with his foot. 'I know we've still got a lot of stuff to do with the house, but . . .'

She cut him off with a grateful kiss. 'We both need a break. Although, yours doesn't seem like much of a break.' She went to the refrigerator and scanned its contents. 'Need me to pick up anything while I'm out?'

'We should be fine. I'll get some razor clams from the seafood market and make linguine alla vongole.'

'My favorite! I'll stop by Betty's and grab a baguette. But what's with this monster pan of lasagna? This thing could feed an army.'

'I threw it together after you went to sleep last night. It'll make for easy meals this weekend. We can freeze whatever we don't eat.'

The lasagna, on top of the linguine, seemed like an embarrassment of riches, but if it meant she didn't have to cook for days, she was all for it. She breezed out the door, momentarily pleased with herself, and then a little shaken as to how easy it had been to play on his trust. She remembered similar scenarios with her husband – the way he was always ducking out to retrieve something he'd forgotten at the office, or to attend a weekend meeting with a client with an unforgiving work schedule, or even just a beer run.

Given the breadth of the suit filed against his law firm for allowing Joe's years of harassment, she had to assume that none of those errands were as innocuous as her meeting with Jeremiah.

She'd envisioned fitting her visit into the smallest of time slots. Now she had most of the day to herself. She grabbed a slicker as protection against the inevitable rain, fitted her cleats into the pedals and treated herself to a long, leisurely ride, heading off the peninsula and on to the mainland, amazed anew at the area's wildness given its relative proximity to two of the region's biggest cities.

A couple of hours' drive would put her amid spaghetti-tangle freeway interchanges, hulking big-box stores and suburbs cut by curvilinear streets and cul-de-sacs. Here was only sky and water and marsh and trees, the narrow road along which she pedaled the only testament to humanity's intrusion. The lingering tensions from Everhart's message and her encounter with Ron shuffled off to the emotional outskirts.

This, she thought, was worth a little rain. Although, she feared, looking at the lowering sky, the day might bring more than a little. She reversed course and headed back toward the peninsula, her appreciation of nature playing second fiddle to her anticipation of a warm and dry place to shelter from the coming storm – and telling herself that anticipation didn't also include her surreptitious meeting with Jeremiah.

But first, she had a stop to make. One that had nothing to do with that night's dinner.

Everhart stood in the doorway of a peninsula cottage so fiercely well-tended that Nora felt she should remove her shoes even though she remained outside on the step. Surely just on the other side of that door sat a mat for shoes and slippers at the ready, and cleaning products nearby to erase any indignities imposed upon the principal's lair.

'I said my office. On Thursday. This is my home. And it's Sunday.'

Peninsula Middle School's staff handbook listed the names, address, phone numbers and online contacts for all the employees in the event of an off-hours emergency. Nora was pretty sure her visit didn't count as such. She tried to suppress an internal wriggle of satisfaction at Everhart's discomfiture.

'I know you did. But I just heard – from someone who doesn't even have kids in the school system – that my class project on the tsunami tower has been canceled. When were you going to tell me?'

'You saw my text. We'll discuss this at the school.'

Everhart started to close the door. Nora stuck a toe into the opening and followed it with a shoulder. 'I'm here now.'

The door mashed against her. Much harder and it would leave marks. Which of them would bear the greater liability for what happened next?

The door fell open.

'Fine.' Everhart's expression said it was not fine at all; that Nora would face retribution into the afterlife for this breach of protocol.

'We can – we will – discuss this further on Thursday. But you must know already that your project has raised concerns around town, so much so that several people have contacted me. In my judgment, it's irresponsible to make young children the focus of such controversy.'

'Before you've even seen the finished project? Don't you want to read their newspaper before you even think about censoring it? Anyway, isn't that illegal?'

Ron Stevenson's grin had been unmistakably shit-eating. Everhart was far too dignified to allow anything more than the slightest, iciest smile to drift across her lips.

'Actually . . .' She proceeded to cite, chapter and verse, the 1988 Supreme Court decision giving school administrators a say over student publications. 'One would think every teacher would have this sort of knowledge at her fingertips when planning such a project,' she finished, almost sweetly.

A project you approved! But Nora knew that fact wouldn't help her cause. If Nora had learned anything during her years in public relations, it was that business of the buck stopping at the top was crap. The alpha dog never took the blame.

Time to fold – or at least, appear to.

She tried to speak without gagging. 'Please. The kids – students – are so proud of their work, and we're so far along. Let me review what we have so far and submit a new, detailed proposal. I'm sure there's a way we can complete this without upsetting anyone.'

She wasn't sure at all. And she'd just given de facto permission for the very censorship she'd objected to moments before. But she'd worry about all of that later. For the moment, she'd do whatever it took to avoid walking into class on Thursday and announcing the project was dead.

She wielded her best weapon.

'With all due respect' – hah! – 'as much as the project seems to have upset some people' – emphasis on *seems* and *some* – 'an equal number of people would be disturbed to hear that it's been killed. The school doesn't need that sort of publicity.'

Nora held her breath. Let it out at Everhart's terse nod.

Extracted herself from the doorway and congratulated herself on not breaking into a dead run as she headed back to her bicycle.

THIRTY-SEVEN

Nora usually coasted through stop signs when she was on her bike.

On this day, the sign at the T intersection gave her a chance to catch her breath. She'd fled Everhart's in such a rush that she'd forgotten to take her usual detour, something she only realized when a raging beast charged out of the shadow of the pines, howling murder.

Nora yanked the handlebars. The bike veered on to the sandy shoulder. The front tire dug in. The rear rose.

Nora soared. Landed hard. The dog went berserk.

Nora curled into a ball, folded her arms around her head, and awaited a slashing death. The dog's howls morphed into a series of strangled coughs.

She opened one eye and peeked beneath a protective arm.

The dog lunged against a chain pulled taut. His collar dug into his windpipe. His eyes, red with lethal intent, bulged.

A door banged. An elderly woman came toward them, entirely too slowly for Nora.

'Are you all right? Did Booyah scare you? Booyah, honey, that's not nice. Honestly, there's nothing to worry about. He sounds mean but he's just the sweetest boy.'

She hauled on the chain and the dog took a reluctant step backward. She leaned forward and scratched his ears. He turned his head, brought those fearsome jaws to her face and licked her from forehead to chin.

'You see?' The woman beamed at Nora. 'Are you hurt?'

Nora clambered to her feet and picked up her bike, keeping it between her and the mass of muscle bunching and sliding beneath a short brindle coat. She fished for the woman's name.

'I'm fine, Mrs Maxwell.' If by fine, she meant she was pretty sure her heartbeat would return to normal in the next week or so.

'But you're bleeding. Let me get you a Band-Aid.'

Nora looked at her knee. Blood welled from a deep scrape and traced a crooked stripe down her shin.

Good God. That meant the woman would leave her alone with that creature again. Who knew how long that chain would hold, especially with the scent of blood in the air?

'No. I mean, thank you, but I'm almost home. I'll be there in five minutes. Bye now!'

Nora hopped onto her bike – well, she'd meant to hop, but it was more like a lunge – and wobbled away, gaining speed with each revolution as she fled yet another bad situation, so that by the time she hit the stop sign, sweat dripped into her eyes and the fire in her calves presaged a double dose of ibuprofen when she got back to the house.

She bent over the handlebars, gasping. A left turn would bring her home. Luke would probably have finished his paperwork. She imagined his reaction when she told him about Everhart's plan for her project.

He'd remind her of her precarious status as a teacher-in-training and Everhart's status as boss. She could just picture him turning from the stove and posing the question: 'Is this the hill you want to die on?' As though the answer were obvious.

Which it wasn't.

Nora put her feet back onto the pedals and turned right, toward Jeremiah's. But first she stopped by Betty's for the baguette she'd promised, pushing away the knowledge that in offering to bring home the bread that would prove the innocence of her jaunt, she'd likely mimicked her husband's behavior during the final years of her marriage.

But her visit with Jeremiah *was* innocent.

So why did she feel guilty?

Because of the way Jeremiah's face lit up when he saw her on his deck.

Really, what was the harm in enjoying another's appreciation? She'd always told herself she welcomed her fifties – a friend had touted them as the give-no-fucks decade – but she'd be lying if she pretended not to miss the ego-stroke of a turned head.

He waved a brush at her. 'Out in a second,' he mouthed through the studio window.

A minute later, he was at the door, holding two glasses adorned with sprigs of mint.

'I made iced tea. And I've got tuna salad, if you'd like a sandwich. Just give me a minute.'

With its unpretentious echoes of childhood, it sounded like the best thing in the world. All she needed was a good book and a porch swing to time-travel to the summers of her youth. But she wasn't there for nostalgic imaginings.

They settled themselves into the deck chairs, balancing plates on their laps.

'What happened to your leg?'

She'd already forgotten about it. 'I had a bad encounter with a scary dog.'

'Booyah? He's a menace. To be fair, I've never heard of him biting anyone. Worst-case scenario, he causes a heart attack.'

Nora wet her finger and rubbed at the drying blood. 'I thought I was going to have one. He didn't bite me. I'd forgotten all about him and when he came at me, I fell off my bike.'

'Let me get something for that.' He rose and returned with a basin of warm water and a clean cloth, dabbing away the blood and grit as she poured out her fury and frustration about Everhart's decision.

Jeremiah wrung out the rag. 'You're right. That's straight-up censorship. Problem is, she's right, too – about her right to censor it, I mean. Not about her reasons for doing it. That's bullshit. But it sounds as though you handled it just right. You've heard that old phrase, right – publish or perish? What's to stop you from showing her a watered-down version and then putting the real one online?'

It was a tempting scenario, and she admitted to having already considered it. But she'd considered something else: 'I'd probably lose my job.'

He tipped the basin's red-tinged contents over the edge of the porch. 'So?'

There it was – the difference between her and Ward's Warriors.

'I've just bought a house. I don't live close to the ground like you and Ward. I can't afford—'

'Principles?' he broke in. 'Sorry. That was unfair. Given your reaction to Everhart, I'd say you have plenty. As to worrying about losing your job, you're like ninety-nine percent of people in the world, with responsibilities like mortgages or rent, and car payments and families and so on. Nothing wrong with that. Only problem is, it gives the Louann Everharts and the Spencer Templetons of the world power over you, and they have zero scruples about using it.'

He'd let her off the hook. 'Thanks. For that and—' She gestured at her leg, now sporting a simple scrape instead of a bloody mess.

'Clean it again when you get home and put some antibiotic ointment on it. Anyway, speaking of Spencer Templeton – and by extension, Ron Stevenson – I want to hear more about your conversation with him. I got your text last night. Why am I not paranoid?'

She hesitated. Thinking it was bad enough. Saying it out loud might make her sound crazy.

'I texted you last night because I thought Ron Stevenson might have something to do with Ward's death.' No. That wasn't right. She'd soft-pedaled her suspicions to a man whose main asset, as far as she could tell, was his plain-spokenness. She tried again, finally giving voice to the vague swirling unease that had coalesced into dread during the previous insomniac night. 'I texted you because I thought he could have killed him.'

She'd expected he might choke on his sandwich, do a spit-take with his iced tea. He did neither.

Jeremiah nodded, chewing thoughtfully. 'Wouldn't surprise me.'

She hadn't seen that one coming. 'Because Ward was so dead set against Spencer's projects? Ron's the supervisor on both of them. That's got to be a sweet windfall for him. If Ward had managed to stop either one, Janie might have had to work at Betty's forever.'

Jeremiah took another bite of his sandwich. 'Yep,' he mumbled around it. 'But that's not why. I mean, it's a pretty good reason. But there's a better one.'

'What's that?'

'Remember how I said Ward had someone new in his life? That he was really secretive about?'

She nodded and took a bite of her sandwich.

'I've finally figured it out. Pretty sure it was Janie.'

THIRTY-EIGHT

Jeremiah hadn't choked, but Nora did.

She bent double as he pounded her back. She finally waved him away. 'I can breathe now. I think.'

'Here.' He held her glass out. 'Drink. But take it easy.'

He watched as she took a sip, then a larger one. 'Better?'

'Much. Thank you. I did not see that coming. Ward and Janie? What makes you think that?'

'Couple of things. But, look.' He pointed to the sky, where roiling dark clouds drew a cloak over the sun. 'We're working up to a storm. Let's go down to the beach and watch it. We can talk on the way.'

Even as he spoke, he gathered up the plates and glasses and took them inside, while she wheeled her bike beneath an overhang. He emerged wearing a slicker and headed toward a gap in the spruce and brambles, barely wider than a deer trail. 'Hurry. You don't want to miss this. A few weeks from now, when the really big storms roll in, people drive all the way over from the cities to watch. Same with the King Tides.'

She nearly jogged to keep up with him, the path so narrow that she held her arms before her face to keep the whippy branches from slapping her. 'What's a King Tide?'

'We get them a couple of times a year during a full or new moon. Tides are always higher then and King Tides are higher still.'

He tossed a grin over his shoulder. 'Kind of like a mini-tsunami. Lot of drama, usually some flooding. That campground where you have your trailer? It'll be under a few inches of water.'

Nora reminded herself to check the tide tables. Maybe she should move Electra to a campground farther inland. But the trailer had survived the previous year's storms with no problem.

Thunder rumbled above them. 'Should we be under trees?' She cast a wary eye upward but couldn't see through the tangle above her and anyway, Jeremiah was too far ahead to hear her. She lengthened her stride and nearly tripped over a root, saving herself only by grabbing a nearby branch.

Jeremiah was just like every other guy after all, rushing toward something without stopping to think how it might affect anyone else, she thought with a thud of disappointment. She should turn around. She even started to, but then caught a glimpse of a break in the trees, the heaving ocean beyond, and Jeremiah, his hand stretched toward her.

His clasp was warm and firm, nothing like Ron Stevenson's bone-crushing statement, and better yet, he dropped her hand as soon as she drew alongside, so there'd be no mistaking the gesture for anything more.

'Look,' he said unnecessarily.

Because she couldn't do anything but.

The ocean, flat and gray on cloudy days, flat and blue on the rare sunny ones, with a soothing whoosh on both, had morphed into a different animal entirely, great crouching waves rushing toward them and breaking with a thunderous crash, the water surging so far up the beach it nearly covered the sand.

Nora took an involuntary step back.

Jeremiah gave her a knowing look. 'It feels like it could snatch you away, doesn't it?'

She gave a sheepish nod.

'Nothing to be embarrassed about. Your instincts are good. Do you have your phone?'

'I left it at home.'

'When we get back, you'll probably have a string of alerts about rogue waves.'

She jumped as lightning traced a lengthening crack in the clouds. 'One-thousand-one, one-thousand-two . . .' she counted, waiting for the thunder. Jeremiah's lips moved, counting along with her. The clap shook them at three seconds.

'Jesus,' Jeremiah said. 'That's right next door. But we don't have to worry about the lightning. These trees aren't that tall, and if the lightning hits anything, it'll be on Highview Hill.'

Raindrops dimpled the water and tattooed the sand. A crashing wave echoed the thunder, sending water hissing closer still. She flinched and tried to cover her reaction with a joke.

'Rogue Waves. It sounds like a band name. Are they related to King Tides?'

He didn't smile. 'They're a real thing. I wish they'd just call them what they are – killer waves. Then maybe people would take them more seriously. Every so often, someone gets too close – these days, they're usually trying to take a damn selfie – and that's the last they're seen until their body washes up miles away. Look there, toward town. There's a whole collection of idiots on the beach right now. Except that' – he squinted – 'I think I see Janie and her kids. And isn't that . . .?' He glanced toward her and cut his question short.

She stepped out of the trees and glanced at the tiny figures running toward the water, and dashing back, always – at least so far – just in time. 'I can't tell. Luke's been telling me for a while I need glasses.'

He narrowed his eyes again. 'Huh. Looks like three kids, not two. Must be someone else. Let's get back under the trees.'

'I'm fine. It's not raining that hard.'

He'd already retreated. 'No. That's not why.'

He stood in the shadows so she couldn't be sure. But she'd have sworn he was blushing.

'Then, why?'

'You've been here long enough to know what this place is like. If we're seen together here like this – well, everybody knows my house is here. They'll say we're carrying on.'

'Carrying on?' She suppressed a smile. 'You make it sound so, oh, I don't know. Old-timey. But I take your point.'

Still, she lingered a moment more, watching the frolickers near water's edge. Idiots, he'd called them, probably correctly. But she got it. As scary as the waves were, they were thrilling in their urgent, unbridled power, as was the lashing wind, full of charged ions. Her skin tingled, goosebumps rising. It was almost sexual – an uncomfortable thought, given Jeremiah's warning, but one that at least brought her back to his intriguing theory.

'You said you thought Ward might have been sleeping with Janie. Why?'

'Just a gut feeling. A belated one, for sure. Ward and I used to hit Betty's pretty regularly. Janie would always throw in some freebies – sides of fries, or dessert, stuff like that. She was pretty flirty with Ward, and you could tell he enjoyed it. You know how it is with married people – sometimes you flirt with them more because you figure they're safe, and you enjoy it without worrying about it going anywhere.'

Someday, Nora thought, she was going to hear a comment like that and not think immediately of her husband. Had the women he'd flirted with thought he was safe, until he wasn't? She yanked her attention back to Jeremiah, who was still talking.

'But when I think back on it, the flirting stopped a while ago. They didn't even make eye contact when she'd come to our table.'

Nora's shoulders shook with laughter. 'That's a total tell. They were definitely sleeping with each other. Or maybe they only slept with each other once, and it didn't go well. But how does that tie into Ron maybe having killed Ward – oh, wait.'

She clapped a hand to her forehead. 'Maybe he found out. But killing somebody is a pretty big leap. From what little I've seen of him, I can easily imagine him getting in Ward's face, maybe even punching him. But lying in wait for the guy and beating him to death?'

Jeremiah shrugged. 'Maybe he hit him just right and killed him. You know, the kind of stuff that only happens in novels and cheesy movies. The thing that made me wonder about it, though, was how quick Janie was to pin it on Harold, who's never punched anybody in his life, as far as I know. What if she was protecting Ron?'

'I think I'm like you,' he said. 'I know it's possible. It's just hard to accept the notion.'

He started back up the path. 'We'd better get going unless you want to get really soaked.'

She followed him back to the house, where she declined an offer of a towel for her hair, and more tea, hot this time. They stood under the roof overhang, watching the rain slacken.

'Your paintings,' she said. 'Now that I've seen that storm, I understand where you get your inspiration. It's weird that every-body buys the sunny scenes for their homes, but that they all flock outdoors to watch the storms.'

'They like the excitement. It's fun for a few minutes, but they don't want a reminder that it's dangerous, too. Not everyone is comfortable with being reminded of our own vulnerability.'

She was relieved when he changed the subject. 'You said you *thought* Ron might have killed Ward. Past tense.'

She'd been wondering if he'd picked up on that.

'Clearly, the man has a temper. And you just gave me another reason, beyond Ward's stance on development, that he might have killed him. But I saw Delilah at Betty's one day. Her face looked bruised and her hand definitely was. She told me she caught it in a car door but what if she hadn't? What if Spencer's temper is as bad as Ron's?'

His face shaded. 'For Delilah's sake, I hope not. Remember what I said about all the shenanigans that go on around here during the winter? I made it sound almost fun – a lot of drinking, a lot of fooling around. God knows, when I was younger, I did my share. But there's a dark side to it. A lot of affairs mean a lot of divorces. And a lot of drinking can lead to a lot of violence. Not necessarily something like Ward getting killed – that's way beyond the pale – but women and kids getting knocked around. It's the curse of all isolated places.'

Nora had left a truly remote – and cursed – place before coming to the peninsula, where the isolation had seemed like sanctuary. Now she wondered.

'Is it crazy for me to think he might have done it?'

'No crazier than anything else. But that's not his style. He sics lawyers on people.'

'That's just what Sheila said.' She looked outside. 'It's letting up. I'd better get home.' She had to remind herself that *home* meant the new house instead of Electra. 'Do you have a plastic bag I could borrow? I've got a baguette that needs to get home safe.'

'We haven't used plastic bags here in a few years,' he reminded her. 'But I've got a cloth bag you can borrow. And, listen. Best-case scenario, we're both being paranoid. But be careful, OK? Don't go saying anything more about this to either Ron or Spencer, at least not if you're alone.'

There was no repeat of their hug. But his caring words left her with the same warm feeling, one that sustained her until she remembered the morning she'd gone to the bakery to pick up Everhart's birthday cake.

She'd mentioned the architect to the wives of both the men he'd told her to avoid.

THIRTY-NINE

Her thoughts revolved along with each turn of the wheels on the rain-spattered ride home, the baguette in its bag tucked inside her jacket for double protection. One thing didn't make sense.

She could see Ron picking a fight with Ward if Janie had been sleeping with him. But the confrontation with Spencer Templeton didn't make sense. Given Ward's antipathy to the construction projects that were both men's bread and butter, they should have been natural allies.

Despite Jeremiah's warning, she'd try Spencer next, preferably with other people within sight – although that would make it tougher to ask about his beef with Ron.

Luke's car was in the driveway as she pedaled up to the house. She'd been gone for hours. She hoped he hadn't been home long. She readied an explanation as to why she'd ridden through such a storm – she'd say she sought shelter somewhere during the worst of it – but she didn't need to explain a thing.

She climbed the porch steps and opened the door and . . .

'Surprise!'

A grin split Luke's face as he rose from the gold sofa, followed a moment later by a dark-haired, dark-eyed boy whose scowl was the storm cloud lurking behind his father's delight.

Nora dropped the bread.

Luke and Murph lunged for it, Murph's teeth closing on thin air as Luke whisked it to safety.

'You-you-you must be Gabriel,' she stammered.

'Duh.'

'Ahem.' Luke nudged him. Gabriel held out a hand.

Nora took it and after a moment in which neither of them moved, gave it a shake. 'I'm Nora.'

'Yeah. He told me. In the car.'

Luke hadn't mentioned her before this?

Luke hurried into the fray. 'Gabriel had a long weekend off from school, too, so I flew him up here. I wanted you two to get to know each other, and for Gabriel to see where he'd be spending the Christmas break and next summer, spend some time on the beach.'

Christmas break? Didn't that usually last two weeks? And the entire summer?

Nora stared at Gabriel. The dismay in his face mirrored her own.

He shuffled a step back, his enormous sneakers trailing sand. He was already nearly as tall as Luke. Those shoes indicated he'd be taller within a year.

'Looks like you've already seen the beach,' Nora said.

Luke gave her a look. 'There's sand everywhere here. We'll go after dinner.'

Murph, still sulking over being deprived of his prize, put his tail between his legs and whined.

'Well!' Luke clapped his hands, his voice ringing loud in the excruciating silence. 'Let's eat!'

Nora tried over dinner. She really did.

She said things like, 'Isn't this good? It's my favorite of all your dad's dinners,' only to hear, 'Don't you cook?'

She ignored that, persisting, 'What grade are you in? Oh, eighth? I teach seventh.'

'Really? Do the kids in your class hate you as much as I hate my teacher?'

Finally, in desperation, 'I guess this place is a lot different than New Mexico,' which earned another of the all-purpose ammo, 'Duh.'

Any moment now, she thought, Luke's going to save me.

But he merely smiled fondly at Gabriel's rejoinders. 'You're just like I was at that age. When it came to my mom and dad, I don't think I spoke in full sentences again until I was in college.'

'And she's not even my mom,' Gabriel pointed out. 'So I probably don't even have to talk to her at all, right?'

'Good one, Gabe. Isn't he funny?'

Nora wished Luke had made something other than linguine, so soft and yielding, with the long narrow clams that slid so easily down her throat. She'd have preferred something like nachos, with their satisfying crunch, or even a steak – anything that required chewing. Because she felt like biting something.

She contented herself with ripping off a piece of the baguette and mashing it into the briny sauce. She would not, she would not, she *would not* tear off bits of bread, roll them into little balls and fling them at Luke and Gabe, no she would not.

'Nora? Are you all right?'

She coughed and swigged her wine. 'Piece of bread went down the wrong way.'

But then she saw the light in his eyes whenever he turned toward Gabriel, a new soft vulnerability in his expression, and guilt chased the bile.

'You have a dog, don't you, Gabriel?' She wasn't sure enough of herself to call him Gabe.

He didn't bother replying beyond a nod.

'What's his name?'

'It's a girl. Llora.'

She wasn't sure she'd heard correctly. 'Jore-a?'

Luke jumped in. 'Short for Llorona. Like La Llorona.'

She shook her head.

Gabriel smirked and, for the first time, looked her in the eye. 'La Llorona is the ghost of a woman who cries all night because she chose a man over her children. She killed them but he left her anyway.'

Luke, hastily: 'Llora is a hound. She howls. Hence—'

'I get it,' Nora said. She made one last try.

'My dog – our dog – is named Murph. He's not allowed to beg treats at the table, and he's finally learned better than to try.'

Murph lay in the doorway between the living room and kitchen, head on his crossed forepaws, eyes following their hands' every move from plate to mouth.

'But you're new to him. He knows that you don't know the rules. Slip him a clam or a piece of bread and you'll have a friend for life.'

Gabriel rolled his eyes and snorted. But a few minutes later, his hand dropped below the table and Murph eased to his side, then retreated to the other room where no one could see him gulping his prize.

Nora started to congratulate herself, but a realization brought her up short. Now the dog would be on Gabriel's side, too. All she'd done was score a single point in a losing game.

FORTY

She finally pleaded exhaustion at 10 PM on the longest day of her life.

Luke and Gabriel were playing a complicated card game – complicated to her, at least – called Conquian.

'It's a kind of rummy,' Luke said. 'Give it a try. We can take turns.'

'It's only for two people,' Gabriel said, giving her an out.

'I'll just watch.'

But instead, she baked cookies, bustling around the kitchen with a smile pasted on her face as she located flour, sugar, peanut butter and cookie sheets, all in places still unfamiliar.

This is what moms do, she told herself as she dropped the dough by spoonfuls onto the sheet and pressed a crosshatch pattern into each with a fork. They bake homemade sweets for dad and the kids, and they do all the cleanup afterward, too.

She'd settled on peanut butter a) because they had peanut butter, which they used to conceal Murph's pills when he was sick, and b) because what kid doesn't like peanut butter?

She should have known.

'Uh, I'm allergic to peanuts,' Gabriel said when she put a plate of still warm, soft cookies between them. She'd barely stopped herself from pouring a couple of glasses of milk.

'I'm not,' Luke declared and helped himself to two. The recipe made four dozen. They'd be eating peanut butter cookies through the rest of the month.

Nora admitted defeat. 'You know, that bike ride today wore me out. I'm going to crash early, if you two don't mind.'

The hell with cleanup, she thought and tried not to slam the bedroom door behind her.

She lay wide awake and simmering with resentment, listening to the easy murmur in the next room. It seemed Gabriel was talkative when she wasn't around. She even heard him laugh a couple of times.

At one point, Murph nudged the door open and wandered over to the bed to check on her. 'Hey, old man,' she whispered as he nudged her cheek. She smelled peanut butter on his breath. 'Traitor.' She rolled away from him and pulled the pillow over her head.

She'd been long asleep by the time Luke came to bed. He curled himself around her, pressing against her back, buzzing with beer and adrenaline.

'Isn't it great having him here?'

'Mmm.' She'd come awake instantly but feigned sleepiness.

'Wait till you hear what I've got planned for tomorrow. I've got a charter fishing trip lined up. Halibut – have you seen the size of those things? Should be a blast. You were smart to go to bed early. We've got to be at the dock at 5:30. But it was just so good to stay up and talk with Gabe.'

She sat up, throwing off the act along with the blankets. Her voice came out in a squeak. 'Five-thirty? In the morning?'

'Early fish bites the worm? Something like that. Come back here.' He pulled her down beside him.

She lay stiff within his arms.

'A charter boat? Like, out on the ocean?'

'That's generally where the fish live.'

'But I get seasick. You know that.' There'd been a disastrous whale-watching excursion, soon after their arrival on the peninsula. She was told there'd been whales. Lots of them. She never saw them, too sick to raise her head from where she hung over the rail, each new roll of the boat bringing up more contents from the stomach she'd thought surely was empty.

'Take Dramamine.' He nuzzled her neck. 'Glad you're awake.'

She wasn't ready to let it go. 'Dramamine from where? Not even the Store of Everything is open at that hour.' Jesus. No way was she getting on a fucking boat, unable to escape the churn of the waves and the disdain of a thirteen-year-old.

'I'll bet the charter dude has it on board. You can't be the only one.'

'But you have to take it ahead of time. Once I'm on the boat, it's too late.' Her voice climbed high again. She fought to get it under control. 'I have a better idea.'

'Is it this?' His lips moved from her head to her breast. She squelched an urge to push him away.

'That, too. But why don't you make the fishing trip a father–son deal? I'll stay here and have dinner ready when you get back.' No, the Susie Homemaker act was a step too far. He knew better. 'Or we can go to Betty's. My treat,' she amended. 'I don't want Gabe's lasting impression to be of me puking my guts out. What do you think, hmmm?'

She was whispering now, returning his kisses, letting her fingers trail along his body, hating herself for the obvious tactic, but hating even more the idea of that boat. Besides, with Luke and Gabriel out of the way, she'd wouldn't have to think up an excuse to sneak out of the house to track down Spencer Templeton.

As for Luke, given what happened next, he thought the plan was just fine.

Among the many advantages to her plan was that she wouldn't have to drag herself out of bed in the depths of predawn dark. She'd imagined a long, luxurious sleep-in, followed by a quick bike ride to Betty's, where she could enjoy her coffee and dough-nuts without having to make conversation.

She and Luke had only shared the house for a couple of weeks, but she already missed the bouts of solitude afforded by Electra. But Luke's presence was one thing. She'd never imagined the amount of noise a grown man and growing boy could make when rousing themselves and making their own breakfast.

'Eggs OK?' Luke hollered from the kitchen. 'How many?'

'Four. With hot sauce!'

'You got it.'

This back and forth between one end of the house and the other was punctuated by the click and scrape of Murph's nails as he ran between man and boy. Nearby, Mooch hissed his own displeasure.

By the time Luke and Gabriel finally cleared out of the house,

Nora was fully awake, with Betty's not open yet for another hour. She opened one eye and beheld Murph beside the bed, head cocked expectantly. Everybody else was up, so why wasn't she?

'Oh, all right.' She clambered out of bed. She might as well make coffee and kill the time before Betty's opened with a run. But the sight she beheld when she wandered yawning into the kitchen vanquished any lingering sleepiness.

Two plates sat on the table, yolk congealing, despite the efforts of Mooch – when had he sneaked out of the bedroom? – to polish them away. Orange pulp had already dried into hard nubbins inside empty juice glasses, and toast crumbs littered the tablecloth. Luke hadn't even bothered to put the dirty frying pan in the sink.

Nora cursed her way through the coffee preparations and drank a full cup before tackling the mess. She gained a measure of satisfaction when it came to the frying pan, one of Luke's cast-iron pieces. He was forever lecturing her on the importance of maintaining its seasoning, cleaning it by sprinkling it with coarse salt and rubbing it away with a sheet of newsprint. She gleefully attacked it with soap and the dish scrubber and headed out on her run with renewed, if waspish, energy.

FORTY-ONE

She had to pass the spaceship on the way to Betty's.

Her idea was to linger at the bakery as long as possible, past the hour when it would be too early to try and talk with Spencer Templeton. Maybe, by the time she'd finished her doughnut, she'd have figured out a pretext for approaching him.

But the gate in the fence surrounding the spaceship stood open, as did the hatchback to the Mercedes SUV within. Beyond it, Delilah dragged an unwieldy cardboard box from the open elevator door toward the car.

Nora paused, her weight first on one foot, and then the other. She looked behind her, then back ahead. No one.

'Would you like some help with that?' she finally called.

Delilah straightened and shook a strand of hair from her eyes. 'Love some. If you could just grab the other side . . .'

Nora hurried to comply and together they hoisted the box into the car. Delilah pressed a button on the underside of the hatchback and it slowly lowered and clicked into place.

'Thanks so much. You're up awfully early, aren't you?'

So was she, but Nora thought it best not to point that out.

'Teachers have lives, too, despite what the administration would prefer.'

Delilah did her the courtesy of laughing at her attempted joke. She shook her tennis bracelet away from her tiny watch. 'I've got putting practice this morning, but not for a while. Come up for coffee? It's the least I can do.'

Nora fought an urge to pinch herself. Maybe, after such a teeth-grinding start, her day was about to get better. She'd planned on using her time at Betty's to figure out a way to tactfully quiz Spencer. Now she'd have to do it on the fly. First, though, she intended to enjoy another espresso from the Templetons' fancy machine.

She told Murph to stay and rode with Delilah in the elevator, which she was disappointed to find more resembled a freight elevator than the elegant hotel variety she'd imagined. It made sense when she thought about it, though. How else to move furniture into the spaceship?

The elevator opened into the kitchen, where the espresso-maker stood at one end of the counter, all gleaming steel, an altar inviting worship by the caffeine-addicted. Delilah pushed some buttons and the contraption gurgled to life, inky elixir streaming into tiny cups. Nora perched on one of the stools at the kitchen counter and sipped appreciatively as Delilah thanked her yet again.

'Even though Ward and I had been divorced for more than a year when he was . . . when he died, somehow all of his possessions went to me. I've been going through them bit by bit and taking what Damien doesn't want to the Mall. So far, Damien hasn't wanted much of anything.' Her voice caught.

The light was so dim in the shaded parking area below the house that Nora hadn't gotten a good look at her. Now, perched on a stool in the kitchen's bright pitiless glare, she saw the puffy eyes, the reddened nose, the lips whose swelling likely owed more to a savage chewing than to Botox.

The bruise she thought she'd seen at the bakery was either gone or maybe Delilah had applied makeup more carefully. But she doubted the latter. The delicate skin beneath Delilah's eyes was still damp. The woman had been crying – not just weeping, but full-on sobbing – just before Nora arrived.

On impulse she reached across the kitchen island and took her hand. 'Delilah, are you all right?

Then searched frantically for something, anything to stanch the fresh flood of tears.

'I don't know why I keep crying,' Delilah said when she'd wept herself out. 'We'd been divorced for a year and things hadn't been good for a long time before that.

She blotted her eyes with the linen napkin Nora grabbed from the countertop and blew her nose into it.

'Before that, though, you must have had a lot of good years together. And you have a wonderful son.' Nora trod carefully, hoping she sounded as though she knew what she was talking about. She and her husband had been married for twenty years and she had yet to cry over his death. But that was because those years she'd thought good turned out not to have been. She just hadn't known until after the fact. And she and Joe had never had children.

'That's the problem!'

Nora waited through another watery outburst.

'Just because things weren't good between us didn't mean I didn't love him anymore. But I just felt like I'd – oh, I don't know how to say it. As though I'd lost myself within the cause, I guess. Do you know what I mean?'

Of course she did. She and Joe hadn't had a cause in common. They'd just had a life, humming along on the well-oiled autopilot of jobs and friends and vacations, and by the time she'd realized they'd diverged from the same track onto parallel ones, it had been too late. She hadn't realized until it was over how few decisions she'd made solely for herself.

'It's not the same,' she said now, 'but yes, I have an idea. I think a lot of women do.'

Delilah dropped the sodden napkin onto the counter. 'I just can't help but think that if I hadn't left him, Ward might still be alive. We were together all the time. I mean, joined-at-the-hip together. It was one of the reasons I felt so smothered. But if I hadn't left him, no way he'd have been wandering alone up on Highview Hill where somebody could attack him. I just don't understand who could have done such a thing!'

Her words amplified the caffeine jolt hitting Nora.

She spent a minimal number of minutes reassuring Delilah that of course her husband's murder wasn't her fault, before summoning what she hoped was an expression of casual concern. 'Do you have any idea?'

Delilah shook her head, and Nora took a moment to admire a hairstyle that immediately resumed its shape. She guessed Delilah eschewed the brisk efficiency of the peninsula's Kut 'n' Kurl beauty shop in favor of the sort of city salon where they served herbal tea to patrons undergoing the lengthy ministrations designed to soothe the stresses of an upper-crust life, as well as flatter aging features.

'I wish I did. I keep asking the police, but they say that while everybody's pointing fingers at everybody else, nothing pans out.'

'I hear those things, too. The last finger-pointing I heard was aimed at Ron Stevenson.'

'Really?' Delilah flapped her hand and Nora was relieved to see a hint of a smile. 'Just because Ward was sleeping with his wife.'

At least Nora didn't have to feign surprise. It was one thing for Jeremiah to have voiced his suspicion, quite another to hear it calmly stated as fact. 'I didn't hear a reason,' she lied. 'Is that common knowledge? Anyway, I'm pretty sure that's one of the top two or three reasons people kill each other. Crimes of passion and all that.'

Delilah took her tiny cup to the sink and rinsed it. 'Want another?'

'Sure.'

Delilah busied herself at the machine. 'Ward was hardly Janie's first rodeo, and Ron's done his own share of cowboying around. If that was the reason, those two would have shot each other a long time ago. Oh, don't look at me like that.'

Nora willed her eyebrows back into place. 'Sorry. So Ron and Janie have an open marriage or something?'

Delilah's half-smile turned into a genuine laugh. 'Nothing so formal. Just sheer boredom. Have long have you been here?'

'Not quite a year.' Nora took her fresh cup and sipped it, hoping it would help her understand. Clearly she was missing something.

'Then you've already been through one winter.'

Nora made a face and Delilah nodded.

'All that rain, right? Day after day after day, and half the businesses shut down and nobody making the extra money they do in the summertime, so they can't go carouse in the city for a break. Nothing much to do for months on end but drink and smoke weed and sleep around and drink some more. If you came to this peninsula with those genetic tests everybody seems to be ordering now, half the people here might find out their dads aren't who they thought they were.'

Nora grimaced. 'Everyone here sings that same song.' She felt a sudden, sharp affection for the casual encounters of her youth, known blissfully only to her and the man in question, instead of a whole town. 'But Ron seems to have a pretty bad temper. He made such a fuss at the meeting. He yelled at me because he thought I sided with the environmentalists. And I saw him arguing with your husband. Something to do with his job.'

At Delilah's blank look, she added, 'Do you know what that might have been about?'

Delilah shrugged. 'Anything. It's a big project being built in a rush. Spencer wants to open the hotel in time for next summer's tourist season. There are bound to be tensions.'

'I was hoping to ask Spencer about it. It seemed like more than your basic run-of-the-mill disagreement. But I guess he's sleeping in today.'

She couldn't believe her clumsy prod produced information. It just wasn't the information she wanted.

'No. He and Damien were out of here early. Male bonding and all that. I think he's trying to balance out my golf lessons with Damien. I'm glad, though. This gave me a little time to get to know you better.'

The warmth of Delilah's smile undercut Nora's disappointment in hearing of Spencer's absence. She nearly missed the sadness in the woman's eyes.

'Seems like you know just about everybody on this peninsula. I'm flattered to be included.'

Delilah grimaced. 'They don't seem to want to know me anymore. Not after' – she spun on her stool and gestured to include the vast room – 'all of this. People liked me a lot better when Ward and I were scrounging and scraping just like everyone else.'

'Human nature,' Nora offered.

'Doesn't make it any easier.'

'No. I imagine not.' Nora couldn't figure out how to ask the obvious: did Delilah marry for love? Or for things like espresso at the push of a button? She turned instead to a non sequitur. 'I think I bought some of your dishes at the Mall.'

Delilah brightened. 'The ones with the local birds? Aren't they beautiful? I'm so glad they found a good home.'

'Someone told me Spencer gave them to you and Ward as a wedding present.' She didn't want to dime out Sheila and was glad when Delilah didn't ask. 'Didn't you want to keep them as, oh, I don't know, some sort of reunification?'

Delilah pointed to her watch. 'Speaking of golf lessons.' She slid from her stool and turned toward the door.

Nora followed reluctantly. Other than more of the seemingly unending supply of gossip on the peninsula, she hadn't really learned anything useful.

'About the plates,' Delilah said. 'I'm really a clean-slate kind of person. Out with the old life, in with the new, you know?'

Oh, Nora knew. She was on her third supposed fresh start in the space of a little more than a year. This one, she'd promised herself, would stick.

Then Delilah surprised her with the same sort of faux-casual question she herself had been posing.

'By the way, who told you about the plates?'

Nora's brain did a quick tap-dance, trying to formulate a not-quite-lie.

Delilah saved her from the effort with a quick follow-up. 'Was it Janie?'

Nora's jaw dropped. She snapped it shut. 'No. Someone else.

Why?' she asked, hoping to forestall further questions with one of her own.

It worked, but in a way that left her gasping with surprise as she waved goodbye.

'Before she moved on to Ward, she made a play for Spencer just as he and I were getting together. I think she pictured herself as lady of the manor. Honestly, can you imagine?'

She closed the door behind her with a laugh, leaving Nora trying to work her jaw back into place.

FORTY-TWO

Nora arrived home to the blissfully silent house she'd earlier imagined.

She hadn't had time alone in it since she and Luke had moved in, and while it was nice to share a bed every night, she hadn't been prepared for the extent of his physical presence, the way it would overlap with hers.

'Any place for my toothbrush?' she said when it became clear that the Guy Stuff spread around the rim of the sink was never going to make its way into the medicine cabinet.

She tripped over his shoes whenever she got out of bed – somehow, they always migrated into her path to the bathroom. She routinely turned her back on the pan slicked with congealed bacon grease in which he'd made his breakfast, just as she stepped around the dirty clothes on the floor in front of the washer – they had a hamper! – as if inviting her to pick them up and start the machine. Which she was no more going to do than she was going to wash that goddamn pan.

To his credit, he mowed the lawn. Picked up after the dog. Brought her coffee in bed every morning. Those, especially the coffee, were not nothing.

But sometimes she missed the ability to just sit and stare off into space without having to come up with an answer to the inevitable query: 'Whatcha doing?'

Mooch and Murph trailed her to the living room, where she

flopped on the sofa, angling her head so she could admire Jeremiah's painting. Every time she looked at it, she noticed something new: a wave's ominous curl, a shorebird's defensive hunch, a surfboard's broken fin.

Mooch leapt up beside her and purred his appreciation. Murph laid his head on the cushions and gazed a query.

'What should we do with our day?' she asked them.

What had she done before Luke came into her life?

Delilah's revelations had startled her out of her plan to treat herself to breakfast at Betty's. Maybe she'd do lunch instead.

'A fried oyster sandwich. And I'll ask for an extra oyster for you,' she reassured the cat. 'And when I get home, you and I will take an extra-long walk on the beach,' she told the dog. 'Maybe all the way to the end of the peninsula.'

In all her months on the peninsula, she'd never gone to its northern tip. She'd tried on a few runs, heading into the mist, thinking that it would take only another mile – or two, or three – before she finally arrived at the spot where ocean met bay uninterrupted by the narrow spit of sand. But the sand stretched on and on, farther than seemed possible, cut by deceptively shallow tidal streams that she feared would be far deeper on her return, forcing her to run in soaked shoes, never fun.

Today, though, she'd check the tides and plan accordingly. She'd just pulled up the tide tables on her phone when an ungodly clatter sounded on the porch.

She jumped from the couch just as a wave of testosterone broke over the room: Gabriel, along with Sheila's boys Lannie and Bill, as well as – she blinked; no, she wasn't mistaken – Damien. Followed by a grinning Luke, lugging a cooler.

'Look who I found!'

'Um.'

'They were all on the fishing charter! I invited the boys over here for a sleepover. Thought we could grill the fish this evening, have a bonfire once it gets dark.'

'Um.'

Even as she tried to process it, the boys' beeline for the refrigerator distracted her. 'We're hungry. Got anything to eat? Hey, can we have this?' Gabriel pulled out a pan of lasagna that Luke had made a couple of nights earlier, ostensibly designed to get them through the weekend as they continued the myriad chores involved in settling into the house.

Now she realized he'd known Gabriel was coming. 'Sure. Have at it.'

They did, yanking open kitchen drawers until they found the silverware, scooping cold forkfuls straight from the pan. Nora felt as though she were watching a video on fast-forward as the contents of the outsize pan disappeared before her eyes.

Did you even think about asking me?

But she couldn't say it. Not in front of the boys. And she couldn't bear to wipe the joy from Luke's face.

'Reminds me of myself at that age,' he said now, watching them. 'My mother used to joke that she needed to take out a loan to afford to feed me. Boys. You know?'

She didn't, never having been one, nor having had one of her own. Even the wilderness program where she'd met Luke had been for teenage girls, who posed a different sort of challenge.

'Hey. Clean the pan when you're done,' Luke called to the boys, who gave no sign of having heard him as they bolted from the kitchen into the yard, a delighted Murph bounding in their wake.

'You were smart not to come, though. The water was a little rough. A couple of people were hanging over the side of the boat. Even I got a little queasy. The boys were fine, though. And Sheila and Spencer – they looked just at home on a boat as they do on land. Makes sense, given that they grew up here. Sheila caught the biggest fish! Speaking of which.'

Sheila was on the trip? Had they planned that in advance? She shrugged the thought away.

He'd just said something, hefting the cooler for emphasis.

'Excuse me?'

'Want to help me clean these?

Oh. Hell. No.

Nora congratulated herself on her admirable restraint. Really, she deserved a freaking Oscar. All she said, with the biggest smile and the breeziest tone she could manage, was:

'You caught 'em, you clean 'em. I'm heading out to the Store of Everything to restock the fridge. Maybe, just maybe, it's got enough food to get that teenage plague of locusts through the next few hours.'

She didn't go to the store, not right away.

She drove to the nearest beach access road and parked the truck, stomping across the sand to the water's edge, trusting the ocean's calming influence.

But it seemed to mirror her own thoughts, churning fierce beneath a darkening sky. Luke had said the waves were rough and, for all that the trip had somehow resulted in a home invasion by a herd of boys, she was doubly glad not to have been on that boat.

She and Jeremiah had fled just such a storm the other day. Now, mindful of his words about rogue waves, she backed a few yards away from the water, but lingered, mesmerized by the storm's growing power. A gust scooped up sand and flung it at her. Thunder growled a warning. Rain swept the sky.

So much for Luke's plans for a backyard barbecue, she thought as she raced for the truck, focusing her attention on practical matters. She texted him that she'd pick up frozen pizzas as a backup plan. When she got home, she'd fall back on her classroom experience to be the sort of den mother the weekend demanded of her. It was Monday. Within twenty-four hours, all the boys except Gabriel would be back in their own homes. And on Wednesday, Luke and Gabriel would be in the car, speeding to catch Gabriel's flight out of Portland.

She could survive that long.

She glanced at her watch. She'd only been gone for fifteen minutes. Luke was probably so busy with the boys that he wouldn't pay attention to the clock. She had time to act on some of the information she'd gleaned from Delilah. She'd find a way to talk with Spencer another time – it would seem too weird to drop by the spaceship twice in one day.

She reverted to her original plan and headed for Betty's instead.

FORTY-THREE

She'd made her snap decision on the chance that she'd hit Betty's just before the lunch rush, and she was right.

She took a seat at a two-top across the room from an elderly couple who were the only other diners. Janie dropped the disinfectant-soaked cloth with which she'd been wiping down tables, grabbed a coffeepot, and poured her a cup without being asked.

'Don't worry, it's fresh. You're not the only one who needs constant caffeination. Oyster sandwich, extra oyster for the cat?'

'You know me too well.'

Janie raced to the kitchen to put in Nora's order as though she were coping with a full house, then hustled back with the coffeepot to top off the mug Nora had already half-drained.

'For heaven's sake, Janie, take it easy. Pull up a chair. Join me.'

Janie started to shake her head, then changed in mid-shake to a nod. 'On second thought, let me just put this pot back on the warmer.'

Nora watched her walk away. Janie wore her usual attire, a black T-shirt with Betty's logo of a coffee cup beside a doughnut with a bite taken out of it, and a short denim skirt that showed off thighs and calves toned by the miles she walked between the dining room and kitchen.

When Nora had seen Janie with her husband at the town meeting, she'd seemed tiny, almost frail beside his bulk. On her own, she looked lithe, strong, with the sort of restless energy that might appeal to a man whose wife had just left him for one of the peninsula's most prominent citizens.

Janie returned with a mug of her own and pulled out two chairs. She sat in one and draped her legs across the other. Her ankles were puffy above her sneakers. 'Ah, God, my feet are killing me. First time I've been off them since six. The bakery person called in sick again today so I'm pulling double duty. Plus, I've got an overnight side hustle a couple times a week working in one of those big warehouses across the bridge. I guess I just wasn't meant to sleep. God, I can't wait until I can quit both these jobs.'

She leaned back and closed her eyes. Nora felt a pang. She looked forward to her own retirement, still more than a decade away. Janie was years younger and working for the kind of paychecks that didn't allow for generous contributions to a retirement fund.

Given her punishing schedule, Nora wondered how she managed the extramarital adventures Delilah ascribed to her. She remembered how tentatively she'd approached Sheila about her fling with Ward. But at least Sheila had been safely single. Asking a married woman, especially one she barely knew, whether she'd strayed with the man who later became the peninsula's best-known murder victim seemed at best inadvisable.

'I bought a painting by someone who lives here. Jeremiah Wendover. You probably know him,' she ventured. Maybe if she started with him, they'd eventually get around to Ward.

They did, but hardly in the way she expected.

Janie's feet hit the floor with a thump. 'Oh, I know that bastard.'

Nora supposed Jeremiah deserved that. If he'd told Nora about Janie and Ward, he'd probably told others.

'When I heard Ward was gone, it was a shock. Not that he died – the way that guy worked, I figured he'd keel over someday – but that someone killed him. I was afraid he'd kill himself after what Jeremiah did to him.'

A bell dinged across the room. Janie jumped up.

'That'll be your sandwich.'

Nora couldn't imagine focusing on the sandwich after what she'd just heard.

'Here. Tartare sauce on the side, and some ketchup for your fries.' Janie was back in dervish mode, spinning on her heel and reaching for the rag she'd abandoned on one of the tables.

'Wait. Janie, wait.'

She spun back, the rag hanging from her hand.

'What was the bad blood between Ward and Jeremiah?'

Janie snorted. 'What it always is with guys.'

'A woman?' Good lord, had Jeremiah slept with Janie, too? A detail that Delilah had forgotten to mention, maybe because it was one degree of separation too far to matter.

Janie shook her head. She yanked two pens from her apron pocket and slapped them side-by-side on the table.

'This.'

'Pens?'

'Oh, come on. Which one's longer?'

Nora shrugged. 'They look the same.'

'To you, sure. But to guys, it's always about measuring dicks. Ward headed Preserve the Peninsula. Jeremiah thought *he* should. Thought he had better ideas than Ward about how to run it. He undercut Ward at every chance possible. Did you meet him when you bought the painting?'

Nora shook her head. It was true, kind of. Jeremiah hadn't been in the gallery when she'd selected it.

'If you ever do, watch your back. Don't let that mild-mannered bullshit fool you. Guy's a snake. Preserve the Peninsula was about to go under because of the way Jeremiah was badmouthing Ward behind his back. Not around here – he's too slick for that – but with the rich folks who help fund the lawsuits, the kind of people who like that ugly shit he paints. Oops, sorry. No offense meant.'

'None taken. Luke's right with you on that front. But, Janie, you don't think Jeremiah . . .' She couldn't bring herself to say it.

Janie had no such squeamishness.

'Killed him? Good lord, woman, why do you think I look so tired? It's not just the work. I spend half my nights staring at the ceiling, wondering if I got the wrong guy when I told the cops I thought it was Harold.'

Nora gaped. 'How in the world could you mistake Jeremiah for Harold?'

Janie twisted the towel in her hands. 'It was dark. Tall skinny guy in a ball cap. Long hair.'

Nora bit back the obvious, the thing that Harold's public defender had pointed out that day at the courthouse: The peninsula – heck, probably the whole country – abounded with tall, skinny guys in ball caps. 'Have you told the cops?'

Janie rolled her eyes. 'Yeah. You can imagine how glad they were to hear from me again, given how credible I was the first time. They wrote his name down, but that was about it. Said they'd add it to their list. Town this size, how long can that list be?'

The door opened and a young couple with a toddler and an infant came in, tourists from the look of them, taking advantage of the cheaper shoulder-season rates. 'Ten to one, that baby screams half the time they're in here,' Janie muttered. 'I gotta go.'

Nora stared down at her sandwich, her appetite gone. She retrieved a to-go box from a table just outside the kitchen door and took it down to the beach, where she plopped down in the sand and ate it while staring at the waves, wishing one would send some comprehension her way.

FORTY-FOUR

The long weekend she'd so dreaded passed more easily than she'd feared.

The invading pack of boys worked to her advantage, far more interested in one another than they were of her. Luke even gave her permission to ignore them.

'The last thing they want is to be forced to interact with us. I can't think of a better way to make Gabe feel more at home here than to spend time with them. Our job is to make sure they don't hurt themselves or somebody else with stupid teenage shenanigans, but to otherwise stay out of their way.'

Which proved to be easier than she'd imagined. The boys alternately ate, watched videos, raced around the yard with Murph, and then came back inside to eat some more until, as exhausted and dirty as the dog, they flopped on various horizontal surfaces in near-comatose sleep.

Nora stepped gingerly around them, picking up empty bags of chips, orange peelings and water bottles. She collected improbably large sneakers into matched pairs and lined them up beside the door, then returned for the sweatshirts they'd shed. Finally, she fetched an armful of blankets and spread one over each boy, gasping when she inadvertently stepped on Lannie's leg.

'No need for quiet,' Luke advised. 'They're down for the count. You could drive a locomotive through here right now and you couldn't wake them. Remember, they've been going since before dawn. Come to think of it, so have I.'

His mouth gaped wide in a yawn. He headed for the bedroom. 'Let's hit the hay. Morning's going to come early.'

Nora looked at the immobile forms on the floor and sofa. 'Surely they'll sleep in, as tired as they are?'

Luke gave one of those fond chuckles that she'd come to read – and resent – as commentary on her woeful ignorance when it came to all things boy.

'They'll be up at first light, rarin' to go. And hungry! I'll try to beat them to the punch and grab a couple dozen doughnuts from Betty's. That ought to hold them, oh, for an hour or two.'

At least he'd offered to take responsibility for breakfast. 'Thanks for that,' she said as she climbed into bed beside him. But he was already drifting into sleep.

She lay awake beside him, her mind gnawing at the threads of information she'd gleaned from Delilah and Janie, unable to weave them into a satisfying whole. She wrote off her conversation with Delilah as simply bizarre, the woman veering from tears of self-pity over the ostracism from her neighbors after her new marriage to unbecoming snark about Janie's alleged play for her new husband.

Janie had described Jeremiah as viciously undercutting Ward at every turn, but Jeremiah himself had sketched an image of easy friendship, the two of them sharing confidences about women and work over frequent beers.

If Ward were still alive and Jeremiah were truly intent upon ousting him, the need for such subterfuge would be understandable. But, even with Ward gone, nothing Jeremiah had said indicated he had any interest in running Preserve the Peninsula.

Nora pushed away the possibility that a nascent attraction to Jeremiah might have made her miss some obvious clue as to his real attitude toward Ward. She rolled over and wrapped an arm around Luke as though to further dismiss the thought – rejecting as well her relief that he was too tired to respond to her gesture.

*   *   *

Despite Luke's prediction, the boys slept until nearly noon on Tuesday, when Sheila and Delilah showed up to retrieve their sons.

'You're a saint,' Delilah said. 'Spencer and I actually had a night to ourselves. We drove up to Portland and ate at this amazing Ukrainian restaurant. They cover the whole table with little plates of delicious things. Such a nice change from these endless oyster dishes. It's a shame there's nothing like that here – although, it gave me some ideas for one of the restaurants in the Mare Vista.' Her voice caressed the name.

She turned to Sheila. 'What did you do with your night off?'

'I stayed in.' Sheila. 'But I bet I had way more fun for way less money than you two.'

Nora shook her head. 'You're incorrigible. Plant Man?'

Sheila winked. 'You should see my place. Every time he comes by, he brings a new plant. It's starting to look like a regular greenhouse in there. Last night, he brought orchids.'

'I love orchids,' Delilah sighed.

'Bet if you let Spencer know, you'd end up with an armful.'

Delilah forced a smile. Nora thought she must hear things like that all the time from people who even as they passed judgment would trade places with her in a minute.

'Anyway, the orchids were a farewell of sorts.'

'What?' Nora and Delilah spoke in unison.

'I thought you two were having fun,' Nora added.

'Oh, we were.' Sadness tinged Sheila's smile. 'But fun only goes so far. He's not into kids. I told him if he wanted to keep seeing me, the kids were part of the package.'

'He bailed? Oh, no.'

'Oh, yes. Believe me, I'm used to hearing it. Not everyone is as lucky as Delilah.'

Her first shot had been a tap. This, a straight-up jab. Nora jumped in to prevent a full-on punch, maybe verbal, maybe not.

'Where is Spencer, anyway? I thought maybe he'd pick Damien up.'

Delilah cocked her head and fixed Nora with a heavy-lidded gaze. 'This is the second time you've asked about my husband's whereabouts. Why the interest?'

'I, ah.'

Saved by the boys, who stampeded into the room, decibel level increasing as they vied to tell their moms about their weekend.

Nora gathered stray belongings, matched them with the appropriate boys, and ushered them from the house, closing the door behind them and nearly collapsing against it.

Luke caught her. 'Congrats. You survived the invasion of four pre-teenage boys. That's no mean feat.' He kneaded her shoulders, knuckling deep the way she liked. 'But it's great to have Gabriel to ourselves for the rest of the day, isn't it? Let's head down to the beach and see if we can find some sand dollars to take back to his friends in New Mexico.'

For once, Nora's enthusiasm wasn't entirely feigned. She'd rather suffer Gabriel's scorn than dwell on Delilah's pointed warning. If she had to guess, Delilah was probably just issuing a retro sort of hands-off-my-man message. But the reason didn't matter.

Delilah's antennae were quivering on high alert, which meant that Nora would have to steer clear of Spencer Templeton. She'd need to find her answers elsewhere.

FORTY-FIVE

B ut first, a beach excursion with Gabriel. How hard could that be?

Plenty, Nora found out.

There was the matter of getting him to the beach at all. 'Aw, man. I'm still fried after yesterday. Can't I just stay here and sleep?'

His bleary-eyed gaze might have been convincing had it not been fixed on his phone, his thumbs a blur over the screen.

'If you're so tired, maybe you want to put that away so you can actually sleep.' Nora's words were bad enough. The tone that accompanied them – the verbal equivalent of a slap – was worse.

Luke, who'd bent to tie his shoes, snapped to attention. He and Gabriel swiveled to face her, their expressions so similar they'd have been funny if Nora hadn't had the distinct sensation of trying to extract herself from emotional quicksand.

Instead, she dug herself deeper.

'Your father's chosen to live here. Maybe you could take the time to learn something about this place, especially if you're going to be spending a lot of time here. So let's put down the phone, put on your shoes and go to the beach.'

That sort of thing generally worked in the classroom.

This wasn't the classroom.

'Who are you to tell me what to do? You're not my mom. You're not even my stepmom.'

This is where Luke was supposed to step in and tell Gabriel that it didn't matter, that Nora was an adult deserving of respect, especially given that Gabriel was a guest in her home and even more especially that she was his father's . . . girlfriend? Ugh, too teenager-y. Lover? No, not with its whiff of illicit sex. Partner? Fine, if they were in business together.

At least Gabriel got one thing right. For sure, she wasn't his stepmom, and maybe never would be, if the expressions on father's and son's faces were any indication.

Luke cleared his throat. 'You go ahead and catch up on sleep. You and I can go back to the beach later. Or you can catch up with us now if you change your mind in a few. Nora?'

Luke made it sound like a question.

She knew it wasn't.

So she left the house on command, sweeping with as much dignity as she could muster past the teenager who'd just shown her exactly where she ranked in his father's affection.

Luke didn't wait until they got to the water's edge.

They stalked in silence along one block, two. Nora was not going to speak first, and she most certainly wasn't going to apologize.

Luke cracked when they got to the main street that ran along the beachfront.

'What the hell were you thinking, talking to my kid like that?'

She spun to face him.

'What the hell were you thinking, letting your kid talk to me like that?'

They stood like mirror images, arms akimbo, shouting to be heard above a wind that whipped froth from the waves. Bits scudded across the sand and rolled across the pavement. Luke kicked at one, scattering it like so much dandelion fluff.

A car coasted past, the driver's head swiveling toward them, hand raised in a wave. Just as Nora recognized Sheila, she saw Sheila's own recognition of the moment's tension. The car sped away.

'You didn't give me a chance to say anything. You jumped on his case right away, like he was one of your students. But he's not. He's my son and I only get to see him a few times a year and now you've ruined one of those times.'

Were those tears in his eyes? *Fuck.*

Nora's vow to herself vanished. 'I'm sorry. I'm so sorry.'

Luke turned his head. When he faced her again, his eyes were dry. 'I'm not the one you should be apologizing to.'

Nora bit her tongue to hold back what she'd been about to say: *I'm not going to apologize to that brat.*

She forced herself to unclench her jaw, her fists. To drop her arms to her sides. To speak in something other than a scream.

'Go back to him. You need your time together. I'll take a walk, and if he wants to walk with us later, that's fine. If not, that's fine, too. Look.'

She pointed up the beach, where three figures left a car and ran toward the waves. 'There's Sheila and her boys. I'll visit with her for a while. That'll give us all time to calm down.'

She held her breath.

'Good idea,' he said finally.

But when she reached for him for a hug, he'd already turned away.

'The nerve of that kid!'

Nora poured out the whole story to Sheila, pausing only to grab ineffectively at the Frisbee when it came her way.

'He couldn't have been more obnoxious. And Luke didn't do a damn thing about it.' She hurled the Frisbee back toward Lannie with such force that he ducked rather than try and catch it.

'Easy there. My kid didn't do anything to you.' Sheila gave

her a funny look. 'This was the first time you'd met his son? How long have you and Luke been together now?'

'About a year.' She waited for the Frisbee, but Lannie and Bill started tossing it back and forth to one another, perhaps opting for safety by leaving the adults out of the equation. 'But I'd never met him. Luke visits him in New Mexico a few times a year.'

'How have you communicated with him up until now? Phone? Well, of course not. I know kids hate talking on the phone. Text? FaceTime?'

Now Nora wished for the distraction of a Frisbee. 'None of that. We'd never talked before. For all I know, this is the first time he realized Luke had someone in his life.'

'Yikes.' Sheila made a face. 'That's not good. Word of advice?'

Nora thought back to Luke's face, so tight with anger he'd gone white around the mouth.

'Anything. I'm in uncharted waters here.'

'Make nice with the kid. Gabriel, right? Grovel if you have to. Yeah, he was being a jerk, but you were, too, and you're the adult here. Make sure when he leaves that you two are on speaking terms. And then start communicating with him. Whatever it takes, a quick text here and there, photos of the dog doing something silly.

'Don't expect an answer right away. Maybe never. But he needs to know that if he ever feels like reaching out, you'll be there without a bit of judgment coming his way.'

Nora dragged the toe of her shoe through the sand, drawing figure eights. 'That's not what they told us in all those teacher-training classes. It was all about polite-but-firm, drawing boundaries, stuff like that.'

Sheila echoed Luke's words of minutes earlier. 'He's not your student. He's the most important person in the world to the man you love. And keep that in mind, too – Gabriel will always come first to Luke, and that's exactly how it should be. If you can't accept that, maybe you two shouldn't be together.'

Nora doubled over with the gut punch of recognition. Sheila had said aloud the thing that wriggled up from the recesses of her brain in the dark of night as Luke lay snoring contentedly beside her.

She felt Sheila's hand on her back, the same calming gesture offered an upset child.

'Are you OK?'

'Sure. I'm going to have to figure it out, right? I mean, we just bought this house together. Splitting up isn't an option.'

She turned to Lannie and Bill. She might as well practice on them before heading back to the house. 'Hey, guys! Throw that thing this way.'

They did, albeit cautiously, in such a slow and gentle arc that she very nearly snagged it, but for Sheila's barking laugh.

'What's so funny?' She chased the Frisbee down. 'Sorry. I'll get the hang of this yet.' She managed a passable throw, with a sense of accomplishment that surprised her.

'You,' Sheila gasped between guffaws. 'Saying splitting up isn't an option. From what I've heard about you' – it figured that Sheila, like everyone in town, had heard about the very public spectacle when Nora left her husband – 'splitting up is your superpower.'

FORTY-SIX

Nora had stomped out of the house furious with Gabriel and Luke.

She stomped back pissed off at Sheila.

Superpower, indeed. She'd show her. She'd make getting along with Gabriel her superpower. She stopped to text Luke.

'What's G's favorite food? Dessert? I want to make his last night here special.'

She held her breath until the three dots appeared, signaling a pending response.

'Honestly? McDonald's. Guess his mom doesn't let him eat there.'

She typed so fast she had to stop and start over again, rather than fix each typo. 'Great! There's one in Seacrest. If it's OK w/ his dad, that is.' Smile emoji.

A thumbs-up came back at her.

She took a moment to visualize the tourist traps along Seacrest's main drag and typed anew.

'There's a video arcade there, too, if you think he might like it. Could be fun for all of us.'

Once again, Luke eschewed words in favor of an emoji. This time, a heart.

Nora shoved her phone back into her pocket and sauntered toward home, a smile on her face and a taunt on her lips.

'Take that, Sheila.'

McDonald's was a hit. Gabriel stowed two Big Macs, two chocolate milks, large fries and a McFlurry somewhere within his skinny frame while Nora made a pretense of nibbling at a plain hamburger.

So was the arcade, although Nora could barely hear Luke and Gabriel's victorious whoops when they scored points in a series of incomprehensible games over the machines' decibel-defying jangling and beeping.

Gabriel exchanged looping swags of tickets for a big Nerf gun, and while he never thanked either of them for the evening, he managed a 'good night' to Nora after he hugged Luke at bedtime.

For his part, Luke was so thrilled with the evening that Nora thought they might finally indulge in some lovemaking unencumbered by resentment. But when she rolled close to him and ran her hand down his bare torso, he pulled away.

'Shhh. Let's just sleep. Gabriel might hear us.'

Because a teenager might be shocked to find out that adults have sex?

A thought Nora – this evolved, understanding Nora – kept to herself.

A wasted effort, she realized the next morning, when Luke and Gabriel left for the airport.

She had a moment's shock, then elation, as Gabriel pulled her close for a hug.

Take *that*, Sheila!

'Bye, honey,' she said. 'Can't wait to see you next time.'

He raised his voice – 'Bye, Nora' – then whispered in her ear. 'You didn't fool me for a second last night. There won't be a next time. You might as well kiss my dad goodbye now.'

He pulled away, hefted his backpack and turned to Luke, still beaming at the two of them.

'Let's go, Dad.'

Their exit belied one part of Gabriel's gibe.

Luke didn't kiss her goodbye.

Nora took Mooch and Murph and fled.

Not far – just to Electra, which had always felt like a refuge, its aluminum walls curving around her like an embrace.

She made coffee, serving it from the silver coffeepot that was the sole remnant of her mother's tea service, willing the extra formality to soothe her vibrating nerves. The animals, who always knew when something was wrong, hung close, Mooch purring on her lap and Murph lying across her feet.

She pulled back the curtain and took in the view of the waves surging and receding just yards away. Farther out, an undulating flash signaled porpoises working their way north on their daily feeding runs. While she appreciated the extra space afforded by the house, she'd missed her sea view, along with the sound of the waves lulling her to sleep on the nights she slept in the trailer.

The house. She'd been quick to cite it to Sheila as the reason she and Luke had to stay together. Why hadn't her love for Luke been her go-to?

Sheila's words played on a continuous loop. 'Maybe you two shouldn't be together.'

And: 'Splitting up is your superpower.'

What if Sheila was right?

As much as the taunt rankled, she couldn't deny the impulse even now thrumming through her veins to hitch Electra to the truck and flee to parts unknown, much as she'd done when she'd caught her husband cheating.

Except Luke hadn't cheated. As Sheila had also pointed out, he'd merely presented her with the person he loved most in the world. To be sure, he'd been clumsy and admittedly even unfair by springing Gabriel on her without warning. But maybe he'd felt that was his only choice, given that she'd never shown an interest in the boy. Maybe, just as she'd spent much of the weekend in simmering acrimony, he'd done the same, given her graceless interactions with Gabriel.

She dropped her head to the table and addressed Murph and Mooch.

'I've really gone and done it this time.'

Murph groaned to his feet and laid his head on her knee. Mooch dug his claws into her thighs as though to cling to her no matter what she might decide.

'Ow.' She jumped. Her elbow grazed the coffeepot. She caught it before it upended and held it high, studying it.

It had belonged to her mother, a woman who'd spent the entirety of her adult life staring fixedly away from unpleasant truths. Until the very end, when she'd squared her narrow shoulders, lifted her delicate chin and faced the worst within herself, acknowledging that she'd ruined entire lives.

And now here was her daughter, wanting to run away again. Why? Because she faced the same problem presented to thousands, probably millions, of blended families around the world?

Nora set the coffeepot aside and bent over her mug, hoping to inhale sense along with fragrance. She wouldn't have to face Gabriel again for a few months. In the meantime, she could do exactly as Sheila suggested, reaching out to the boy in the most minimal, noncommittal ways.

She'd ask Luke to tell her stories about Gabriel. Instead of dancing around the subject, they'd *communicate*. Wasn't that the linchpin of all successful relationships?

Besides, although she probably shouldn't have cited the matter of the house to Sheila as her first reason for staying with Luke, the fact was undeniable. When she fled her marriage, she and her husband had already quit their jobs and sold their home. Now, she was committed to half a mortgage. A job. And even a place. For all its cloaking dampness, the peninsula had grown on her, with its mercurial mood shifts from storm to sun, its restless winds, its murmuring waves.

But was she truly committed? Because no matter how she tried to deny it to herself, she'd indulged in a silly flirtation with Jeremiah. What did they call it? Emotional infidelity? It hadn't even gone that far – at least, she didn't think it had – but the fact that she'd been sneaking around to see him spoke for itself. She'd set him up in her mind as the sympathetic foil to Luke's occasional sternness. But if what Janie said was true, Jeremiah was capable of the same sort of ruthlessness she'd seen in Ron and Spencer. He just hid it better and employed it for a different cause.

All this time, she'd thought Jeremiah simply wanted to find out who killed his friend. It hadn't occurred to her that he could wield such knowledge in a way that would make him Ward's heir apparent. And he'd used her to obtain it.

Nora knocked her head against Electra's aluminum wall. 'Jesus, I'm a fool.'

The animals tilted their heads. She rose, dislodging them, and poured the rest of the coffee down the sink and rinsed and dried the silver pot.

'Crisis over,' she informed Mooch and Murph. 'Let's go back to the house. I mean, *home*.'

Maybe, when Luke returned, she'd even find something good to say about the gold sofa – a thought that prompted a laugh so loud Mooch and Murph skittered away. Even the most well-intentioned compromise had its limits.

Still, as she left the trailer, her hand lingered on its silvery flank. No matter how resolute her intentions, Electra's presence meant she still had an escape.

FORTY-SEVEN

Luke had vowed to wait at the airport until he was sure Gabriel's flight had departed, a wise precaution given the increasing upheaval of air travel. He wouldn't be home for hours.

The energy of renewed purpose surged through Nora. She decided not to waste it. She dropped the animals back at the house and drove to Jeremiah's. She needed to get something straight.

He saw her through the window and waved, greeting her at the door with a brush in his hand and a wide smile on his face.

'Nora! I was going to call you, but this is even better. You won't believe what I have to tell you.'

He stepped aside to let her in. She stayed on the deck.

'I don't want to hear anything you have to say. This isn't a social call.'

The smile faded. 'What do you mean?'

She'd spent weeks tamping down her confusion and frustration – everything from the veiled threats over her students' projects to Damien's constant needling and finally the debacle with Gabriel – none of it caused by Jeremiah. But he was the one standing before her and when the dam on her emotions broke, he took the resulting flood full force.

'All that bullshit about your friendship with Ward. What was that about? When you were doing everything possible to undercut him?'

The brush dropped from his hand, daubing the floor with the color of rain-streaked sky.

'What in God's name are you talking about?'

'Knock it off.' Nora paced a circle on the deck. 'I am so tired of everybody playing me for a fool. Why did you want me to find the architect? Did you think he'd tell you something that would finally discredit Ward? Even though Ward was already dead? Wasn't that enough for you? Did you have to go and trash his memory, too? Some friend.' She practically spat the words.

Jeremiah stooped to retrieve the brush and ventured onto the deck, holding the brush at arm's length before him as though to fend her off.

'What. Are. You. Talking. About.'

Nora knocked the brush from his hand. 'Cut the crap. You wanted to run Preserve the Peninsula. Ward was in the way. And from what it sounds like, he was sleeping with half the women on the peninsula. Was that part of the problem? He had the job you wanted and all that sex, too?'

Jeremiah's eyes darkened to the shade soaking the tip of the unfortunate brush.

'Cut the crap yourself. I have zero – less than zero – desire to run anything. Do you see me stepping into Ward's job? As far as I can tell, Preserve the Peninsula is about to go under and while I think that's a shame, I don't begin to have the kind of skills needed to save it. As far as women, all I know about are Janie and Sheila. I don't know what kind of math they teach at

your school, but in my book two hardly counts as half. Maybe
it does in yours, though.'

Nora pressed her hands against the heat rising in her face.
She'd also slept with two people since her marriage ended, and
hardly viewed herself as the swath sort.

'May I?'

When she didn't answer, Jeremiah took her hands and pulled
them away, peering into her eyes. Concern creased his face. 'I
don't know where you're getting this stuff, but it's crazy talk.
Next thing I know, you're going to accuse me of killing Ward.'

'Did you?' She'd already gone so far overboard the question
seemed like a foregone conclusion.

He jerked away as though she'd slapped him. 'I'm not going
to dignify that with an answer. You need to leave.'

'Gladly.' She tried to infuse her voice with ice, to walk in a
near-saunter to her truck, replaying the conversation with Jeremiah
on a continuous cringe-worthy loop on the short drive home.

She'd let her emotions get the best of her, accusing when she
simply should have asked. Because he'd seemed genuinely
puzzled with none of the defensiveness she might have expected
from a guilty man. She probably owed him an apology.

A thought she abandoned as soon as it arose. Because despite
his evident bewilderment – whether real or masterfully feigned
– Jeremiah had not denied killing Ward.

Luke returned from Portland with a driving rainstorm at his heels.

He stood dripping just inside the door. 'Coming down in
buckets doesn't do this justice. Dumpsters, maybe. Tanker-trucks
full. I got soaked just running from the car to the house.'

Nora handed him a towel. 'Those are awful metaphors.' She
raised her voice to be heard over the drumbeat on the roof and
held out another towel.

Luke shed his shirt and took it, rubbing his skin red. 'It's
supposed to be like this for days. School is going to be a
nightmare.'

'Don't remind me.' After a house full of boys for a single
twenty-four-hour stretch, Nora had relished the prospect of the
merely mild chaos of the classroom. But the kids would be wild
without the pressure release of recess. Peninsula schools were

like most in their rain-soaked region: Recess usually meant taking an extra few minutes to don slickers and rubber boots. This, though, was the aqueous equivalent of a high plains blizzard.

Once the kids arrived in the morning, they wouldn't set foot outside again until the final bell – bad enough on a single day. She couldn't imagine a longer stretch. At least, thanks to the long weekend, there were only two schooldays left. And unlike her time with Gabriel, she'd be able to escape her students each night.

Luke looked at his sodden shirt on the floor and then at Nora. 'Crazy idea here.'

Nothing, she thought, could be crazier than the way he'd sprung Gabriel on her.

'Try me.'

'I'm exhausted from the drive back. I barely got up to fifty miles per hour the whole way home. The last thing I feel like doing is cooking. You?'

As if Nora ever felt like cooking. It was good to laugh with him again.

'Betty's it is,' he said. 'Even though it means going out in' – he pointed to the window, vibrating under the deluge – 'that.'

They weren't the only ones braving the storm.

'Bad weather brings everybody out of the woodwork,' Janie said as she filled their water glasses. 'My guess is, they can't stand the idea of being cooped up with one another. And for some strange reason, they tip better on nights like this. I'll be dead on my feet when I get home tonight, but it's worth it.'

Nora and Luke had snared the last table, a four-top. The door edged open and two men squeezed through as fast as they could, but not quickly enough to prevent a damp gust from sweeping the room.

Clark Stevens and Gerry Fields, the art gallery owner and his biologist friend, shed their slickers and hung them on the over-burdened pegs beside the door, Betty's futile attempt to limit the puddles to a single corner.

They surveyed the room, their glances stopping on the only two empty seats. Nora tried not to make eye contact but it was too late. Luke waved them over.

'You don't mind?' Gerry asked, even as he pulled out a chair.

Nora decided to make the best of it. If nothing else, she had two experts in all things peninsula at hand.

'How often does it get like this? I don't remember this happening last winter. A bad day here and there, sure. But a whole week?'

'Specials for everybody? Would make my life easier.' Janie was back, daring them to order differently.

'Um, sure.' Nora looked to the others, who nodded assent. 'Just for the record, what is it?'

'Spaghetti and meatballs.'

Clark brightened. 'Score! I like seafood as much as the next person, but it's good to get a break. Thanks, Janie.'

She met his hopeful smile with a scowl. They were, Nora remembered, on opposite sides of the hotel development.

Clark sighed and turned to Nora. 'As to your question, this isn't typical. You can thank climate change. We got lucky last winter. But for the last few years we've seen more and bigger storms. Just for good measure, they last longer, too.'

'Oh, for the love of God.' Janie was back. 'We've had big storms here forever. Remember 2011? That was a damn mess. What about the floods back in '96? And that storm hundreds of years ago that supposedly drowned all the trees? How is it climate change if it keeps happening? Sounds like "climate same" to me.'

'Those were one-time events, not week-long storms like this one is supposed to be.' Gerry's voice had something of the teacher in it. Nora supposed he gave lectures in his role at the research station. 'And the one around 1700 was a tsunami trigged by an earthquake, not the atmospheric changes we're seeing now.'

Janie tilted her pitcher precipitously. Water sloshed over the rim of Gerry's glass and pooled atop the vinyl tablecloth.

'Maybe some more napkins, Janie?' Gerry called after her. But she gave no sign of having heard.

Clark threw his own napkin atop the puddle. 'Face it, Gerry. You're never going to win her over. Remember how Ward tried? Got him nowhere.'

Nora bit her lip. From what Jeremiah had told her, Ward might not have changed Jamie's views on development, but he'd won her heart, at least for a while. Which reminded her. First she'd felt guilty about enjoying Jeremiah's attention. Now regret nagged at her because of the way she'd lobbed her poison-tipped accusations. Maybe Clark could help her decide whether she'd been justified.

'How are things at the gallery?' she blurted.

Clark brightened. 'Did you find the perfect place to hang the painting? I'm so glad it found a home with you. It was one of my favorites. How do you like it, Luke? Nora has excellent taste.'

'It's, ah . . .'

The spaghetti's arrival saved him from a reply, at least momentarily. Luke took an immediate bite of a meatball, chewing long and thoughtfully. But when he finally swallowed, Clark still beamed his way, eyebrows raised.

'Interesting. It's interesting.'

Clark and Gerry laughed knowingly. 'Don't worry,' Clark reassured him. 'Jeremiah's work isn't for everyone. But I'm glad Nora enjoys it.'

Nora tried again. 'About Jeremiah. I thought all of you warriors marched in lockstep. But it sounds as though he and Ward had quite the rivalry.'

Clark and Gerry looked at each other, then back at her.

'Rivalry?' they asked in unison.

'I heard somewhere,' she started to say, but stopped. That would only invite questions as to where she'd heard it. 'I guess Jeremiah didn't like the way Ward ran Preserve the Peninsula.'

They were like mirror images, eyebrows shooting up, jaws hanging open.

'Why in the world would you think that?'

'B-b-because Jeremiah wanted to run Preserve the Peninsula. He thought he'd do a better job than Ward, especially since Ward's divorce.' OK, that last part was pure embroidery but it lent – she thought – probable cause to Jeremiah's doubts.

Gerry twirled a forkful of spaghetti so savagely the sauce splattered his shirt. 'Oh, this is getting out of hand.'

'What is?'

Gerry dipped his napkin in his water glass and dabbed at his shirt while Clark took over.

'This whispering campaign against Ward and everything he stood for. My personal belief is that Chairman Bailey is behind it. He'd never admit it, but he's running scared from Melanie and has convinced every developer and every fan of development that she'll regulate them right out of business. He won't come right out and attack her personally. Preserve the Peninsula is a dog-whistle. Now that Ward's out of the picture, he's going after his friends.'

Nora's own spaghetti lay untouched. She ran a fork through it, trying to appear at least as interested in her meal as she was in the conversation. She even took a bite and mumbled through it, oh so casually. 'So they really were friends?'

'The best. Besides, anyone who knows Jeremiah knows he doesn't have a vicious bone in his body. He's always been that way. Look at us.'

She did, baffled. Gerry lay his hand atop Clark's. 'When we were growing up, not everyone was, let's say, as evolved as they are today. Kids were cruel. But never Jeremiah. Nor Ward, for that matter.'

What about Spencer, she wanted to ask. Or Ron or Janie or even Delilah?

But she'd heard enough. She looked across the room at Janie, laughing obligingly at something a customer had said, even as her eyes skittered around the room, keeping track of which table needed attention next.

Janie had wanted her to think ill of Jeremiah. Why?

Maybe, in the clumsiest way possible, she'd been trying to protect Nora, to warn her away from Jeremiah. She might have seen them together, despite their precautions, or at least seen Nora steering her bicycle off the main road toward his house. Maybe, just as Jeremiah had predicted, the peninsula was already buzzing with talk about their presumed illicit pairing, something to lend a little sizzle and spark to the dreary days ahead.

Damn. It seemed she owed Jeremiah an apology, a big one. Yet she dared not approach him, not in public and apparently not even in private.

'You've barely touched your spaghetti. You feeling OK?' Luke, eyes full of concern.

No, she was not.

'A little sick to my stomach.'

Which, finally, was the truth.

FORTY-EIGHT

Nora waltzed – as much as one can waltz in Wellingtons and flapping slicker – into Everhart's office on Thursday morning with a stack of printouts and a straight face.

She'd combed the kids' surveys for every positive comment they'd received about the tsunami tower and excerpted them as 'proof' the project was nearly universally loved. She'd fallen back on her days as a public relations specialist and prepared a list of talking points that she memorized and then practiced until they sounded unrehearsed.

The only thing she lacked was a shovel to spread the bullshit she'd be laying upon Everhart.

'As you can see, there's overwhelming support for the project.' She wasn't stupid. She knew a complete whitewash wouldn't fool Everhart, so she'd included a few negative comments. 'Aside from a predictable and insignificant minority, you'll find that my students' survey accurately reflects the views of the community.'

Nora made her voice high and hopeful.

'Please, Mrs Everhart. They've worked so very hard on this and learned so much in the process. We're on track not just to meet the goals we set for the project, but to exceed them. Once we're done, I've even thought about contacting the *Peninsula Press* for a story about their work. Maybe they could even run the students' stories. It would be nice to see some positive press about the school.'

That last said with wide-eyed innocence. Because how could Nora possibly know about the last time Peninsula Middle School had been in the news for anything other than sports stories or features about the annual holiday pageant? She hadn't even been living on the peninsula when a custodian opened the utility room door and saw the school psychologist and a teacher engaged in some very hands-on therapy.

She hoped Everhart wouldn't realize the obvious: She'd heard about it within days of arrival at the school, if for no other reason than that the scandal created the job openings that allowed her and Luke to be hired.

Whatever the reason, she left Everhart's office so relieved she walked into her classroom with a smile, one that vanished within minutes. By midday, Nora had questioned nearly every single belief she had, especially concerning the innate goodness of children. It hadn't occurred to her that they'd already been cooped up for days at home, and that school – for all that they were still indoors – represented a release of sorts.

By lunchtime, she'd already foisted a pop quiz on each of her classes and had handed out three after-school detentions – a punishment that applied equally to her, given that she'd have to stay late and supervise.

She fell onto the sofa next to Sheila in the break room. 'I've already tried everything I know to try and get them to settle down and not a single one has worked. And this weather is supposed to continue through tomorrow. How do you handle this? Dose their juice boxes with Xanax?'

Sheila lifted her hands. 'If I thought I could get away with it, I would. I wish I could help. There's enough pent-up crazy in this building – and that goes for us teachers, not just the kids – to blow the roof right off it. We're just going to have to tough it out.'

Nora's lunch awaited in the refrigerator across the room, but she didn't have the energy for the few steps it would take to retrieve it. 'That's what I was afraid you were going to say.'

Sheila went to the fridge, found the Tupperware container with Nora's lunch, and lobbed it toward her. 'Eat. You're going to need your strength.'

Nora pried off the top. Luke had re-created the hand pies they'd enjoyed at the coffee shop in Portland, filling them with a ground lamb and potato combination. She took a bite, then another bigger one. Sheila was right. It helped.

'I'm going to need my strength for more than dealing with the kids. Does everyone in this town hate everybody else?'

Sheila twisted to stare at her. 'Why in the world would you ask that?'

She'd thought it over during the night, huddling against Luke as the house shuddered in the wind. Her first impulse had been to attribute Janie's words about Jeremiah to an awkward warning. But Janie had homed in on his friendship with Ward, and her slander had been particularly vicious.

And it wasn't just Janie talking smack about Jeremiah. She thought the woman's frostiness toward Delilah, Delilah's snark about Janie in return, and of Ron and Spencer's confrontations.

'Just . . . people seem cranky.'

Sheila relaxed against the sofa's ratty cushions. 'You think it's bad now? Wait until February. It's a miracle Ward's the only person who's been murdered here. Oh, God.' She dropped her head in her hands. 'Did I just say that?'

'Say what? I didn't hear anything.'

Sheila threw her a grateful smile. 'Thanks, friend.' She pointed to the clock. 'We'd better eat our lunches. We've got fifteen minutes before the bell, and as bad as those little monsters are now, they'll be worse on an empty stomach.'

She stood and held out her hand. Nora groaned but took it, letting Sheila pull her from the safety of the sofa toward the table.

She knew Sheila was right; that the dreadful week launched a lingering winter that would test everyone's mettle. But the harsh words that so troubled her had been uttered in the waning golden days of summer, including her own unforgiveable treatment of Jeremiah.

Gossip be damned, she needed to apologize.

She'd go to him, olive branch in hand. But first, she needed to procure said olive branch, something that would prove she'd made an effort to win back his trust. She was pretty sure she knew what would suffice.

She hadn't gotten the name of Kirk Lopez's daughter during their too-brief phone call. But it was in the obituary and, in a rare stroke of luck, the woman turned out to be nearly as prominent as her father, with her own boutique firm with a website that – hallelujah – listed a phone number.

Nora called as soon as she got home from school.

Martina Lopez Meadows was out, a frosty-voiced receptionist informed her.

'When do you expect her back?'

'Not for some weeks.'

Of course. According to the obit, she was an only child. In addition to her natural grief, she'd be dealing with her father's house and finances.

'It's really important that I talk with her. It's about her father.'

The woman's sigh was long and aggrieved. Nora wondered how many phone messages, to say nothing of emails and texts, had piled up in Lopez's absence.

'Fine,' she said in a tone that told Nora it was anything but. 'I'll take the message.'

Nora doubted Martina would ever see it. It had been a Hail Mary, anyway. She'd hoped Kirk Lopez had told his daughter whatever he'd apparently told Ward, and that maybe the daughter would pass that information on to her – something she could bring Jeremiah, along with her apology.

But it seemed as though she was going to have to grovel empty-handed.

She checked the clock. Just 4 PM. Luke had a meeting at the high school in Seacrest that he expected would keep him until about 5. Plenty of time for her mission, especially as she was driving. No one rode a bike in this weather.

She reached for her still-damp slicker by the front door and stuck her feet in her boots. Murph, usually alert and eager at the least sign of a walk, took one look and ran for the bedroom as fast as his aging joints would allow. 'I don't want to go, either,' she called to him.

Her phone buzzed as she opened the door. She slammed it shut and answered.

'Am I speaking to Nora Best?'

Nora glanced at the number. Not the one she'd called earlier, but a Portland exchange nonetheless.

'Is this Martina Lopez Meadows?'

'Yes. And you are . . .?'

'We spoke earlier. I'm from the peninsula. I'd visited with your father . . .'

'Oh, this is unbelievable.' Martina cut her off. 'Don't you ever quit? Dad told me someone had shown up at his house twice – twice! – bugging him about something on the peninsula. But at least now I have your name. Which I'll be happy to pass on to the police.'

The line went dead.

FORTY-NINE

T wice, Martina had said. And, 'someone'.

But she'd immediately assumed that someone was Nora, which meant the person probably was a woman.

Which meant . . .

The morning in the bakery came back to her. Janie and Delilah giving each other the stink-eye. Janie ignoring Delilah, homing in on Nora. 'Are you still trying to track down that architect?'

Janie, who'd been sleeping with Ward, but who was dependent on the income her husband earned from the projects Ward opposed. What had she found out about the tower that threatened Ron's paycheck?

Tumblers shifted and turned within her brain. A few slid into place.

The fight she and Luke saw between Ron Stevenson and Spencer Templeton. Spencer: *Don't forget who gave you this job.* Ron: *Don't forget why you gave it to me.*

Why, indeed? Because of something Janie had found out? What was wrong with the tower?

Nora's fingers twitched on her phone. She wanted to text Jeremiah, or even call. This information felt like the olive branch she'd been seeking. But he probably wouldn't take a call.

Anyway, her suspicions were just that. The mental padlock guarding the answers remained stubbornly closed. She'd wronged Jeremiah too grievously to go to him with anything less than concrete evidence. Hadn't she?

The phone jumped in her hand.

Later, she'd blame her foolishness on the worst kind of wishful thinking. She swiped into the call without looking into the screen, gasping: 'Jeremiah?'

There was a pause. A grim chuckle.

'Am I speaking with Nora Best?'

That voice. So familiar. But she couldn't quite place it.

'Yes?'

'You don't sound sure. If I remember, there were a lot of things you weren't sure about.'

She knew this person, and not in a good way, not given the crawling feeling along her spine.

'Who is this?'

'So soon you forget. This is Detective Eberle. I just got a call from Portland PD. They – and I – would like to talk with you about . . . well, I'd like to talk with you about a couple of things. But for now, let's discuss your, ah, pursuit of a man named Kirk Lopez.'

If Nora had learned one thing in her previous encounters with law enforcement, it's that she didn't have to say a goddamned thing.

She said a few things anyway.

'Pursuit is hardly the word I'd use. I'll save you some time, Detective Eberle. I did visit Mr Lopez – once.' She gave him the date and approximate time. 'I doubt I was there even five minutes. We spoke briefly. I never set foot inside. Let me stress again that it was the only time we spoke. If I understood Mr Lopez's daughter correctly, I'm not the only person from the peninsula who visited Mr Lopez. Perhaps you should seek out that person and then decide whether you still need to speak to me. I can assure you that if you do, it will be in the presence of my lawyer.'

Bold words.

She rang off, hoping he hadn't heard the tremor in her voice. For good measure, she turned off her phone.

She could have given Eberle Janie's name. Maybe she should have. But if she were wrong, his suspicion would only deepen. Just as with Jeremiah, she'd need more information.

She'd have to go back to Portland. Her only hope of talking with Lopez's daughter was to do so in person. If she tried another call, the woman would go right back to the police.

She wanted coffee but needed calm. She dug a tin of loose herbal tea out of the back of the cupboard, made herself a cup, stirred in honey and tried to think it through.

Martina might call 9-1-1 the minute Nora introduced herself, but at least Nora would have a prayer of a chance of getting the information she needed before she had to fend off Eberle again.

But how in the world would she explain another trip to Luke? Something that quickly turned into the least of her worries.

'Nora? Nora!'

Luke banged into the house, not bothering to shed boots and slicker, puddles in his wake. 'Nora, what the hell is going on?'

He stood over her. Rainwater sluiced from his slicker onto the table.

She hadn't told him about Everhart's plan to kill her class project. That had to be what he was talking about, right?

Wrong.

'I just got a call from that detective. The one you said Spencer mentioned. The one who kept bugging us after . . .'

After. It was still unspeakable.

But that wasn't what troubled Luke. 'He said you went to Portland and bugged some guy. A dead guy now. When in the world did you go to Portland?'

Nora slid down in her chair. 'We went there together. Luke, you're getting water everywhere.'

He unzipped his slicker and let it slide to the floor. Watery tendrils probed their way across the kitchen floor. Murph nosed at one, looked from Luke to Nora, and wisely retreated.

Luke's face worked through degrees of puzzlement. It was still contorted when he said, 'I don't get it. We didn't go to anyone's house.'

Nora lifted her mug, took a sip, and kept it to her face, an inadequate shield.

'It was when we went to the coffeeshop. You were reading your book.'

Comprehension dawned slowly.

'You left.'

'Yes.'

'You said you were going to get a book. And' – understanding flashed, wiping away the previous confusion – 'you came back without a book.'

He sat, so suddenly and so hard she feared for the chair creaking beneath him.

What the hell no longer sufficed.

'Nora,' he said, 'what the fuck?'

She told him.

Sort of.

She reminded him of her first encounter with Ron, of the argument they'd later seen between Ron and Spencer. She told him how Ron knew before she did that Everhart wanted to cancel her project.

She didn't tell him her growing concerns about Janie. And she never mentioned Jeremiah's name.

'Somehow all of this has something to do with the architect. I just wanted to find out.'

He shook his head throughout.

'I just don't get it.'

'What don't you get?' To be fair, given her abbreviated version, there was a lot not to get. But he focused on something else.

'We talked about this before. A long time ago, if I remember correctly. This doesn't have anything to do with you. With us. You told me you'd dropped it.'

'I never told you that. You assumed.'

'And you let me think it.'

They glared at each other across a widening divide.

At what point, Nora wondered, does the gap become too immense to leap? She chose to sidestep.

'What did you tell Eberle?'

The anger drained from Luke's eyes, replaced by a pain so naked she looked away.

'The truth: that I had no idea what he was talking about.'

His words hung in the air between them.

She was supposed to say something now. 'I'm sorry.' 'Let's talk this through.' Or even the unthinkable: 'Here's the rest of it.'

She thought all of those things.

But she didn't say any of them.

Luke made a small, helpless motion with his hands. 'I'm too tired to even think about dinner. I'm turning in.'

Nora closed her eyes and waited for the slam of the bedroom door.

She heard footsteps, back and forth, followed by the click-click of Murph's nails across the floor, trailing Luke. Rustling. The click of light switch. A deep masculine sigh, followed by a canine one.

She opened her eyes and leaned from her seat so that she could see into the living room, where Luke, wrapped in an old quilt, had just settled himself on the sofa, with Murph on the floor by his feet.

Nora sat in the kitchen until she was sure he was asleep.

Then she tiptoed past him into the bedroom, where she slept alone and woke to see he'd already gone.

FIFTY

The only saving grace to the school week was that it was short.

Nora had spent all day Thursday putting out behavioral fires of varying strengths. On Friday, she turned to a teacher's time-honored last resort: movie day. With a straight face, she announced *Jurassic Park* as a movie about the consequences of development – especially development meant to draw tourism – without considering the disadvantages.

'How might this play into our project about the tsunami tower?' she asked. Uselessly. They didn't care, and truth be told, neither did she. She shrugged off their protests that they'd all seen the movie before – some several times.

'We're only watching half today. We'll watch the rest on Monday.' As she expected, the promise of starting the week on an equally easy note calmed them. She dimmed the lights and clicked the 'start' arrow. She patrolled the aisles during the early, boring parts and held her breath when, despite knowing what was coming, they squealed in delighted horror when the cute little dinosaur flared its frill and zapped avaricious Nedry with deadly venom.

Nora slid along the wall until she reached the door and cracked it open, expecting to see Everhart heading toward her classroom with the same alacrity with which the *Dilophosaurus* pursued Nedry, ready to douse Nora with verbal venom.

But the hallway was empty and echoey, and Nora took her desk at last, making a note to herself to have the kids research the ways in which the movie's *Dilophosaurus* varied from the real one. Because this was an education exercise, dammit.

She smiled to herself, knowing that just down the hall, Sheila was showing her own students *Hidden Figures*, tailor-made for math class. She looked at her watch. Only twenty more minutes until the end of this dreadful day. The minute the bell sounded, she'd happily walk hatless and coatless through the downpour to get to the nearest strong drink. Because she still hadn't solved her Saturday problem. She and Luke had made up, sort of, which meant they'd taken the path of least resistance by acting as though nothing had happened.

They moved gingerly about the house, speaking in short sentences about safe topics: His day. Hers. And always the rain, whose ongoing barrage had become so familiar Nora could – almost – tune it out.

They'd shared a perfunctory, embarrassed cheek-kiss Friday morning before getting into separate vehicles to drive to school. Which Nora welcomed except that it left her with the problem of finding a believable excuse to be away from the house long enough on Saturday or Sunday to drive to Portland and back – alone – in order to confront Martina Lopez Meadows and find out who else from the peninsula had so badly wanted to talk with her father.

She toyed with the idea of coming clean to Luke about her intentions to pursue another conversation with Martina. But each time she mentally rehearsed broaching the topic with him, reality gave her a swift kick and she fell back on the idea of simply leaving the house without explanation on Saturday morning and facing the consequences when she returned – a thought that made her grateful Electra remained as a retreat.

Then Friday night brought a pair of miracles.

Nora had curled up on the sofa after another stilted but civil conversation over dinner, decompressing with her favorite medical show on her iPad.

Footsteps vibrated across the floor. Luke yanked out her earbuds and pulled her to her feet.

'Nora. Listen.'

She covered her ears with her hands. 'Please, Luke. It's been a rotten week. I'm not up for a talk now. Can it wait until tomorrow? I just want to chill.'

He lay his finger across her lips. '*Listen.* What do you hear?'

She shook her head. 'Nothing. Not a goddamn thing.'

Luke beamed. 'Exactly.'

'What the . . . Oh, my God.' She ran to the window. She could see things through it – the yard, trees. The *sky.* All of it hidden for days behind draperies of rain.

She ran to the door and flung it open. Held out a hand and pulled it back, examining her palm.

'It's dry!'

Luke had followed her. She spun into his hug. 'It's dry!'

'It's dry.' He buried his face in her hair. 'Nora, let's promise something.'

She stiffened. 'What?'

'From now on, full transparency. No more hiding things from each other.'

'Um.'

He must have taken it for assent, because he released her and whistled for Murph. 'Come on. The weather app says this is just a little break. Let's hit the beach while we can.'

He tugged her hand – her wonderfully dry hand – and headed for the door. 'Anyway, it's just as well it'll rain again tomorrow. They dropped an all-day training on the county's guidance counselors tomorrow. We'll get extra pay, but it doesn't make up for losing a weekend day.'

Miracle Number Two, Nora thought. She went full Supportive Partner. 'We both committed to these jobs. If a weekend training day is part of the deal, so be it.'

She ran ahead of him onto the sand, fearing he'd rightfully question her if he glimpsed the elation on her face. Her sort-of-agreed-to transparency was going to have to wait a day. She no longer needed to think up an excuse to drive to Portland.

She was in her truck and gunning for the mainland minutes after Luke's departure the next morning.

As predicted, the rain was back, although gentler, a mere atmospheric pout after days of full-on tantrum.

The all-news station continued its wearying recitals of records broken, along with associated destruction: mudslides that swallowed homes, gaping sinkholes that made roads impassable, the costly halt to construction projects. The broadcaster rushed through a recital of national and world news – Congress already into its year-end wrangling over a spending bill, a volcano on an obscure island chain in the far reaches of the Pacific, the state legislature trying to figure out how to wrangle still more tax money out of legal weed – before launching into a lengthy interview with a local psychologist who delivered the dog-bites-man fact that the prolonged rain played hell with people's emotions. The psychologist suggested ways of combatting it, including daily light therapy.

'Maybe you'd like to fund twenty of those lamps for my classroom,' Nora challenged the disembodied voice. She tried to imagine her classroom aglow with manufactured sunshine, something that purported to spark more energy in its recipients. Just what she needed.

Nora shut down the radio. She needed to focus before she spoke with Martina – if, indeed, she was lucky enough to find Martina at her father's house. It was the only place she could think to look, given that an online search for Martina's home address proved fruitless.

What if she found her? And what if Martina confirmed that Janie indeed had visited her father? What would it mean? All Janie had done was warn Nora away from Jeremiah. She'd sniped at Delilah – the wife of the man who'd appointed Janie's husband as his foreman. Maybe Janie had become caught up in whatever bad blood boiled between the two men. And even though she was one of the most outspoken proponents of those projects, she'd slept with their chief opponent.

Nora had tossed and turned so through the night that at one point Luke rolled over to ask what was wrong. She'd briefly thought about sharing her confusion as part of their next-level openness. But he'd never seemed particularly interested in the fallout surrounding Ward's death, beyond the ongoing uncertainty around how he died and who might have killed him.

'People are complicated,' he'd probably respond, which is what he usually said when she questioned him about some of the classroom dynamics, an answer so bland it made her grind her teeth.

She could just imagine his incredulity if she dared to voice her wavering suspicion about Janie.

He'd make some smartass remark – 'What'd she do, brain him with her menu pad?' – that would only echo her own doubts.

There had to be a logical explanation. And if Martina didn't slam the door in Nora's face, please God she would supply it.

Martina didn't slam the door.

Nora barely recognized the polished professional in the website photographs. Martina Lopez Meadows was small, haggard, face free of makeup and hair pulled into a messy ponytail. She wore sweats that had seen better days and the hand gripping the door was clad in a thick yellow rubber glove.

'Yes?'

'I'm Nora Best. I called . . .'

There it was. The door swung hard against Nora's hastily extended foot.

'Ow. Look, I know I'm bothering you at the worst possible time, and I'm sorry for that, truly I am. But you said your father told you someone had bugged him twice about the peninsula.'

'And now you're going at it a third time.'

'No. I only visited here once. And I never went inside. I've told the police the same thing. I don't blame you if you don't believe me. But if I'm telling the truth, it means someone else was here the day your father fell.'

Martina let go of the door but folded her arms across her chest and continued to block the opening with her body.

Nora spoke fast. 'I know this sounds crazy, but apparently your father knew something about the tower being built on the peninsula.'

'What tower?'

'Sort of a platform. For if – when – there's a tsunami.'

The anger faded from Martina's face. Recognition replaced it.

'Oh, that tower. Right. He said someone had talked with him about it a couple of months ago.'

Ward.

'My father didn't have anything to do with it.' Martina started to close the door again.

'Wait.' Nora wanted to grab the woman and shake the answers out of her. 'There was something wrong with it. It threatened an endangered species, maybe. Something like that.'

Martina shook her head. 'No. That wasn't it.'

'What was it?'

Martina told her.

Nora grabbed the doorjamb for support.

'Does that mean what I think it means?'

Maybe Martina said something else. All Nora registered was her long, slow nod.

Nora happily would have collected speeding tickets all the way from Portland back to the peninsula – if only she'd been able to speed.

The weather forecast turned out to be all too accurate, the previous week's rain seeming like spring showers compared to the volume of water battering the truck, in fierce competition with a wind that seemed determined to shove her off the highway.

At one point, she joined a line of vehicles that had pulled to the side of the road, hoping for either a break in the weather or to gather their courage for a fresh attempt at getting wherever they were going.

Nora guessed most of them lived in the area, with only a few miles to their destinations. On a unicorn day with light traffic and dry roads, she faced a two-and-a-half-hour-drive home. Now she doubted she'd get home before Luke.

It didn't matter, anyway. She was done keeping information to herself. She intended to share what she learned with the world.

But she'd start with Jeremiah. She owed him that much. A wavery light, blinking red, caught her attention. The car ahead of her pulled back onto the road, its driver signaling like mad to warn the nonexistent oncoming traffic.

Nora tapped Jeremiah's number into her phone and got a mechanical beeping in return. She held her phone to her face. Zero bars. The storm must have knocked out a cell tower.

'Damn it!' She pounded the wheel.

Farther ahead, another car turned onto the road. If she exercised all the powers of her imagination, she might see the storm's strength lessening. She took a breath. The information would hold until she got back. The important thing was to get home safely.

If phone reception returned on the way home, she'd call Jeremiah. Luke, too. Or she'd tell each of them in person. But after that, she'd go straight to the police.

FIFTY-ONE

Nora's speed crept up – thirty-five miles per hour. Forty. Fifty. At which point, she realized that while winds still dragged her truck back and forth across its lane, the rain had slowed to a near drizzle.

She was almost home. She tapped the brake and eased through the sharp turn from the mainland onto the peninsula, where she found herself in the kind of traffic she hadn't seen since Harold Wallace's court appearance. Where in the world was everyone going?

The wind howled louder and Nora clenched the wheel, ready for another wrestling match. But the truck cruised straight and true. Only her thoughts swerved, away from the reality that the sound came from the tall speakers placed at intervals the length of the peninsula, wailing their warning.

Luke ran from the house as soon as she pulled into the driveway, Murph giving him a run for his money.

'Nora!' He pulled her into his arms. The dog pressed himself against her legs. 'I was so worried about you. Where have you been?'

'I don't even know where to start. I have so much to tell you.' She shouted over the sirens. 'What a crazy time for a drill.'

'It's not a drill.' He sprinted back to the house, reached inside and grabbed a carrier containing a yowling Mooch. 'Come on. I was just about to leave for Highview Hill. I've been trying to text and call but couldn't get through.'

'Same here. I think the storm hit a cell tower. What's happening?'

He opened the truck door, helped Murph in and practically threw Nora in behind him. He sat the cat carrier on her lap.

'There was a volcano somewhere—'

'In the Pacific. I heard about it on the radio. About a zillion miles away.'

'Maybe that's why this is just an advisory, not a full warning.' He pulled up at the base of the hill, next to a few other cars. 'Looks like not everybody thinks it's worth the effort. I didn't want to take any chances. If nothing else, it's good practice. Plus, it'll be fun to watch the wave come in.'

Nora huffed up the hill behind him. 'You've got a weird idea of fun.'

'I'm not the only one.'

People stood in knots facing the ocean, which as though exhausted from the week-long beatdown by rain and wind stretched gray and nearly motionless but for listless riffles against the sand. Nora scanned the beach for the campground where her trailer rested along with a handful of others, not so much as even a low dune between them and the beach and the water beyond. She pointed. 'Will Electra be OK?'

Luke shrugged. 'Should be. Depends on how high the wave is. They're not expecting much, according to the alerts I'm getting on my phone.'

Nora cursed herself. She'd meant to set up the tsunami emergency app but had never gotten around to it. She saw Jeremiah among the onlookers. She'd thought to try and give him her news in private, but maybe this was better. He couldn't hang up on her, shut the door, ignore a text. She took a step toward him.

Luke tapped her arm. 'No wonder we're so lonely up here. Everybody's on the tsunami tower. Look.'

Nora spun back. '*What?*'

Work on both the tower and the hotel project had stopped days earlier, the successive storms too much even for Ron Stevenson's rain-adapted crew. But the tower stood nearly completed, stairs climbing to platforms at forty and fifty feet, only the safety railings lacking.

People packed both platforms, as others no doubt crowded the bluff at the peninsula's southern end, everybody eager for the spectacle promised by Mother Nature.

'They've got to get down! It's not safe!'

Luke shook his head. 'I know it's not finished. Looks like the storm knocked down the security fence. They'll get a way better look at the wave this way. Anyway, as long as they keep back from the edge, they'll be fine. Nobody's getting blown off today. The wind's finally stopped.'

Luke was right. Flags drooped sodden against poles, and the whippy sea grasses that bent prettily beneath the slightest breath stood tall and proud.

'No!' Nora screamed. 'They've got to get down!'

'What in the world are you talking about?'

Another voice sounded behind Luke.

'Nora?' It was Jeremiah.

But she'd already started back down the hill, slipping a little on the muddy path. An inarticulate roar went up from those atop the hill. Luke caught up with her and dragged her back. 'Too late. The wave's coming. Holy shit. Just look at that.'

'But . . .'

Nora cast a last glance toward the tower, then steeled herself to face the ocean.

A hump rose on the horizon, long and very low. The tightness in Nora's chest eased. 'I've seen bigger waves during a full moon,' she blurted. Maybe things would be OK.

Jeremiah moved beside her and spoke low, an unnecessary precaution given the rise and fall of the sirens, the excited chatter of the crowd. 'Nora, what's wrong?'

'Ward wasn't worried about an endangered species. The tower's not safe. Something to do with the soil beneath it, combined with its height and the weight of people on it. That thing never should have been built. Those people shouldn't be up there. But that little wave . . . Still, do you know anyone who might be over there? We need to call, tell them to get down.'

Luke stepped between them. 'Who's this? Nora, what are you saying?'

'This is Jeremiah, one of Ward's friends. The guy on the beach who bugged Abby that day . . . oh, never mind. Whose numbers are in your phone? I've got Sheila's – I'll call her and tell her that if she's up there, to get down and make sure everyone else does, too. You guys call everyone you can think of . . .'

They shook her heads at her in unison.

'Too late.'

'What do you mean?'

The crowd roared, nearly drowning out the sirens.

She didn't know whether Luke spoke, or Jeremiah. 'They can't come down. They'll be in the water. It's almost here.'

The silly little blip on the horizon rolled toward them, a sheet unfurling but somehow growing larger at the same time.

'It's not that big. It's not that big.' Nora might have been praying.

And indeed it wasn't, not even a foot high, a judgment Nora made as it hit the campground and swirled around the base of her Electra, which rocked and bobbled as the water rushed past, but somehow remained upright.

It swirled across the road, jostling cars, catching up loose objects like trash cans and bicycles and signboards and carrying them along.

'It's not that deep,' she whispered as it surrounded the supports for Spencer Templeton's luxury cabanas and then the legs of the tower and still it came on, slower now, thoughtfully, as though choosing what to swallow next. It drowned the school playground under several inches of water and climbed the two steps to Betty's front door. Faint cheers reached her from those on the tower as Betty opened the door and shook a broom at it, as though to shoo it away.

All around her on Highview Hill, people wielded cell phones, capturing photos and videos. The water slowed to a trickle, the crowd turning as one to watch as it wandered inland, hesitating at the edge of Nora and Luke's lawn.

Then, slowly, slowly, it retreated, hesitating intermittently as though about to change its mind, wrapping itself around a less fortunate house, probing for a way in, nudging aside a few final things. A toddler's pink plastic playhouse drifted back toward the ocean.

Nora sagged in relief. 'It's going to be OK.'

Jeremiah reached for her arm. 'No. It's not. Oh, Jesus, Nora. Look.'

A scream arose from those around them, the shrieks from the tower sounding a faint echo.

Nora's own wail joined the chorus as the tower shuddered sideways, hung for an agonizing moment, corkscrewing as a support sank deep into the sand, flinging people from the platforms, bodies soaring with arms outstretched toward the nonexistent railings before splashing into the roiling water below.

FIFTY-TWO

Jeremiah moved first, sprinting past the frozen onlookers and heading down the hill.

'Come on!' Nora followed, losing her footing halfway down and ending up on her ass in the six-inch-deep lake that now surrounded the hill. Luke ran past, reaching down to grab her arm and hauling her in a half-crouch behind him until she finally regained her feet.

He flung open the truck door, threw in the cat carrier and gave Murph a boost onto the seat. Nora started to climb in, but he pulled her away.

'It might not start or it'll quit on the way,' he yelled. 'All that salt water – quicker like this.'

She splashed behind him, pushing through the water in a waking version of a leaden-legged nightmare, one whose true horror dawned as they reached the fallen tower. Bleeding people stumbled past them, heading inland. Other simply sat dazed in the water. Jeremiah and Luke lifted one inert form after another, draping them across car hoods and in pickup beds.

The utter silence, but for the gurgle and splash that accompanied each movement, unnerved Nora more than any scream or moan. Luke, once they'd ascertained no one else lay sneakily submerged, fell back on his training as a wartime medic, going from one person to another in a hasty triage. The onlookers from the hill belatedly arrived, their vehicles having betrayed them as Luke predicted.

'This is a nightmare. We shouldn't be moving them. But the

unconscious ones would have drowned otherwise. Nora and – what's your name again? – tell all these so-called helpers not to touch any of these people on the cars. God knows who has spinal injuries. And try and steady the kids. Where are their parents?'

Child-free Nora, so recently judged and found wanting in the sort-of-step-parent department, rushed to their defense. 'Living their lives. Doing things people do on weekends – running errands, doing all the things they can't do during the work week. Do you see any little kids here? No, it's just the bigger ones who safely could be left at home alone. Who knew there'd be a damn tsunami? Don't you think they feel guilty enough already?'

She turned her back on him, checked her cell phone and finally saw a signal. She headed for a boy with blood cascading down his face. 'Luke. Your bandana.' She took it and wiped the boy's face, only then recognizing her student Matthew Dexter. He didn't even look at her, his eyes wide and staring at some point past her.

'Matthew, it's Ms Best. There's a lot of blood, but you only have a shallow cut. That's how it is with head wounds. They look a lot worse than they are. I'll keep pressure on it. You take my phone and call your mom and let her know you're OK. Just promise not to FaceTime her.'

Someone splashed through the water toward them.

'Luke? Thank God you're safe.'

Sheila's voice came high and thready, her face bleached of color.

Luke took her hand in both of his. 'Nora and I were on the hill. We got here as fast as we could. Where are your boys?'

Sheila's laugh wobbled. 'Never again will I complain about those stinkers being plugged into their headsets on their stupid video games all day. I was on the mainland, loading up at one of the box stores, when I got the alert. The boys said they never even heard the sirens and God forbid they should check their phones. Once I knew they were safe, I tried to call you guys. Panicked when I couldn't reach you.'

Nora took her phone back from Matthew and guided his hand to the makeshift bandage on his head. 'Keep pushing against that. And try and clean your face off a little better before your mom gets here.'

She rinsed the blood from her hands in the water, wishing she could as easily rinse suspicion from her mind. Sheila's children had been safe at home. But she'd rushed to the scene not to check on her own students or her children's friends but to see if Luke and Nora were all right. Or, maybe – Nora scrubbed harder at her hands – just Luke.

In the end, nobody died.

'It's a fucking miracle.' Melanie James turned toward Nora, coffeepot in hand, then sat suddenly and burst into tears. Nora gently took the pot from her hand and filled both their mugs.

Nora remembered Melanie's barely concealed agitation the day she'd asked Melanie for a meeting about Abby. Now Melanie made no attempt at concealment. 'Abby's going to be all right. But she could have died,' she managed to say. 'And I voted to approve that damn thing.'

Abby lay wan on the couch in the next room before a television playing an endless loop of the Disney classics – *Frozen*, *Beauty and the Beast*, *Mulan*, *Coco*. Neon-green casts held her arms rigid. She'd rocketed head-first from the tower, throwing her arms up at the last moment to break her fall.

George James rubbed his wife's back. 'She probably saved herself from a head injury. We need to count ourselves lucky, Melanie. Even if nobody died, so many have it worse.'

Broken limbs abounded. Janie was in traction in the convalescent center with a broken hip, which at least would heal with time, unlike her household finances. Neither the waitressing at Betty's nor the moonlighting gig at the warehouse came with health insurance. Likewise, Spencer Templeton hired his crews on a contract basis, so Ron also lacked health insurance and his cracked ribs and broken tibia meant it would be a long time before he could climb scaffolding or swing a hammer again. A GoFundMe account was their best hope, but they were hardly the only ones who'd taken that route.

Nora was on her second day of visiting injured students – or at least, their families. Zeke, the budding financier, had landed safely atop the relative cushion of other bodies, only to be side-swiped by a steel beam. 'His parents are with him at HarborView in Seattle,' an aunt, white-lipped with worry, told Nora. 'They've got doctors there who specialize in these things . . .' Her voice trailed off. 'I'll let them know you stopped by.'

Sworn enemies Jeannie Graves and Matthew Dexter had grabbed one another's hands and clung together until the last possible minute, launching into midair and somehow falling free of the cascading bodies and metal as the tower finally collapsed completely. Both suffered concussions, but no worse.

'Jeannie refuses to sleep in her bed. She wants to be on the floor so she can't fall,' Belinda Graves said. 'And she wants to be with him every waking moment.' The two sat side by side on the sofa, hunched over their Switch games. Under any other circumstances, Nora would have laughed. Now the sight made her want to cry.

Nate Gilmore had a ruptured spleen. Madison Everett's ankle full of pins forever ended her dream of becoming a placekicker for the Seattle Seahawks.

And several students would need plastic surgery to realign smashed noses and jaws. Classes had been canceled for at least two weeks because so many students, teachers and staff were injured. Water damage meant the school building itself would remain closed through the end of the semester.

Meanwhile, a second flood inundated the peninsula, this one of news vans roaming the streets, where they found no shortage of residents willing to opine on the disaster, whether they'd been there or not.

'Lucky, my ass.' Melanie's tears stopped as abruptly as if she'd cranked an internal faucet. 'This never had to happen. I want every last bastard who had anything to do with this put away.'

'I hear Spencer has already lawyered up.' Oh, Nora had heard plenty while making her rounds, laced with so much vitriol she'd not have been surprised to see a mob with pitchforks and torches marching on the spaceship.

Melanie blew her nose into a napkin. 'For once, it'll be a fair fight. All those trustafarians among Ward's Warriors, the ones who got tired of underwriting the cause over the years? They're back in full force, and they won't hear any talk of an out-of-court settlement. It'll take years, but some of those kids' injuries are for life. Put them in front of a jury, and all the money in Spencer Templeton's world won't make a damn bit of difference.'

She toed the trash can pedal and dropped the napkin inside. 'You know the saddest thing?'

'I can think of a lot of sad things. What's the worst?'

'It took a disaster of this magnitude to bring this town together. All the pro-development types are just as hot to go after Spencer as everyone else. Meanwhile, it seems Brock Bailey has very quietly let it be known he won't be running for re-election.'

'Does that mean you're going to be our new commission chair? Should I offer congratulations or condolences?'

Melanie rewarded her with a smile, even as Nora wondered at the single-minded focus on Spencer. It felt almost as though everyone had forgotten about Ward.

FIFTY-THREE

B ut she hadn't forgotten him, and she knew who else prob- ably hadn't, either.

Luke had done her the favor of not asking where she'd gone the day the tower collapsed; or of how she knew of the danger. Nor did he ask where she was going when she wheeled her bike away from the house a few days later.

'Want company?'

Guilt, already occupying far too much real estate in her psyche, claimed new territory. 'No, thanks.'

He shrugged and turned away.

Not a good sign, she knew. They'd have to deal with their shit sooner rather than later. But first, she had to deal with her own shit.

Cycling was a challenge. Debris still littered the road, every- thing from broken glass that threatened her tires to patches of sand carried inland and deposited across the roads, no problem for cars but so deep that at one point she got off the bike and carried it across.

The exertion took the edge off the anxiety she felt as she tapped at Jeremiah's door. She backed away before he answered, standing just off the deck, holding on to her bike, ready to pedal away the minute he ordered her off his property.

But he didn't. Nor did he invite her in. He simply stood wordless in the doorway.

'I was an ass,' she began.

He lifted an eyebrow, his meaning clear.

'*Am* an ass.'

A nod.

'But I was even more of an ass that day. I was all worked up over a whole bunch of things and took it out on you . . .'

The nod became a head-shake. What would it take to draw even a single word from him?

'Damn. I'm sorry. I promised no excuses. Just an apology. I was wrong. Really wrong. That's all I came to tell you. Actually, there's one other thing. The day the tower collapsed? I'd gone to Portland. I talked to the architect's daughter.'

Now both eyebrows shot up. Nora took it as encouragement.

'Someone else came to see Kirk Lopez the day he fell. Or the day he was . . . whatever happened to him. He called his daughter to tell her about my visit. Then he told her he had to hang up. That there was someone at the door. She thought that because of what he'd just said, that it was me. But I didn't go back after I left. Someone else did.'

Jeremiah cocked his head.

'A woman.'

She'd hoped for a single word. She got it.

'Janie.'

It wasn't a question.

'Remember how I said I had something to tell you? Before you went Defcon One on me?'

Nora covered her face with her hands. 'I'm so sorry. I'll be sorry forever.'

'Forever might be overkill. A decade or so will do.'

She peeped between her fingers, hoping for a smile. She was pretty sure she saw one. She dropped her hands.

'Done. What did you have to tell me?'

'Why don't you come in first? Get comfortable. I suspect this will take a while.'

She realized as she followed him indoors that she'd never been inside his house. It was small and spare but for the riot of color covering nearly every inch of wall space. Paintings, pen-and-ink drawings, rough sketches and photographs hung from floor to ceiling. Nora stopped and stared.

She recognized Jeremiah's work among them, but most were unfamiliar.

'They're from friends' work,' he said. 'Say I help someone knock out a wall so he can turn a room in his house into a studio. Or I stay with a single mom's kids so she can go to the opening of her show in a Seattle gallery. None of us has any money to pay for work like that. So they give me a painting or two. I do the same thing. Look.'

He pointed to an oversize image of a woman's face, so daubed with gray in a way that suggested shadows – or bruises. Her eyes stared into the viewer's, her gaze flat and disinterested – or dead.

Nora couldn't tear her own gaze away. The woman's lips were slightly parted. A final breath? 'Whoa. That's really disturbing. And interesting.'

'That single mom? It's her early work. I could sell it tomorrow and pay my bills for the rest of the year. And theoretically, that's what I should do with some of these. Problem is, you get attached. I know there are people who buy art as an investment – I've been lucky enough to make some of those sales – but for me, it's an emotional thing.'

'Same,' Nora murmured. She felt that way about his painting that hung over her sofa. She liked to stretch out and stare at it, noticing something new each time.

She forced herself to sit. As much as she wanted to hear what Jeremiah had to tell her, she could have stayed for hours, moving from one work to the next, absorbing the emotions evoked by each.

He waited until she'd settled herself.

'Remember how I offered to go through court records; to see if I could find something, maybe some old lawsuit, that would explain why Ward was so against the tower?'

'Vaguely. So much has happened since then. Did you find something?'

He nodded. 'But not what I expected. Sure, some of those suits filed by Preserve the Peninsula are still hanging around, just one appeal after another. But one of them involved Spencer.'

Nora sat up straight. 'About the tower?'

'No. Some small project, years ago. I wanted to make sure it was over and done with so I plugged Spencer's name in the system. Man.' He shook his head at the memory. 'It was like hitting the jackpot.'

'I don't understand. In what way?'

'Lawsuit after lawsuit, all of them against Spencer.'

'By Preserve the Peninsula?'

Now she was sure. He *was* smiling. But not in a good way. In a grim, should-have-seen-this-coming way.

'By pretty much every contractor Spencer's ever dealt with. Dude doesn't pay his bills, or at least not on time. And he countersues, claiming shoddy work, so things get tied up in court forever, meaning he doesn't have to pay until it's settled.'

'Genius,' Nora sighed. 'In an evil way. But how are you the first one to find this out? As claustrophobic as this place is, I'd have thought it would be common knowledge.'

His smile became scarier still.

'He always used mainland contractors, from about as far away as he could find them. He must've run out of options if he's using Ron's crew. Anyway, Ron's only the subcontractor. The bottom line is, Spencer Templeton is up to his eyeballs in debt.'

The tumblers in Nora's brain spun again, clicking like mad, her words barely able to keep up with her thoughts. 'Ward somehow found out the tower was unsafe. But Spencer needs the money from the project.'

She got the silent treatment again, in the form of a decisive head-shake. He sat back as she worked it out.

'Wait. That's not it. Spencer donated the tower to the peninsula, so he's not making any money on it.' She leapt from her chair. 'It was to sweeten up the commission so they'd approve the hotel. Which he *does* need. But where does Janie come in?'

Again, he waited.

Nora paced the room, thinking aloud. 'Ron and Janie need the project as much as Spencer. They're really struggling financially. But somehow Ward found out the tower was dangerous. That would have killed it – and probably would cast doubt on the hotel project as well. But he didn't go directly to the commission with that information. Why not?'

She waited for another 'click' of that internal lock. Nothing.

'I don't know either,' Jeremiah said, to her relief. 'My best guess is that he didn't have proof yet. But he must have said something to Janie. Pillow talk, maybe.'

Of course. That delicious interlude, lying together afterward, whispering into the dark about nothing – and everything.

'That's it! It finally makes sense!'

'What makes sense? Because I haven't gotten to that point yet.'

'The fight I saw between Ron and Spencer. Spencer said something about how Ron owed him his job. And Ron said – I think this is right – "Remember why you gave it to me."'

Comprehension lit Jeremiah's face. 'Janie and Ron were blackmailing him. That's why Spencer went with a local crew. They could have told him that if he didn't hire Ron, they'd take what they knew to the commission. He wouldn't have known, at least not right away, that they didn't have proof. He would've been afraid that the commission wouldn't award his permit.'

Clickety-click-click went the final tumblers. The lock fell open. Nora's elation vanished. 'Blackmail or no, they all had the same goal. The projects had to go forward. Nothing could get in the way.'

They looked at each other a long moment.

Jeremiah spoke first.

'Ward.'

They'd come up with a motive. Only problem was, three people shared it.

FIFTY-FOUR

'We should go to the police,' Jeremiah ventured.

Nora flinched, a residual effect of her own encounters with law enforcement. 'I was going to, when I found out about the tower. But that was before it fell. And now that I think about it, it would have been premature even

back then. I feel like we need to know more. We're like Ward.
We need some kind of proof.'

The last thing she wanted to do was to attract even more of
Detective Eberle's attention. She'd asked Martina Lopez
Meadows not to mention her visit, but the woman had agreed
so reluctantly Nora figured she'd only bought herself a brief
grace period.

'Janie probably knows the most and is the easiest to talk to.
I can visit her in the convalescent center.'

Jeremiah peeled a long strip of cobalt-blue paint from his
pants. 'What are you doing to do? Hand her flowers and ask if
she killed Ward?'

'I'll figure it out.' Nora was nowhere near as sure as she
sounded.

'Be careful. The minute you talk with Janie, it'll get back to
Ron, if not Spencer, too.' He hesitated. 'You don't have anything
like a gun, do you?'

'Anything *like* a gun? You mean an actual gun? God, no.'

'What about Luke? Isn't he ex-military?'

He was, but she'd never seen a gun. 'I'll look.' Although, she
probably wouldn't. Even if she found a gun, what would she do
with it? She didn't know how to shoot one, and where would
she carry it? In a purse? Was her small bag even big enough for
a gun? How big was a gun, anyway?

'What about you?' She tried to smile, make a joke of it. 'Do
you have something like a gun?'

He played along, extracting a paintbrush from a jar of clean
ones on an end table.

'My only weapon. Picasso said all art is a form of power.'

Which didn't make her feel better at all.

Nora brought something better than flowers.

She stood beside Janie's bed and held out a paper bag.

'It's a fried-halibut sandwich. I just picked it up so it should
still be crisp.'

Janie grabbed the bag, dug out the sandwich and wolfed down
half of it before she said a single word.

'God.' She fell back against the bed cranked into its sitting
position. 'If I had to eat one more cup of green Jell-O I was

going to kill somebody. I'm serious. They can't keep me trapped like this forever. I've got a list of every single orderly who showed up with that crap.'

'I'm telling myself that's the drugs talking and that after you're out of here, you won't remember a word you said.' Nora couldn't help herself from joshing along with Janie. The woman's energy, despite the contraption immobilizing her leg, was infectious.

But she couldn't put off her questions any longer. The good thing was that no matter how mad she made Janie, the woman couldn't come after her. Still, she backed away a step.

'Ward knew the tower was dangerous.'

Janie took a savage bite of the remainder of the sandwich and chewed. Her glare promised retribution that would go beyond anything inflicted upon the purveyors of green Jell-O.

'So?'

Nora had decided ahead of time not to insult Janie's intelligence by dancing around the subject, a strategy that had seemed great when it was only theoretical.

'For Chrissakes, Nora. Spit it out.' Which is what it looked Janie wanted to do with the remains of her sandwich.

'You and Ron would be screwed if that project – and the hotel – got canceled.'

Nora braced herself.

But Janie only nodded. 'Good and screwed. But that wasn't going to happen.'

'Why not?'

'Ward didn't have the goods. He couldn't find anything to document it. Just some old man's say-so. The only way he could have gotten the information was to commission a study himself – well, himself in the form of Preserve the Peninsula – and Preserve the Peninsula had bigger fish to fry. Sorry,' she said to the remaining shreds of halibut in her sandwich. 'They'd bid on some land to add to the wildlife refuge at the tip of the peninsula. Just a monster purchase. Ward knew the board wouldn't go for any more expenses.'

Nora wondered what sort of painkillers Janie was on to make her so forthcoming. But since Janie was talking . . . 'Maybe you can clear something up for me. I saw Ron and Spencer really getting into it one day. Do you know what that was about?'

Janie's matter-of-factness surprised her yet again. 'Probably Ron was hitting him up for more money. Chance like this comes along, you gotta make the most of it.'

'But you didn't have proof! What did you think would happen when Spencer figured that out?'

Janie fished around in the paper bag and found a napkin. She blotted her lips and wiped her fingers. 'By then, Ron would have already pulled down a bunch of paychecks. What was Spencer going to do, take us to court to get his money back? Then he'd have to admit his own part.'

'You guys deserve each other,' Nora said. Even though it made a practical sort of sense. She could almost accept it. But she couldn't accept something else. 'You tried to put blame for Ward on Harold. Did you even see anyone arguing with Ward that night? And then you hinted maybe Jeremiah could have done it. That was shitty, Janie.'

As had been her own treatment of Jeremiah as a result, but Janie didn't need to know that. Anyway, Janie had the grace to look ashamed.

'From the start, we figured it was probably Spencer, and that they'd probably pin it on him eventually. We just wanted to string this thing out as long as possible. As to Harold, I honestly thought it might have been him. It was so dark I really couldn't tell.'

So far, so logical. But one thing wasn't.

'You knew, and Ron, too, that the tower was dangerous. Why in the world were you on it that day?'

For a minute, Nora thought Janie might cry. 'We're not monsters. It was one thing to squeeze Spencer. The guy could afford it. But when we saw everybody heading for the tower, we tried to get them to come down. Ron was yelling at them, saying that safety fence was there for a reason. But some kids managed to pull a section apart. And I went partway up, trying to get everybody to come watch it from Betty's. Told 'em free nachos. Guess our nachos aren't as good as I thought they were. I'd started back down but the water came back in a lot faster than I expected. I'm just glad nobody got killed.'

'Not nobody,' Nora reminded her. 'Ward's still dead. Same goes for the architect – the guy you called "some old man". He fell down his basement steps that same weekend I was in Portland. Or maybe he was pushed.'

She watched Janie work it out. If the woman was acting, it was a fine performance. She did not, however, expect laughter.

'I get it now. You think I did it. First, I killed the man I'd been sleeping with.' It was Janie's turn for close observation. 'Huh. Looks like you already knew about that. Jeez, this peninsula. Just for your information, Ward and I were polar opposites in terms of all his environmental shit, but we'd known each other since we were kids and we figured it was finally time to give prom night a do-over – this time in a bed instead of that goddamn beater he drove back then. Also – do I have this straight? – I drove to Portland and pushed over some old dude I've never met and killed him, too.'

When she put it that way, Nora thought. But she wasn't ready to let Janie steamroller her.

'You knew I was going to Portland. We talked about it in the bakery that day when Delilah came in. Maybe you thought I might try and talk with him.'

Janie put her hands to the mattress and tried to push herself up. She fell back, cursing. 'Goddammit. I may as well be in a straitjacket here. When did you go to Portland?'

Nora counted back. Got out her phone and checked the date.

Janie rolled her head to one side and stared Nora in the eye. 'I can't believe I'm saying this because it sounds like I'm taking you seriously. I pulled extra shifts that weekend. No way I could have gone to Portland. You'd better doublecheck with Betty because I can tell you don't believe a goddamn word that's coming out of my mouth. And what about Delilah? She knew you were going, too. You think she drove there in her Bimmer and put one of her fancy-ass high heels to that guy and shoved him down?'

'Mercedes,' mumbled Nora.

'What's that?'

'She drives a Mercedes.'

Janie just looked at her. Nora knew when she was beaten. She fled.

FIFTY-FIVE

She emerged from the convalescent center to see Jeremiah leaning against her truck.

She stopped in confusion. 'What are you doing here? I thought I was supposed to try and talk with Janie. Although in retrospect, it might have been better if you had. That was a disaster.'

She gave him an unsparing summation. Maybe it wasn't as bad as she thought. He winced. So it was that bad.

'I probably just should have gone to Betty's and asked first. Janie is one pissed-off human right now and she's going to be even madder when the drugs wear off and she realizes everything she told me. You can bet she's already called Ron. We'd better steer clear of him.'

'Too late.'

Nora mentally matched his spare frame to Ron's musclebound bulk. Her hand went to her mouth. 'Oh, no. Are you OK?'

'It wasn't so bad. Guess I got to him before Janie did. Believe it or not, I ran into him coming out of Betty's. I stopped by to fortify myself with some coffee.'

'And here I thought you only drank herbal tea.'

At least he smiled. Nora desperately needed someone, anyone, not to be mad at her.

'He was on crutches but moving pretty well. I told him I was sorry about the tower and that I'd kicked some money into the GoFundMe account. He said his bills, and Janie's especially, are going to take way more than GoFundMe, and that he was suing Spencer. I believe his exact words were, "I'm gonna take that asshole for every cent he's got." I didn't have the heart to tell him that Spencer is damn near bankrupt. I don't know what he might or might not have done to Ward, but he didn't have anything to do with the architect.'

Nora slumped against the truck next to him. The sun had come out just long enough to warm its metal flanks and it felt good against her back. She didn't ask the obvious, wanting to take just a few seconds more to enjoy the heat easing muscles kinked by tension, to delay the next bad-news bomb headed her way.

Jeremiah answered her unspoken question. 'After he finished a whole diatribe about suing Spencer, he said, "I've worked straight through the last two months on these projects. Not a single day off. Now look at me. I don't know when I'll be able to work again. I could end up like Harold."'

Clouds covered the sun. The truck cooled.

'Strike two,' she said. 'You know, I didn't think I could be any more upset with myself than I already am. But I was so quick to assume Ron or Janie. They fit all those blue-collar stereotypes. I just couldn't imagine Spencer getting his manicured hands dirty. But Janie said something that made me think. She made a crack about maybe it was Delilah who hurt Kirk Lopez. I laughed it off. Actually, no I didn't. I was beyond laughing at that point.'

Jeremiah didn't laugh, either. But his smile was genuine. 'I have to say, as much of a stretch as it is to think about Spencer – and let's leave aside the reason for a minute – Delilah seems like a stretch too far.'

'But it brings me back to Spencer. Janie said that all along, she figured he might have killed Ward. That's why she pointed to Harold' – she didn't tell him that Janie had also named him as a possibility – 'to keep Spencer from being arrested, so as to keep the money coming.

'And then it occurred to me that he and Delilah were taking Damien to a child psychologist in Portland every weekend. He would have been there the same weekend I was. I don't know why, but I assumed the other person who went to Lopez's house was a woman, too. Maybe because she thought I had come back. Now that I think back on it, though, Martina didn't specify.'

He did the chivalrous thing. 'Want me to try and talk with Spencer?'

Nora's gaze said it all, sweeping his Hawaiian shirt, his paint-crusted pants, his bony feet in their Birkenstocks, toes blue with cold on this blustery day.

He offered a wry grin. 'I know what you're thinking. Spencer wouldn't give the likes of me the time of day. But we did grow up here together. That has to count for something.'

'Sorry to be so obvious. But I don't think either of us will be able to get to Spencer. I've heard he's been in Seattle for days, huddled up with lawyers. But—'

She had an idea. It had worked with Melanie when she'd first tried to find the identity of the architect, a move spurred by Jeremiah himself. At the time, she'd thought it almost goofy. Now a second man was dead and dozens injured.

'I can try to talk with Delilah. I'll tell her it's about Damien. It's about time I finally got some good out of that kid.'

FIFTY-SIX

D elilah surprised her twice. First, by responding immediately to her text and second, by saying that Spencer was on his way home from Seattle and would be able to sit in on their talk.

'I know it's after hours, but can you stop by now?'

Nora pumped her fist. 'Score!'

Luke looked up from the sofa and lowered the volume on Monday night football.

'What?'

'I was able to set up a meeting with a parent.' Nora figured this met the standards – almost – of their avowed transparency.

Which was the bigger danger sign? The fact that she'd withheld the whole truth, or the fact that Luke didn't ask? Just as he hadn't asked about yet another extended absence when she'd brainstormed with Jeremiah and visited Janie in the convalescent center.

They were going to have to deal with their shit. And they would, they truly would, she promised herself, just as soon as she and Jeremiah figured out what had happened to Ward Austin and Kirk Lopez. *If* they figured it out. She'd reluctantly agreed with Jeremiah that if the Hail Mary meeting with Delilah was a bust, they'd go to the police with what they knew.

Nora gave Luke another chance to ask where she was going, or even who she was meeting. 'I'm heading out now. This shouldn't take too long.'

'At this hour? Who are you going to see – oh, goddammit. Ref just gave the Eagles a touchdown when anybody could see the guy was out of bounds.' Luke shook his fist at the screen. 'Uh, sorry. Catch you later,' he said without looking at her. 'Hey, ref!' he shouted at the television. 'Who makes a call like that?'

Nora tiptoed away. She stuck her head out the door for a reality check. The sky was fast darkening, but a few stars glittered, a good sign.

She took a second to text Jeremiah. 'Heading out to talk with Delilah – and Spencer, too!'

She pulled on her cycling shoes, hopped on her bike, switched on its blinking safety lights and headed for the spaceship.

Delilah, silhouetted against luminaria in ceramic containers set atop the wide, flat railing, waved to her from the rooftop deck as she rode up.

'Halloooo! I thought we'd meet up here. It's such a lovely night. Do you mind taking the stairs? The elevator's broken and we can't get a repairman out here until the end of the week.'

Nora wheeled her bike into the parking area beneath the home and eyeballed the spiral staircase. She patted the bicycle's seat in gratitude. At least the hours of cycling had toned her legs for the climb ahead.

She went up and up and up, hesitating occasionally as her cleats caught in the stairs' metal slats. She considered removing her shoes but didn't want to linger any longer on the steps than necessary. The stairwell was in shadow, somehow making it seem even narrower, higher, the concrete floor farther below. At the landing, a door opened, flooding the steps with welcome light.

'Hey, Ms Best.' Damien stood within. Behind him, she glimpsed a predictably chaotic room – unmade bed, clothes and sneakers in piles on the floor, walls covered with posters of bands she didn't recognize.

But he'd called her Ms Best, not Miss Worst, something she took as a good sign.

'Hi, Damien. How's the wrist?' He'd survived the tower collapse with a mere sprain. Tape immobilized his hand and arm. He nodded at the stairwell. 'You seem out of breath. My mom runs up those every day.' He gave a brief laugh and shut the door.

So much for détente. Annoyance fueled the rest of Nora's climb.

She stepped onto the deck, bracing herself against the expected breeze off the ocean. Instead, fire blazed in an outdoor hearth.

'Come sit here.' Delilah padded in soft slippers to cushioned rattan chairs pulled close to the blaze. Nora followed, her shoes clacking against the floor. She stopped with a gasp.

'I'm sorry,' Delilah said somewhere to one side of her. 'I know it's a quite a climb.'

'No. The view!' She'd seen it through the second-floor windows on previous visits. This height made those earlier vistas seem pedestrian.

Nora walked to the edge, leaned on the rail between two of the luminaria, and took it in. A full moon had emerged, laying a shining slash across the water.

A hand on her arm eased her back a step. 'Careful. I've asked Spencer to replace that railing with a four-foot wall. I can't help it. I'm a little afraid of heights.'

Nora tore her gaze away from the water. 'Not if you can run up those stairs, you're not. Damien dimed you out,' she said to Delilah's look of surprise.

'Up is all right. Down is a different matter. I usually take the elevator down. You can bet that tonight, I'll be hanging on to the stairway railing the whole way down. Come on. Let's sit. I've opened a bottle of wine. I hope you like red.'

She'd set a low table with a charcuterie tray and two glasses.

'You didn't have to go to all this trouble,' Nora said even as she reached for a cracker and a wedge of Manchego.

Delilah handed Nora her glass. She'd poured generously, something Nora feared would make for a precarious descent of the stairs.

'Why only two glasses? I thought Spencer was joining us.'

'Oh, he's been detained. It's just us girls.'

But Delilah looked anything but girlish. Maybe it was the firelight, hitting her full-face as it flared, cruelly finding the fissures Botox had failed to stretch taut, the red veins threading her eyes. Nora wondered if she knew about Spencer's debts, knew tarnish was fast darkening the lifestyle Delilah's ex-husband had derided as 'shiny'.

Nora dutifully recited her excuse for the visit. 'I've been making the rounds of my students' houses, making sure they're caught up on homework, that sort of thing.'

Delilah started to reach for a bit of Brie but at the last minute popped a grape into her mouth instead. Probably she had a calculator in her brain that assessed calories, carbs, fats and all the other things that made life worth living.

'Funny,' she said. 'I would have thought you could take care of that with the online classroom site. That's what Damien's other teachers are doing.'

Nora twirled her wineglass, pretending to admire its contents. 'Damien's already been through so much this year. That's why I think the personal touch is important.'

Delilah ran a finger around the rim of her own glass, circling, circling. Nora forced herself to look away, suppressing the crazy thought that the woman was trying to hypnotize her. But when Delilah spoke, her low, confiding tone only added to the impression.

'Yes. I've noticed you like what you call the personal touch. Visiting Kirk Lopez in Portland. That was pretty personal.'

Nora set down her glass with extreme care and knitted her fingers in her lap. *How did you know?* She didn't dare ask, not trusting her voice. It didn't matter. Delilah told her.

'Imagine my surprise upon seeing you at his door.'

Nora had so many questions. Had Delilah and Spencer trailed her all the way from the peninsula? No, that was crazy. They must have slipped away while Damien met with his therapist and stumbled upon her just as she made her own visit to Kirk Lopez.

Anyway, it didn't matter. She and Jeremiah had wanted proof. This wasn't it. But it seemed as close as she would get to the inescapable conclusion that Spencer Templeton had blood on his soft, manicured hands.

Why was Delilah handing it to her?

She answered her own question. 'Spencer's hit you, hasn't he? You're scared of him. And God knows what he did to Kirk Lopez, but I can make a guess. Maybe you saw it. Maybe you didn't.

But you know enough that the walls are closing in on Spencer. Why don't you go to the police? Even if you were there that day in Portland, they'll go easy on you if you can help convict Spencer. If it will help, I'll go with you.'

The tightness in Delilah's face relaxed all at once. It hadn't all been Botox. She even smiled.

'You're so smart. You've got it all figured out, don't you? You're right. I'm afraid of him. If you'd go with me to the police that would make everything so much easier.'

The words were right. But the tone. Nora rubbed her arms, trying to smooth down the hairs pushing against her sleeves. She voiced a belated thought.

'Spencer's been gone for days. You could have gone at any time. Why haven't you?'

Delilah spoke as one used to being obeyed. 'Come with me.' She rose and – when Nora remained seated, mouth agape – pulled her from the depths of the cushioned chair and steered her to the railing.

'Look at this view. I love living here. It makes up for all the years I spent in that rathole with Ward. I made a mistake then.' She shook her head. 'Maybe you've done the math. God knows, everyone on this peninsula did. Ward and I passed Damien off as a preemie, as though that made any difference. Pretty sure half the babies here are' – her fingers wriggled air quotes – "premies."'

Nora tried to pull away, Delilah's fingers dug into her arm. 'I was supposed to marry Spencer. State schools were good enough for the rest of us, but not for him. He wanted to go away to college.'

The way she said *away*, it sounded as though Spencer had been bent on going to hell. 'Spencer and I started having sex when we were fifteen. God, we were careful. So careful. Well, he was. I used to tease him about whether he'd bought stock in Trojan. He went off to college and Ward was still here and he didn't give a damn about being careful. We were *wild*.' Her eyes glittered.

Nora didn't even try to pull away again, rooted by a squirmy fascination.

'And then there was Damien. All of this' – she waved the

hand not latched on to Nora – 'had to wait. But it's been worth the wait. Spencer built this house for me as a wedding present. Now that I've got it, do you think I'd let anything take it away again?'

She yanked Nora's arm, spinning her around so their faces were within inches of one another. Nora's elbow struck one of the luminaria, sending it over the edge. She heard the ceramic pot shatter against the concrete parking pad below.

You think you're so smart, Delilah had said.

But she wasn't. She was a fucking idiot.

'Spencer didn't hit you, did he?'

Delilah smiled.

'You didn't catch your hand in a car door.'

A gull's crazed shriek echoed Delilah's laugh,

'Kirk Lopez did that to you. Oh, God.'

Delilah reached for her other arm.

Nora brought her foot, shod in a cycling shoe with its metal cleats, down on Delilah's slippered instep.

Delilah yelped and let go.

Nora bolted for the stairs – and nearly pitched forward when her cleats caught in the grate of the first step.

'Jesus!' She grabbed the railing for support and clattered down the steps as fast as she could. Fast, light footsteps followed her – Delilah, having a far easier time of it in her slippers, although like Nora she clung to both railings.

Delilah had been right. Down was scarier. Far below – too far – lay the concrete parking pad against which Nora's head would split open like the doomed luminaria if Delilah caught her and gave her the sort of shove that must have felled Kirk Lopez.

Already Delilah's fingers brushed Nora's back, grasping at her jacket. Nora jerked away, giving thanks for its slick fabric – but almost fell in the process. Delilah might not have to lay a finger on her. She could trip on her own, flip over the slender railing and plunge to her 'accidental' death.

Delilah reached for her again and this time gained purchase. Nora clung to the railings and sank onto the step. Delilah would have to pull her up and over, which she immediately tried to do, her hands under Nora's arms, hauling at her, both of them screaming now, Nora's 'Stop! Stop!' nearly drowning out Delilah's 'Let go, you bitch! Give it up!'

Then, a third voice.

'Mom! Mom! Stop it!'

Both women froze. Damien stood on the landing below, his face chalky.

'Damien. Call 9-1-1.' Stupid, Nora thought, even as she gasped her plea. She'd be splattered all over the concrete below before even the fastest cruiser would arrive.

Delilah spoke with a mother's calm authority. 'Go back in your room, Damien. Miss Best fell. I'm trying to help her up.'

He hesitated. Half-turned back toward his door.

'Damien, no,' Nora moaned.

He squared his shoulders. Looked up again and despite her own terror Nora's heart broke at the look on his face.

'Mom. It's OK. You don't have to do this. I threw it away.'

Delilah's grasp loosened.

Slowly, slowly, as imperceptibly as possible, Nora put her right toe to her left heel and edged off one shoe, praying it wouldn't tumble into the abyss and land with a sound that would alert Delilah.

'Threw what away?'

'Your putter.' His face went from white to a patchy scarlet. He spoke through a sob. 'I found it. In the garage. It's gone.'

Delilah. Tall, slab-thin, always in that golf cap. Seen at dusk, from afar, raising a golf club high, could someone mistake her for a man wielding a stick or a steel rod? Because who would think a woman capable of such a thing?

Delilah said something Nora had often thought. Hearing it aloud made her realize why – beyond the certainty of getting fired – she never would have voiced it. It was even more obscene coming out of a mother's mouth.

'Shut the fuck up, Damien.'

Nora kicked off her other shoe, sprang to her feet and bounded for her life down the stairs.

FIFTY-SEVEN

S omeday, Nora would be able to wrap her head around the fact that the boy who'd devoted himself to making her life a living hell had likely saved it.

Because Damien called 9-1-1.

There was some confusion when police intercepted a barefoot Nora sprinting away from the spaceship, her feet cut and bleeding from the shards of shells embedded in the sand. It seemed Damien had given a confused account, intimating his mother was being attacked, resulting to a near-hysterical Nora being detained in the back of a police cruiser until a laconic message crackled across the radio.

Delilah had been pulled over in her Mercedes, speeding onto the mainland, leading to the obvious question: if she was the victim, why had she fled?

Nora told her story over and over. Jeremiah – who'd left a string of increasingly panicked responses to her text – was called in, presumably facing a similar ordeal in another room. At one point, through a smudged police department window, she saw a shaken and bewildered Spencer arrive. Luke, she was told, waited in an anteroom.

She found him there hours later, asleep in a hard plastic chair. Two paper coffee cups sat on a scarred table nearby. She stood a few feet away.

'Hey.'

He startled awake and began to get up but fell back into the chair. 'Leg's asleep. Give me a minute.' He looked at the cups. 'I got you coffee. I figured you'd need it. That was hours ago. What time is it?'

She shrugged. 'No idea. Both my phone and my watch ran out of juice. Dawn, I guess, from the looks of that. Although . . .' She pointed at the filthy, rain-streaked window. 'That shade of gray could be any time between 6 AM and 6 PM.'

Luke tested his leg, putting a little weight on it, then more.

'OK, I'm good to go. How about some coffee that's actually hot. Betty's?'

Nora shook her head.

'We need to talk. Something we should have done weeks ago. Let's go home.'

But they didn't talk, not right away.

Luke insisted, rightly, that first they both needed long, hot showers and then, sleep. Lots of it.

They got the former, more restorative than Nora could have imagined, although the soap and water stung the crosshatched cuts on her feet. She crawled into bed, leaving her feet sticking out from under the covers, even the light pressure of the sheet unbearable. She was asleep within moments beside an already-snoring Luke. But they'd made the mistake of plugging in their phones to recharge them and, within the hour, both were blowing up with texts and calls.

Nora fumbled to mute hers.

Luke groaned. 'What if it's important? What if it's the police again?'

'Then I definitely don't want to take it. I've had enough of those guys to last me forever.'

Eberle had sat to one side during her endless questioning, never saying anything, just watching, watching. At some point, he'd left. She wondered when he'd return. Because he always seemed to.

Someone banged on the door.

'Jesus, what if that's him?' Nora pulled the pillow over her head.

'Who? Never mind. I'll get it. We'd better get dressed. Looks like sleep is going to have to wait.'

Nora left the bedroom a few minutes later to find Luke making a pot of coffee and Jeremiah sitting at the kitchen table.

'Uh, Luke, this is Jeremiah. Jeremiah, Luke.'

'We've met. You introduced us the day the tower fell.' He took three mugs from the cupboard.

'Jeremiah usually drinks tea.'

He turned to her, mugs in hand. 'You seem to know a lot about Jeremiah.'

'Luke, we should talk.'

'I'm good with coffee,' Jeremiah interjected.

Luke poured. Put the mugs before them. Sat. Looked at Nora.

'We're talking now. Go.'

They took turns, Nora starting with Abby's encounter with Jeremiah on the beach, Jeremiah jumping in with his own fears about why Ward was killed.

'So, because you felt it was dangerous, you tried to get Nora to find out for you what was going on?' Luke started to rise from his chair.

Jeremiah held up his hands. 'That's how she reacted, too.'

'I was ready to tell him to go pound sand—'

'Which, in effect, you did. Several times.'

'– but then both Ron and Spencer gave me a hard time and I couldn't help but be curious.'

The darkness that settled over Luke's face had the same unyielding quality as the rain. 'You two are like an old married couple, jumping in on each other's sentences.'

'Luke, it's not like that.'

'It isn't? Whatever. Just finish your story.'

Jeremiah looked to Nora. She shrugged. 'Might as well.'

They went through it all, the deepening suspicion, her first visit to Kirk Lopez's house – 'which I only just found out about,' Luke grimaced – and then the second. The tower's collapse, before Nora could warn anyone. Jeremiah's discovery of Spencer's financial woes. Their zeroing in on Janie and Ron, then realizing their mistake. Turning their focus to Spencer.

'We never would have guessed Delilah,' Nora said.

Both men started.

'Delilah?'

Which was when Nora realized that while the police had questioned Jeremiah, and made Luke wait, neither man knew of the previous night's events.

So she told them.

'And then I ran,' she finished. 'All the police told me was that they caught her headed out of town. Guess she should have driven a Ferrari instead of a Mercedes. Maybe then she'd have gotten away.'

Her feeble attempt to lighten the mood fell flat. Both men stared aghast.

'I should have headed over there as soon as I saw your text,' said Jeremiah.

'You texted him and not me?' said Luke.

Nora was very, very tired. She'd had too much coffee and too little sleep. Any impulse toward generosity had long fled.

'Knock it off, Luke. You're making something of this it isn't.'

'Isn't it?' Luke picked up his phone and tapped at it.

Jeremiah mouthed a question her way. 'Isn't it?'

Nora already felt as though the coffee she'd drunk was burning a hole through her insides. But she needed clarity more than she needed her stomach lining. She poured another cup.

Luke put his phone away. 'It doesn't really matter.' He got up, took the basket out of the coffee machine and emptied the grounds into the trash. 'We're going to need a lot more of this.'

'What does that mean?'

'Wait a few minutes. You'll see.'

Nora glanced toward Jeremiah and caught her breath at the mixture of hurt and hope in his eyes.

She looked away, keeping her eyes fixed on the table during the interminable moments before the knock on the door.

FIFTY-EIGHT

Sheila rushed in, spreading rainwater and questions.

'Have you guys heard what's happening? Children, Youth and Families went to the spaceship and took Damien away. Somebody said Delilah's been arrested. Do you know what for?'

She stopped and caught her breath. Nora watched her take in the scene before her: Three people seated at the scarred-but-serviceable table she'd helped Nora and Luke select at the Mall, two of them at least freshly showered but all three worse for the wear, shoulders sagging in exhaustion, hands clinging to coffee cups like lifelines. Her eyes narrowed as her gaze flicked from Luke to Nora to . . .

'Hey, Jeremiah. What are you doing here?'

'It's a long story,' Jeremiah said.

'What are *you* doing here?' Nora asked.

'Coffee?' Luke offered.

'Sure.' Sheila shed her slicker but barely committed to a chair, perched so precariously on the edge Nora feared she'd fall. 'Luke texted me.'

Nora looked from Sheila to Luke. 'Why?'

Luke cleared his throat. 'Before we get to that, there's really nothing going on between you two?'

'Drop it, Luke. For the last time, no.'

Jeremiah said nothing.

Nora noticed. Luke didn't seem to. Sheila sure as hell did.

'Well.' Luke drummed his fingers on the table. 'Well.'

'Well?' Nora wished they'd had the foresight to go to a motel after leaving the police station. At least no one would have bothered them there and she could have gotten the sleep she so badly needed to enable her to cope with a situation like whatever this was.

'That's going to make this doubly awkward,' Luke said.

'Make what doubly awkward?' Although Nora thought she was starting to understand.

'You know how much I miss Gabriel.'

She hadn't known. More precisely, she hadn't wanted to.

'And then, living here, we got to know Sheila's Lannie and Bill.'

Nora couldn't have named Sheila's sons if someone offered her fifty bucks.

'I started hanging out with them.'

'Just casually,' Sheila said. 'Frisbee on the beach, mostly.'

Mostly? 'What else?'

Jeremiah slid his chair back at Nora's tone. He glanced toward the door.

'No,' she said. 'Don't go. I want you to hear this, too. I'm so exhausted I'm not getting everything straight. You can be my backup.' Even though, having also spent the night at the police station, he was probably nearly as fried as she.

'Sounds like he's been your backup for a while,' Luke muttered.

'You were saying,' Nora reminded him.

Jeremiah's chair moved back another inch.

Sheila spoke up. 'Really, Nora, it was good for my boys. My ex is not the greatest role model. And God knows, the guys I date don't seem to want to do much with Lannie and Bill. Luke's been a terrific positive influence in their lives. They've really bonded with him.'

'Bonded? Jesus, how much time have you all spent together?'

Dumb question. Because she already knew the answer. All those after-hours and weekend 'meetings' at the school. Stupid, she berated herself. Stupid, stupid, stupid – an inner pummeling that did nothing to vanquish the memories of all the times she'd sneaked away from him. But not for this! Whatever *this* was.

'Let me turn your own question back on you: there's really nothing going on between you two?'

She'd addressed Luke.

Sheila answered, drawing a finger down her chest, then across. 'Honest.'

'It wasn't until . . .'

Here it comes, Nora thought.

'. . . when Gabriel came to visit.'

When Luke sprung him on me.

'He and my boys got along so well,' Sheila said.

Jeremiah, silent all this time, came to life. 'That day on the beach. I thought I saw all of you. But then I wasn't sure because there were three boys. And a woman and man with them' – he turned to Nora – 'although I didn't say anything to you about that part. It was the day of the storm. Remember? I was so glad you didn't recognize them.'

'Meaning you and Nora were together that day,' Luke said.

Goddammit. He was going to find a way to make this her fault if it killed him. Nora placed her hands flat on the tabletop, bracing herself against the too-lateness of it, all the things left unsaid finally bursting forth.

'You brought Gabriel to meet Sheila before introducing him to me.'

'Yeah. Which was a good thing because at least somebody was glad to see him.'

'Whoa, whoa.' Sheila switched into teacher mode. 'Let's dial it down a notch or three.'

'Good idea.' Poor Jeremiah. Three sets of eyes lasered his way, all with the unmistakable message: butt out.

'So everything was above board until it wasn't. Which was after Gabriel's visit.'

'It's still above board,' Luke insisted. 'Nothing's happened.'

Men, Nora thought. *They have such a funny definition of nothing.* 'You mean you haven't slept together. Yet.' She glimpsed the longing beneath Sheila's professional mien and knew she was right. Especially about the 'yet' part.

'We agreed it was best for all concerned that we do not see each other unless other people were around,' Sheila said. 'Other people beyond the boys.' Nora wondered who else they'd managed to rope into their faux family unit to enable their continued contact. What it must have been like to try and conceal their growing feelings. Probably fooling no one except for her. Like Ward and Janie, had they suddenly grown cool toward one another in public? Had everyone else on the peninsula already figured it out?

Gabriel's whispered farewell came back to her. *There won't be a next time.*

'Hell, Nora,' Luke burst out. 'You were always off somewhere doing God knows what, although I've got a pretty good idea.'

Nora held up her hand. 'I don't think Sheila was finished.'

Sheila's face crumpled. 'We tried. We really tried. And we might have gotten to a safer place, might have found our way back to just being work buddies. But then the tower fell.' She spoke directly to Luke now.

'I couldn't reach you on the phone. I went to your house, but the truck was gone. I was afraid you were . . . I was afraid you were . . .'

Luke didn't rise. Didn't reach across the table, take her hands in his. All he said, so softly Nora had to strain to hear, was: 'But I'm not. I'm right here.'

Fuck, she thought. They're in love. That's that, then.

She rose. Took her slicker from the peg by the door, stuck her burning feet into her wellies. Whistled up Murph. Mooch quick-stepped behind,

'Where are you going?'

'Oh, Luke,' she said, trying to project the forgiveness she knew she should feel. Forgiveness for him, and for herself, too. Because her next words conveyed the thing each should have recognized long ago, that should have made it clear all along that despite real affection and a shared secret history, they weren't right for each other and never would be.

'I'm going home.'

She closed the door behind her and headed for Electra.

FIFTY-NINE

The smart thing would been to hitch up Electra and leave. But that proved impossible after her first night back in the trailer, when despite everything she slept longer and more soundly than she had in weeks, lulled by waves sighing languorously after their recent cataclysm.

So she dug in, holing up in Electra, grateful for the fast-shortening daylight hours that made it easier for her to walk Murph in the dark, doing her best to avoid human contact beyond supervising her students' work via the online classroom.

She returned from one of those predawn strolls to find a basket of pastries from Betty's on Electra's step, with note signed simply in Abby's rounded hand, 'Your news crew.'

Other offerings appeared, from parents, colleagues, strangers. Casseroles. Fruit. A tiny tin, hand-painted with violets, of truly sinful truffles. And a Thermos with a jar of Sicilian olives beside it. An unsigned note read: 'Shake. Sip. Someday forgive me?'

Despite herself, she smiled – and drank down every drop.

Her stealth benefactors showed her the courtesy of not knocking. Maybe some tried to call, but she'd turned off her phone and, for good measure, let the battery run down. Which wasn't to say her refuge went unmolested.

Through much of the first week, reporters tried repeatedly to roust her, knocking, wedging their cards into Electra's doorframe with their cell numbers circled and chirpy notes in tiny printing: 'Look forward to hearing from you!' As if.

Some even lurked for hours in the campground, sitting in their cars and typing away on laptops on their knees, swiveling their heads occasionally toward Electra. In the end, it didn't matter that she wouldn't talk to them. Plenty of other people did, resulting in stories with clickbait-y come-ons like 'Hero teacher tried to warn of tower danger'.

But the details supplied by the people who described Nora's screams on Highview Hill as the water rushed toward the tower were so limited that those stories paled next to the headline-grabbers about Delilah.

So far, she'd been charged only with speeding and obstruction of justice, minor enough offenses that a judge released her on her own recognizance, albeit with the humiliation of an electronic ankle monitor. Police had found her fingerprints in Kirk Wilson's house, although she'd apparently told them he'd invited her inside and who could prove otherwise or even what had happened once she was in the house? As for Ward, authorities continued to seek the source of his head injury, which police slyly allowed was possibly 'some sort of metal object, possibly a piece of rebar or maybe a golf club'.

And, as much as Nora loathed the reporters' attention, she had to give them credit for one thing – they dug into the details of the tower's approval, far deeper than the county documents that Nora and Melanie had examined. A Seattle newspaper discovered that when Lopez retired, he'd given his old firm permission to use his seal of approval on projects in exchange for a regular stipend.

'These were people who'd worked for him for years,' his daughter told the newspaper. 'It never would have occurred to him the agreement would be misused in this way. And when he realized what had happened, that his name had been put to a project that was patently unsafe, he was—' At which point, according to the newspaper, the interview ended in tears.

As with the case against Delilah, authorities were tightlipped as who might have done some sort of bait-and-switch with the firm to obtain the seal, but Spencer was their obvious focus. The story did due diligence in pointing out the structural differences between the tower and Spencer's grand hotel project, noting the wider footprint of the latter's bungalows and the fact that they'd never hold hundreds of people – something the soil beneath the tower was too unstable to handle.

The pillars meant to support those bungalows stood like lonely sentries, looming ghostly when Nora passed them on her predawn and nighttime walks with Murph. So far, she'd read, no one had stepped forward to take over the project.

'What do you give it, Murph?' she asked him. These one-sided conversations were the only time these days she heard her own voice. 'A year? Five?' Because at some point a developer would visit the peninsula and gaze across the seductive stretch of sea. Maybe it would be a sunny day, wavelets glittering innocuously, kids splashing in the shallows, a whale breaching in the distance. *Ka-ching.* Who could resist?

Meanwhile, the County Commissioners – pushed by chair-in-waiting Melanie James – were looking into other tsunami safety measures, including abandoning the middle school building entirely and moving it to the peninsula's southern end, with better access to higher ground. Perhaps predictably, despite the devastation wrought by the tower's collapse, people were already pushing back against the anticipated cost.

As for the rest of it, Jeremiah filled her in.

The reporters had finally gone away. Nora had enjoyed enough days of peace and quiet that the rap on her door, coming just as darkness descended, startled her. She peeled away a corner of the duct tape she'd used to secure the curtains to the wall and eased the heavy fabric back a couple of millimeters.

He stood on her step, holding a flat, wrapped packet that he held up when she opened the door.

'I hear there's been a regular food chain going on, so I knew you didn't need anything to eat. But maybe this will help sustain you?'

He'd brought her a miniature painting – 'I wanted it to fit in your trailer' – a rendering of the sea the morning after the wave, the shore littered with debris, the tower wreckage off to one side, the felled steel beams catching the sun's rays and reflecting them back. Because the sun *was* shining, the water calm.

'I get it,' she said. 'At least, I think I do.'

They sat and he told her how Children, Youth and Families had released Damien to Spencer's custody, but that for the time being, the boy was staying with Sheila and her sons.

'They all get along,' he shrugged in response to her surprise. 'Spencer's occupied twenty-four/seven with his legal issues, and Damien refused to go with his mother. For now, this works.'

'Poor Delilah.' Her words shocked her nearly as much as they did Jeremiah. She tried to explain. 'In a way, it's the perfect punishment. She wanted all those creature comforts and when she finally got them, she was willing to kill – allegedly – to make sure nothing took them away. She still has the big shiny house. But that's all she has. She's lost her husband and her son and she's rattling around in that place all alone and she can't show her face anywhere outside it because the whole town hates her. She'll probably end up in prison but I wonder if, in its own way, this isn't worse.'

'Where are you going to end up?' His tone was so casual as to reveal what it cost him.

'Nowhere. I'm staying right here.'

The dinette shifted as he sat upright. 'Have to say I didn't see that coming. I thought you'd want to get away from all this. Everybody thinks that. Sure, they're all talking about you – about all of it – but from what I hear, other than the food chain they've left you alone.'

'You heard right. And I'm grateful. Believe me, my first impulse was to get the hell out of here and not look back. But here's the thing. I like it here. I even like my job and my students, as crazy as they make me. I actually can't wait to see them again. For now, though, thank God we've got the technology for remote learning. We'll use it through the end of the semester and go back to in-person learning next semester. By then people will have moved on.'

He chuckled. 'Haven't you lived on this peninsula long enough to know better?'

She laughed with him. After the days of self-imposed isolation, it was surprisingly good to talk with another person.

The sun had long gone down. They sat in the dark, as they had the first time she'd gone to his place. He'd brought out a candle at some point. Nora didn't have any candles and, when he posed his next question, she was grateful for the darkness.

'What about Luke?'

'We're working it out.'

'Oh,' he said, and she wondered how a single syllable could contain so much emotion, packed as it was with resignation and a struggling sort of acceptance.

'He's staying in the house while it goes back on the market. I imagine it will take a while to sell – that wave didn't exactly do wonders for property values here – but it's good because it gives everyone time to settle down. But I'm sure once it's sold he'll move in with Sheila and her boys, and I guess Damien, too, if they can work it out with the Children, Youth and Families folks. And Gabriel will spend summers with them. Can you imagine? I barely survived an overnight with four boys in the house, but Luke will love it.'

'That's awfully generous of you.'

'Oh, I'm still pissed. But at myself as much as Luke and Sheila. I knew we weren't ready to move in together, but I did anyway. Serves me right.' Words she'd said to herself over and over, to the point of almost believing them.

She sensed Jeremiah gathering himself, a tension so palpable that Murph slunk to his side, whimpering sympathy.

'What about us?'

Damned if she'd let him know she'd wondered the same thing. But she'd repeated another mantra during the long days alone.

'There is no us. Listen, Jeremiah. When I came here, I didn't think my life could get any more screwed up than it was. But it did. I've proven stunningly bad at relationships. To the extent possible, I just want to *be* for a while.'

She braced herself for a reaction ranging from sadness to anger. She didn't expect laughter.

'You've proven yourself stunningly bad at *traditional* relationships.'

'What do you mean?'

'Is there a light in this place? I want us to look each other in the eye.'

Nora wasn't sure she wanted that at all. She compromised by

rising and flipping on the light in the trailer's bedroom area, leaving the dinette in mere semi-darkness.

'I suppose that'll do.'

He waited until she sat again. She grabbed Mooch and pulled him into her lap, seeking comfort, always a mistake with Mooch. He gave every outward illusion of providing it, curling up and purring audibly, but repeatedly flexing his claws against her thighs to remind her who was boss.

'You're right. It was a mistake for someone like you to move in with Luke and play house.'

She flicked a finger against Mooch to make him stop. He responded by digging in harder. 'What do you mean, someone like me?'

'That sort of thing works for a lot of people. Most people, I guess. It's what's supposed to happen when you couple up. You move in together, get married – in whatever order – and do the happily-ever-after thing. Which is great if you're most people. But what if you're basically a loner like me? Or like you?'

'I'm not . . .' she started to say. Then she thought about it. There'd been one constant amid the calamities that had followed the end of her marriage: She'd loved living in Electra, in a tiny space all her own, with the freedom to go anywhere and anytime she pleased. And, beneath the humiliation of seeing a second partner stray, even if under vastly different circumstances, lay the undeniable relief of solitude.

'You love this trailer just as much as I love my place, which is more studio than house. Can you for a minute imagine living there?'

'God, no,' she blurted. 'Sorry. That was rude.'

'It wasn't rude. It was true. As true as my never being able to imagine living in a place like this. What I can imagine, though, is getting to know its occupant a lot better. Slowly. Over a long period of time.'

'How long?'

There was enough light for her to see the slow smile that spread across his face.

'As long as it takes.'

She tried to suppress a smile in return. Failed.

He held out his hand. 'Deal?'

Melanie had said the same thing, when she'd asked Nora to chase down Kirk Lopez in Portland. As had Luke, when he'd pushed her to buy the house with him. She'd had misgivings each time.

Now, her hands remained in her lap while she did a gut check.

Nothing.

Really?

She checked again.

Still nothing.

She shoved the cat from her lap and took Jeremiah's hand.

'Deal.'